Jeff Abbott is an internationally bestselling author and has been published in twenty languages. He is a three-time nominee for the Edgar Award. He lives in Austin with his family.

ADRENALINE

Sam Capra lives an idyllic life. An American, living in London, he has a perfect job with the CIA and a perfect wife, Lucy — who is seven months pregnant with their first child. But then it all goes up in flames. At work, Sam receives a call on his mobile from Lucy. She tells him to leave the building immediately, which he does — just before it explodes, killing those inside. Lucy vanishes, and Sam wakes up in a cold, dark prison cell. Why did Lucy call him? Was she a loving spouse or an enemy operative? Is Sam's unborn child safe? Now, he's in a frantic race against time to save his life — and discover the truth about those he thought he knew so well . . .

Books by Jeff Abbott
Published by The House of Ulverscroft:

PANIC
FEAR
RUN
TRUST ME

JEFF ABBOTT

ADRENALINE

Complete and Unabridged

CHARNWOOD
Leicester

First published in Great Britain in 2010 by
Sphere, an imprint of
Little, Brown Book Group
London

First Charnwood Edition
published 2010
by arrangement with
Little, Brown Book Group
London

British Library CIP Data

Abbott, Jeff.
Adrenaline.
1. Intelligence officers- -United States- -Fiction.
2. Kidnapping- -Fiction. 3. Suspense fiction.
4. Large type books.
I. Title
813.6–dc22

ISBN 978-1-44480-498-0

Published by
F. A. Thorpe (Publishing)
Anstey, Leicestershire

Set by Words & Graphics Ltd.
Anstey, Leicestershire
Printed and bound in Great Britain by
T. J. International Ltd., Padstow, Cornwall

This book is printed on acid-free paper

For Beth and Emmett Richardson
who got me hooked on crime
Thanks for the felonies

PART ONE

14 NOVEMBER–10 APRIL

'In the flux that defines the world of the illegal, beginnings are often endings and vice versa . . . Trillions of dollars move around the world outside of legal channels . . . They ruin the lives of some and create vast empires of profit for others.'

— Carolyn Nordstrom, *Global Outlaws*

1

Once my wife asked me, if you knew this was our final day together, what would you say to me?

We'd been married for all of a year. We were lying in bed, watching the sun begin to shine through the heavy curtains and I answered her with the truth: anything but goodbye. I can't ever say goodbye to you.

Two years later, that final day started as most of my days did. Up at five, I drove and parked near the tube station at Vauxhall. I like to use the public housing a few blocks away for my little adventures.

I started the run with a long warm up in the open, exposed concrete courtyard of the old public building, slow running in place, gathering pace, elevating my body temperature by a few critical degrees, then took off. You want your muscles and ligaments hot. A brick wall lay directly ahead of me, three feet taller than me. I hit it with a step that launched me upward, my fingers closing on the edge of its top. I pulled myself up with one fluid movement I'd practiced a thousand times before. No hard breathing, no creak of joints. I tried to move in silence. Silence shows that you're in control. Over the edge of the wall, running across the ground, and then a vault over a much shorter wall, one-handed, my legs clearing the bricks. Into the main building. A stairwell, smelling of piss and decorated with a finger of black and white graffiti lay ahead of me. I hit the painted wall with my left foot in a careful jump, using the energy to launch me rightwards to the railing at the turn of the stair. A hard move where I'd fallen before, but today, sweet, I landed with care onto the railing, holding my balance, heart pounding, mind calm. Adrenaline thump. I jumped from the railing to an extended steel bar that stretched into the construction site, used the momentum to swing myself over to a gutted floor. The building was being torn apart and redone. I would damage nothing, leave no sign of passage. I might be a trespasser, but I'm not a jerk. I ran to the opposite side of the floor, launched into the air, caught another bar of steel, swung, let go and hit the ground in a careful roll. The energy from the fall spread across my back and butt rather than jamming in my knees and I was up and running again, back into the building, looking for a new, more efficient way to enter its spaces. Parkour, the art of moving, gets my adrenaline going while, at the same time, a slow calm creeps over me. Make a misstep and I fall down the brick walls. It is exhilarating and settling all at once.

I made another three passes through the building's interesting web of space — broken floors, gaping stairwells, equipment — using a mix of runs, vaults, jumps, and drops to find the line — the simplest and most straightforward path through the half-ruined walls, the low brick rises, the empty staircases. Energy burned my muscles, my heart pounded, but the whole time I tried to maintain a distinct and separate calm.

Find the line, always the line. Around me, in the distance, I could hear traffic beginning to build, the sky lightening for the new day.

People think that what the British call council housing is an eyesore. It's all in how you look at it. To a parkour runner the old square buildings are beautiful. Full of planes and walls to run up and bounce off, railings and ledges to walk and jump from, neighbors who don't call the police at the merest noise.

The last route, I dropped from the second story to the first, grabbing a bar, swinging, letting go in a controlled fall.

'Hey!' a voice yelled at me as I slammed through the air. I hit, rolled, let the energy of impact bleed nicely through my shoulders and bottom. I ended up on my feet and took three steps and stopped.

Not a guard, a teenager, watching me. A morning cigarette perched on his lip. 'How do you do that, man?'

'Practice,' I said. 'Long, boring hours of practice.'

'Like a spider,' he said, smiling. 'My mum and I been watching. She wanted to call the Old Bill. I said no.'

'Thank you.' I really didn't need the police in my life. Time to find a new place to practice. I waved at my benefactor and decided to cool down with a long, straightforward run. Twenty minutes in a long looping circle, a normal jogger out for his paces, and I jumped back into my car to drive home. Most Americans living in London don't have cars. You don't need them.

I have one for security.

I headed up to our apartment off Charlotte Street, not far from the British Museum. I slipped inside, trying to be quiet, hoping that Lucy was still asleep.

She was up, drinking juice at the small kitchen table, frowning at an open laptop. She glanced at me.

'Good morning, monkey,' she said, putting her gaze back to the laptop. 'Out making mischief?' I'd forgotten to take off the hand coverings I wore to protect my palms on the parkour runs. I could hear the disappointment in her voice.

'Hi.'

'You didn't fall off a building,' she said. Like it was a good thing.

'No, Lucy.' I poured a glass of juice.

'What a relief. When you miss grabbing the edge of a wall and plummet to an untimely end, I can tell The Bundle you died getting your morning fix of crazy.'

'The walls aren't high. I don't take stupid chances.' Defensive.

'When I'm expecting, Sam, any chance is a stupid one.'

'Sorry. Mostly it was a normal jog.' I took off the palm protectors, stuffed them in my pocket. I went to the fridge and found a cold bottle of water. I took refuge in it, drinking slowly and steadily. Shower, coffee, then a long day at the office. The adrenaline rush was gone for the day.

'Sam?'

'Yeah?'

'I love you. I want you to know that.'

'I know that. I love you, too.' I turned from the refrigerator, looked at her. She was still studying her laptop, her hand perched on the soft fullness of her belly. The Bundle was seven months along and I suppose, with the imminence of parenthood, Lucy and I were both more serious these days. Well, she was. I hadn't yet been able to give up parkour runs, interspersed with my regular miles.

'I wonder if you might find a less dangerous hobby.'

'My job is more dangerous than my hobby.'

'Don't joke,' she said. Now she looked at me. In her morning rumple, she was beautiful to me, brown hair with auburn high-lights, serious brown eyes, a heart-shaped face with a full red mouth. I loved her eyes the most. 'I know you can do your job better than anyone. I'm scared you'll take a stupid fall doing these runs. I don't need you with a broken neck with a baby about to be born.'

'Okay. I'll learn golf.'

She made a face that told me she didn't take my promise seriously. But she said, 'Thank you. Remember, tonight we have dinner with the Carstairs and the Johnsons.'

I smiled. They were her friends, not mine, but they were all nice people and I knew our regular dinners out in London would become much rarer once the baby arrived. And maybe they knew a golf instructor. 'Okay, I'll be home by five, then.'

'We're meeting them at six at the tapas bar in Shoreditch. Do you have a big morning?'

'A PowerPoint-heavy one,' I said. 'Briefings all day with Brandon and the suits from back home.' I looked at her, standing to stretch, her hands on the swell of her belly. 'But I could cancel. Go to the doctor's with you.'

'No.'

'Save me from the PowerPoint. Let me go with you and The Bundle.' We kept skirting the discussion of names so I'd given our imminent child a pseudonym.

'The Bundle.' She patted the top of her swell.

'Actually, I may have to meet you at the restaurant. I might have to go drink a quick pint with the suits after the meetings.'

She laughed and smiled and said, 'Oh, such a tough job you have.'

I thought *thank God I don't have my parents' marriage*. Lucy and I didn't fight, didn't glare, didn't inflict long, painful silences.

'Go and bar-hop without your pregnant wife.' She smiled and closed her laptop. 'But not quite yet.'

She came to me and slid hands up my back. Pregnant women are full of surprises; it's like living with a breeze that can't settle on its direction. I loved it. She kissed me with a surprising hunger, almost a ferocity, her belly big between us.

'I'm hot and sweaty and gross,' I said. 'I'm a yucky husband.'

'Yes,' she said. 'Yes, you are, monkey. And I'm enormous.'

'Yes,' I said. 'Yes, you are.' And I kissed her.

When we were done, the sweetest start to that

final day, I made us a breakfast of toast, coffee and juice, showered, dressed, and I went to our office. Before I walked out, I looked back at her, at the breakfast table, and I said, 'I love you,' and she said, 'I love you.'

Famous last words.

2

London's skies that day shone blue as a bright eye; a rare sunny day for November after two weeks of grey, looming clouds. I had been in London for nearly a year. That final morning, in my somber suit, taking the tube to Holborn, I might have looked like one of the young lawyers heading for a firm or for court. Except my briefcase carried a Glock 9mm, a laptop full of financial information on suspected criminal networks and a ham and cheese sandwich. Lucy is sentimental; she liked to make my lunch for me because I made breakfast for her. She would be in the office later, when her doctor's appointments were done. We'd worked together for nearly three years, first back in Virginia where we'd met and married, and then here. I liked London, liked my work, liked the idea of The Bundle being born here and spending his early years settled in one of the world's great cities, not jumping latitudes like I had. Some kids start each year in a different school; I'd often started in a different hemisphere.

Holborn is a mix of new and old. Our office building was close to where the street goes from being High Holborn to plain Holborn. It was a contemporary glass and chrome creation that I don't doubt irritated architectural purists; next to it was a building undergoing a major refurbishment; scaffolding studded its façade. In front, a walkway funneled pedestrians into two lines and I avoided it when I could. The space opened up in front of our building and I worked my way through the spilling crowd.

The office building was mostly occupied by small firms — solicitors and marketing consultants and a temp agency — except for the top floor. The sign on the elevator read CVX Consulting. The initials had been picked by the throws of a dart at a newspaper stuck to a dartboard one night. I joked with Lucy and my boss, Brandon, that CVX stood for Can't Vanish eXactly.

I stepped into a bare room with a guard named John, a thicknecked Brooklyn expatriate. He sat at a desk with enough firepower in his drawer to blow several holes in me. John was reading a book on cricket, and frowning. Me, I'd long given up on deciphering that game. I walked to the door facing me, scanned my ID card; the door unlocked and I walked inside. The CVX offices were deceptively spare. The walls and windows were reinforced steel and bullet-proof glass; the computer networks were moated with the strongest firewalls available. Offices and a few cubicles, a staff of eight people total. It smelled like all offices: a bit like ink, burned coffee and Dry-Erase.

And the meeting I thought started at ten was apparently already underway. My boss, Brandon, was sitting in the conference room with three other suits from Langley, frowning at a PowerPoint display that was three days out of date.

11

Oh, hell.

I stepped inside. 'Not at ten?'

'Eight. You're twenty minutes late.' Brandon gave me a forced smile.

'My apologies.'

Two of the suits were older than me and already looked doubtful. The other was younger than me, and he had a page filled with scribbled notes. An eager type.

'If Lucy's in labor, you're forgiven,' Brandon said. He was originally from South Carolina and he'd kept the slow cadence of his speech during all his years aboard.

'I have no baby and no coffee,' I said. 'But I have a more up-to-date presentation. Give me five minutes?'

The suits nodded and all stood and introduced themselves, shook my hand, and went out to refill their cups with bad American-government-approved coffee and I set up the laptop.

'I don't like late, Sam,' Brandon said, but not with anger.

'I don't either, sir, I'm sorry.'

'I hope you have good news for us. These guys are from the budget office. They think we might be wasting time. Convince them we're not.'

Nothing so concentrates the mind as the possibility of the job being scrubbed.

When the suits returned with their bad coffee, I had jumped past the insomnia-inducing series of bulleted slides and stopped on a blurry photo that filled the presentation screen. The man's face was florid, a bit heavy, with small ears. His hair was dark and curling, as though it had just been ruffled.

'Gentlemen. We are hunters. Our game is international crime rings, operating with impunity across borders because they have managed to get their fingers deep into governments around the world.' I pointed at the photo. 'Think of us as lions, chasing antelope. This man is the weakest one in the herd. We're closing in on him. He might be the CIA's most important target.'

'Who is he?' one of the suits asked.

'He's what we call a 'clear skin' — no name, no confirmed nationality, although I believe he is Russian, due to other evidence we've received. We believe he moves and handles large amounts of cleaned cash to these global criminal networks. I call him the Money Czar.'

Brandon said, 'Tell us about the networks, Sam.'

'Sure. The Mafia is an old-school criminal network — a distinct leader, a bureaucracy of muscle and money cleaners that support him. New-school networks are highly specialized. Each part — whether muscle to enforce security or to intimidate or kill, or financial to clean money, or logistics to smuggle goods — is autonomous. Each is only brought in for specific jobs, and each time it may be a different set of people to do the work. It's therefore much harder to break the network down, to get any detailed information on how it works as a whole.'

'I know we've been paying particular attention to certain networks that might have government ties,' the youngest suit said. 'There's a Croatian gunrunner network we might infiltrate, the Ling smuggling family in Holland, the Barnhill network in Edinburgh . . . '

The young suit was on my side. I took that as a good sign. 'The Feds were able to break the Mafia because it was a hierarchy — lower-level thugs could testify against the big guys. But the only weak links here are the common elements that move from network to network.' I tapped the Money Czar's ugly face on the screen. 'This guy is the glue between some very bad people. It goes beyond crime. It moves into threats not only to our allies, but to the United States. This man may represent our best hope of uncovering some of the biggest threats to Western security.'

'He doesn't look that scary,' Brandon said and everyone laughed. Except me. I was prepared to scare the hell out of them when I told them what I knew.

'So the question is how do we find this Money Czar and . . . ' My phone beeped. When your wife is seven months pregnant, you get a free pass on taking calls in meetings.

'Sorry,' I mouthed to Brandon. 'Pregnant wife,' I said to the suits. I stepped out in the hallway. I didn't recognize the number. 'Hello?'

'Monkey?' Lucy said. 'I need you to meet me outside.'

'Um, I'm in a meeting.'

'I need you to step outside. Now, Sam.' Then I heard it: an awful undercurrent in her words, like a shadow eddying under summer water.

I started to walk to the door. 'Did you get a new phone?'

14

'I lost my old one this morning. Just bought a new one. It's been a rotten morning.'

I heard the shaky tension in her voice. 'You sick?'

'Please, just come outside.'

Bad news, then, to be delivered face to face. Not in the office, where emotion might be seen. A coldness gripped my heart. The Bundle. She had gone to the doctor. Something was wrong with the baby.

I hurried out of our offices; past John the guard, who had abandoned his cricket book for a British tabloid. Down the hallway. 'Where are you?'

'Out on Holborn.'

'Are you okay?'

'No . . . just come find me outside. Please.' I raced down the stairs, six flights, not waiting for the elevator. I came out into the lobby.

No sign of Lucy.

'Come out into the street,' she said. 'Please, Sam. Please.'

'What's the matter?' I headed out onto the busy street. It offered a steady stream of pedestrians — office workers, couriers, shoppers, the inevitable London tourists. Two young women leaned against the building in fashionable coats, smoking, sipping tea from plus-sized paper cups between gossipy laughs. I scanned the street. No Lucy. 'Where are you?'

'Sam, now. Please. Run.'

I ran, even before Lucy said to, because it was all so wrong, I could feel it in every cell of my body. I headed under the covered scaffolding of

15

the building next door, hurrying along the steady march of people. Finally I pushed past a man in a suit, past a woman in a hooded sweatshirt.

I stopped when I stepped back out of the temporary tunnel; there was no sign of Lucy, on the sidewalks, in the herky-jerk of London traffic. None. I turned, looked every way.

I heard my pregnant wife crying on the phone.

'Lucy? Lucy?' I gripped the phone so hard the edges bit into my fingers.

Now I heard her sobbing: 'Let me go.'

My eyes darted everywhere and I heard a car honk. I turned and saw a truck whip around an idling Audi, thirty feet away, the car facing me on the opposite side of the road, Lucy in the passenger seat. My office building stood between me and the Audi. My first thought was: no one stops on Holborn. The car was silver gray, like the sky in the moments before rain. A man sat in the drivers' seat, bent toward Lucy. Then he straightened and I could see him better. Late twenties. Dark hair. Dark glasses. Square jaw. I saw a flash of white as he turned his head, the pale curve of a scar marring his temple, like a sideways question mark.

Lucy looked right at me.

Then the blast hit.

3

A roar, an eclipse of the sun like God stuck his hand between me and the sky. I turned and the top floor of our building was shattering, flame spouting out, reinforced glass and ash and steel carving and falling through the air. The ground shook. A person, halved, burning, fell to the street, right by the pretty tea drinkers, who cowered and staggered for the doorway's cover as debris rained down.

My office of fake consultants was gone. Brandon, the visiting suits, the scribbling rookie, my friends and colleagues. Gone. Rubble covered the street, people, landing on cars, cabs and buses, and London itself seemed to give out a scream, formed of the thundering blast's echo against glass tower and stone courts, the keen of car horns, and the rising cry and stampede of the bystanders.

I couldn't see the Audi any more and Holborn was a mad jumble of stopped buses, cars and chunks of concrete, stone, and steel.

I couldn't see. I didn't think. I vaulted onto the construction tunnel roof, monkeyed up the bars. I had to get above the haze. I climbed fast, then I saw the flash of steel gray. The Audi, with my wife in it, revved forward. I saw the back of Lucy's head, bent slightly as though to catch the breeze in the window. Driving with the window down helped her cope with her morning

17

sickness, I remembered. It was a crazy thought.

'Lucy!' I screamed. 'Lucy!' I scrambled up the scaffold. I had to keep her in sight, find her above the cloud of grit. Below me was chaos. I had to keep the car in sight. I hurried up the scaffolding, found the Audi again. The traffic thickened like smoke from a fire, everyone trying to flee the blast.

I saw the Audi turn right onto a side street, revving onto the sidewalk to escape the impassable jam in the road, nearly running down two women.

The scaffolding moaned, heat surging through its joints. I heard a massive roar, turned, saw that the edge of the scaffolding closest to my office building had been savaged by falling debris. It was collapsing, thundering down onto the pavement.

I vaulted from the railing, bursting through the sheeted plastic onto a reconstructed floor. I hit concrete, coughing, tried to roll. I wasn't in the right shoes for this and my roll was rough. I ran across the empty concrete, glanced back to see the scaffolding twist and shred and tumble into the street. The building shuddered and I thought: it's next.

I ran across the unwalled floor to the back of the building — it cut all the way to a parallel street — and looked down, past a web of scaffolding on the north side of the building that was intact. I saw the Audi forcing its way onto the narrow sidewalk, a man in a suit kicking at the door in fury as it nearly ran him and a woman down. It was thirty feet below me.

My wife looked up. Through the sunroof. She saw me, her eyes wide and her mouth a perfect little shock of O. She started to reach upwards, her jaw moving, and then the scarred man hit her. With a solid punch across her mouth. She slammed into the door.

I dropped down through the web of the scaffolding, my blood turning to adrenaline. I braked my descent with grabs but I let gravity do the pulling and I had never been so afraid in my life. Not for myself but for Lucy and The Bundle. I couldn't lose the car. He was taking my wife, he had killed innocent people. Then I was on the ground and I dashed into the traffic.

A Mini Cooper barreled into the street, right into my path, and I wasn't even thinking, I was only running for all I was worth. I timed it, going over the roof when I should have been run down by the car, sliding with purpose, and then I hit the street, rolled down to my shoulders, back onto my feet, not crippled by the impact or the force. The pain came later. I didn't even know I was hurt.

The Audi surged ahead into the crowd and I ran hard and saw it turn a corner. I couldn't fight my way through the thickened crowd driven out from offices and shops, the jam of cars and two buses, paralysing the traffic between me and the Audi. I saw the Audi make another right.

I ran, my foot a hot, bright glow of pain. I made it to the corner. In the distance the Audi inched past a delivery truck, tires exhaling smoke for a moment in the tightness of its turn, and then it surged forward. I ran down the block and, when I reached the intersection, the car was gone. The scarred driver had found an empty side street, one unstuffed with panicked traffic.

With shaking hands, I tried to redial the number she'd called me from. There was no answer.

Lucy was gone. My office was gone. Everything was gone. Training bubbled to the surface in place of thought. My fingers dialed an emergency number in Langley. Words came to my mouth but I couldn't remember what they were.

Help me. My mouth moved.

She'd gone, everyone had gone. In the heart of London, the smoke rising like a pyre's cloud of a life ended, the sirens starting their mad kee-kaw blare, a thousand people rushing past me, I was completely alone.

4

I had been in the cold dank prison for over a week when a new man sat across from me in the cell. Fresh talent to try and break me. Fine. I was bored with the last guy.

'My name is Howell. I have a question to ask you, Mr Capra. Are you a traitor or a fool?'

'Asked and answered,' I mumbled through the desert of my mouth.

'I need an explanation, Mr Capra.' The new interrogator leaned back in the chair. He crossed his legs, but first he gave his perfectly creased pants the slightest yank. So they wouldn't wrinkle. I hated that little yank; it was like a razor against my skin. It told me who had all the power in the room.

I had had no real sleep for three days. I reeked of sweat. If grief has a stench, that is what I smelled like. The new interrogator was fortyish, African-American, with gray spiraling in his goatee and stylish steel-framed glasses. I told him what I told interrogator one and interrogator two. I told the truth.

'I am not a traitor. I don't believe my wife is a traitor, either.'

Howell took off his glasses. He reminded me of one of my old history professors back at Harvard. A calm coolness surrounded him. 'I think I believe you.'

Was this a trick? 'No one else does.'

Howell rested the end of the glasses' earpiece against his lip. He studied me for a long, uncomfortable silence. I liked the silences. No one called me names or accused me of treason. He opened a file and he started the old litany again, as if any of my answers might change. He would keep asking me the same questions to wear me down, to wait for my mistake.

'Your full name is Samuel Clemens Capra.'

'Yes.'

He raised an eyebrow. 'Samuel Clemens was Mark Twain.'

'He's my dad's favorite author and my mother vetoed Huckleberry and Tom Sawyer as choices.' Normally that story would make me laugh but nothing was normal any more.

'I want to call my father before I answer your questions,' I said. I hadn't asked for this in the past three days of questioning. What would I say to him? But now I wanted to hear the tobacco-flecked warmth of my dad's voice. I wanted to find my wife. I wanted to be out of this awful, dark, stone room that had no windows. It was stupid to ask. But it felt like fighting back after the endless questions, making my own modest stand.

'I didn't think you got along at all well with your parents.'

I said nothing. The Company knew everything about me, as they should.

'Your parents didn't even know you and Lucy were expecting, did they?'

'No.' It seemed a shameful admission. Family strains should stay private.

'You haven't spoken to your parents for three years, except for a brief phone call at Christmas. None of the calls lasted more than two minutes.'

'That's correct.'

'Three years. Some have suggested that's how long you've been working against us? You cut off your parents so they wouldn't be suspicious of your activities, would not be involved in your treason.'

'You just said you believed I wasn't a traitor.'

'I'm telling you what others in the Company are saying about you.' He leaned forward. 'A classic sign of treason is emotional distance from extended family and friends.'

'I didn't cut my family off. My parents stopped talking to *me*. It wasn't my choice. And I wasn't going to use my own child to get back in their good graces. Can I call my father? Will you let me do that?'

'No, Sam.' Howell tapped the earpiece against his bottom lip and considered my file, as though mining it for further pain. I wondered what else was inside those few sheets of paper. 'Your wife called you and warned you to get out of the office before the bomb exploded.'

'She was being kidnapped. I saw her struck by a man.'

'And why would her kidnapper allow her to call you?'

'I don't know. Maybe he wasn't in the car then, maybe she had a phone.'

'But she didn't say she was being kidnapped.'

'She was trying to save me. To get me out.'

'But not the rest of the office. She didn't say,

23

'Evacuate, Sam', did she?'

I closed my eyes; the stone of the cell floor chilled my bare feet. 'No.' I was sure I was no longer in the United Kingdom. Back in London the Company — the term used for the CIA by me and my colleagues — and British intelligence had heard my story and questioned me for three days. I was given no advocate or lawyer. Then four thick-necked men came with a syringe, held me still, and I woke up on a plane. I was in a Company prison, I guessed, in eastern Europe, most likely Poland. These secret prisons were supposedly closed several months ago.

'She got you, and only you, to safety. You see that's our problem. You walked out alone and then the office was destroyed.'

'Maybe Lucy didn't know about the bomb then. The scarred man must have told her to call, to get me out.' I had described the scarred man in detail but no one had brought me photos to look at, a suspect to identify. That scared me more than their questions and their needles.

'Why spare *you*?' Howell asked.

'I don't know.'

Then he surprised me. The next question should have been about the briefing on the man with no name that I'd been giving Brandon and the suits. That had been the pattern of the first two interrogators. 'Tell me about the money.'

5

'What money?'

He slid paper toward me. An account number at a bank in England where Lucy and I didn't have an account. I studied the transaction history. It included transfers to a bank in Grand Cayman. A quarter-million dollars.

'This is not our money.'

'This Cayman account was used in a Company operation last year; Lucy was the operations tech, she was supposed to close the account when the job was over. She didn't. Money was parked in this supposedly dead Company account and then moved into this UK account with both your names on it, and then moved out to a numbered account in Switzerland where it was transferred to private bonds. Now we don't know where it is. This is why people are having a hard time believing you, Sam.'

'I have no idea about this money!' This was bad. Very bad. 'I didn't have access to or knowledge of these accounts.'

'Conventional wisdom says the spouse always knows when the other is a traitor, Sam. Always,' Howell said quietly. He sounded like a teacher, one with patience to burn, no need to raise his voice. The last two interrogators screamed at me. Howell's calm was scarier, like a still blade held an inch above the throat. You don't know when

25

the cut will be made. 'Always. Usually it's the husband who turns traitor and the wife learns about it and then keeps her mouth shut. Either because she likes the money or because she doesn't want to see her husband go to jail. Was Lucy recruited first? Or you? Or did they hook you together?'

'Neither. Neither of us is a traitor.' I couldn't believe this of Lucy. I couldn't. Not my wife. I didn't care what evidence they showed me, it could not be real. To believe it was to commit treason against the woman I loved. My brain pounded with exhaustion; my chest felt thick. Air in my lungs felt coarse as sand.

'Beyond hope. Do you know that term, Sam?'

'No.'

'It's what's used to describe the state of being a traitor's spouse. We want to hope that the spouse is innocent, that they don't know that their loved one has betrayed their country. But we know, realistically, that they probably know about the treason. They are therefore beyond hope. Right now, Sam, that is you. Only I can help you. Tell me the truth.'

'I did nothing wrong. I knew nothing about this money.'

'I've made it easy, Sam.' He held up a slip of paper. 'A confession, short and to the point. You only need to fill in who you worked for. Sign it and we're done.'

'I won't. Ever.'

He lowered the paper. 'One of you is a traitor, Sam. Either her or you. Tell me about this money, Sam. The money.'

26

'I don't know.' The coldness spread to my skin.

'You and Lucy are both alive and everyone in your office is dead and she warned you out.'

'The scarred man hit her. She hadn't gone willingly. I can tell.'

'Who's the money from? The Chinese or the Russians? A crime network like the ones you were investigating? Did you get turned while you were undercover? Who are you working for?'

'No one. No one.'

'You were giving a presentation to a team from Langley on the work you were doing.'

'Yes.'

'Tell me about it.'

I tried not to laugh. My notes for my talk were still vivid in my mind because of the terrible thought that maybe my work had gotten our office targeted. 'We're looking for a Russian criminal I call the Money Czar. He cleans funds for various networks. I worked undercover for a few months last year, making contacts in these networks, mostly posing as an ex-Canadian soldier based in Prague who could provide smuggling routes for everything from knockoff cigarettes to guns bound for warlords in Africa. An informant in our employ in Budapest got the job to courier cash and gold from the Money Czar to a Russian scientist. Five million equivalent.'

'What was the scientist being paid for?'

'We don't know. This scientist was kicked out of the Russian military's research programs because of his heroin addiction; he set up shop

27

as a brain for hire in Budapest, doing contract work. The informant was the one who told us that this Money Czar had a Russian accent.' I paused. 'The informant and the scientist were both found dead a week later.'

'What kind of scientist was this man?'

'He used to work on nanotechnology.'

'Heard the term nanotech but don't really know what it means,' Howell said. 'Sorry. History major.'

'I was a history major, too,' I said.

'Then tell me in English.'

'Simply, nanotech is the study of the control of matter on an atomic or molecular level. Most of the research today has beneficial commercial applications — such as more effective means of delivering medicines into the body, or to specific organs. It could have huge implications, for instance, in the fight against breast cancer or brain tumors. Or we could create medicines geared to specific people's DNA, or much more sophisticated sensors to detect serious illnesses in our bodies, or vastly expanding the number of hours a computer battery can be charged.'

'And there are military and weapons applications to this?'

'Absolutely,' I answered. 'Nanotech builds machines or materials on an incredibly small level and makes them powerful. Theoretically. Creating new kinds of armor to repel bullets, or much stronger tanks, or much more efficient guns. Creating bullets that could self-correct on a course once fired. Smaller nuclear weapons that have incredible guidance systems and produce virtually no fallout. Or imagine a bomb that releases a swarm of miniaturized robots that aim for human flesh or body temperature and inject a fatal toxin into every person in a two-mile radius.'

Howell swallowed and his throat made a dry click. 'So this Money Czar could have been financing weapons research?'

'Yes.'

'And maybe whoever killed the scientist and the informant to protect your Money Czar came after you.'

'Yes.'

'Or, more likely, you got turned by the people you were chasing. You're good at your job, Sam. *You* could have found this Money Czar. And maybe he offered you and Lucy all that cash in this Caymans account.'

'No.'

'They didn't want you and Lucy talking and they've taken her and you decided to keep your mouth shut, maybe to protect her. I can see the thoughts going across your tired, beat-ass face, Sam.'

'No.' I wanted to drive Howell and his insane theories through the stone wall.

'Your only hope is to deal, Sam, with me. Tell me everything.' Howell leaned in close to me and he put a large hand on my shoulder. 'Think how easy it will be. All the weight will be gone, Sam. And then we can work on finding your wife. Your child. You want to be there when your child is born, don't you? Lucy's due date is in six weeks' time. Tell me where we can find the people you work for and we'll find Lucy. You can see your wife, hold your child.'

He leaned back. 'We checked with her doctor. You and Lucy didn't want to know what you're having but I know. It's a boy, Sam. Don't you want to see your son?'

My son. I was going to have a son, if Lucy was still alive. Howell was laying brutal trumps on the table, one after another: this unknown money, my child. Maybe Lucy . . . No. I could not believe it of her.

Each word felt like a pebble in my mouth, spit out one by one. 'I can't tell you anything because I am not a traitor.'

Howell studied me in the long silence. 'Then you're a fool, because your wife is the traitor and she's left you to take the blame.'

'No. No. She wouldn't. She loves me.' The words sounded weak in my throat but I remembered that last morning with my Lucy, her shuddering atop me, my hands on the curve on her bottom, her breath warm against my throat. Talking to me about not taking chances running parkour, and telling me she loved me, and reminding me of dinner with the nice couples. Calling me monkey, to soften her criticism of my running. That was not a woman preparing to vanish from her own life.

He looked at me as though he were a teacher disappointed with his student's performance. 'She doesn't love you. She left you holding the bag. Happy Thanksgiving.' Howell got up and left, the lights went out, and I sat in total blackness.

6

Time, unmeasured, passed. My throat was molten, parched, like I'd reached in and raked the flesh with my own fingernails. A knot of hunger tangled my stomach and I felt like I had fever. I slid from the chair and lay on the cold floor. I ate bread and water when it was brought to me. I slept and I awoke, unsure if minutes or hours had passed, shivered against the stone. I dreamed I was running parkour, vaulting over walls, flying between buildings, every muscle afire with glory, my mind clear and clean and precise. Then the wall where I was to land was gone and I plummeted toward a pavement covered with burning wreckage, helpless, out of control.

The lights snapped back on and Howell was sitting in his chair; as though he'd been there the entire time in the dark. But the suit was different. I looked to see if he had any water for me to drink. He didn't.

'Help me, Sam.'

I looked at him. 'How?'

'Help me understand this most interesting information I've come across,' he said.

'Did you find Lucy?' Confusion clogged my brain; my head felt thick with sleep. 'The baby. Lucy is due soon. You have to find her.' My voice grated like rock against sand.

'The bomb,' Howell said, as though I hadn't

spoken. 'I have the forensic analysis of the blast pattern, Sam.' He pulled out a photo of the London office, after the explosion. The desk arrangement had our names on it. S. Capra. Brandon. Gomez. McGill. The conference room, with the names of the three suits. In the computer room, a desk labeled L. Capra. Lucy's desk. My dead friends. The photo painted a horror: the smears of gore, viscera blasted and cooked on the walls, the blackened, gaping holes in the floor, in the center.

The smallest circle, painted in red, marked my desk, in the center of the office.

'The bomb was planted right under your desk. It was disguised to look like a small external hard drive, plugged into your system.'

I stared at the map of destruction.

'Lucy handled all the hard drive installs in the office.'

'No.'

'How *easy* it must have been for her. Did she set up the bomb right under Brandon's nose, James's nose, Victoria's nose? *Your* nose?'

Each word felt like a knife sliding under my skin.

'The bomb is placed where Lucy can most easily hide it without anyone noticing. Did she feel some guilt, sentencing her husband, the father of her child, to death? So she warns you. You walk out right before the explosion.' In case I didn't understand the implication.

'Shut up,' I said. I had not snapped or growled at anyone. I had focused and kept my calm while pleading my innocence. But this. Now. I couldn't take it. 'Shut up, shut up, shut the hell up.'

'Help me prove this woman a traitor. Think. Think of what you must have known. Try to remember.' This woman. Not calling her Lucy, not calling her my wife. Trying to establish an otherness for her, a separation between us. No.

'Lucy is innocent.' My voice wasn't calm. The bomb being planted under my desk unnerved me.

'Then maybe you're the one who's the bad guy,' he said. 'Maybe *you're* framing *her*. Maybe *you* planted the bomb. Did you have someone take her away? Kill her and your own child?'

The rage, buried in me, surged like a killing fever. I wanted to strangle the lies out of his throat. *I am starting to crack*. I saw my hands start to shake. I felt heat rise in my eyes. But I couldn't break. He wanted me to surrender control. I wouldn't. 'There has to be another explanation,' I said.

'That explanation is Lucy. The money. The bomb. It points to Lucy. She had the access to the account. She could have smuggled in the bomb.' His voice slid, low and soft. Howell had the barest Southern accent. 'I am your only friend left, Sam. The rest of the Company and our British friends want to see you burn. I will help you but not unless you help me.' I saw how damned I was in their narrow gaze. The evidence of the financial account. The bomb, hidden in a way that Lucy or I could have done it. That was all they needed. I was screwed, even being innocent.

'You will never see the outside of this prison

33

again if you don't tell me what you know. Stop protecting Lucy, or stop protecting what you thought she was.'

He wanted me to call Lucy a traitor. To agree with him, to accept this impossible possibility. 'No. She's innocent. That man took her.'

'She got you out of there and then she left you behind. She betrayed her country and then she betrayed you.'

'No.'

Howell slapped me. Hard. I didn't expect it because he looked like a professor and professors don't slap. 'That's reality, coming and waking you up, Sam. Tell me what you know.'

'Don't be an idiot. If I wanted to bomb the building I wouldn't have been there. I would have been long gone. You know I'm innocent and you're just going through the motions because it's easier to lean on me than to go find the real bad guys. I have no deal to make because I have nothing to give.'

'Then you are a prize fool.' He left and then he came back five minutes later with a cold bottle of water. Beads crowned the plastic. And I wanted it so badly. He set it down in front of me but I didn't reach for it.

'I want you,' he said, 'to entertain the possibility that nothing you knew about Lucy Capra was true.'

Tears welled at the back of my eyes. I won't let him see, I thought. But cameras were pointed at me, all the time. He would see me weep on tape. I kept my face still; kept the tears inside. For now. I would wait for the darkness, for the safety

34

of the crook of my elbow. I would not let them see me hurt.

He watched me, like he'd trumped my hand. 'I know you're thirsty. You haven't had water in three days. Did you know it had been that long? Drink up, Sam. I want your throat working. You have things to tell me.'

I took the water. I drank it. And as I finished, he pulled out the earphones, the eye covers. Two women wheeled in the cart with the meds.

Sodium thiopental, scopolamine, experimentals. Say hello to my blood. Maybe they gave me all of them — I felt more than one needle slide under my skin. Howell asked his soft questions again, and this time I heard other voices asking me the same, and I told them the bone-marrow truth: I do not know. I am not a traitor. I never did anything wrong. I babbled answers to every question about my life with Lucy. I told them about our love-making, our friends in London, our trips back home, any times she went to the Continent to explore on her own. I didn't know what she did in those weeks I was undercover, playing a role in Prague, pretending to be a smuggler looking for illicit goods to ship. I told them whatever was in my brain. I became an oil spill of words.

But there was the bomb, and there was the Caymans account, and that was enough. I must have known more, they decided. I must have had suspicions. Howell kept saying he wanted to believe me, like that belief topped his Christmas list. I said I knew nothing.

So they moved on past the chemicals.

35

The eye covers — which completely cut off my vision — made me feel like I'd been dropped into a hole that never ended. The earphones blasted music into my head: a hell's jukebox of saccharine ballads, brain-crushing psychedelic rock I didn't recognize, teeth-rattling rap. The rest of the time the sound was this high-pitched noise that made every nerve feel like it was sparking, like a broken cable. I lost all track of time, of place, of any sense that I remained tethered to the world.

The cure for that was pain. Howell wasn't there when guards came in and they beat me for a solid ten minutes. Fists and feet. It was an expert ass-kicking. They didn't mar my face but the rest of me purpled into a bruise. I curled into a ball. They gave me water, let me spit out a gob of blood. They looked at the gob as though gauging how much more I could take before passing a limit. Then they beat me again, kicking me harder. My spine and my legs felt on the verge of breaking. They were delightfully precise, careful not to break my ribs or my chin or my spine.

They asked the same questions. I gave the same answers.

I don't know how long I resisted the sensory deprivation treatments. Minutes under the noise and the blackness can feel like endless hours.

Lucy. The Bundle that was a boy. That was the thread I seized, the scant hope that I would be believed. They had to be searching for her, desperately. They would find her, and when they did, they would find the answers. The explanation as to why Lucy and I were framed, why they took Lucy, why they destroyed the Holborn office. Find the line, just like in the parkour runs. There was a line to the truth. I just had to find it.

They left me alone with my pain for a few hours and then they returned and they dragged me into another room. They strapped me to a flat piece of wood. It moved. I felt my feet rise. My head descended toward the stone floor.

No, no, no. I fought against the straps. The sensory deprivation was allowed. It remained legal. This, no.

It wasn't Howell standing above me, a cloth in one hand, a bucket in the other. The man wore a hood. I didn't know his voice. I screamed for Howell.

'Mr Howell isn't here,' the hooded man said.

'Please don't. Please.' I'd been through this before, in training. I knew what horror was coming and I struggled against the bonds, panic exploding in my chest like a mine. Because with the water on your face, you say what you have to. And if you know nothing, you truly know nothing, you will babble any torrent of words to get it to stop. You will tell any lie.

The truth of my life was about to die in this room.

'We've reached a moment of true unpleasantness, Sam.'

He waited for me to answer. All I could say, in a broken voice I didn't recognize, was 'Please don't do this. Please. For your sake.'

I didn't know where the last words came from.

Like I cared about this stupid, heartless bastard who was nothing but a tool. I didn't care. If I could have got off that board I'd have strangled him with my own hands.

'Tell us. Who did you and Lucy work for?'

'The Company.' I used the insider term for the CIA. 'No one else.'

He shifted the words: 'Who gave you the money that Lucy moved through the accounts?'

'I didn't know about the money.'

'Why did you bomb the office? Who was threatened by the office's work?'

I thought of all the networks we tried to study, the Money Czar who had no name, his face displayed on the presentation screen in the final moments before the office was destroyed. 'I didn't do it! I didn't!'

'Where is your wife? Start with any of those questions and we don't have to dance this dance.'

'I don't know. Please.' I hated myself for that *please*.

'Why was the Holborn office a threat to your employers?'

'I have no employers! Jesus, please believe me. Please!'

My voice told him he was so close to breaking me. So close.

He draped the cloth over my face. 'You're not going to make it out of here to see your kid, Capra.'

'No!' I yelled. 'No!'

He gushed the water over my face. I felt the water closing in on my lungs. I writhed against

38

the straps, trying to move away from the awful, steady flow. The gush surged into what felt like a river.

I was drowning.

I started to babble. Nonsense. Random words. Lucy. The Bundle. God, no. The scarred man. Innocent. Innocent. I knocked myself nearly unconscious, slamming my head against the water board. He hadn't secured me correctly. He slowly dragged the wet fabric off my face. I begged for air. Then he put the soaked shroud back over my nose and mouth.

And then he started again. I resumed screaming and babbling.

I was glad, when they kicked me to the cold embrace of the cell floor, that I cannot hear or remember what I said. Some things are best lost to memory.

7

December came. One of the guards mentioned to me that it was Christmas Day. He did not use the word merry. Then January marched by me. The baby's due date, 10 January, came and passed. Maybe my son was born now, drawing his sharp breaths, needing me. And I was stuck in a rocky hellhole.

That day, Howell came into my cell. 'Your child was due today.'

I looked up from the black bread and the potato soup I was having for lunch.

'Cooperate and maybe we can find her. We have every hospital in Europe on alert for her. You could see your son, Sam. Don't you want to see your boy?'

My face set into steel, no matter how torn my heart felt. 'Yes. But I've told you everything. Let me go, Howell. Let me go. Let me help you find her.'

'What would you have named him?'

I didn't want to talk to Howell about my lost son. I didn't want to talk to Howell period. 'Screw you,' I said. 'What the hell would you care what we wanted to name our kid?'

'You're really angry today, Sam.'

'I'm sick of you. Of all of you. Of your utter stupidity.'

Howell studied me, and then he stood. 'Here's the thing. I've fought for you. I believed you

40

when you said you knew nothing. I think you are an innocent man. For what that's worth.' He dropped a piece of paper on the stone floor. A photo of one of the ultrasounds, The Bundle in all his glory. Howell walked out.

I studied the picture. My child.

Am I a father? Has he been born? I have to get out of here. My kid needs me.

But I stayed sitting on the cold stone floor, thinking.

8

A winter spent with cheek against stone. I kept insisting on my innocence into February. Every day, every aspect of my life was questioned, dissected, dissolved. Every day, I was doubted.

Do you know what that is like? To not be believed? To not be believed by the people who are your peers, your friends, your sole support, when your family has gone missing? To have your colleagues sure that you are capable of treason and murder?

You cannot build a crueler jail.

March came. Howell was gone; there was no more water-boarding. Four different interrogators asked the same questions and listened to my litany of innocence. One morning two thick-necked ex-Marines came in and held me down and slid a needle into my skin and part of me hoped: this is it, the forever dark, the end. Now they're done with me.

I woke up back in America.

The television mounted in the corner played Comedy Central. I jerked around to look at the walls. No window. Just white walls, the hospital bed, a chair, the television with a standup comic roaming the stage, screaming into a microphone, making fun of newlywed guys for being lame and uncool. Restraints bound my arms to the bed. The room smelled of disinfectant and lavender air freshener. I was washed and clean, for the first time in weeks. Cold against my butt I felt a bedpan, and poking into my flesh I felt a catheter; in my arm was an IV drip.

I stayed very still but all I heard was the soft, dreamy hum of hospital equipment and air conditioning. I didn't call out for the nurse. I was clean and in a bed and not in a dank, forgotten cell and no one was kicking me.

The comedian on the TV bitched about his wife. He poked fun at the insane demands of his kids. I wanted to strangle him for his blind ingratitude. He didn't know how lucky he was. Then I just closed my eyes and I slept again, clean and comfortable, on sheets instead of stone.

When I woke my mouth tasted sour with sleep. Still bound. Bedpan and catheter. A nurse entered the room and inspected me. She didn't let her eyes meet my gaze.

'Hello,' I said.

She didn't answer.

'Where am I?' I croaked.

She still didn't answer. She checked my vitals and made her notes and then she left. I tested the strength of the restraints. I wouldn't be breaking loose . . . On the table now, pushed to the side, stood a green bottle of Boylan Bottleworks Ginger Ale, my all-time favorite soda. It's made in New Jersey and you can't get it everywhere. And a bottle of Heineken, although since I'd taken up parkour I didn't drink very often. Both bottles glistened with beads of cold. Stacked next to it were books by my favorite authors. Pecan pralines, my favorite candy. A Hubig's fried pie from New Orleans, a childhood treat from one of the few times when my folks lived in the States when I was a kid. A prickle of sweat formed on my back. This was some new torture.

Then a man stepped into my room. Broad-shouldered, dressed in a neat, bland gray suit, gray tie, blue shirt, his hair cut down to a burr, slices of gray in the goatee. Howell.

'Hello, Sam. How are you today? You've slept quite a bit, which is just what you need to get back on your feet.' His voice sounded kind, like he really cared how I was. Soft, quiet, and immediately I hated him again. The past months had taught me that I had no friends and no patience with those who pretended to be my friend.

He saw the fire in my eyes and for a moment he glanced away.

'Where am I?' I said.

'You're in New York City. I will be your liaison.'

'What do you mean, liaison?'

'You're being released.' He flinched a smile at me.

I didn't believe it. It must be a trick. I made myself breathe. 'You found my wife?'

'No.'

'Then why . . . '

'Your innocence has been established.' Now Howell's voice stiffened, and the words felt a shade rehearsed. 'We regret the inconvenience.'

I could neither laugh nor howl at the four small words, their pitiful sentiment, their

44

complete inadequacy to the hell I had endured. When I found my voice it sounded cracked. 'Established how?'

'It doesn't matter, Sam. We know you're innocent.'

I closed my eyes. 'Then you're lying to me, you must have found Lucy.'

'No,' he said. 'I swear to you, we do not know where she is.'

The silence between us, broken by the comic's rantings in the background. I reached for the remote and my fingers fumbled for a grip. Howell picked it up and turned off the television.

'I don't believe *you* now.'

'This is no trick, Sam,' Howell said. 'We know you're innocent. Just be grateful for your freedom.'

Grateful. Freedom. The words sanded against each other in my brain. 'You people tortured me. You held me prisoner, without a lawyer, without cause.'

'It didn't happen, Sam.' Slowly, Howell unbuckled the straps binding my legs to the bed. He moved with caution, like he was removing the top of a basket holding a cobra. He looked up to catch my stare and swallowed, as though realizing he should not show fear. 'You will be integrated back into civilian life, Sam. Think of me as a parole officer.'

'Innocent people aren't on parole.'

'The Company asked me to serve in this role. I'm the only one who believed you, do you remember? I said I thought you were innocent. I

45

was your only advocate, Sam.'

'You were a piss-poor one.'

Howell gave a long, low sigh and sat on the side of the bed. 'I told the directors I thought you were telling the truth. Finally they believed me when . . . '

'When what?' I leaned forward.

'I can't discuss it.'

'You owe me.'

'No, we don't owe you a thing,' Howell said. 'You were too blind to see what was in front of you.'

'You know Lucy is guilty? Tell me.' Oh, God, confirmation of the impossible, that my wife was a traitor.

'Do you want your freedom back, Sam?'

'Yes.'

'Then shut up. Swallow down every question and don't ask me about Lucy.' He cleared his throat. 'We need to talk about your immediate future, though.'

I sat up slowly. 'My future is I'm going to find my wife. And my child.'

'You are not. She remains a national security matter. As do you. You will do as you're told.'

And I would, until I did what I wanted. I could play the game. I swallowed my questions. 'My parents . . . '

'Your parents think you want nothing to do with them, Sam. Let's keep it that way.'

I was silent. This was my shame. Normal people had normal relations with their parents. Mine weren't quite normal, at least where I was concerned.

46

'Of course your parents were thoroughly investigated. They are a bit . . . unconventional.'

'Stay away from them.'

'Oh, that would be a loss for me. I find them charming; we like to sit in the garden and drink tea. I've visited with them several times. My division at the Company bought the house next to theirs in New Orleans; I'm their manufacturing representative neighbor who travels a great deal. We've had their house bugged for months, tapped their phones, watched them. Just in case their pregnant daughter-in-law contacted them or they attempted to make inquiries about you. But only silence. Since they didn't hear from you at Christmas, they are a bit worried that the gulf between you cannot be bridged.' He shrugged. 'Don't take it hard. We sometimes don't like the people we love.' He told me this like he was handing me a gift.

'My parents — just leave them alone.'

'Then do as I say and the surveillance, the investigation of them, will end.' He raised his hands, palms toward me. 'I don't want to involve your parents. They're fine people, Sam.'

I was being bribed. Fine. I would protect my parents. 'Deal.' I cleared my throat.

'It's your lucky day. You were never technically fired. You are still under Company command. You have been assigned to my group. I am your boss.'

I wanted to say *I resign* but: 'Then let me help you look for her.'

Howell raised an eyebrow. 'Do you really want your job with us, Sam?'

47

'Yes.' It was the first rational lie I'd told in months. I didn't count any lies I had screamed during the waterboarding. Apparently none of my false information worked out for the Company.

'Then here are your orders. You stay put here in New York. There is an account at a bank that has been opened in your name, with a sizeable initial deposit. Enough to live on, although I suggest you find work. If only to keep your mind and hands busy.'

'Work. But you said . . . '

'You remain on our payroll. But your clearances are gone, Sam. So find a job to keep you busy. One that requires no travel and is not demanding.'

'I can't sit still. Not with my family in trouble.'

Howell rode right over that speed bump. 'You want to help find Lucy? Then do what you're told. Sit tight. Get a job. A simple one.'

'I've only ever worked for the Company. I started straight out of college.'

'You tended bar in college, though. Pour beers, mix martinis. The jobs are easy to find.' He shrugged. As though all my training, all my field experience in Company work meant nothing.

I steadied my voice. I was caught between rage and knowing that if I throttled Howell I'd be back in the cell. Slowly, unbound now, I got off the bed. Howell steadied me. I felt woozy from the drugs, from inactivity. 'I cannot put this more plainly. I am going to find my wife. My child.'

'You are going to follow orders, or you will regret it, Mr Capra.'

'You can't keep me . . . '

'If you break parole you will be back in prison, facing charges ranging from money laundering to treason. Any proof of your innocence will be eliminated and you will be prosecuted.' It was a nasty bit of leverage. Anger colored his voice and I shut up so I could hear the deal.

The rest of my life hinged on what he offered.

'You hunker down, you don't let yourself get bored, and you don't go to the press, you don't go to your friends in the Company — not that you have any left. Not everyone knows that your name has been cleared. You let us look for Lucy and you don't get in our way.'

'So what am I now? Worthless?'

For the first time I saw in that horrible flinch in his eyes what I had never seen in the past months: pity. 'How are you worth anything to us, Sam? You either knew she was a traitor, and did nothing, which makes you pure evil in the Company's eyes; or you didn't know she was a traitor. And that makes you a pure fool.'

I looked at him and then I looked at the spotless tile floor. We were back to his original question to me. After all my pain.

'You'll recuperate here, gain your strength before we send you out into the world. You lost a bit too much weight,' Howell said. 'Let's go see what clothes we have to fit you. Then I'll take you downstairs.' He got up and opened the cold beer for me. He handed me the icy bottle. 'We've made all your favorites. Spicy corn soup, salad

49

with blue cheese, roast beef with horseradish, mashed potatoes, asparagus, key lime pie, coffee. Doesn't that dinner sound good?'

My mouth watered, to my shame. I hoped the food would taste like ashes. 'It sounds like a last supper.'

Now Howell risked another very slight smile. 'Just do as we ask.'

'And forgive the months you made me suffer?'

'Let's all just pretend it didn't happen.'

'It didn't *happen*? God.'

They needed me out in the world. Why?

'There are clothes for you in the closet. I'll ask the nurse to get you all disconnected, if you like, and I'll let you get dressed.'

I started to pull off the medical sensor glued to my chest.

'I do have one question for you, Sam,' he said.

I left the sensors alone. 'What?'

'Novem Soles.' He said the words so softly I wasn't sure I heard.

'What?'

'Have you heard that term before?'

'Novem Soles? Sounds Latin. Novem is nine, what is Soles?'

'Suns. Nine suns. Did Lucy ever use those words with you, ever mention them?'

This wasn't a casual question. I stopped and I considered. He watched me. 'No. What does it mean?' It sounded silly. But the Company gave computer-selected codes to every job, operation or project and this sounded like one of those code names. Nine suns? It meant nothing to me.

He studied me and I wondered if the sensors

50

on my chest were being monitored to see if I was lying. Howell smiled. 'It means let's go eat that good dinner.'

He went to the door and the nurse came in. She removed the catheter and the sensors and put the IV on a trolley. She helped me into a robe. I was weak and now starving and I shuddered at the thought of accepting these bastards' kindnesses. Food on a plate. Edible food, not the slop they'd given me. I'd eat it. I needed my strength.

I stood up from the bed. Howell offered a steadying arm and I shook it away. Fine, I would take their food and their clothes and their false solicitude and I would get back on my feet. But I had no illusions. I was not Howell's friend, or someone that he wanted to help, who might ever get his life or his job back. His words *it didn't happen* rankled in my ear.

They hadn't found Lucy in these long months, or the man with the question-mark scar. So they still needed me. Howell and his superiors had found something called Novem Soles, whatever that was, and they thought putting me back out in the real world might lead them to it.

I knew the truth: I was bait. Bait for whoever set up me and Lucy.

9

August Holdwine drained the trace of whisky from the glass in front of him, centered the glass back on the napkin on the oaken bar, and studied me. 'I'm not here to spy on you,' he said. 'In case I need to state the obvious.'

'I know,' I said. 'Howell has people to follow me and make sure I look both ways before I cross the street. They have a van and I think they call their moms three times a day. You want another?'

'No. I have to work tomorrow.' But he didn't stand up to rise. August was a big guy, about six-six, old college muscle that hadn't morphed all the way into fat but was considering the option. He had blondish hair and apple cheeks and heavy muscles under the shirt. He said, 'Uh, maybe I shouldn't say anything about work.'

'I'm not bothered that you still have a job and I'm serving drinks,' I said. 'Bartending is honorable.'

'I think I would rather be serving drinks. Less stress.'

'Want to trade?'

August and I had gone through training together at the Company, me straight from Harvard, him fresh from the University of Minnesota. He was my opposite: a farm boy who'd spent most of his life in one place, on land that had been in his family for seven generations.

I couldn't imagine such stability. He had a broad open face, the kind decent people trusted, and a gravelly baritone voice. He worked stateside, in a satellite office in Manhattan. He'd landed me the bartending job at Ollie's. I was grateful. None of my other friends in the Company had bothered to call or express condolences. I was tainted. Like Howell said, conventional wisdom dictates the spouse always knows treason is under the roof. So I was beyond hope, as Howell put it, suspect, irreparably damaged goods. Except to August. But that was fine; August was the perfect friend to sit with in a bar. You could talk to him about your darkest secret and know he wouldn't judge you or you could be silent with him and just watch sports and never share a thought. Either was cool with August.

I wanted to trust August. But I couldn't. Either he was under orders to be Howell's tool or he wasn't, and if he knew anything he would get in trouble once I put my plan into motion.

'So. Early morning tomorrow,' he said. 'I should go.'

'You got cows to milk?' I enjoyed teasing him about his farming past.

He didn't stand up from the bar.

'Do you want another drink?' I waited.

He looked up at me with his watery blue eyes. 'What are you doing, Sam?'

'Pouring beer mostly.' I glanced down the bar; no other customers. It was a Monday night, always the slowest at Ollie's. Odd, because Mondays sucked so bad that you'd think most people would want a drink to wash the

53

beginning of the week out of their mouths.

'You're very quiet.'

'I don't have a lot to say, August.'

'I don't know what you were told, but not everyone at the Company believes you turned. Most of your friends are still your friends.'

'Most? That warms the heart.'

He shrugged. He meant well but I guess he just didn't know what to say. Thousands upon thousands of people work for the Company; the traitors in its history are very, very few, and rightly unforgiven.

'And yet there's no crowd here tonight, what with my many friends.' I wiped down the already clean bar.

August picked up his glass and set it down when he remembered it was empty.

'Are you being brave in staying my friend, August, or are you just doing your job?' I'd intended not to push the subject but my patience was thinning.

'I'm not here because anyone told me to be. Howell said you were cleared but you couldn't go back to work, not yet.'

'I'm a lure to draw out whoever took Lucy. The idea being that I wasn't supposed to survive the explosion and she messed up that plan.'

August said, 'I know all that. Be bait, then. But don't think you're alone. You're not.'

'We stirred up a pot, August, the office in London. On this Money Czar guy, on a bunch of criminal networks. If you could help me . . . find out if there's been any new evidence come to light on who was behind the bombing.'

'Sam. I can't. I don't have that clearance.'

'But you could access the files . . .'

He held up a hand. 'I cannot. End of discussion. Let them investigate. Be glad they've cleared your name.'

'If they have.'

He cleared his throat. 'You have to consider the possibility Lucy set you up.'

'For three years? No.'

'Maybe she wasn't dirty three years ago. Maybe she turned much more recently.'

It's very *Twilight Zone* to have a talk with your oldest friend from work that revolves around the theme *my wife is not a traitor*. 'Because pregnant women are notable for wanting to put themselves at risk of arrest and imprisonment.'

August turned the glass in his hands. 'I'm just saying.'

'Then why save me?' I couldn't let the argument go.

'Don't be an idiot, Sam. You're alive, the sole survivor, the Company focuses on you. Not her. You're in their grip. It gave her a chance to run.'

'I can't think that.'

'Because you're being a good husband?'

I stared into his watery blue eyes. 'Because if she was dirty, she still lived with me for three years and she knows that if she betrayed me and killed our friends and I'm alive to come after her, I will. So if she was dirty, she'd want me dead.' I kept my voice steady and calm.

'So all this energy, and you're still sitting here in Brooklyn?'

55

'If I run, they grab me and I'm back in a jail cell.'

'Unless you're smart about how you run.'

'August. I just got out of a Company prison. I'm not risking a return ticket. We are not having this conversation.'

August put his money on the table and said, 'Don't worry about the change.'

'Okay.' I watched him leave. It's awkward to tip a friend and I didn't want him to, but I slid the change into the tip jar. I got back to work, which involved making a pot of decaf for Ollie and serving a group of wannabe artists who came in five minutes later for a round of Pabst Blue Ribbon beers.

Most people at Ollie's Bar drank beer and wine. But at least six times a day I made vodka martinis; five times a day I poured whisky; and now and then I made a margarita on the rocks. There wasn't a frozen margarita machine; it wasn't that kind of bar. Usually a couple of early customers at the lunchtime opening wanted Bloody Marys and I made them extra spicy and got bigger tips. I made drinks and kept quiet and gained back weight I'd lost and slept a lot. August came and drank during my evening shifts. A few questions to my fellow barkeeps told me that he didn't come in on my days off. I felt myself getting stronger but I was only running very basic parkour, vaults onto railings and low walls, because I was too out of practice and I didn't want to risk an injury. I pretended not to notice the surveillance Howell had put on me. Three rookies, two on foot, one in a van, were nearly constant whenever I left the bar or my apartment. They were testing me, seeing what I might do, how close to their orders I would stay. Or, conversely, waiting for someone to kill me.

10

I like bars. I don't drink a lot but I like the air of a good bar — the ripe wisdom of animated conversation, the cutting smell of fine liquor, the sound of laughter among friends. Ollie's was a good, simple bar. Quiet most nights, a wide oaken bar surface, stools topped with leather that bore the imprints of loyal and regular customers, not a lot of kitsch on the walls — just mirrors from the beer companies and framed photos of Ollie's father, the original owner, with many of his longtime customers. The regulars were a bit of a mix, older folks who'd been in the neighborhood a long while, younger folks with a bohemian bent who might be borrowing money from parents to pursue art or internships. Now and then the Manhattan-commuting professionals would slum at Ollie's, and they tipped well and drank imports and more lavish cocktails. But the people, most of them, were nice. No one asked me questions. I just served the drinks, made idle talk when required, and no one knew my hell.

The Company got me an apartment three streets over from Ollie's, on the edge of Williamsburg, in Brooklyn. It wasn't cheap, but I wasn't paying the rent, and the building I was in was seeing several units remodeled, so I didn't have many neighbors. Howell, no doubt, liked my isolation. I assumed that Ollie's and my place were being bugged, perhaps even with cameras hidden inside. Probably installed by August. I found the bugs, four of them, and the next morning I walked straight to the van and, as they stared at me in surprise, I laid the bugs on the van roof, in a nice straight line. Then I walked away. The next day they had a new car to follow me in and I didn't find any replacement bugs. Didn't mean they weren't there, though.

It was like life in a cage. But it wasn't the stone prison cell. I wondered how long Howell's men would keep an eye on me, and, if I didn't draw out Lucy's kidnappers, if they'd shutter me back behind bars.

I thought about how to escape. I would do myself no favors by rushing. I was still in a cage, but a cage where I could move. I did not want to be back in the Polish prison.

And when I wasn't serving drinks, I thought about Lucy and The Bundle.

In late March one day, I arrived a bit hurt. A bicycle courier had sideswiped me while crossing a street and I'd fallen, scraping my forearm. My shadows did nothing to help me. I rolled up my sleeve to keep the shirt clean and went into the front; it was early afternoon on a Saturday and only one customer sat along the bar.

She was a few years older than me, maybe thirty. Pretty but eyes of hard quartz, a slash of a mouth. Her cheekbones would have made a photographer contemplate a next great shot. She wore black slacks and a dark sweater. Her hair was blondish, the color of fresh straw, and cut to just above her shoulders. She picked up her neat whisky, drank it carefully. She moved with precision. She was not looking at me but I thought she was entirely aware of me. My first thought was: she's major trouble.

'Do you have a first-aid kit?' I asked Ollie.

'Yes, in my office.' Ollie sounded irritated. I'd interrupted a discussion between him and the woman. He jabbed a thumb at me. 'This one. Runs like a maniac, bouncing off stairs and buildings and such. He'll fall and break his neck and then I'll be out a halfway decent bartender.' Ollie felt self-esteem to be overrated.

The woman surveyed me. '*L'art de displacement?*' Her voice was low and cool, like a summer breeze coming out of a tree's shadow, and she had an odd accent I couldn't quite decipher. She was beautiful to look at — although I had no real eye for any woman but Lucy — but I did not like her.

But she'd used the original French name for parkour running. I nodded. 'Are you a *traceur?*' I asked. A term for parkour runners, drawn from the French term for a special kind of bullet that leaves a trail.

'Oh, no. I used to live in Paris. I used to watch the kids trying parkour, running along the edges of buildings, throwing themselves from rooftop to rooftop, amazed that they didn't break their legs.' She smiled the slash-smile again. 'I wished I had their nerve, their fleetness.'

'I say if you want to run an obstacle course, get on a track.' Ollie poured more whisky in the woman's glass, although she hadn't asked.

'But life's an obstacle course,' the woman said.

'The runners run in the world we live in, not an artificial one.' She turned back to me. 'I always thought they looked like animals.'

I raised an eyebrow.

'In their grace. Wolves on the street. Hunters. The runners looked to me like a pack, closing on prey.' The woman sipped her whisky. 'I have a fondness for wolves.'

It was exactly the sort of bizarre comment you hear in a bar that would make no sense anywhere else but seems reasonable in dim light with the sting of booze on your lips. Ollie stared at the woman, auditioned an unsure smile, and decided to end the discussion of wolves with introductions. 'Hey, Sam, this is Mila.'

Mila offered a hand. I shook it. 'Are you a regular, Mila? I'm still learning who's who in Ollie's kingdom.'

'She's a wandering regular. Stops in when she's in town, which is only like three times a year. And then I can't get rid of her for a week,' Ollie grinned. 'She keeps wanting to buy the bar from me but you know I will never sell.'

'I can work on him for you,' I said with a polite bartender smile. 'I'm sure he wants to retire to Florida.'

'Oh, God, no,' Ollie said. 'New York till I die.'

'He won't sell, but he listens to my proposals because he sells me a bottle's worth of Glenfiddich during that week.' Mila kept her hands folded on the bar in front of her, primly.

'Nice to be able to travel,' I said.

'The world is a smaller place these days. Much smaller.' Mila shrugged — a small, elegant

61

gesture. 'Be careful on your parkour runs, Sam. Ollie will not spare the whip if you're on crutches.'

'Sam I don't need to whip. The others, Jesus, Mila, you can't believe it. How hard is it to pour neatly and quickly and accurately into a glass? To pour? Gravity does the work. This is not surgery. I tell you, that day-shift guy, he sloshes my profit margin onto the floor and I mop it up . . . '

I raised my arm. 'I better bandage this.'

I found the first-aid kit in Ollie's cramped office. There was a desk, with scatterings of papers, an ancient, grinding PC Ollie had never quite mastered (I'd had to help him do searches on the web and also recover a lost spreadsheet), and a safe. He'd mentioned he kept a gun inside, and, in case I ever needed a gun, I was glad to know where I could borrow one. The safe would not be difficult to crack; it had a keypad, and, considering Ollie's general loathing of technology I suspected the pass code would be a simple one to guess.

Arm tightly bandaged, and dressed to work, I went back out to the bar. Mila was gone, bills tucked under her glass. She was an excellent tipper.

'She completes me,' Ollie said. 'Damn. I like her but there's no hope.'

'Where's she from?'

'Everywhere.'

If Howell wanted to have me followed by someone other than his normal teams, or wanted to insert someone into my life, he might pick a person like Mila. Or if the Money Czar was coming after me, *he* might send someone like her.

But. But she had a history with Ollie. Unless Ollie was lying about that, and was in Howell's pay. Hello, madness. You see how your mind starts to twist: you suspect everyone. I went back to wiping down the bar, trying to blank my mind.

'Hey, I got this for you.' Ollie pushed a thick book at me. I looked at the cover. A bartender's guide. I opened it to the end to see how many pages it was: 508. Very comprehensive.

'Preparation is key so you don't mix drinks wrong and waste liquor,' Ollie said. 'Take it home.'

'I will never make most of these drinks.'

'You strike me as a guy who likes to be prepared.' Ollie was right.

The week inched past. Dave with his Budweiser, Meg with her pinot grigio, the Alton brothers with their pints of Guinness every Friday night; they'd watch the pour you did as though you were splitting a diamond. I worked, I ran, and Howell's two shadows followed me everywhere I went. At night I lay in bed and I flicked through the five-hundred-page bartender's guide. It relaxed my mind to consider the thousands of cocktails crafted by humanity; each a perfect little mix of what was at hand to produce a desired result. That was the pattern of thinking I needed to solve my own problem. What elements, mixed together in what order, to create a sublime result.

How to get a gun, how to get documentation to get overseas, how to escape Howell's constant watch.

11

Ollie fired a bartender he didn't like, hired a new one so he'd have a fresh face to bitch about. August showed up twice, watched part of a basketball game, didn't have much to say to me. I felt he was trying to summon the courage to broach a topic but didn't know how to start.

Then there was the lovely Mila. She came in for four more nights, discussed world politics with Ollie and asked me about my parkour runs and nothing else. But I felt her watching me as I worked, as though taking my measure. Ollie's mother in New Jersey got sick and he had me manage the bar for two days; one night I lifted prints off the safe's keypad, found prints on only four keys. Same four numbers as the bar's street address. I tested the code; the safe opened. Inside was a cash bag, a Glock with three rounds of ammo and Ollie's passport, used once three years ago to visit Ireland. I left everything where it was, cleaned off the keypad, and felt relief I could get to a gun when I needed one. Because I thought the time had come to move. Howell's followers had been a bit lazy, not coming up on me when the bicyclist hit me. They were slacking or Howell was loosening the leash on me. They'd convinced themselves that I was willing to sit still. That was the key to escape.

Now I knew where I could steal a gun. But I had no passport. And I needed to get back to

Europe. Lucy's trail started there.

But I didn't know where I could obtain fake documentation in New York. Passports now have digital watermarks and subtle chips and they can't be forged as easily as they used to be. You need someone who can acquire the special paper used in the passports — usually by bribing someone who might send in a diplomatic pouch or works in government printing. It didn't have to be an American passport; in fact, it would be easier for me to have one from Belgium or the UK or Canada. Belgian papers particularly are known for being easy to forge.

So. I had to find a way to find a contact who could get me a passport that could pass muster. I knew the street value of a false passport was around eight thousand dollars. I would have to either save or steal the money and I'd have to lose my tails to find a seller. I bought a cellular phone, prepaid, close to the Brooklyn Flea Market, using the crowds to lose Howell's shadows for a few minutes to make the buy. I made some discreet ventures, calling my non-CIA contacts in Prague and Paris and London, looking for someone who could help me get back to Europe.

No one I called knew I was part of the Company. I used an old identity from the Prague sting, a former Canadian soldier named Samson — close enough to Sam so I wouldn't ever tongue-stumble using it — who operated as a smuggler and hired gun.

I got stonewalled for three days until a friend in London mentioned a broker in New Jersey named Kitter who could set me up with Belgian papers. I called Kitter to arrange a meet in Bryant Park in midtown Manhattan the next day.

I dodged my shadows by going into Ollie's — the tails did not sit in the bar, they watched from outside — and then heading out the back of the building, down a side alley through a deli. If a shadow there saw me, and I had to assume they would, it made sense to dodge into a department store and exit out the back, hurrying into a hotel across the street. I watched for familiar faces — it's easy to dump out of a suit into casual wear, you can't rely on clothes as identifiers, you can only rely on the face. I felt clean and I grabbed a taxi to Manhattan an hour early. Got off at Grand Central, felt I was still walking clean. I kept scanning the patterns of people's movements for any followers as I walked through building lobbies and hotel lobbies, in and out, cutting through, doubling back, not spotting Howell or any of his regulars following me.

The man fitting Kitter's description sat on the edge of a bench, iPod earphones in place, wires trailing inside his jacket. He was reading *The Wall Street Journal*. Thin blue jeans, flannel shirt. I sat on the other edge of the bench.

He pulled out his earphones but he didn't look at me.

'Our mutual friend sent me,' I said. 'I need documentation.' A tickle surged at the back of my throat, I felt the need to rush. Stupid. But I'd been waiting days, weeks, months for a chance to track Lucy. I was like a dog, straining at the leash, ready to run. How could I wait any more? I dreamed of my family every night.

'You have the photos and the money.'

'Four thousand and the photos.' Half up front, half when I got the finished passport.

He took the envelope from me and told me to wait. 'Meet me at the Starbucks on the north side of Grand Central in three hours.'

Kitter stood and walked off. I sat for a moment, thinking, good. Then I stood and started to walk and my stomach wrenched. Forty feet away stood Howell, hands tucked inside his overcoat. I turned around; Kitter and my money were gone.

I sat back down. I stayed on the bench and Howell walked up to me. He didn't sit.

'I don't blame you,' he said. 'My wife, my child, I'd be doing whatever I could to get to them.'

'Can I have my money back?'

'No. Let it be a lesson learned.'

'You're the one who needs a lesson,' I said. 'I could draw out Lucy's kidnappers if I could get back to London. I know I could.'

'We can't trust you. Look how you've disobeyed instructions.'

'But you said you don't blame me.'

'You have not been fired, Sam, and your job classification has been reassigned so that you cannot resign without the permission of the Director. You do not have that permission. You're ours. Do what you're told and be glad you're not locked in a cell for the rest of your life. We have

68

been generous to you. Go back to that charming neighborhood bar, smile at people, be glad you're not sucking cold soup out of a wooden bowl and being beaten every night.'

I shook my head. 'I dream about my son,' I said. 'Did you have that in your file, Howell? I dream about my wife and my child because I know she's innocent and I know she and my kid are out there and . . . you are in my way.' I heard the iron growl in my tone, for the first time in a long time.

He was unimpressed. 'You're in your own way. Go home, Sam. Play nice. I won't be so forgiving next time. There was a debate in the office about whether to shoot you on sight for attempting to acquire forged documents. Your actions could be the act of a desperate man or a guilty man. I argued for desperate and thank God for you I won. But desperation fades. Do this twice, then you're guilty.'

'You don't have the balls to arrest me because you need me out here as bait,' I said. 'I call your bluff. Stick me back in the cell. I'm not sitting still, Howell.'

'Go home, and we'll pretend it didn't happen.'

'That really is your favorite phrase, isn't it? *It didn't happen.* But sticking my head in the sand doesn't work for me.'

Howell turned and walked away from me, lighting a cigarette as he walked, blowing out an annoyed plume of smoke.

He was wrong. Desperation doesn't fade. It just gets stronger. I watched him walk away and then I got up and walked in the opposite direction.

I took the bus back to Brooklyn. I didn't bother to try to shake any shadows. It made the trip much faster. I went to work, listening to Ollie tell me the same stories he'd told me yesterday, drawing lunchtime half-pints of Harp and Budweiser, jetting sodas into glasses, listening to regulars prattle on about their problems with difficult clients or troublesome bosses or wives who just didn't understand, and when Ollie bitched about not getting full shipments of Glenfiddich — he was a crate short — I thought of an escape from this second prison.

12

August was sitting on the stoop at my apartment building when I got home.

'I'm in trouble,' I said. 'Are you?' I sounded like a fifth-grader caught skipping school.

He looked out onto the street like he was back home surveying the windswept plains. 'From what I heard, it didn't happen.'

'Howell is, if nothing else, consistent.'

'I think you're lucky you're not dead. You owe Howell big time.'

'I am never going to be in that man's debt.'

'Plus, I didn't know what you were up to,' he said with a shrug. 'Can I have a beer?'

'You could have gotten a beer at the bar.'

'I'm tired of hearing Ollie's opinions,' August said.

'Sure.' We walked up to my apartment. It was bare, furnished only with the second-hand stuff the Company had bought before I moved in. I opened the fridge and handed him a cold Heineken.

'You can't run, Sam,' he said, popping the little keg-shaped can.

'You should have told me that this morning,' I said.

'Your stunt set off a wildfire here. Some people wanted you put back into jail. Others took it as a clear sign that you were dirty. Howell fought for you. I thought you should know. You have one other friend than me, and that's Howell.'

'What is Novem Soles? Howell asked me about it. It connects to Lucy somehow and the London bombing.'

'Never heard of it. And you shouldn't be asking questions. Not today, when you're lucky to be out of a noose.'

'Maybe this is the group that has her. I want you to see what you can find about it. Please.'

'You know I can't share any classified stuff with you.'

'Then why are you here, August? A free beer?'

His cheeks reddened. 'I am here to give you a warning,' he said. 'You're a horrible embarrassment, Sam. The cover-up that was involved in London to keep from the press that it was a CIA front that was bombed was enormous. Nearly two dozen people dead, we're lucky it wasn't worse. The British are furious and they'd just as soon kill you if you set foot back on their soil. And for the few that think you might be telling the truth, no one's taking a bullet for you. I'm telling you, watch your back. Higher-ups who normally get their way have argued for you to be terminated. A hungry soul's bound to pick up on the sentiment and will figure they might get a promotion if you conveniently disappear or die, Howell using you as bait and Howell's defense of you be damned.'

'Has the order been issued?'

'It won't *be* an order. Nothing written. Just a wish made and a wish granted. Like King Henry talking about Thomas Becket: 'Will no one rid me of this turbulent priest?'' He finished his beer. 'Watch your back, turbulent.'

'I'll be fine.'

He pulled two phones out of his pocket, handed one to me. 'Here. Only you have this number. If someone comes after you — call me. I'll help you.'

My only friend. I didn't want him to see the heavy swallow in my throat. 'Thank you, August.'

I watched him leave, and then I went to bed. I think best in bed. I cleared my mind by paging through the thick bar book Ollie had loaned me. Every success in life was like a cocktail; a careful blending of elements in exact proportions, done in correct order.

I put the bar book down and I lay watching the ceiling, hatching a plan.

13

I awoke to the barest sound. I didn't move. It was a footstep and then the slightest click of a door closing.

I was bait, and someone was hooked.

I could lay still. I could get up and see who it was. I could wait for one of Howell's rookies to crash in the door and save my ass. But Howell, for all his warm words to me, didn't need me alive after the bait was taken. If this was someone from the scarred man, he could dispatch me and the watchers could catch him later. I wasn't sure the shadows were even listening to me since I'd tossed them their bugs.

Or maybe it was someone like August had said, ridding the Company of their great embarrassment.

I listened for the next footfall. Didn't hear it. I got up from the bed with enormous care, scooted the pillow where I should be, moved on cat feet to the corner of the room behind the door.

I heard nothing else. Maybe I had dreamed the footfall. I stood in the darkness and a crazy thought wormed its way into my head: it's Lucy, come home, finally she's gotten away and she's found me. It was lunacy to think it, but I did.

The air conditioner kicked on. The soft, somnolent hum masked the intruder's movements. I had no weapons. Nothing. I waited.

I expected the intruder to kick in the door and lay a round of fire into the bed.

Didn't happen.

Slowly — as slowly as a door opens in a nightmare that floods you with dread — the door opened. The hinges moved in silence. I waited.

No convenient glow of moonlight lit the stage for killer or victim; the dark in my bedroom was nearly total.

Then a tiny flash of light sparked, seeking the bed. A snap of silenced bullet hitting the mattress.

I slammed the door into the intruder. Hard. I heard him fall back onto the floor and in the thin gleam of light from the den window he swiveled the gun toward me. I powered my foot into his wrist and the bullet skimmed along the expensive hardwoods. I kicked the gun loose, then away.

The intruder stayed as silent as his gun. No yell, no cry out. He was taller than me and I felt hard muscle power into my chest as he drove me back into the bedroom. We landed on the bed and he, with crisp efficiency, yanked a length of sheet around my throat. I hardly heard his breathing increase in heaviness from the exertion.

He started strangling me and I seized the pillow and pressed it hard into his face. Silent standoff as the oxygen deprivation kicked in for both of us. The darkness deepened. I let go of the pillow and he tightened the sheet around me with a renewed vigor. I pile-drove fists hard and sharp into ribcage. Harder. Sixth blow I felt bone crack and the intruder gasped and eased on the strangulation. I was sick and dizzy, struggling to breathe, but I launched myself free of the sheets and aimed a shattering kick into the face.

The intruder fell off the bed and I grabbed at the lamp. I missed, and my hand closed on the bartender's book Ollie had given me. I slammed its five-hundred-page hardcover spine hard against the intruder's throat and pressed downward as he struggled on the floor. He tried to kick me loose but now I had breath and I had fury; there is a primal flutter about killing someone who comes into your house intending you harm. Awful atavistic shudders; I could feel waves of energy pouring from the ganglia at the base my spine, that ancient seat of instinct. I gritted my teeth.

Harder. His struggles grew more frantic. I put all my weight onto the bartender's book. I pressed my knees against him. I wanted him unconscious so he could wake up bound and answer my questions. But then I felt his windpipe break and the crack sent a sick tremble up my arms.

The kicking stopped and I yanked the book off him. The intruder said his first words, just a gurgle of breath. Maybe he called for his mama; maybe he called me a bad name; maybe he cursed whatever boss sent him to his death.

I expected Howell's rookies to crash in if they'd eavesdropped on murder but no, no one was coming. They hadn't put in replacement listening devices. I went and stood in the corner of my bedroom and looked at the splayed body and considered the problem. After a few moments my head was clear.

I had a dead body in my apartment. I dragged him into the bathroom, shut the door, and turned on the light. I eased him into the bathtub; easier to clean. Dead bodies release stuff.

I had never killed a man before. Ever. The body count on my jobs had been, well, zero. I fooled people into telling me things and then I left them. I did not kill them. I never had need.

I am a killer now, I thought, and another calming voice rose in my head: stop it. You did what you had to do. Keep doing what you have to do.

Killing slices your life into a before and after. I was firm in the after, because the alternative was to be the body lying in the cool porcelain tub.

I leaned against the wall and let my gaze focus on the intruder's face. He was around my age, mid-twenties. Olive-skinned, with dark, short hair. Big ears, a wide mouth, a Roman nose that I'd broken with one of my kicks. He wore black jeans, a black T-shirt, a black denim jacket. Dark, heavy boots. I searched him. A heavy knife in the boot he'd never had a chance to go for, of Swiss manufacture. An extra clip for his gun in the jacket pocket. A cell phone, small, light, not packed with features, just a plain, cheap phone that was practically disposable. No passport, no ID, so presumably he'd left those stashed someplace. On his upper arm there was a small, delicately crafted tattoo. A stylized blue nine, in a curving beauty. The top curve of the nine was an orange sun, with short spiky rays.

Nine and sun. Nine suns. Novem Soles. My head felt a little swimmy.

I checked his wallet. A wad of dollars, another wad, of euros. Wedged in the folded corner of one of the euro bills I found a rail ticket, used, from Paris to Amsterdam.

The ticket was three days old. He'd come to Amsterdam from Paris and then here, one could presume.

A man, sent from Europe, to kill me.

I had a problem. Someone had taken the bait. Howell would want to know. But given August's warning, maybe this guy wasn't from the scarred man. He could be Company, stationed in Europe, dispatched by one of my detractors who still thought me a traitor.

I opened his phone. The only referenced activity was a text, sent from the phone six hours earlier. The text read: *arrived at JFK*. I recognized the country code for the Netherlands. I pressed the number to send another text. What the hell.

Let's play, I thought.

Capra done, I typed. *But problem. Followed by surveillance. Clear now but they may have seen face.*

Within one minute the phone vibrated in my hand.

14

The text message displayed: *Do not return now. Lay low. Destroy this phone & I will destroy mine. Call backup number in three days. Good luck.*

Well, that was not helpful. English sent to a Dutch phone number meant little. Practically everyone in Holland spoke English; including any Company operatives there who might consider me a traitor worth killing. And if the person on the other side decided to call this number and saw that the phone still received calls or texts — hmm, he'd realize his buddy had disobeyed orders and figure out that said buddy might be dead.

Understood, I texted back, hoping to get more.

I hope he suffered was the answer.

Wow.

He did I texted back. I knew this was a huge risk; it might raise suspicion that I wasn't following orders.

The call failed. The other end had broken or dismantled the phone; I was texting to ether.

I turned on the lights in the apartment. I found the bullet buried in the bookcase; it had sliced into a copy of *Great Expectations*. I pocketed the bullet and threw the shredded book in the trash under the kitchen sink.

I went and stared at the body. How was I

going to get it out of here? There was not only the matter of the neighbors but Howell's watchers might check the apartment at any time when I was at work and I wasn't inclined to call Howell and say someone took the bait until I knew who this someone was.

My link to Novem Soles, whatever it was, was that someone in Amsterdam wanted me dead, and thought they had gotten their wish.

I could call August. But what could he do?

For the next hour, I retrieved the bullet from the mattress, made the bed, tidied the apartment and then sat and then I paced and I thought about what to do with this dead body.

There was a quiet knock at the door. It was four in the morning. I took the intruder's gun and went to the side of the door.

Howell's soft voice came through the wood. 'Sam?'

'Yes.' I wasn't sure I wanted to open it.

'Are you okay? I got a report your lights have been on for a while.'

'I can't sleep.'

'Open the door.'

I tucked the silencer-capped gun in the back of my pajama pants and made sure the T-shirt covered it. I opened the door. Howell stood there, in jeans and a black sweatshirt. 'Is everything okay?'

I let him step inside and then I shut the door. I hoped he didn't have to use the bathroom.

'You get a call if I leave my lights on?'

'Yes. Especially on a day like today. When you tried to run.'

'I couldn't sleep.'

'You're not up thinking about a new way to run?'

'No. It's just standard-grade insomnia that is the curse of accused traitors. I hope to get an Ambien endorsement next week.' I kept my voice steady, so unbelievably I-am-a-statue steady.

'You're tense.'

'You showing in the middle of the night reminds me that I'm basically still your prisoner. Tension is a by-product.' I shook my head. 'Honestly. I can't believe you get up out of bed in the night to come check on me.'

'You matter to me, Sam. I know you want to believe the whole world is your enemy, but *I'm* not.'

I wanted to believe him. I could hand over the intruder's phone and, you know, validate Howell. Show him the Novem Soles tattoo and say, well, you asked if I'd heard of it and now I have. Make him happy. But Howell and his peers had been so ready to believe the worst of me for so long, I had no reason to trust them. And whoever was gunning for me thought that I was dead. I had to take advantage of that temporary illusion.

I had to move. Quickly.

Howell said, 'Well, if you're all right.'

'I appreciate the concern.' I didn't look at him. It just occurred to me that maybe I had marks on my throat from the intruder's attack or bruises on my face. I hadn't looked in a mirror. 'I think now I can sleep. I mean, knowing that your team is watching over me. You all are better than a nightlight.'

He shook his head at my sarcasm.

If they'd watched everyone enter the building, then they'd notice on their logs that a guy in dark clothes who'd entered at some point hadn't left. Questions would be asked, probably by the morning. I didn't have much time. I met Howell's gaze.

Howell looked at me and he tried, God help him, a smile. 'I know this is a pressure cooker. Just be patient, Sam. The truth will come out.'

'I'm sure of that, Howell. I'm all about the results.' The results were in the tub. And I smiled at him, the tentative way you do when you want a job and you're not sure the interview went well.

He left. I went back into the bathroom and I looked at the dead guy for a minute. I looked at the useless phone number on his cell and then I took apart the phone. I didn't want whoever wanted me dead to be the least bit suspicious. I went next door to an apartment under renovation and I picked the lock, then I carried the body there and put it in the bathtub. I cranked the air-conditioning to its highest setting. The body would start to stink in the next day, which was Saturday, but the remodelers didn't work weekends so as not to disturb the current tenants, so I might have two days before the body was found, if I was extremely lucky. Fine. I would be gone by then.

I disassembled the cell phone and put the pieces into a plastic bag I could throw away after I left the apartment. I didn't want the Company finding it after I was gone; I didn't want them on my trail.

I went back to bed, and I thought that, having killed, I would never sleep again. But I slept the deep and restful slumber that comes after making a hard decision.

* * *

My spark of inspiration came from a complaint Ollie had made about some missing imported whisky. Because there are thousands of containers holding crates of fine whiskies shipped from Ireland and Scotland, and nearly nine billion metric tons of all sorts of cargo shipped on the seas every year. These goods are mostly carried in two hundred million containers — twenty-foot or forty-foot long steel coffins you can fill with whisky or shoes or computers or frozen meat or whatever. Even me.

Many cargo ships carry six thousand containers or more. Almost none of these containers are inspected for contraband. A busy port may see thirty thousand containers a day enter and then be loaded onto rail and trucks. As the ships arrive to deliver their cargo — whether in New York or Boston or Los Angeles or Houston — they are met by a fleet of trucks. Stop the containers to conduct detailed inspections, which involves offloading a container onto a truck, hauling it to a scanner, having bureaucrats complete paperwork and watch the inspection, unpack and then repack if any anomalies are found, and then reload and return to a truck, and you get a logistical and financial nightmare. Any inspected container creates a delay, strains a link in the surprisingly delicate economic chain. Trucks bring cargo or empty containers to the port and they take away cargo from the port.

Stop for inspections, and the trucks and the trains moving the raw goods and finished products stop. The stores don't have necessities on their shelves. The shoppers complain, the stores lose profits, the shareholders scream bloody murder, the politicians listen.

This is the big, gaping hole in our armor.

The security people brag that six per cent of containers get inspected. That math means ninety-four per cent don't. But that number lies. Six per cent at a major port would be nearly two thousand containers a day. It simply doesn't happen.

I could get to Europe if I could get inside a container. The odds of being caught in an inspection were very low. Hide in the steel box for seven to ten days, get spit out in London or more likely Rotterdam, the biggest European port. Then hitch a boat into London. Start looking for Lucy and my son.

All I had to do was smuggle myself.

16

Amsterdam

Edward loved fear. The smell of it in the skin, the taste of it in the saliva, the feel of it in the drumming heartbeat. Fear was the most powerful force in the world. Edward knew fear was the engine for religion, the spark for war, even the kindling for love — because people are all afraid to be alone.

Fear had been the key to breaking the young woman's soul.

Edward sipped his coffee at the kitchen table and considered the past two weeks. His experiment had proved to the malcontents and low-level criminals he'd formed into a loose gang that a careful application of abuse, drugs, isolation, coupled with a consistent dose of rape and frequent threats of execution, could produce desired effects. He could tell each morning that the group's nervousness about the kidnapping had lessened: the ransoms were paid, and the young woman had begun to drift into their circle. It wasn't so different from his student days as an actor: you created a character and stepped into the skin. Now he'd done that for the young woman. He had remade her into a new character.

Edward made it clear to the others that no one else was to touch her; no one else was to speak to her without his permission.

She was his clay. He knew, though, that they listened at the closed door as he told her of her evils, and the evils that she and her father had done, while he held the knife to her throat and pushed himself inside her. He knew they eavesdropped on the disintegration of another human being. And he'd told her they were listening, and it made her more afraid.

It was lunchtime and most of the group had gone for a walk around Amsterdam to enjoy the sunny cool of the day. The others were eating in the main room.

He could talk to her alone now. Alone was best. He opened the knapsack and looked at the most interesting gear that she had rigged for him. It had taken a long while to get all the materials, but now it was done and there was only the final step. His only worry was Simon, who had to lay low in Brooklyn now that Sam Capra was dead, but would be in touch, no doubt, in a few days.

He put down his coffee cup and went upstairs. She was kept in a small closet in the corner. He told the gang she was frightened of enclosed places and her claustrophobia had played a critical role in her unraveling. Research was so important. He unlocked the door and inched it open.

She lay curled in the dark, holding her stomach, trembling. The room was not cold but still she shivered. She stared at him, not drawing away, just lying there, waiting to see what he would do.

'It is an important day,' he said. He did not climb atop her, pushing her legs apart and easing down the sweatpants she wore for his pleasure. He did not yell at her about why everything in her Old Life was bad, and disgusting and criminal, and an affront against human dignity, and how they fought against injustice. He did not play her videos showing the burned people, the shot families, the results of her father's commerce. The rest of the gang loved his speeches; they leaned against the door and listened to him preach to the girl. He had read a book on how the Symbionese Liberation Army had brainwashed Patty Hearst and it held many useful and fascinating tips for reshaping a woman into a pawn. So far his approach had borne fruit: after a few hundred hours of careful torture the young woman was quiet and pliant now, a textbook victim of intimidation and fear. Suffering was a condition that forged strength and Edward needed her to be strong. 'What do you want to tell me?'

She glanced at the door.

'They're not out there,' he said. 'It's only you and me.' He smiled; it would let her know that it was okay to smile. 'So you can use the toothbrush today, and the toilet. And then we will take a walk.'

'A walk?'

'Yes. I have a job for you, one that is very important.'

Edward helped her to her feet and steered her into the small bathroom. She stank of sweat; she would need a shower before she could venture into public. It was important she not be noticed or remembered. He opened the door and told her to clean herself. She nodded, not looking at him.

He went downstairs and into his bedroom, where he had bought new clothes for her; modest slacks, a plain blue scarf she could pull over her mouth when needed to help mask her face, a gray pullover. She would be practically invisible. He came out and glanced in the kitchen. Demi stood at the sink, frowning.

'What's the matter?' he said.

Demi said, 'Piet went upstairs. He said you are handling the woman wrong. That you don't know how to break her entirely. That he will do it.'

Edward turned and ran up the stairs. He tried the bathroom door. Locked. He kicked it in and he could see Piet, bending her over the lavatory, starting to inch his pants down. He held an antique short Japanese sword in his hand, a *wakizashi*, teasing its sharp edge along the woman's back as though her spine was a whetstone. She shivered in silence. Screaming for help was long past her abilities.

Edward pulled his gun from the back of his pants and put it at the base of Piet's neck. 'I beg your pardon,' he said. 'That's my science project.'

'She needs to be properly broken,' Piet said. 'And it's not fair you get all the fun.'

Edward's hand trembled. 'Pull your pants up and go downstairs. She has a job to do today. Critical. You would traumatize her now?'

'If you break her right, nothing'll traumatize her, and that's the point. She feels nothing then.' Then he said, looking at Edward in the mirror. 'What job is she doing?'

'A job for which she is uniquely qualified.' Edward fought down the urge to splatter Piet's inconsequential brains across the faded paint of the bathroom wall. He wiggled fingers in Piet's face. 'Touch her again and her skin is the last thing you will feel.'

'Why don't you want to share Little Miss Succulent here?'

Edward didn't like the glint in Piet's eyes. Piet was useful, but only to a point. However, he could make trouble and it was important there be no trouble, not now. Not when he was so close. So he said, 'Because I don't have to.'

Piet took the small sword away from the woman's spine and walked out of the bathroom, Edward holding the gun at his side. Piet turned and smiled back at the young woman who looked away from him, covering her nakedness. Edward closed the door behind Piet.

The woman started to shudder, and Edward closed the bathroom door. He put a protective arm around her shoulders. 'Did he? Did he?' He didn't finish the question.

She shook her head. He inspected her back; a scratch, but the *wakizashi* sword that was Piet's pride had not made a serious mark.

'It's because you're so important to me, that he wants you,' Edward said.

'You're not here all the time.' She spoke very softly.

'I'm everywhere. All the time,' he said, his voice cold. 'I'm even in here.' He tapped her forehead. 'Now clean yourself.'

He went downstairs. Piet sat alone in the kitchen. People always seemed to clear a room when Piet entered. It was time to get leverage over Piet so he made no further trouble.

'Your initiative inspires me,' Edward said. 'Come along on the job. Since you're curious.'

'Where are you going?' Piet sounded a bit nervous; Edward smiled.

'Centraal Station.' It was Amsterdam's main train hub, on the north side of the city.

'Are you letting her go?' Piet asked. Demi, the thin Dutch blonde, stepped back into the kitchen, arms crossed.

'Don't be silly; she doesn't want to leave me. You will walk with us. Demi, you too. Go get the handheld camera. We have footage to shoot.'

Piet looked uncomfortable.

'I want you there. Because I trust you. And if you are there, I think she will do whatever I say.' Piet would be a spur to her to do what must be done. And Piet would then be in his power.

The woman came downstairs, slowly. She glanced about, uncertain, her hands trembling. She had not been left alone outside of the closet since being brought to the house three weeks ago. But she had made no trouble now, Edward thought, and he flicked a smile at Piet. The Hearst approach worked: break, tear down, and give her the barest bit of hope to rebuild.

She glanced once at Piet and her mouth

90

trembled. 'Are you making me leave?' she asked Edward.

'Of course not, Yasmin, you belong to us now, and we to you.'

'Yes,' she said, her voice small. She'd fought back hard the first two days. That memory of defiance in her face seemed distant now.

'Today is about your father.' Edward made a click in his throat. 'He is dead to you. Do you remember, Yasmin?'

'Yes,' she said after a long silence. 'He's dead to me.'

'He's a bad man, Yasmin. Your old world was very bad, isn't that right? We've saved you from that evil.' He lingered on the last word. Evil wasn't a word you got to use in every conversation. 'But we are the ones who do good.'

'He's a bad man. He needs to pay for what he's done.' More strength in her voice. 'He's bad. Like you said. Very bad.'

Edward shot Piet and Demi a scowl of triumph. Then he gave Yasmin a smile. 'You are nothing to him, and you are everything to us. Yes? This is true. This is your home now. We are your family. Forever.'

She didn't speak.

'We are going for a walk, Yasmin, outside the house. You'll be good, won't you, Yasmin? Or I'll have to put you back into the closet, for a week or a month or maybe a year, I'll have to visit you there for a long time, play with you and my little knife. Maybe Piet would visit you, too.' He ran a finger along her jaw line. She stared past his shoulder at Piet.

Then she nodded. She rubbed her arm and he could see the needle marks from the drugs he'd given her.

'You don't need to be afraid,' he said. 'I'll be with you every step of the way. We're going to use your expertise. You should be proud, us taking the bad you made and using it for good.'

She nodded again.

'We're going where there are a lot of people, Yasmin,' Edward said. 'All very bad people.'

'Very bad people,' she repeated.

'We're going to the train station,' Edward said, and he held out his hand with a smile. With Piet and Demi watching, he put her hand in his. He could feel their gaze on him, like an audience in a darkened theater. And then he started to crush her fingers.

A slow moan escaped her mouth.

'I didn't say you could make a noise,' Edward said, squeezing harder.

She went silent. He continued to increase the pressure. 'Now you may speak.'

'When do we leave?' Yasmin gasped. But the best part was she didn't try and pull her fingers away. She was broken.

Behind him, Piet laughed.

He released the pressure and interlocked her fingers with his.

'In a few moments. If you do as I tell you, you don't have to go back into the closet. You can stay outside. All day. And tonight you could sleep in a bed, Yasmin. With me. Like man and wife.'

Her mouth moved like words might spill in a flood, but she was silent.

Edward put his lips close to her ear. 'Will you do what I tell you, Yasmin?' But he already knew the answer.

'Yes,' she said quietly. 'I'll do what you ask.' For a moment he saw the strong woman she had been, before her ordeal in the hellish closet, and then that sense of steel vanished as she glanced at Piet and Demi. Now she showed the others that she was a broken, desperate shell, trying to survive to the next hour. Just as he'd planned. Fear. He'd seen it in the faces of the men he'd killed in Hungary, in Sam Capra's blind panic as he tried to find his wife in the smoke and noise of Holborn.

Fear worked.

He released her hand. 'Everything changes for you today, Yasmin. Today, you're the most important person in the house.'

Edward smiled. This was going to be so much better than London.

17

On Saturday I had a day off from Ollie's. I had been careful to spend my days off at home, sitting quietly, watching TV or reading books that sharpened my mind. My only outings were an occasional jog or a trip to the library.

A typical trip to the library meant browsing for an hour, killing time in the stacks, checking out books that would not raise red flags (no non-fiction, no books on the Company; I usually picked thick historical novels). I would log onto the web and do a search on Lucy's name; I felt sure Howell monitored the library's internet connection since it was my only avenue to the web. Lucy's name never resulted in any news. I would visit her abandoned personal page on Facebook and I lingered over the few pictures of her: our first Christmas in London, her walking on a beach during a long weekend in Majorca, us having coffee in Kensington Park during a glorious summer morning. I have no photos of her; nothing left from our apartment in London. The Company had taken and kept it all, for evidence.

In some of the pictures she smiled, in others she wore the intense competitive frown I'd seen in her. I stared at the old photos, looking for any trace, any sign, that she could turn traitor. As if it could be read in a face. She had not put up any photos since she became pregnant; most of her

Facebook friends were from her college days at Arizona and their wall postings remained unanswered.

So, no surprise to my watchers, when, on Saturday at noon, I stopped by Ollie's for a minute and then went to the library. I dropped my checked-out, unread novels into the return chute. I smiled at the librarian behind the desk, who ignored me as she spoke into a phone. I moved along the shelves for five minutes, determining the relative positions of the staff and the visitors. I took off the cover of the alarm system sensor — it was close to the door — and with a pair of scissors I snipped the wire that connected the back exit door to the alarm. I replaced the cover. No one looked at me; story time was going on in the children's section, a hearty reading of *Where the Wild Things Are*.

Then I took the deepest breath of my life and eased open the door. The alarm didn't blare. I walked straight out into the cool sunlight. I waited for a bullet to pound the pavement in front of me, or to cut into my kneecap. I waited to be hurt and fall and for a man to hustle me into a car at gunpoint and call on Howell to say I'd been a bad boy, asking me to explain the dead body in the neighboring apartment.

Silence. The bars were widening, just a bit.

I walked to a nearby car I'd noticed parked on a side street, same place every week, in front of a strip shopping center. The model was one that was easy to boost, and had no GPS system to track it remotely. I hotwired it, and was gone in less than the proverbial sixty seconds. No sign of pursuit in the mirror; any watchers used to my routine were probably keeping their eyes on the front door or considered themselves clever by monitoring the internet searches.

I drove north, making a stop at a Wal-Mart for the rest of my disguise, then I drove on and found a truck stop about thirty miles south of Albany. I parked the car in the far corner, went inside for coffee. Many ate here because it was cheaper to eat a couple of hours out of New York than in the city. I drank three cups of excellent coffee in unhurried progression, watching the truckers come and go. Mostly they sat and listened to the news: a bombing at a train station in Amsterdam that had killed five, a dive in stocks yesterday, an indictment against a Congressman for bribery.

In the hush of the commercials I listened to them chat, in their varying levels of sociability; I wanted a talker. Talkers don't ask as many questions. They like to discuss themselves, not you. You are just there to drink in the wisdom. Often they talked about their cargos, a conversational opener the same way one might ask about the weather. Forty-five minutes after I came in a trucker, silver-haired, with a slight Southern accent, sat next to me and wolfed down a hamburger and fries, half-drowned in ketchup. When his plate was clear, he mentioned to the uninterested trucker next to him that he was hauling flannel and buttons to be shipped overseas for fashioning into shirts.

'Why they can't stitch together shirts here is

96

beyond me,' the talker said. 'We got sewing machines.'

'Yeah,' the other trucker said, 'Japanese sewing machines.' He shrugged at the shrinking world. He got up and left.

The talker ordered a cup of coffee.

After it had been poured and the first curl of steam was rising from it and he'd taken an ample sip, I asked: 'Are you heading to the port, sir?'

He gauged me with a look. 'Yeah.'

'I'm trying to get there. My car broke down here. My brother's working on a ship sailing out of New York and he got me a job.'

'Usually it's not American boys working those ships.'

'I know. He's a supervisor. He got me the job.' I tucked my teeth over my lip, all small-town sheepish. 'I'm a little desperate. Ship's coming in and leaving tomorrow and I'm stuck here, drinking coffee. I kept asking for rides earlier and I think I asked wrong. Everyone said no.' I let a shade of heartbreak show on my face.

'That's tough.' He looked at the empty, ketchup-smeared plate like it was a painting.

'I know, sir. I wouldn't ever ask but I need the job bad.'

'I'm not supposed to take on riders. You understand.'

'Sure, of course. But this wouldn't be out of your way.' Then I went for the knife. 'Like you said, wish they'd make shirts here. I'd have a job where I could stay on dry land. I got to take what I can get.' I had been careful to count out sparse change for the coffee in front of the waitress. I wanted to look like I was what I said I was the moment I walked into the truck stop. You have to play the role to the hilt. The waitress, listening since the crowd had slowed, put a bit more coffee in my cup without me asking.

The trucker set down his coffee cup. Thinking it over. Most people are decent and are inclined to help. 'Well . . . '

'I could chip in some gas money.'

'What's your name?'

'Sam. Sam Capra.' I had no fake ID; there was no point in lying. I did have a driver's license and he asked to see it. I showed it to him.

'Capra like the film director?'

I laughed like I'd never heard the question before. 'Sadly no relation. How much royalties could I get off *It's A Wonderful Life*?'

'That's a good movie,' he said, like I had confirmed a connection to the most famous Capra. 'Says you live in New York: why are you up here?'

'I was looking to get a job in Albany. Didn't get it.' Could I be more hard luck?

He studied the license some more, like it was a long book. He handed it back to me then downed the rest of his coffee.

'Then it's a wonderful life, Sam Capra, you got a ride,' the trucker said, and he laughed at his own joke. So did I.

18

I was now part of the flux, the river of goods going out into the wider world. I just wanted to be swept along by the current and hope I didn't jam up in an eddy or byway.

The denim delivery truck paper-worked its way past the Port of New York's checkpoints, the terminals, the inspection sheds, all at a steady clip. I thanked the trucker, slipped him his bribe (which we called gas money) and stepped out of the cab.

Ports are busy. People are intent on their work. From my Wal-Mart stop I was dressed in jeans and a denim shirt and work boots and a Yankees baseball cap. I carried not a knapsack but two duffel bags on which I'd marked FACILITIES along the side with a Sharpie pen. I could have come from a ship; I could have come from an office inside the port complex. I hoped I was invisible.

I watched containers being hauled off the docks and craned into the bowels of the ships and, when the holds were full, stacked along the flat decks. The loadings were as graceful as a dance. The trucks inched forward, were relieved of their burdens, then turned around and joined another line to be loaded again with goods from Europe and Africa or from American ports to the south: Charleston, Miami, New Orleans, Houston.

I walked past a line of cargo ships. There was an entry gate, with a guard. The line of fencing curved away as I walked out past a loading area and within a few hundred feet the guard shack lay out of sight.

I climbed the fence fast, dropped over the other side. No one yelled.

I walked, without haste, past towers of containers. I faced a choice. Pick a ship or pick a container. If I tried to board a ship and then hide, I was going to be dealing with people. Not good. It was taking a risk to enter a container; I might end up at the bottom of a shipment, unable to force open the door. I had tools inside my duffel with which I could cut open an air hole, but I preferred to pick my own coffin for the next ten days.

No one was paying any attention to me. But my chest felt tight. Anyone could stop me; anyone could challenge me. If I looked the least bit suspicious I would draw attention. Howell and his watchers knew by now that I had run; I could make no assumptions about how close they were on my tail.

'Hey!' a voice called.

A guy, twenty feet away, hurried toward me. I froze. He wore a shirt, indicating he worked for a shipping contractor. He carried an electronic hand-held bar reader and he said, 'Where's the closest john, man? First day — and this place is too goddamned big.'

I jerked my head toward the nearest building and I hoped I was right.

'Thanks.' He took off.

If there wasn't a bathroom there — would he remember me? I watched him walk off toward the building. I might have a lot less time to find what I needed than I thought. *Yeah, I asked this guy, but he told me wrong. No I didn't notice if he had an ID clip on . . .*

I knew what kind of container I was looking for. The sides showed a stenciled shipping company ownership mark tied to an individual number. Containers were routinely bought and sold and bartered among the shippers; I could see on some of the containers that they had been restenciled, the shadows of old paint edging the new numbers.

Most containers I saw boasted a so-called 'tamper-proof' seal. But I could see a few of the seals dangled from the openings, broken. Again, these seals are not quite up to the ironclad image that politicians feed the public masses. The seal is often a strip of plastic, sized like the wristband a patient wears in a hospital. The number matches the ID number on the side of the container and the seal is simply fed through the door's levers. I saw a few that had no seal at all: the moving, positioning, emptying, loading, and moving again of a multi-ton container means that these strips of plastic can easily be torn off or brushed away during the process.

And no one checks; no one cares. The rivers of commerce cannot be dammed.

A line of big ships lay ahead. The ownership marks disclosed a shipping company based in Rotterdam, in the Netherlands. It would have to do. Unfortunately the containers headed for the UK did not have a large neon sign marked London over them. But I could hide and slip away, unseen, in the chaos and the maze of Europe's largest and busiest port. I chose a container on the bottom of a large stack — it would be the last to be loaded. The door faced away from the crane and I didn't care what was being shipped — as long as it wasn't snakes or scorpions. This was my chance.

The seal was in place; I sawed through it with a knife from my bag, leaving ragged edges so it would appear that the seal had been damaged in transit. I opened the door, stepped inside, closed the door.

It took all of five seconds. I knelt close to the door. Listened. I waited to hear footsteps running toward me, but there was only the sound of the continual movement of goods, the screech and grind of the containers above me, slowly being hoisted into the air. I dug in my duffel and found a flashlight. I clicked it on and scanned the container. Stacks of boxes. I had half-expected it to be empty — after all, what does America build anymore that the rest of the world uses? Maybe I'd find leveraged financial products or sub-prime mortgages.

I inspected one section of boxes. They all read CLEAN-PAK HAND WIPES. Others read VER-MONTER HERBAL SOAPS HANDMADE IN USA, with a stylized landscape scene of a New England farm on the boxes. Eight to ten days stuck in here; at least I wouldn't smell as bad as ten days with no shower.

I hunkered down away from the door. Eventually I felt the container rise, leave earth, swing toward the ocean, and then settle down — slowly.

I leaned against a box of Vermont soap, wrapped a blanket around me, and slept.

19

Ten days in a steel coffin. No way to pass the time, except to think, and to plan. Imagine if you had ten days shut off from the world; no phone, no web, no television. Cutting the electronic cord separated me from the incessant twittering chatter of modern life. The quiet might drive many people mad but I welcomed it. The only good thing about the prison in Poland had been, after the initial weeks of questioning, the long silences, just me and the stone walls. The power of time to think is a forgotten pleasure in today's world. This was not so different from the stretches of useless quiet in the CIA prison, except no one was torturing me. But the line I'd crossed weighed on me in a way it hadn't when I'd thought out the plan. Howell might well issue a kill-on-sight order on me. I had broken away from the invisible cage. No second chance now.

Waking, I used the flashlight and established my tiny camp inside the steel coffin. Inside the duffels, I had the Glock and two clips of ammo I'd stolen from the safe in Ollie's office. I had a hopefully delicious assortment of protein bars and fruit. Bottles of water. Extra batteries for the flashlight. Toothbrush, toothpaste and toilet paper. A small container for waste. A first-aid kit and sleeping pills. A charged iPod with Mahler and the Rolling Stones and an extended battery. Two changes of clothes: gray shirts, jeans. All the cash I'd saved after the passport fiasco, a few hundred dollars.

It wasn't much with which to start a long and dangerous journey to find my lost wife and child. I checked my watch. The cargo ship should have departed by now. A constant hum of engine played. But I didn't want to risk opening the door and being spotted — although with thousands of containers, I thought the odds of being seen low — until we were at least a day out of America. The ship wouldn't turn around for a stowaway at that point; they would just arrest me and throw me in whatever small room they could improvise as a brig. They would alert the port authorities when they arrived in Rotterdam. But it was best of all if I wasn't seen. I could keep my sanity without seeing the sky.

The container was like a womb, I told myself. Maybe when I got out I'd be reborn, ready to kick ass.

I closed my eyes again.

Felt nothing but an utter loneliness that one cannot find easily in today's world. Nothing to do but sleep and dream about what I had lost. It couldn't be healthy, to dream so much.

★ ★ ★

I dozed and it wasn't a dream: it was a memory rising to my brain like a bubble.

'What do you want to name him?' Lucy asked me. She stood by the window of our Bloomsbury flat, staring out at the rain. Gray clouds scudded low over the city, and my normal life was ticking five days to zero.

'Him. You're sure it's going to be a him.'

'He kicks like you.' She placed her hand on the little swell of stomach.

'I have never kicked you.'

She put a hand on my cheek. 'In your sleep. When you have bad dreams. About Danny.'

My brother.

Mention of Danny always brought a silence. Maybe it only lasted a moment, but it marked a cold pause in everyday life. And the inevitable sting. At the back of my eyes, in the bottom of my throat.

I lowered the book I was reading. 'Well, how about Edwin, for your dad?' Lucy's parents had died in a car crash when she was ten and I had thought she might want to honor her lost father or mother. She had been raised by an aunt after her parents died, gone to college on full scholarship and studied the elegance of data-bases, joined the Company fresh out of school, just like me. She spoke fondly of her aunt and little of her parents, almost as if they were characters she'd read about in a novel.

'I appreciate the sentiment, monkey, but Edwin's too old-fashioned for me.'

'Um, okay.' I stared at her, my mind a blank.

'How about Samuel junior?' she said

'I don't want him named for me. Let him be his own person, entirely.'

Lucy tucked feet under her. 'I'd like to honor a loved one.'

'Well.' I loved my parents, very much, but

106

relations with them were frosty at the moment. 'How about we'll name him for you, Lucy. Call him Lucian. He'll have to be the toughest kid on the playground.'

'No. My mind's made up. Daniel, for your brother.'

'You don't have to do that. You never even knew Danny.'

'I know what he meant to you. It's an awesome name. Let's honor him.'

(If I could put a sticky note into my memory, it would read: This was the woman the world wanted me to believe was a traitor.)

'Then let's put Daniel on the list.' I picked up my book again.

'Daniel. Okay. What if I'm wrong and it's a girl?'

'Capri, for the island. Capri Capra. She'll love us forever.'

She laughed. 'Sam?'

'Yes?'

She didn't answer me and I glanced up at her, still watching the slow slide of rain along the glass. And then she said words she never said in real life: *Do you think I could let you die?*

I awoke with a start. The dark was nearly complete and for a moment I forgot I lay nestled in the container's cocoon.

I lay listening, wondering how long I'd slept. Today had been the first time in a long while I'd slept like a free man — no listeners, no cell, no one watching me or my dreams for evidence of betrayal. I slept again, woke again, slept again.

For how long I didn't know.

But my brain jerked me awake at a sound. An approaching buzz, sounding hard, above the soft steady thrum of the engines. An interrupting roar.

I knew the sound. A helicopter.

Lowering toward the deck.

20

I risked cracking open the door. Daylight hit my eyes, the dawn, rosy-fresh. I could smell air unsullied by city, salt water, the tinge of rust. The light stung my eyes; I blinked the pain away. My container stood near the top of a stack — another stack stood next to it. I could barely open the door and squeeze through, and I had to hold onto the side of the adjoining container. I looked down. I was roughly four stories up — if I slipped I would fall into a narrow canyon created by the containers. I pushed the door open as far as I could and pulled myself up to the top of the container wall.

Thin clouds streaked the sky. The helicopter's whoosh faded as the rotors powered down. I inched along the top of the containers and looked down. At the ship's stern, a jet helicopter squatted. I saw four men, armed, exiting the helicopter as the rotors slowed. One figure — a woman in a suit — stood at a distance, conferring with a group of men who appeared to be the captain and members of the crew.

The arrivals must be Howell's people.

Jesus, how? *How?* Finding people who didn't want to be found was hard; I'd hit my head against that wall a number of times. Yet no matter how carefully *I* hid, here came the Company. My heart trip-hammered against my chest and then I thought: six thousand containers, they can't open and search them all. It would take weeks.

Well, if the Company was seizing the ship, they would *have* weeks. They could commandeer the vessel, sail it back to New York or to Boston, pay off the disgruntled shippers. They could take as long as they wanted to find me. If they'd found the intruder's body in the apartment, they'd never give up. Howell would know I'd killed the guy and run, presumably with highly useful information.

The helicopter rose again. It hovered over the stern of the ship, then began to work its way slowly over the deck. I could see two men sitting in the copter's open door, peering at a laptop. Hanging from each side of the helicopter was an array of lenses, shaped like a rectangle.

The helicopter passed low over the first stack of containers, keeping up its flying speed, but just barely. It wasn't in a hurry. It was searching.

My heart sank. Infrared scanners tied to thermal imagers. My body temperature would stick out like a flame against the coolness of shipped goods like my Vermont soap and New Jersey hand wipes.

I had to find somewhere else on the ship to hide. Now.

I couldn't go down. My body heat would stick out like a blister. I had to go up and then find rapid entry into the ship. I'd be spotted, but they were going to find me within minutes anyway. I ducked back down to my container, grabbed my gun and the ammo, and the cash. I put the cash and the ammo in a belt bag and tucked the gun in the back of my pants then went back out the door. The containers' surfaces were damp from the ocean breeze and I tested my grip carefully; a slip would be fatal. I hoisted myself up high. The helicopter was about a hundred meters away. The ship had stopped and dropped anchor; the white noise of the engines had faded.

The helicopter was turned away from me, its nose pointing back to where the suit from the helicopter and the captain (I presumed) stood. I crawled out onto the top of the containers. I was five stories in the air, laying flat on the cool steel of a blue container. I could see that the container stack here stair-stepped down, then rose again. The loader had not done a neat job and it gave me ledges and walls, just like back in Vauxhall.

The helicopter began its turn. I hunkered low and ran. I eased myself over the lip of the first stack and dropped down to the next.

I made a clang when I hit. The helicopter couldn't have heard it. But a crewman, standing near the railing toward the bow, turned, either at the sound or at the flash of color I made as I ran.

I saw him turn and point. Right at me.

I rolled and ran toward the edge again, and I heard the increasing whine of the helicopter. I slammed off the edge of one container, slowed my descent, hit the top of another and rolled to my feet. I glanced back as I ran the twenty feet to the edge and saw the helicopter bearing down on me. One of the men jumped from the copter onto the container stack, gun in hand.

I ran. Metal hit metal — a bullet pinging against the container. I had to get off the stack

111

— the helicopter roared above me, circling, keeping me in sight as the gunman narrowed the gap between us.

I was caught between man and machine, boxed, now three stories above the deck, and I could see another thin crevasse between shoved-together stacks of multi-colored containers.

I wriggled inside the gap. I had maybe thirty seconds to navigate down thirty feet to the deck before the gunman caught up to the canyon. I'd be a dead target if I wasn't out and clear by the time he reached it. He could simply fire a bullet into the top of my head.

I bounced down, my feet catching the edges of the containers, just enough to break the descent, then dropping again. Find the line, I told myself. It was like a parkour run inside a pipeline; my shoulders bounced hard against the steel.

Twenty feet. I hit a skid, lost my balance. I slammed into the metal side, caught the edge of a container with my hands. I could hear the helicopter drumming above me like a hammer.

I focused and let go and managed to drop to the deck in a controlled roll. I spilled free from the container stack, out of shadows, into the weak, ocean-guttered sunlight. Fifty feet ahead of me was a railing — and beyond that the uncaring gray of the sea.

I ran, staying close to the edge of the containers. I needed to get below decks. On a ship full of warm bodies and heating pumps and heavy engines, they'd have to do their thermal scans by hand. And hundreds more containers should be below. I could become the needle in the haystack for a while. I was going to make them work to find me, because I was sick of being stymied, of being pushed away from finding Lucy and my son.

I crashed into a crewman, a young Filipino who cried out in Tagalog for help. I showed him the gun and he froze. I pushed him away hard and ran through a doorway, started hammering down the steps.

Behind me I saw the gunman take a hard run, slide off a container, hit and roll with enough grace to hold his balance as he came off the front of the container stack.

I vanished into the depths of the ship. The crew was not likely armed; this ship wasn't sailing past Somalia. I didn't want to shoot an innocent person, and the sound would betray my location to the hunters. Best to be silent and vanish.

I ran down a long, narrow corridor, turning back and slowing to look for pursuit, and I slammed into a wall of a man as he bound out of a doorway. I staggered back and the man — heavy-set, Asian — snarled and launched a flurry of blows at my face. He used Muay Thai: hard, sharp, brutal blows, a Thai fighting form designed to knock an opponent down and out with the smallest amount of effort. It hurts. A lot.

He landed two precise blows on my jaw and my throat before I could parry and I fell to the ground.

Then he flicked open a switchblade. A

switchblade? The eighties want their weapon back, dude. 'They pay for you,' he hissed. He sliced the air between us, smiled his hard awful smile. 'You get up, slow, and — '

'That's cheating,' I said. I pulled my gun free and shot the knife out of his hand. He shrieked; the broken knife clattered along the deck. I glanced behind me, saw the gunman launching himself into the hallway behind us, so I cheated some more and I closed arms around the crying, bleeding sailor and made him my shield. The gunman held fire. Hurray for morals. I yanked the sobbing sailor back along the hall. We finally hit a door; it opened into the main container hold.

'Let him go, Mr Capra, we want to talk,' the gunman called.

Mister? So polite. I acted like I hadn't heard. I hurried the sailor down toward the hold floor. He didn't struggle, moaning as he clutched his hurt hand. But two can't move as fast as one, and as we reached the hold floor, I aimed at the lights above us. I needed the blanket of darkness. The gunman appeared at the steps and aimed. He fired as I tried to pull sailor back behind the angle of a container while squeezing the trigger, and my shot missed the light.

I'd moved too slow. The gunman's shot caught the sailor in the upper back and he screamed and sagged to the floor.

I glanced down at the sailor — and instead of a spread of blood on his shirt, a small metal dart protruded from between his meaty shoulder blades. Not a bullet. An anesthetic dart, like we were on a nature show, tagging tigers to trace their roaming. The dart was so I could be dragged back and put into whatever cage Howell wanted. They wanted their bait to be functioning.

I fired at the gunman, who took cover behind the edge of a container, then I turned and I ran into the maze of containers. Hard right, hard right. I needed to take out the gunman. I was trying to get behind him when he descended the stairs. I hoped his adrenaline would make him rush, make a bad decision to my profit. Dim lights illuminated the stacks.

I stopped, risked a glance around the corner. The containers were more tightly packed down here; less room to move, longer lines of sight, which meant that there was a better chance of getting caught in the open. I could hear more voices, raised, feet thundering on the steel stairs. A crowd was coming. If I shot I'd betray my position.

I broke the seal on a container, slipped inside, left the door open less than an inch. I counted slowly in my head. At nineteen the gunman went past me moving quickly but silently. I watched him move past the door. I stepped out of the container, slamming a kick into the back of his head like he was a wall I was running up. He collapsed and I caught the back of his shirt so he wouldn't make a noise. With my other hand I grabbed the dart gun, fired it into his back. He rag-dolled and I eased him to the floor. I hurried to the intersection and looked down the long unbroken gap in the containers and saw another man in black, accompanied by a crewman. I ran along the aisle, hearing their echoing voices clang against the steel.

They would expect me to hide in the stacks. I would have to find another part of the ship to make my own. I had to keep moving, use the crew's thermal signals as camouflage. Hide where the heat of the engines would mask my body's signature. I had to hold out and get to Rotterdam. There I could vanish.

I stopped at another intersection, for just one single moment, getting bearings, and a sting aced my throat, hard, like a hand's swat.

A dart. I had maybe seconds before the anesthetic worked its juice. I raised my gun at the approaching gunman. The woman in the suit now stood behind him, watching me, unafraid.

Mila. The woman from Ollie's bar. The whisky drinker with the fondness for wolves. Blonde hair pulled back severely, eyes of quartz, a hard smile. She liked Glenfiddich whisky, and my own blood felt like a bottle had been injected straight into my heart.

The steel of the gun slipped from my grip. I laughed as I fell to the deck.

21

I opened my eyes to starlight. I heard the slush of water, the soft whistle of a breeze. I lay on my back, steel for a pillow. On a container, on the deck of the ship. Above me the moon hung, ripe with light. The whistle was the wind slicing through the gaps in the container stacks. The stars lay in a diamond spill across the sky. You didn't see the stars so clearly in a city, ever.

Mila sat next to me. Legs crossed, wearing a trench coat, cigarette in hand, watching the smoke slide into the moonlight.

I sat up. My arms and my shoulder ached but I wasn't hurt.

A darkness of ocean lay all around. I'd been out for most of the day.

'Good evening, Sam,' Mila said.

'Howell sent you.' My God, the trouble they had gone to.

'Howell. Name does not ring bells for me.' Mila took a drag on the cigarette, crushed the embers against the steel. She looked out over the long expanse of the Atlantic. The helicopter was gone.

She opened a bag and pulled out a bottle of Glenfiddich and two small glasses.

'Well, that's one true thing about you. You actually do like Glenfiddich,' I said.

'And my name is actually Mila,' she said. 'A doctor might say it's not good to drink after a

117

sedation dart, so I only give you a bit.' I held my glass and she clinked it against mine. 'For medicine.'

'What are we toasting?' I asked.

'Freedom,' she said. 'Yours. Mine. The world's.' Mila sipped at her whisky. I didn't want any but I took the barest taste.

'Ollie will be missing you, his best bartender. If the wind shifts we may be able to hear his bitching.'

'Who are you?'

'Mila, I said.'

'And who is Mila?'

'I am your friend, Sam.'

'I can find my own friends.'

Mila gestured across the expanse of the ship. There was no sign of the crew, no indication anyone was watching us. 'Forgive me. You have so many friends. Where's the back of the line and I'll wait there.' Sarcasm suited her.

But I was not in the mood for moonlight and whisky and wit.

'Who do you work for?' And who had the considerable resources to do it, I didn't add. Teams of men, thermal imaging, a jet helicopter. It *had* to be Howell.

Or maybe Mila was part of the people who grabbed Lucy, who framed us. They might not want me coming to Europe. The frame against me and Lucy had been elaborate. But . . . I was just one man. This was a lot of trouble for anyone to go to. And if Mila was connected to the intruder, well, then I should have been dead already — taken back aboard the helicopter, shot, and dropped into the cold gray of the Atlantic.

Mila took another sip of Glenfiddich. 'My employers prefer to remain anonymous.'

'Are they the same people who grabbed my wife?'

'No.'

'Are you from the Company?'

'I said no.' And she made a slight face. 'I do have an offer to make you.'

That wasn't hard to figure. Someone who hoped I was pissed enough at the CIA for treating me like a traitor to turn me into an actual one. 'I'm not interested.'

'I've arranged for cabins. Let's go down and talk.'

The night air on the open Atlantic was cold. I nodded. I followed her down to a cabin. The two crew members we passed stared at me with barely disguised hostility.

'Speaking of friends,' I said as Mila closed the door behind us.

'Your fighting them has cost me several thousand in bribes.'

'Sorry.' There were two beds. I sat on one. 'All right. I'm listening.'

'First of all, I wanted to talk to you, not hurt you. And I wasn't going to spend weeks searching containers for you.'

'You *are* Company.'

Mila fingered another cigarette in her pack, but then seemed to reconsider. 'Are you dense? I have said no, I am not CIA. I have been many things in my life but never that.'

'So who are you?'

'The question, Sam, is who are *you* going to be? The government spent a great deal of taxpayer money to train you, and it wasn't to refill pretzel bowls and bruise gin in martinis and phone taxis for drunks.'

'So you want to make the most of that investment. You and whoever you work for.'

'Let's discuss your wife.'

'What about her?'

'You must have your theories about what happened to her,' Mila said. 'You don't believe she betrayed you. Framed you.'

'Framing me didn't require me surviving the blast. She didn't have to get me out of the building.'

'But if she was a captive, why was she allowed to save you? Why would her captors help you?'

'I don't know.'

'Perhaps she made a deal with them. Spare you, and she would cooperate.'

I said nothing. The thought of Lucy sacrificing herself for me weighed on me like rocks tied to a drowning man.

'But there is the question of all the money she had, all the money she moved before she vanished.'

'How do you know?'

'I know about the money she moved. It doesn't matter how.'

I studied Mila's face. I could grab her, throw her against the wall, force her to tell me who she was. But I could tell force wasn't the way to deal with her. She had a lot of resources and she'd chosen to speak with me alone. As an equal, not as a prisoner. It was the first time in a long while someone acted like I could be trusted. 'I can't explain. I think she's alive.'

'I think Lucy Capra was a traitor, paid for her work,' Mila said evenly, 'and, once she was pregnant with your child, she decided to get the hell out of the situation, while she could. She was going to have to go on maternity leave in a matter of days. Her work logs, her computer activities would have been under another agent's direct scrutiny in your office. Her trail could have been discovered.'

I let the words settle. 'You're wrong.'

'The alternative is a monster under the bed,' Mila said softly. 'The alternative is that she never loved you, she used you, and then she framed you to look like a traitor. She murdered your friends. She made you a pawn.' Mila pulled a face. 'I want to know what you truly think, Sam. You worked some of the most dangerous jobs in Europe. You cannot be a man easily fooled and have survived. Tell me what you really think.'

No one had asked me that in so long. 'She's not a traitor. We were *both* framed. They took her, to find out what she knew. The Company's been trying to break the back of the new order of transnational crime rings, especially those with ties to governments, whether friendly or not.'

Mila waited.

'Lucy would be valuable to those kinds of criminal networks. She knew more about our infrastructure, our computer systems, our ways

121

of tracking financial data. She would be more useful to them than I would be. They would have targeted her. I think she warned me to save my life.'

'Yes, she is useful to them,' Mila said. 'And you are useful to no one now, except me.'

'Useful to you. How?'

'I could give you the freedom to find the truth.'

'Freedom?'

'Time. Resources. It's hard to conduct an international search for your wife and child when you're ordering tonic water by the case and cleaning the beer taps and under constant surveillance. And if they catch you now?' She shrugged. 'You'll be in their prison for the rest of your life. The waterboarding was a bitch. I've seen the tapes.'

'I won't be free as long they're hunting me. And as long as I don't know what's happened to my family.'

'They made you into a soldier for the shadows; they made you play a role where you would have been tortured to death if you'd been discovered. Smuggler, hired gun. They made you their weapon, and they don't need you any more, Sam. How long did you last on the waterboarding? A minute? Most people don't make it past the twenty-second mark. You are strong.'

'How are you not Company but you're watching Company tapes? Did you find it on YouTube?'

Mila risked a smile. 'According to the file, you were never waterboarded. According to your file,

122

your wife is considered missing in action and you have resigned from the CIA. Your file indicates you did not do field work, but were a minor administrator with limited duties. They've rewritten your history to make you unimportant.'

'All neat and tidy. It never happened, like Howell likes to say.'

'If Lucy was a traitor, she may have compromised a hundred agents in Europe and beyond. She might have given them secrets in trade for your life. Maybe that's why they let her save you.'

The thought was crushing. 'Please don't say that.'

'Sam. You are aimless. That's a waste. You should be aimed, like a hand-crafted bullet.'

'So where would you aim me?'

'At some very dangerous people.'

Recruitment. Mila wasn't Company, but she was . . . big. Mila was capable of accessing my no doubt top-secret file and could have a jet helicopter intercept and search a ship, with an armed team. 'I'm offering you a chance to do the work you've been trained to do, with support, and to regain your credibility and dignity.'

'I'm not worried about that.'

'Of course you are. The Company believed for months that you were a mass murderer and a traitor. Now they simply believe you're an idiot who was played by his traitor wife.'

'They said I was innocent, that they had proof.'

'The only proof in your file was that you never

broke. That you never changed your story. Howell argued for you to be put out as bait. That Lucy, if a traitor, would come out of hiding to kill you to eliminate you as a loose end or to keep you from coming after her. Or if Lucy had been kidnapped, then putting you out was no risk. If you ran, you ran, and they would find you.'

'If she wanted me dead, she didn't have to get me out of the office.'

'Unless you living was useful to her, in the moment and its aftermath,' Mila said. 'Traitors are not rational. They live in a bizarre limbo. Not poster children for the good adjustment.' Her English was nearly perfect but not quite.

'She's not a traitor.'

'I should get you a T-shirt with that on it,' Mila said. 'And then my Christmas shopping is done.'

'You're brutal.'

'I am the first person in months, Sam, telling you the truth. Love me for it, okay?'

'Whatever you're peddling, I'm not interested.' I set my empty whisky glass on the table. I had hardly realized I'd downed it. 'My wife is gone. I don't care what they think. I just . . . don't . . . care.'

'The TV, you watch the news yesterday?'

'Yes.'

'Train station bombing in Amsterdam yesterday.'

It had been mentioned on the TV in the truck stop near Albany. 'I heard about it.'

Mila slid another picture to me. A stack. I flipped through them. Several of the pictures

124

caught the magnified face of a young woman. Attractive, dark-eyed, much of her face masked by a scarf around her throat, pulled high to her nose as if warding off the chill. She wore a long-sleeve shirt and jeans.

'Who is she?'

'The daughter of a man I know. A nice young woman. Yasmin Zaid. She's from London. She has never been in any trouble; she has a doctorate from Oxford. Blameless life. She's been missing for two weeks and yesterday she shows up, walking through Amsterdam Centraal, with a backpack on her shoulder. It had the bomb inside, I believe.' Mila slid another photo out. 'The man walking four feet behind her . . .' Her voice trailed off.

I felt a jolt in my chest. It was the same man who'd driven my wife away in the Audi. The hair was cut into a short burr, makeup smeared over the scar that lay near his eye. But I knew the shape of his face, the question-mark scar seared into my head.

22

'I see a slight resemblance,' Mila said.

I looked up from the photo. 'You think this young woman bombed . . . '

Mila handed me another picture. The same woman, hurrying out of the station, no backpack, the man who took my wife close behind her. I glanced at the time stamp.

Mila followed my gaze. 'The bomb detonated two minutes after Yasmin Zaid left, in a store inside the station.'

I studied the girl's face. A blank canvas, waiting for the delicate touch of the brush. She didn't look afraid or excited about her bombing mission. She was . . . blank. Behind, the scarred man was grinning ever so slightly.

'He certainly matches your description. He has . . . affected or influenced Yasmin Zaid. Perhaps as well your wife. Gotten good people in his thrall. To commit violence.'

'I don't understand. Is he a terrorist?'

'No. I don't believe he is. No one has claimed responsibility for the blast, and it wasn't placed on a train, where they could have killed many more people. They could have blown up Yasmin if they were simply using her as a tool. Instead, they blew up a little newsstand that sells candy and paperback books and magazines. It makes no sense, from the standpoint of an extremist. Like the London office bombing.'

I thought of the Money Czar — I had always been sure our investigation of him drove the London bombing. From her accent, Mila was Russian — could she be connected to him? But she wouldn't be hiring me; she'd just kill me. I put the picture down. 'I imagine the Dutch police are looking for them.'

'The Dutch have not identified her, but they will be using face-recognition software. Even with only a partial match on her face, it's only a matter of time before she's identified. Perhaps days.'

'How did you get these photos? Have the Dutch authorities released them?'

'No.' And she didn't say more.

'Why tell me your troubles?'

'I want you to find Yasmin and bring her back to me.'

'I'm not going to work for you. I can't.' My voice sounded hollowed, like a ghost's. 'The Company . . . '

'Bah,' Mila spat, like the word was a nail. 'Stop pretending to be such a nice guy. Stop playing by their rules, Sam. Their rules put you in jail when you were innocent. Their rules presumed your guilt, when they should not. If you could, you'd want to find the man who took her, to know why he killed your friends, what he's done with your wife and child. Don't lie to me. It's a fever in your blood. To find them.'

A slow awful fire burned in Mila's voice.

'Lucy and your child are your holy grail, Sam. I know you.'

'You don't know me.'

'Of course I do. You are all about fighting the evil, Sam. You joined the Company for revenge. A revenge you can't ever get.'

I froze. Mila raised an eyebrow at me.

'The desire for revenge drove you to the Company, and now revenge can drive you to find the man who tore apart your family. Oh, what a shrink could make of you.'

'I just want Lucy and the baby back,' I said. 'I don't want revenge.'

'Don't believe revenge isn't fantastic,' Mila said, 'until you've actually exacted it.' She shrugged. 'I find revenge absolutely thrilling and satisfying.'

I reached for the Glenfiddich, refilled our glasses.

Mila sipped the whisky. It was a nice big, comradely gulp. 'If you come to work for me you will have a free hand to look for her. I am best boss ever.'

I didn't say anything for a long minute.

'What do you think?' she asked.

'This could be a Company trap. A test to see if I'm willing to sell my services. I don't know who you are and I don't care. I cannot help you. I am practical.'

She made a face at the word. 'Practical is what Soviet architecture was. Practical is not always the answer. The offer expires in one minute.'

'And if I say no?'

'I'll get you to Holland. But then we part ways and you never saw or met me, and be certain you will be back in prison within days. With no hope of ever finding your family.'

'And if I say yes?'

Mila tasted the Scotch. 'Find Yasmin. Bring her back to me, and you may exact whatever revenge you like on the scarred man. If he knows where your wife and child are, it's your concern. But Yasmin is saved first.'

'She's killed people.'

'No. You can see it in her face — she has been drugged or broken. Break this group of kidnappers for me, and I will give you every resource to find your wife.'

'And then what? The Company will be after me.'

'Not if you produce evidence of your innocence. The scarred man might have information that clears the name.'

'Who are you?' I said, so quietly I wasn't sure that she heard me.

Mila set down the glass. 'I work for a group that prefers to remain anonymous. You have no reason to trust me, but via this group I am bringing you the best hope you have of finding your wife. I am giving you freedom and resources. Do you care so much for little questions that have little answers?'

She had a bizarre way of talking but I saw her point. It didn't matter who these people were; all that mattered was Lucy and my son. Daniel. I wondered if she'd been able to give him that name, if they were still alive.

I decided. 'And if I get caught?'

'You're on your own. We can't acknowledge you, we can't help you.'

I waited in silence for her thin smile to fade.

She wanted a response. 'Why are you doing this?' I asked.

'I dislike seeing your talent wasted. You should be put to good use.' Mila lit a cigarette; she was not the kind of person to ask if I minded in the close quarters of the cabin. 'Not just good use. Extraordinary use.'

I picked up the photo from the train station. Stared hard at the man's scar.

'How many seconds left in that minute?' I asked.

'Ten.'

'Yes,' I said.

23

Whatever bribes Mila tossed among the ship worked: the crew left us alone. I was surprised, as I had nearly shot one of them.

I had decided Mila was part of some group within the government, unleashed to do dirty work without the boundaries of law and, since I was damaged goods, I was a perfect recruit. They had limited access to Company information like my file but the Company didn't know about *them*.

I didn't care who they were as long as they helped me get Lucy back.

So. I exercised in my room, lifting myself on a bar, running in place, thinking, clearing my head. I endured a self-imposed captivity for three days, then I couldn't do it any more; not after the long weeks in the Polish prison. So I went up to the deck and I ran among the containers in the bright open sunshine. The crew watched me. I waved. They didn't wave back.

I thought about the best ways to try and find the scarred man. I had to assume he knew my face. This was going to be the most dangerous job I'd ever undertaken, and I was doing it with an unproven ally in Mila.

When I turned past one stack of containers Captain Switchblade was there, helping to clean the deck.

'Hello,' I said.

He stared at me in surprise.

'You okay?' I tried in Spanish.

After a moment, he nodded.

'Good.' I wasn't going to say sorry, since he'd pulled the knife on me, but I didn't want more trouble with this guy. We were still days away from the Netherlands.

I went past him and kept jogging. I didn't look behind me and no knife landed in my back. I wondered how much his forgiveness had cost Mila and why she'd bothered to pay it. I was lying on the cot in my cabin when Mila knocked and came in.

'The Company has sent your face to every passport point of entry in Europe and Asia. They're telling people your passport may have been taken and be in use by a fugitive.'

'If they're looking for me, they might consider that I'd use an earlier legend.' Legends are cover identities used by field operatives. I'd played the part of a Canadian smuggler, a German money-launderer, an American mercenary who wanted to make quick money guarding blood diamonds. The people who could have said, 'He wasn't really any of those guys' were all dead or in prison. The legends could still be counted as clean. I had no documentation in those names — passports, or credit cards — but I could get that from Mila. Those names were known in the criminal underworld. But the risk of using one to infiltrate the scarred man's ring posed serious consequences. The Company could have 'burned' all my old names; told any contact or informant that I was not to be trusted. Worse, they could be listening, watching for me to try to step into my old shoes.

The only sure way to know if the legends were still good was to try and use them.

I gave Mila the background on my old names and we went into her cabin where she broke out a kit full of diplomatic paper, cameras, a small but powerful printer and a laptop. A forger's paradise.

'So what's the first step when we arrive?'

'We meet Yasmin's father in Amsterdam.'

'Her father?'

'Mr Zaid can tell you more about Yasmin and her kidnapping.'

Mr Zaid? Was he Mila's boss? '*You* tell me.'

'I'd rather you hear details from him.'

'What does he know about me?'

'Just that you can help him get his daughter back. That's all he needs to know.'

'Where will we meet him?'

'At a bar.'

'You sure like bars,' I said.

'Yes,' Mila said. 'I sure do. Now. I want to be sure you are not rusty. The rest of the day, we only speak Russian. And how is your Dutch?'

'Poor.'

'I will expect it to improve quickly.' She rolled her eyes. 'I hope you won't embarrass me with poor verb choices.'

I watched Mila build the new versions of me. I was like Frankenstein's monster crafted out of watermarked paper and credit histories and life histories. She made me a Canadian, an American, a German and a New Zealander. All

133

under different names. I watched her use backdoor entries into what should have been iron-clad government databases in Washington, Berlin, Ottawa, and Christchurch to insert the codes for the passports into the appropriate government databases, making me a legitimate traveler. She slid with ease into banks, issuing credit cards to me in my various old identities.

'The Company could be looking for my old names, too,' I said.

'They could. A risk we must take.'

I wondered again — who was this woman? Mila whistled a Bananarama tune as she worked.

★ ★ ★

Rotterdam. The port accommodated around four hundred ships a day, both ocean-bound and for inland waterways, and a labyrinth of rail and road. The port itself was like a city, loading cranes the jagged skyscrapers, vast avenues of water the streets. This was a critical artery between the hundreds of millions of people in North America and the hundreds of millions of people in Europe and beyond.

I rode out in the same container I rode in on. Mila was unwilling to risk that passport control at the port hadn't received the alert on my passport. And she was worried about the crew talking. She spent the morning of our arrival greasing more palms. Silence cost money.

I waited for the container to settle and for her to come and open the door.

When she did, a uniformed man, a port

inspector, stood with her.

'Everything is fine,' she said to me in Russian. The inspector stepped inside and displayed great interest in the Vermonter soap. Mila spoke rapidly to the inspector in Dutch; he nodded, didn't look at us.

Mila and I walked out into the gray cloudy day.

'You are very handy with the bribes,' I said to her as we hurried across the busy docking area.

'I am beloved and popular,' Mila said. 'I have friends in every corner of the world.'

And we vanished into the flood of goods and people coming into Europe.

25

We took the train to Amsterdam, fifty-six kilometers away and I watched the flatland of Holland unpeel before my gaze. I was back in Europe, where I had been happiest with Lucy, and imprisoned by the Company. I thought of the dead intruder and his own ticket to Amsterdam.

I leaned back against the train seat. I'd traded one chain, from Howell, to another from Mila. I watched the brief stretch of Holland pan out in silence. I'd had months to sit and think about what I'd do if I got the chance to find Lucy, and here it was, and my skin felt like lit matches lay under it. The possible truths: that Lucy and our baby were dead, or that Lucy had betrayed me, loomed large, the monsters I didn't want to see and yet had to see.

Fine. I was going to find the man with the scar, force him to tell me where my wife and child were. Then I was going to be the last thing he ever saw on this earth.

PART TWO

10–14 APRIL

'The most powerful weapon on earth
is the human soul on fire.'

— Marshal Ferdinand Foch

26

The bar in Amsterdam was called De Rode Prins, the 'Red Prince', and it was located along a lovely old canal called the Prinsengracht, the Prince's Canal, with many small cafés, hotels, stately residences and offices on both sides of its long curve. The Anne Frank Huis stood a few blocks away (usually with a quiet, respectful crowd snapping pictures), and the only boat on the canal was one of those get-on/get-off tour numbers, purring forward while the tourists took their snaps of the waterside buildings and soaked up the charm.

The air smelled of morning rain but the sun had scattered the clouds. The second thing you notice about Amsterdam — after the canals, of course — are the bicycles. They are everywhere, and on an early spring day they swarm like bees rising from hives. The bicycles are not at all fancy, since they are often stolen, but you will see them ridden by lawyers in suits, mothers with the kids balanced on the back or on the handlebars, students and office workers hurrying along. No one wears a helmet. A steady stream of bikes — although rush hour was over and lunch not yet beginning — zipped their way past the small Rode Prins. A few tables perched on the outside and two gentlemen sat drinking spring beers, watching the light dance on the water beyond the parked houseboats.

Mila and I stepped inside and I could see, from my couple of trips earlier to Amsterdam, that the Rode Prins was a prime example of a dying art. It was a 'brown bar', so-called because in the olden days an incessant stream of tobacco smoke stained the walls. Now there was no smoking in the bar and the walls were brown because they'd been painted that way. The room was narrow, with a long-running leather banquette with several tables on one side, a large table near the window, and a beautiful bar along the opposite wall. Red-shaded lamps hung from the ceiling. A painting of some forgotten royal hung on the wall, and there was a red smear across the canvas — across face and finery and hands — as though a glob of blood or paint had been hurled at it years ago. The painted prince looked very alone. To me, Rode Prins sounded like Road Prince, a king of the wanderers.

I glanced at a menu while Mila waited for the barkeep. They offered beers especially brewed for each season. This was my kind of bar. It surprised me that Mila would choose such a spot for a meeting.

A bartender, tall, bald, heavy-built, with a small gap between his front teeth, appeared from the back. Mila and the man spoke rapid Dutch; he gave me the wariest of glances. Then Mila said to me, 'Sam, this is Henrik. Henrik, this is Sam. Sam will be staying upstairs. Give him whatever he needs.' Henrik shook my hand; a solid, firm grip. Where Mila seemed all exotic secrets, Henrik seemed like a bartender to whom you could talk. I was staying here? I didn't say anything but Henrik just gave me a polite nod.

He gestured toward the back of the establishment, to a narrow hallway, decorated with black and white photographs of the Prinsengracht through the years. I followed Mila as she headed for the rear of the bar, and up a flight of stairs.

Mila stopped and looked at me. 'Bahjat Zaid is a man who is absolutely terrified for his daughter. He doesn't know you and he's trusting his daughter's life to you. Don't rattle his trust. We're his only hope. He can't go to the police.'

'Why?'

'He can explain.' Mila turned and I followed her up the stairs. In a private apartment above the Rode Prins, a tall man sat, shoulders hunched, as though he'd played at Atlas carrying the world, and failed. He stood as we entered, smoothing his palms on his tailored suit jacket.

'This is the man I told you about, Bahjat,' Mila said. 'Sam Capra.' I was surprised she used my name but I didn't let the shock show. A woman like Mila had a reason.

Bahjat Zaid shook my hand, measuring me with his eyes. He had a firm grip and a firmer stare. He looked at me like a boss looks at an employee who may be about to give him bad news.

We sat; Mila asked if I wanted coffee. I said no.

Bahjat Zaid had a narrow face, worn with anguish, and he spoke his English with the faintest of Beirut accents. His navy silk tie was perfectly knotted at a collar of snow-white cotton. A cup of coffee, grown cold, sat

141

untouched at his elbow. He was immaculate and enraged, all at once.

'Tell me about your daughter, Mr Zaid,' I said.

'Yasmin. She is my pride. My only child. Last year she completed advanced degrees in both chemistry and physics. She is twenty-five. She is about one point seven meters tall. Her . . . ' He stopped suddenly, as though embarrassed by the spill of words.

'Yes,' I said, 'but Mila can tell me all that. Tell me about *her*.'

He blinked, and opened a manila folder next to him. He seemed to gather himself.

'This is Yasmin,' Bahjat Zaid said, pushing a photo toward me.

I studied it. The young woman was lovely. A spill of dark hair; eyes alive with joy and intelligence; a narrow smile. She wore a pretty blue sweater and jeans and the sky behind her was gray, pregnant with rain. She was pushing a wind-blown hank of hair from her eyes. Behind her a large estate stood, trees swaying in the wind.

'That's a nice house.'

He swelled with pride.

'My estate in Kent. It is historically important. It was to serve as a redoubt for the government should England be invaded. It has underground offices, a bunker, that would have housed Churchill in the event of a Nazi occupation. The house has been in my wife's family for many years. We have a town house in London, but we love living in Kent. So did Yasmin.'

I didn't say that if England fell to invasion,

142

Kent, being in the southeast corner, would likely go first. 'How interesting for you,' I said. There were more photos, Yasmin with her family, Yasmin with the estate staff, Yasmin on horseback, Yasmin graduating from university.

The next photo was Yasmin as a small child, looking up from a book. She was smiling, her two front teeth missing. 'She indicated from an early age she wished to be a scientist. You see? She is reading a picture book about Madame Curie. Given my business interests, I felt a position in one of my companies would suit her and I began to prepare her for such a career.'

I thought *You decided her future when she was still missing her front teeth?* 'Your companies?'

'Mr Zaid is one of the partners in Militronics. A major firm that does a great deal of business with Western governments,' Mila said. I knew the company; they made a large variety of small-scale military equipment. Digital binoculars, night-vision goggles, bulletproof vests and specialized military software and hardware. Their technology was considered among the best in the world; the Company was a client.

'Yes. Yasmin works in a research facility near Budapest. Mostly on defensive technologies: building better armor, more efficient weaponry and equipment. Her research centers on using nanotechnology.'

'And how long has she been missing?'

'Twenty-five days.'

'Has she ever gone missing before?'

'No. Never. She was always a most obedient daughter.'

Obedient. Not a word you heard every day. It was up there with *nanotechnology* on the rare-word scale, and my own words from telling Howell about the Money Czar thundered in my ears.

'You haven't reported her disappearance to the police,' I said.

'No. I was told not to.'

'A ransom call?'

'Not exactly. Yasmin left work at our Budapest research facility on a Friday evening. As usual, she worked late — she is a devoted employee.' He pushed a printout toward me; it was from a calendar application. Nearly every hour was blocked out, for research or work or, in some cases, self-improvement projects. Learn Chinese. Read up on Puccini operas. Study macroeconomics. 'You see, her days are highly structured. She works best that way, so I have cultivated this fine habit in her and she agrees.'

'You keep her organized,' I said.

The dryness of my comment went past him. 'I didn't hear from her on the weekend but that is not unusual. Then on Sunday evening I received this message.' Bahjat Zaid tapped on the laptop and a video unfurled on the screen. Yasmin, fiddling with a key at her apartment building's entrance. The angle of the camera suggested the video had been shot from across the street, zooming in for detail on the young woman. The doorstep light gave off a feeble glow; there was little ambient street noise, no traffic cutting

144

between lens and woman. Late night. Yasmin dropped her keys and as she knelt to recover them, two men moved into the picture, seizing her arms, stuffing a cloth over her face. The camera caught her gaze, wide with terror. She struggled and the men rushed her away from the door, into the back of a waiting van. The van peeled away. No license plate in the shot. The cameraman had been very careful.

But not careful enough.

'Could you play that again for me?' I asked. My throat dried and I felt the ache of my near-strangulation in the apartment in Brooklyn. He nodded and did so. I watched it carefully. 'Again, please.' He replayed the clip. But this time I studied Bahjat Zaid. His mouth worked as he watched his daughter's abduction.

'Do you recognize those men?' he asked me. 'You look as though you do.'

One of the kidnappers, I felt sure, was the man who'd tried to kill me in my apartment, with the Novem Soles tattoo. 'Yes, I do. He's dead now.'

His gaze met mine.

'My Yasmin, being manhandled by those animals. It makes me sick.' He pinched the tip of his nose with his fingertips. 'They have no right. My daughter belongs to *me*.'

I didn't like that last comment at all. 'What happened next, Mr Zaid?'

'There was a phone number included with the emailed video. I phoned it immediately. A man spoke to me. He had a slight Dutch accent. I was instructed not to call the police or report her

145

kidnapping, otherwise they would kill Yasmin.'

'Was there a ransom demand?'

'Yes. I was asked to transfer five hundred thousand euros to an account in the Caymans. I did so immediately.'

'And all they asked for was money?'

'Yes. I complied and they did not return her.' Pain flashed in his eyes.

'And then. The next email. Another video.' He moused over a window on his laptop; another video began to play. The Centraal train station in Amsterdam; I recognized it from the photos that Mila had shown me. A dark-haired woman entered the train station, a knapsack on her back. The video jumped to her walking out the doors. Without the knapsack, the scarf concealing the bottom half of her face. The scarred man walked four feet or so behind her now.

The clip stopped.

'The train station explosion hit four minutes later,' Mila said. 'Five dead.'

'They have made Yasmin look like a monster.' Exhaustion framed Zaid's face. He got up and paced the floor, pale with worry. 'Her face — it is so blank. Like it has been wiped clean and a nothingness put behind her eyes.'

'You haven't heard from her or the kidnappers again?'

'No.' Zaid shook his head. 'I have heard nothing.' Ice coated his words. 'They don't need to ask me for anything. They have destroyed her, and if this video gets out, they will have destroyed my family, my company as well.'

27

'You think she's still alive,' I said.

'I have to hope — if they wanted her dead, they would have exploded the bomb while she carried it. This video is leverage against *me*.'

'Why not call the police now? They haven't returned her.'

'And I would tell them what? That she has been kidnapped, but that she planted a bomb that killed people? If I go to the police, the kidnappers will release that video, and that will be the end of my business.' He wiped a hand across his brow. 'I do a great deal of business with NATO governments, with the United States, with Russia. My daughter as a bomber? It would destroy everything I've built.'

'People would understand that she was brainwashed. Think of Patty Hearst,' I said.

Zaid's voice was iron. 'Patty Hearst was convicted, Mr Capra. The world did not see her then as a victim: it saw her as a good girl turned anarchist and bank robber. The world is an even less forgiving place now. There will be enough doubt to undo my entire business. Even the mere suggestion that my daughter could be a bomber would destroy my company.' He closed his eyes. 'My company gained billions in contracts when Western governments wanted to show they held no bias against Muslim-run firms. You see the trap they have set for me? I cannot go to the police. I dare not defy their demands.'

'Maybe this isn't about Yasmin, or the ransoms. Maybe they want to bring you down.'

'Then they would release the video now and destroy Bahjat,' Mila said quietly. 'But they haven't. They're using Bahjat's hope against him.'

I glanced at Mila. 'So you want me to find and rescue Yasmin.'

Zaid's stare was steel. 'Oh, more than that. I want you to find these people who took her . . . and kill them.'

'Kill them?'

'Kill her kidnappers. I don't care if there are only two or two dozen. No one who could tie her to this act can live to indict her name,' Zaid said. 'If she is rescued, and any of them survive, they could release the tape in revenge.'

But I needed the scarred man alive to answer my questions. 'If I get Yasmin out, surely that is the primary goal.'

'Of course. But all of them must be dead. That is non-negotiable.'

'You're afraid once she's rescued that the kidnappers might come after you?'

'Yasmin has seen their faces. They won't let her go. Ever.' He looked at me, a long measured stare, and then he looked at Mila. 'You said he could rescue Yasmin. I am not sure.'

'I don't rush in like a fool, Mr Zaid. This is not a suicide mission, especially since you want to be sure no one escapes your wrath.'

He raised an eyebrow at the dryness of my tone.

'Bahjat,' Mila said quietly. 'Let Sam do what Sam does.'

'I would like to ask you both a question. Have you heard the term Novem Soles? Or Nine Suns? Does it mean anything to either of you?'

Both of them shook their heads.

'I would like to know how you propose to take action,' Zaid said.

'You don't need to know. It's better you don't.'

He swallowed. 'I want to be sure Yasmin is safe . . . '

I sighed. 'Mr Zaid. Yasmin may not even be in Amsterdam any more. In which case I've got to find where she's gone. I have no leads to follow right now. And if her face is on the cameras in the train station, and the Dutch forensics teams figure out she planted the bomb, then the police are going to be looking for her. We're on a deadline. I am not spending my time asking your approval or permission.'

'It is just . . . I feel I failed her. I failed to protect her.' The words came from his mouth as though pulled by force. He was a man used to iron control of situations and I guessed his helplessness ate at him.

I leaned forward. 'I know what you're going through. I know what it is to be missing a loved one. I will get your daughter back for you.'

Bahjat Zaid looked at me and then he smiled: an awful, stressed smile that held no joy. Like a dog showing its teeth. 'If you fail, or you take an action that results in Yasmin's death, there will be consequences, Mr Capra.'

He was probably good at handling contracts

149

and subordinates and accounts. I was none of those things. 'Don't threaten me, Mr Zaid. I crumble under pressure.'

He opened and closed his mouth and his stare turned to a glare.

'I need all the information you have on your daughter and the kidnappers.'

He handed me the laptop. 'It's all there.'

'Thank you. Why you?'

'Pardon me?'

'Why did they target you?'

He blinked, once, twice, glancing at Mila. 'My money. Why else?'

'If money was all they wanted, then they could have asked for more. They want more. I'm wondering what it is you have that they want.'

'I expect,' he said, 'being savages who are intent on violence, they could ask for arms, for military equipment.'

'They haven't?'

'No.' He folded his hands on the table.

'What kind of research did Yasmin do?'

'It is classified, and not pertinent to this discussion. And nothing she is working on relates to current weapons systems. I doubt they know or care that she is a researcher. They have shown no interest in her work to me.'

'What about future systems?'

'Yes, like ten years down the line. This is not about her research, Mr Capra. This is about her belonging to me. That is why they took her.'

I stood.

'I was told you were one of a handful of people in the world who could do this incredible work,'

Zaid said. 'Yasmin is all that matters.'

I made no promises to him. We shook hands, awkwardly, and Mila walked him downstairs.

I opened up the laptop. Files on Yasmin's life, photos, listings of friends in London and Budapest and the United States. The emails and the video files he'd received. An electronic portfolio of a kidnapping, and I hadn't an idea where to start looking for her here in Amsterdam.

Mila came back with two steaming coffees and set them down on the small table. 'You don't like him.'

'He strikes me as the worst kind of control-freak parent. And I don't think he's telling us the whole truth,' I said. 'Same as we're not telling him.'

'Pardon?'

'They produce this video to rip his guts out and don't demand a ransom? Bull. They've asked him for something and he's not telling us. He's just hoping I can find them and kill them before he has to deliver.'

'They simply may not have asked for ransom yet.'

'You didn't tell him I had a personal stake against the scarred man.'

'He might be concerned you have two agendas. He only cares about Yasmin. Not about your wife.'

'I can't decide if he's more worried about Yasmin or his reputation.' I drank some coffee. 'How do you know Zaid?'

'Does that matter? I know him and I want to

help him. And I want to help you. Tell me why you asked about the name Novem Soles.'

I explained. She leaned back in her chair. 'It cannot be a coincidence. The CIA's interest in this term and the tattoo. There are groups that mark the members.'

I studied the photos. I tapped the scarred man's face. 'There has to be a history on this guy. He's somebody somewhere.'

'I have access to government databases around the world,' Mila said, 'and we've found nothing since that photo arrived. It's like he's been . . . erased.'

She claimed access that even people inside governments did not have. 'You can work all sorts of magic. You own this bar, too?'

'My employer does.'

'I like this bar a lot,' I said. 'It's nice.'

'When all this is done, then you and I shall have a drink together. Not before.'

'I'm going to get to work now,' I said. The scarred man was within a few miles of me if he was still in Amsterdam; it is an amazingly compact city. Which meant, just maybe, I was far closer to Lucy and my son than I had ever hoped before.

Hang tight, babe, I thought, I'm coming to get you.

28

I was going to break the scarred man's world.

This was what I knew. The scarred man had conducted two bombings, including one in a highly secure Company office. He had kidnapped both a prominent scientist and my wife, a Company agent. He had stayed off the grid; he had kept his identity secret. I suspected he might be in the employ of the Money Czar I'd been investigating, who had been tied to serious government corruption. He had resources, including dispatching a man to find me and kill me in Brooklyn. He'd made no political claims, so one had to assume all this was done for profit.

He was part of a network.

Every world has an opening. The new world of how criminals operate has more than most.

Law enforcement broke much of the Mafia in the United States because the Feds could pressure people on the inside — offer them witness protection, indict anyone connected to the illegal trade, not just those actually conducting it.

The post-modern criminal networks come together for a particular function — smuggling in ethnic laborers, muling heroin hidden inside televisions from China that were diverted first to ports in Pakistan, or setting up a train bombing to short-sell a transportation stock price. The cells are small and nimble and they snap together and break apart into new shapes, like a child's plane or tank or wall made from the little plastic blocks.

But because the glue of the bricks is temporary, they can be isolated. Where you cannot break a wall, you can shatter a single brick. I just needed to find the right brick.

I sat and I drank a soda at an outside table at a café near the sprawling street bazaar of the Albert Cuypmarket, on the south side of Amsterdam, in the dim gleaming sunlight. The air smelled of fish, of herbs, of flowers. I read a Dutch paper and tried to put myself in the mind of Peter Samson, the Canadian smuggler I was on a Company job a year earlier. Samson was a nice guy as smugglers went: paid his fees, paid his bribes, didn't kill people. I'd stung two Ukrainian weapons traffickers who were attempting to ship contraband uranium to a radical group in New York. The uranium turned out to be fake (counterfeited by them), as was the radical group (counterfeited by me). Samson was held blameless in the grapevine of the criminal community when the two men ended up dead in a Prague apartment, killed by their business partners who didn't take their failure well. They were screwed by their carelessness and greed and breaking of the barebones trust. Networks form because of necessity and a distant trust.

As Samson, I would still be distantly trusted by the man I wanted to see. I'd found him by calling my old contacts in Prague and learning

154

that one of them had moved six months ago to lovely Amsterdam.

I was on my third soft drink when he came ambling along, walking past the tent stalls, shoulders hunched, a cigarette dangling from his mouth like a long broken fang. I'd positioned myself because I figured he would come this way, through the street market, to reach his little store. I could imagine the smell of the lavender oil in his hair, the slightly rotten smell of garlic on his breath. I remembered he chewed garlic capsules with enthusiasm because he was scared of colds.

He went inside one of the doors close to the corner. A sign announced a watch repair shop called, in tribute to his craft and his adopted homeland's national color, CLOCK-WORK ORANGE. He closed the door behind him.

I crossed to the door, counted to thirty. It opened up onto the ground-floor business: a tiny old CD and record shop, where guitar riffs of an old Clash album drilled the smoke-scented air. In the store a bored punk sat at the cash register, waiting for Punk to come back. Stairs led up to the Clockwork Orange. I went up and tested the door. It swung open. He hadn't locked it, his hands full of bags.

I stepped inside. I saw Gregor setting the bags on a wooden counter. Glass counters showed vintage and collectible watches. A table, covered with black velvet, held a snowfall of gleaming gears and next to them lay watch repair tools, craftsman's tools, laid out in straight lines, ready for work. Gregor was very good at bringing order to chaos.

I shut the door behind me.

He turned and stared at me for twenty long seconds, and then he said, 'I know you.' He had seen me only a few times, but watchmakers are detail people. 'From Prague.' He did not look overjoyed. 'You knew the Vrana brothers.'

'Yes. They tried to cheat me. But I guess I wasn't as pissed about it as their partners were.' The Vranas had been the morons trying to grab money from me that didn't exist, for goods that didn't exist, and the sting I'd run helped the Company empty their bank accounts. Their business partners took it hard. They expressed their disappointment with an ax.

'They buried them in a single coffin,' Gregor said. 'No need for two.'

Gregor had been a bit player with the Vranas, a guy whose business they used as a cover to mule goods out of eastern Europe to Britain.

'I remember you were always worried you'd catch a cold. You like the climate in Amsterdam better?' I asked.

'It's hardly tropical, but I sneeze less.' He was nervous because he couldn't know what role I'd played in the death of the men he'd known. His eyes narrowed. 'Samson from Toronto. Is that still your name?'

I smiled. 'It's the only one I got.'

He didn't smile back. He tested whether I was armed by saying 'I need a lozenge' and slowly reaching into his pocket. I tensed but I didn't pull a gun yet. Gregor pulled out a package of garlic capsules. He slid one between his thin lips.

156

A test. I wasn't here to kill him. I was here either to offer a deal or get information. He'd provided the setup for the smuggling route for the fake uranium, but, since it was never smuggled, the Company had decided to leave him alone, in play, to be useful again. But he'd moved to Amsterdam for what I guessed was a fresh start. Amsterdam had better smuggling routes, and more of them, tied back to the massive port in Rotterdam.

'How do you like Amsterdam?' I said.

'Lovely. The Dutch are very pleasant people.' He sucked hard on the capsule, drawing out every bit of the garlic's restorative powers. 'They have an excellent healthcare system.'

I gestured at the small shop, brimming with inventory. 'Business looks good.'

He shrugged. 'Watches are a leftover from an analog world. Books, records, movies, everything goes digital.' He sniffled, clicked his tongue. 'But analog watches, people still like them. They are both necessity and luxury. We must always know what time it is and we must look good doing it.' He cleared his throat, wiped at his lip with the back of his hand. 'How may I help you?' Like I was here to look at his Rolexes.

You don't ever answer a question when asked. At least, a man like the one I was pretending to be wouldn't. Instead I invaded his privacy. I peeked inside the bags. Party stuff, for a kid, a girl. Napkins, plates, wrapped candies. 'A party?'

'I married a woman here four months ago. I have a stepdaughter. My life is . . . calmer. I don't think I can be of help to you, Samson. I

157

am no longer connected.'

'You have a website for your little watch business, Gregor. You probably do a lot of international trade here — ordering from Switzerland for inventory, and shipping goods all over Europe. Great front for smuggling.'

'Get out, I don't know what you mean.' A touch of panic bruised his voice.

'Oh, I can get out. I could head straight to the Czech embassy and tell them that one of their wayward sons has set up business in this nice country and maybe, if they don't want to be embarrassed by whatever idiot scheme you're up to these days, they should keep a careful eye on you. Look very carefully at your books, at your shipping manifests, see where your customers are.'

'I don't smuggle no more. I am legit now.'

'Hard to make a living with used watches.'

I opened up my wallet. Pulled out and inspected an impressive wad of euros, courtesy of Mila. Everyone has a price.

Gregor looked at the thickness of the wad and stopped ordering me out.

'I need to find someone, Gregor.' I pulled a photo from my pocket. It was a print of the scarred man from the video of Yasmin at the Centraal Station. 'Now. I need to know if you've seen this man.' I handed him the photo.

Gregor didn't push it back right away and say, *don't know him*. That would have been too obvious a lie. He inspected him the way he might peer at damaged gearwork, a narrow pianist's finger tracing the circle of the man's face. Finally

158

he said, 'I don't know this man.'

'Think. I don't want your stepdaughter's birthday present to be finding out that her shiny new dad used to be a smuggler. Or still is.'

'*She* wouldn't mind me being gone. She acts like she's allergic to me.' But Gregor studied the picture again. 'I don't know *him*. But this man I know.'

'Who?'

He looked at me. I peeled off a couple of bills and slid them onto the counter.

'Him. The big man with the dye job. Behind the first guy you pointed at.'

I looked at the picture. A few feet behind the scarred man was a big, broad-shouldered man with dyed white hair. He looked as though he might have Asian ancestry, mixed with European.

'Him I know,' Gregor said. The edge of the photo trembled ever so slightly, as he tucked it back into my hand. Watchmaker hands don't tremble.

'Do they owe you money?' he asked, and that was his second mistake. He wanted to know why I was looking for the blond. So he could tell the blond about it.

'Who is he, Gregor?'

'Uh, I have to think about his name.' He backed away, toward the gear table.

'No more money. Who is he, Gregor?'

'Tell me first why you are looking for these men.'

'I have a business proposition for them.'

'You can take their picture but not walk up

159

and introduce yourself? I don't know, this looks like a police photo. It's been cropped.' Of course it had. I'd cropped out Yasmin.

'Gregor, just tell me the blond's name and where to find him.'

'The blond — look, I'll do you a favor and give you some advice. Stay the hell away from him. Whatever job you've got lined up, find someone else.'

I stepped forward and said, 'Tell me.'

'No, no. If I tell you, then I've sent you to him. That means he comes to see me. No thank you.' Terror colored his tone. 'He cuts up people who get in his way. No. I'm a family man. I'll tell you his name, but you can get someone else to put you close to him. Not me.'

I touched his shoulder.

And he tried to slice my throat open.

29

The blade was a small thing; but then, so is a vein. I wasn't sure if it was part of his watch-mending gear or if it was simply a weapon he kept close at hand. I heard the hiss it made as it sliced the air and I flinched back and it parted only the air close to my skin.

'Oh, hell,' Gregor said, hesitating. 'Sorry. I just want you to go.'

'I'm insulted you're more afraid of him than of me.'

He dropped the little blade. 'It wouldn't have hurt you really.'

'That's between me and my carotid,' I said. 'Why's he got you so scared?'

He didn't answer me and so I decided that if he was afraid of violence I'd show him a little. Just a taste. I shoved him back toward the watchmaker's repair table. I knocked him with a hard blow to the throat into a chair.

'You're a bully,' he coughed. 'I just wanted to run you out of here. Leave me alone.'

'That is entirely unfair, Gregor.' I inspected the craftsman's tools. They were designed to hold gears in place, remove bits of metal. One had a curved point to it; like an instrument you would see in a surgery. I picked it up.

I put a fingertip on each side of his left eye. I held up the vicious little tool.

'I don't know the scarred man!' he yelled.

161

'Oh, I believe you. But you know the blond.'

'Please, please!'

'Gregor. I don't want to hurt you. I want you to go to your stepdaughter's party and enjoy your 20/20 vision.'

'I have to pick up the cake,' he said, sobbing a little. 'For the games, the *koekhappen*.'

'The what?'

'The game the kids play, sticky cake hanging on a string, you try to eat it fastest . . .'

'Oh, Gregor, that sounds like fun. I want you to go to that. I want you to go get the cake and win the race. I hope it's an awesome party. And you *can* go, soon as you tell me his name and where he is.'

Gregor tried to wrench away from me.

'Is the blond an old friend?'

'More . . . friend of a friend.' He gave in. 'The blond's name is Piet. He is close to an acquaintance of mine.'

'And your acquaintance?'

'His name is Nic ten Boom. I haven't known him long. He and I had a beer a week ago, this Piet came with him. But Nic is connected, and Piet carries himself like he is, too.'

'And what did you talk about during this beer.'

'Ajax — that's the Amsterdam football team. And we talked about women.'

I put the edge of the tool closer to his eye. 'Then what? You just hung out and drank beer?'

'We went to the Rosse Buurt — the red light district.'

'And you a newlywed, Gregor.'

'I . . . I didn't partake. Neither did they.'

162

'You just went and looked at the whores?' I said this in approximately the same tone as a disbelieving spouse.

'That was what Piet wanted. He was a little drunk; he likes his beer. He wanted to see the hookers standing in the windows.'

'Is he a pimp?'

Gregor's tongue flicked along his lip. 'No. No. I don't know why Piet wanted to go. He was insistent. We just went and we laughed at them, the women standing behind the glass. I don't know. Piet laughed and so Nic and I laughed, too. You do whatever Piet likes. He takes over the room.'

Laughing at prostitutes. I didn't believe him.

I cut him a little, close to the eyelid. 'What else did you talk about?'

He yelled, gritted his teeth. 'Okay, okay. Piet wanted to know about moving goods to North America. He asked me questions. How did I sneak goods into the States? I told him but I think they decided I was too small an operation for what they wanted. I don't ship watches in big enough quantities, I guess.'

'Have you seen either of them again since?' Now I put the instrument so close to his eye I could see the eyeball tremble, shake in its socket.

He didn't answer right away and I jabbed the small blade into his palm. He gasped. A little blood welled up from his hand.

'Next the eye. I am serious, Gregor. You do not want to get in my way right now.'

'I haven't seen Piet again. I had a beer with Nic two nights ago.'

163

'What's Nic do?'

'He works with Piet — but I know him just through friends in the business, he does stuff with computers — he's a bit of a geek. He runs internet scams, you know, bank letters from Nigeria kind of stuff. I don't know how he's gotten involved in smuggling.' His face was tense under my hands. 'He's . . . he's odd. I don't really want to be friends with him but he always has good email lists for marketing.'

Oh, a spammer. True evil. 'Where can I find Nic?' I touched the pointed end of the instrument to my tongue. Wet the metal.

Gregor shuddered under my grip. 'He lives above a coffee shop over in the Jordaan neighborhood. But mostly hangs out at a bar. Called the Grijs Gander. It's down near the Rosse Buurt. They know him there.'

I let him go. Slowly. 'You tried to cut my throat,' I said. 'If you want me to forget that bad idea of yours, you'll forget we talked. You don't mention me unless I need you as a reference with these guys. Then we're buddies, got it?'

Gregor nodded. 'You're after Piet. Piet, I don't like. Piet can fry in hell.' He clutched his hurt hand close to him, but carefully, so he didn't besmirch his suit with the blood. He didn't look at me. They're always ashamed after they talk.

'If you tell anyone about our visit, I will be back, Gregor. I mean Nic no harm. I just want to talk to this Piet. But you nark on me to them and I'll make a phone call and you'll be on the next plane back to Prague.'

'I'll say nothing.'

I tucked a little extra wad of euros in his pocket. He nearly sighed with relief. Then I extracted his cell phone and said: 'What's your wife's name? Your stepdaughter's?'

His eyes were bright with fear. 'Leave them alone, Samson, please.'

'Their names.' I made the words sound limed with frost.

'My wife is Bibi. My stepdaughter is Bettina.'

'I hope you and Bibi are happy, Gregor. Tell Bettina I said happy birthday.' I gave him a long look and said, 'If they ever make a film about Peter Lorre, you have a lock on the lead.' I turned and walked out.

I was not used to terrorizing people, and if Gregor hadn't tried to cut me I would have been a lot gentler. But a scared Gregor was a useful Gregor.

On the street I checked the call log on Gregor's fancy smart-phone. Two days ago, a call from a Nic, late in the afternoon. Probably the invitation to have the beer at the Grijs Gander. I checked the other phone records. Nothing of interest that jumped out. Many calls to Bibi, a few to Bettina. Nothing else.

I checked the voicemails. One from Bibi, in rapid-fire Dutch, reminding him to pick up the party decorations for Bettina. Bibi sounded impatient and drunk, and she told Gregor twice in the voicemail that he was a useless piece of crap, but it was not up to me to question Gregor's choices. True love was blind, I thought, with a sudden and sharp sting in my chest, thinking of Lucy.

The other voicemail, from a week before, was from Nic: and, bonus, there was a picture of Nic next to the voice mail. Thick-necked, red hair gathered in a short ponytail, no smile. 'Grijs Gander, tonight, if you can slip from Bibi's chain. See you there at six. I want you to meet a friend of mine,' Nic said in the unerased voicemail.

Said friend being Piet. Gregor was good at slipping all sorts across borders, under the authorities' noses.

What did Piet want smuggled into the States?

30

The Grijs Gander was not as nice as the Rode Prins. It wasn't as nice as a broken urinal.

It sat on the edge of the Rosse Buurt, a block or two from the neon-kissed windows where the hookers pose. It was hard to remember that families and regular working people lived in this district, but they did, and the Grijs Gander wasn't the kind of bar that opened around lunchtime.

I walked, stuck in a mass of Japanese tourists. In the early evening the streets throng with nervous gawkers who simply want to look and have no designs to touch. The girls standing in the windows mostly pose and preen for the tourists like it's a warm-up game; they know the real dealmakers will come by soon.

The Grijs Gander wasn't just a dump bar. It was a karaoke bar. That made it about a thousand times more evil. Think *American Idol*, except that all the judges are drunk and might be handy with a knife.

It was only nine, early by Amsterdam standards. On the karaoke stage a drunken young Spaniard was slaughtering Michael Jackson's 'Off the Wall' as his friends applauded. A few men stood in the back, playing pool; a few others sat in booths. Two young women sat at the bar with their young boyfriends. I cast my bartender's eye over the drinks: most favored vodka or beer; no fancy cocktails. Then I profiled the room. This is a bartender skill. Trouble has nothing to do with gender or age or economic status.

It has all to do with where people sit, where their gaze goes. Most were here just to get drunk and sing and laugh at the bad singers. The pool players seemed to know each other, which made it less likely for cues to be swung like swords. One trouble spot was in the back; a group of big, dark-haired guys who spoke Turkish, and who kept scanning the bar as if waiting for a bubble of trouble to rise. The other was one of the young girls on the opposite side of the bar, who looked exquisitely bored and kept glancing about the room as if looking for bigger muscles or a firmer ass or a brighter smile. Her checking out of the other men was pissing off the boyfriend.

Those were the hotspots, and so I avoided both by sitting at the bar, facing the front and looking at the beer taps. I ordered a pint of Amstel. The bartender, a thin, sallow guy with five piercings in his left ear, brought it to me. He gave the quickest of once-overs and set the beer in front of me. I slid the right amount of euros to him, rounded up for a small tip. He did not offer to start me a tab. I sipped, made eye contact with no one, and listened.

My Dutch wasn't superb but I'd spent four months in Suriname, the former Dutch colony in South America, so I had enough to get by and with any language, hearing it spoken revives the command of it. My parents worked with Episcopal Relief — my father as an administrator and auditor of the charity's funds and my mother as a pediatric surgeon specializing in cleft palates — and they and my brother Danny and I traveled the world for all my youth. My Spanish, Russian and French were fluent, my Chinese and German okay. I could say 'I am an American and I need to call the embassy' in about three dozen languages, although that phrase would do me no good with Howell and the Company hunting me. I'd broken scores on speed of learning back in Langley's language immersion programs, but I'd never studied Dutch that hard and I didn't doubt that my words sounded ragged and colonial.

I heard a mix of tongues in the bar: Dutch, English (widely spoken in Amsterdam), French, Spanish. I gave the Turks a careful look again; they noticed me looking at them and I quickly put my gaze up to the moonwalking (or moon-stumbling) Spaniard. I could wait in this drunken Babel for hours and Nic might not show up. And someone, someone in Dutch intelligence, was going through the Centraal Station bombing tapes and was going to see Yasmin Zaid enter the station with a back-pack on her arm and then leaving without that knapsack.

I had an overwhelming sense that my time was running out.

I had forgotten the virtue of patience. Spying was waiting. And the sudden dull weight of trying to find Nic hit me. But he was the only link I had to Piet, and Piet was linked to the scarred man and Yasmin. And the scarred man to Lucy.

This was the only chain I could tug on.

I sipped my way, slowly, through my beer. The next karaoke singer delivered an accurate version of 'Knockin' on Heaven's Door' that drew hearty applause and then a drunken girl got the giggles halfway through a screech of Madonna's 'Like a Prayer'. She didn't get booed because her top was tight and the crowd was more forgiving.

I hated this place. I missed the clean smells of Ollie's bar. He was no doubt mad at me for running off. I missed hanging out with August. I hoped that Howell and the Company hadn't leaned on him. Ollie knew nothing; not even that Mila played him for a friend. Interesting though, that she'd been a regular visitor at Ollie's. That couldn't be coincidence; not with me getting a job there. Another thread to pull on, but later.

I watched one of the girls lean close to her date, nuzzle his cheek with a kiss.

I missed Lucy.

Third beer. You had to drink in a place like this. Order a soda or coffee and you were instantly noted as someone worried about keeping his senses. You were suspect. You had to drink.

The girl with the roving eye was suddenly sitting next to me. 'Don't you want to sing?' she asked me in English, slurring her words. She hadn't even tried Dutch with me. I guess I look more American than I thought. I glanced over at the boyfriend. He watched me right back.

'I'd be out of tune,' I said.

'You and everyone else. Hmm. What should you sing?' She studied me, as though you could tell what a man's musical taste was from his face. 'Nirvana? You look a little angry.'

'Uh, no.'

'Ah.' Now a smile crept onto her face. 'Prince, I think. I have a purple scarf you can borrow.'

'Maybe Radiohead.'

'They're too solemn. Maybe Justin Timberlake? You could bring some sexy back.'

I didn't look at her. The boyfriend had turned his attention to the stage. 'No, I'm not a singer.'

'What are you then?'

'Just a guy having a beer who doesn't want to sing and doesn't want to talk. Sorry.'

Her smile turned to a frown. 'Asshole. Faggot.'

'Go back to your boyfriend,' I said. 'He's willing to put up with your bad behavior. No one else will.'

She got up in a huff and then I saw the man had sat down two stools from me while the girl was chatting. Nic from Gregor's phone, with his red ponytail and his dour face.

I put my eyes back to the karaoke stage, where the crowd had turned on a Filipino guy singing a Kings of Leon song, with hearty boos. He flipped off the crowd and an empty pint glass nearly hit him. The bartender started yelling at the offending table; they all shrugged like kids caught lobbing spitballs in class. The lazy bartender stayed behind the bar.

Either I was lucky, and Nic had decided to sit near me — or Gregor had warned him, and given him a description of me, and he'd come to see who the hell I was.

I watched him from the corner of my eye and ordered another beer. I could see Nic pulling a smartphone from his pocket, studying it. He tugged nervously at the ponytail while he did so, thumbing through messages. He cursed quietly in Dutch and got up suddenly and headed for the bathrooms, which led in a hallway toward the back exit. He'd only drunk half his lager; so I followed him.

He turned into the bathroom and glanced back. He saw me. Knowing he was just going to the toilet, I would have retreated back to the bar. But now I couldn't.

The bathroom was cleaner than the bar. Nic stood at a urinal, talking on the phone. I hate that. Don't you think the other side can't hear the crash of your pee against the porcelain?

I washed my hands, threw cold water on my face.

'I got the goods, the cops don't know,' he said in English. He stopped talking. He finished and flushed the urinal and put the phone back in his pocket. Two of the Turks from the drunken table stood by the toilet stall, talking, smoking.

And they moved to blocking his way out. Sudden tension. Nic murmured words I couldn't hear in Dutch; the men moved, but slower than they had to. They left. Nic rinsed his hands; there were no towels so he dried them on his jeans. I followed him at a distance.

He was already back on the cell phone when I got back to my pint. I was careful not to look at him; but movement caught my eye. The Turks at the far table were glaring at Nic, frowning, with a clear and ugly rage.

Nic stayed on the phone, not paying attention. His voice was too low to hear over the surge of a bad Journey imitation wafting from the beer-soaked stage.

Four of the Turks got up, headed toward Nic. Lost in his conversation, he didn't see them coming. I finished my beer; you could sense the karaoke was about to be eclipsed as the entertainment. A glass is easier to use as a weapon if it's empty.

The four filled the bar space between me and Nic. I glanced at them, but no one had eyes for me. One man's thick finger tapped on Nic's shoulder.

'Hey, you been ignoring me?'

'Maybe,' Nic said. He closed the phone without saying a goodbye.

'You give a message to your friend Piet that's he's a piece of shit and I want my money.'

'I told you, later. Later. Not now.'

I hadn't been the only one waiting for Nic, it seemed. 'I got him his route. I want to be paid. Now.'

I didn't really want these Turks beating up Nic and breaking my chain. I set the glass down and got ready to move.

31

Nic said, 'Did you not understand? I'm not his messenger. Tell him yourself.' A snideness — very much *I'm better than you* — undercut his words. He was a thin sliver of a guy and he seemed to notice, only after the snotty words hung in the air, the stocky strength of the gathered Turks.

'No, you call him now, he keeps dodging us on the phone. Now. You tell him I got to know where the delivery point is to finish the arrangements. And I want my money.'

'You agreed to the conditions. You don't like the deal once it's done, that's your problem.'

'He won't be getting what he needs, then.'

Delivering what, I wondered. This might be what Piet wanted smuggled into the States.

'You're crazy,' Nic said. 'Go drink your beer and leave me the hell alone.'

'I'm done taking the risks,' the Turk said. 'You get me my money and the rendezvous point from him or I'll break your goddamned neck.'

'Are you threatening me?' Nic hissed.

'You call him. Now.' The biggest Turk grabbed at Nic's cell phone, Nic jabbed it down into his jacket pocket, face reddening with anger.

Hello, needle — I'm the thread. 'Excuse me,' I said to the Turk. 'Do you have a problem with this guy or with his friend?'

'It's no business of yours,' the Turk said,

staring at me as though I'd been stupid enough to stick my hand in a pot of snakes. I am more lean than massive; the Turks were all my size or bigger, muscles and hands hardened from work.

'But you're beating him up to send a message to Piet?' My every word was a poke, a prod, and the Turk knew it. The most brutal bar fights erupt after whispers, not drunken hollers. A yell is a flail, a whisper is a fist. I readied myself to take the first punch and thought: every step is closer to Lucy and The Bundle, and so you can take this, because you can't let these bastards kill him. 'Go find Piet yourself.'

'What do you care?' the Turk said.

'Because Piet already owes me, and I'm going to get my money first,' I lied. I love a good lie that acts like a miniature bomb. It shut them all up, shifted the tension.

Nic stared now, unsure if I was just a loon or someone spoiling for a beating at the hands of a bored and drunk gang. I felt sure now that he didn't know me. Gregor had kept his mouth closed tighter than a watch spring.

The idea of someone getting payment before them raised the group's temperature by about a dozen degrees. On the karaoke stage, the girl who'd flirted with me launched into Depeche Mode's 'Enjoy the Silence'. So I used it.

'Listen to the song, dumbass,' I said to the Turk. 'I'd really like to enjoy your silence.'

'Why don't I call Piet?' Nic started, 'and we'll just see . . . '

I got hit. Hard, from behind, and even being ready my forearms slammed into the wood of the bar. I lashed out hard with a sharp kick that caught my attacker in the groin.

Rule number one of a bar fight: you make it short. The brew of alcohol and machismo makes for a heady mix, and a fight can quickly draw in people with no connections, other than proximity, to the combatants. I did not want a ripple effect. I wanted efficiency, I wanted it over in ten seconds, and I wanted both Nic and me to be on our feet when this was done.

My attacker went down and I took a step and powered the base of my palm twice into the face of the man next to him. He was bigger than me and he wasn't expecting a frontal assault. Nose, throat, very fast, just as his fist grazed my jaw, and he reeled back, blood gushing from the fractured nose, gasping.

One of the others seized me from behind, pinning my arms, and I twisted, trying to throw him off balance. Nic fought with the fourth Turk, slugging without grace or economy of action. He took a hard punch to the mouth and sagged. He wasn't nearly as tough as his phone talk. Consider me unsurprised.

My attacker rammed me into the bar. He slammed the front of his head into the back of mine and my head hammered into the wood. It hurt. A lot. I wasn't going to be done in ten seconds.

'I gonna mess you up so bad,' he hissed. Oh, so original.

I didn't answer because I don't waste breath talking in a fight. No one is listening. A long-burning ember of rage exploded in my

176

chest. These men were between me and Nic, and therefore between me and Lucy. I kicked away from the bar, planting both feet below its shelf, propelling myself and the Turk clear. He thought I was going to try and break free, so he tightened his grip. Stupid. Right now I wanted him bound up with me.

We spun.

I kicked off against the floor; now he was between me and the bar. I slammed him back into the wood. Threw my head back and cannoned it into his face while kicking back. Clutching me close, he didn't have a place to dodge. He sagged on the fourth blow and let me go, so I grabbed Nic's full pint glass and hammered it into the side of his head in a spray of beer. The heavy glass didn't break but the man crumpled. Done.

Three of the other four Turks sitting at the table approached; one stayed behind, watching, arms crossed as Nic's man got the better of him, pinning him to the floor.

The three threw themselves at me since I was open and available to dance.

I leveled one with a kick to the throat, took two hard punches from his friends. I stumbled and then I parried the next punch, drove a knee into the groin (you see how I prefer the throat and groin? They offer a substantial return on investment) of the next guy. He withdrew to the floor.

Young Turk number three swung a broken beer glass at my face. I blocked it with my forearm, and with my other hand yanked a rag from the bar, whipped it over the mug. If you can't take a weapon away you neutralize it. This isn't rocket science. The move surprised him and I powered the covered glass back into his own face. The glass didn't cut him but it scared him, knowing the edge was jagged. Uncertainty is your friend in a fight. The guy stumbled back and left himself open; four hard, fast punches, to the eyes and the stomach, and he was done. Four to keep him down, and to make a statement to anyone in the bar eager to enter the fight.

Nic was still grappling with his original opponent like it was first day of fight school. I seized the man, yanked him off Nic, and positioned my arm just so, his head caught in the crook of my arm.

'I'll break his neck,' I yelled in Turkish, and the slowly regathering Turks stopped. Seriously, there is no point in fighting if you do not have to. The man in my grip went very still and I could feel the panicked panting of his breath. The bar could see I meant what I said and I stood like a man with a knowledge of leverage. It got quiet. Even the girl stopped singing and the Depeche Mode melody thrummed ahead in its lonely beat.

'Let him go,' the bartender called in Dutch.

I said, 'You call the police?'

The bartender's gaze slid to Nic, and I saw Nic shake his head, ever so slightly.

'No,' the bartender said.

In Turkish I said: 'Back off and I'll let him go. Your friends started it. Not me. You saw him hit me first.'

The Turks stayed put. Hands still in fists. Then one sat, and the rest of them followed.

'Gggaaggghh,' the man in my grip said.

I said; 'Shhhhhh.' Then I yelled at the girl on the stage, 'Start singing, please.'

She stared and then her gaze caught the karaoke prompter. She mumbled and then broke into that last bridge of the Depeche Mode tune with a nervous, bright smile on her face.

'Outside,' I said to Nic and, looking a bit stunned, he got to his feet and obeyed.

I shoved the guy I was holding to the floor. I followed Nic into the cool of the Amsterdam night, the girl crooning about vows spoken to be broken.

Nic waited for me. 'Thank you,' he said.

'You're welcome,' I said and I stopped by him to catch my breath.

And then he put the gun in my ribs.

32

'Take the gun down,' I said. 'You'll get arrested in about five seconds.'

He kept the gun under his jacket, me close to him. I didn't pull away because I didn't know if he'd shoot me.

'Walk,' he said. 'Just walk normally.' He kept glancing back to see if the Turks were surging out in pursuit — and yes, here they came.

'You might point that at them,' I said.

He dropped the gun and I grabbed the first Turk by the throat. There was a window with a hooker standing in it and I gestured, with a slash of my hand, for her to move out of the way. She got the message and bolted behind the red velvet curtain that was her backdrop. I pushed him through the glass and ran like hell. Because once the hookers are in danger, here come the police, and they closed in fast, talking into shoulder-mounted mikes, hurrying past me and Nic.

'You put that gun back in my ribs, I'll break you,' I said. 'Let's go talk. Someplace quiet.'

★   ★   ★

Near Dam Square we found a quiet bar/café. No karaoke, no drunken Turks, no fights brewing.

I had blood on the front of my shirt and the bartender's gaze widened slightly as we came inside. She was an older, brittle-smiling woman

180

and she started to shake her head no. Nic went to her, spoke softly in rapid Dutch that I couldn't catch, and she nodded after a moment. We sat across from each other at a corner table, out of sight of the street in case the Turks kept roving, my back to the wall so I could see the entire room. But we were blocks away now and I hoped they'd decided to drink away their anger and embarrassment if they'd dodged the police.

He ordered us two beers from the waitress. She looked at me and I had blood in the corner of my mouth. She brought me a wet napkin and no questions. I cleaned my face. She set beers down in front of us, with a tall shot glass of clear liquid. '*Kopstoot*,' Nic said, pointing at the chaser. 'It means a blow to the head. You'll like it.'

'At least it's not a hole in the head,' I said. I wasn't done with the fighting — I wanted to hit some more. I am not proud of that. But it is what it is. I used to prefer quiet nights at home, reading, watching good movies with Lucy, going to bed early and making love. Now I just wanted to hit fist against flesh, boot against jaw. The brutal dance of the fight shook awake a darkness slumbering inside of me. I tamped it down with a long draw on the tall shot — it tasted a lot like gin — before I even bothered with the beer. A drunken bar brawl; wow, I was really sliding into smooth gear here. I had to clear my head.

'That's backwards,' Nic said. 'You drink the beer first, then the jenever. Do you do everything backwards?'

'Huh?'

'Usually you get to know a man before you risk your life for him in a bar fight.'

'Those guys were assholes. I don't like assholes. And you're an asshole for sticking a gun in my ribs when I helped you.'

Nic took a sip of his beer.

'Forgive me. I am a cautious man,' he said. 'Who are you?'

'Peter Samson. My friends call me Sam for short.'

'You fought like you are a soldier.'

'I was, once. Now I'm not.'

'Does Piet really owe you money?'

'I don't know who Piet is,' I said.

He stared. 'What, you just decide to . . . ' He fumbled for the right English word. 'Insert yourself into a fight?'

'I was bored. I don't have a job to go to tomorrow.'

He took a long hard sip of his beer and rubbed his jaw. He followed it by a sip of jenever. I saw his glance wander over to a family sitting a few tables over: father, mother, little girl about eight. He watched the girl laugh and take a bite of her mother's dessert. Then, reluctantly almost, it seemed, he pulled his gaze back to me, as if he'd decided on his questions. 'Where were you a soldier?'

'Canadian Special Forces.'

'You left them?'

'They asked me to.'

'For fighting in bars?'

'No. I stole some stuff and sold it on eBay.

Dishonorable discharge but no jail time once I paid them back. My commander wanted to avoid the embarrassment of me implicating him.' I shrugged. 'I did it. I can't blame them for giving me the boot.'

'Well, a fighter and a thief. Aren't I lucky?' He gave me an odd, crooked smile.

'I prefer to think of myself as an entrepreneur.'

'You said you don't have a job. Maybe you want a job?'

'What, fighting your fights for you? Dude, you don't even say thank you.'

He took the slap of the insult well. 'I haven't thanked you. Fine. Thank you, Sam. I could have handled them, but thank you.'

'You didn't pull the gun.' I'd missed wherever he was carrying. It must have been strapped on his lower leg. Nowhere had I seen a broken drape in his shirt or his jacket.

'No, you seemed to eliminate the need to do so.'

I didn't say anything and I drank, slowly, the rest of my beer. He wasn't very smart, to be a poor fighter and not produce the gun when threatened by an angry group. There was only one reason he might have hesitated: he did not want the attention. He wanted to stay below notice, and pulling a gun even in a rough bar would result in unwanted interest.

Silence is my most powerful weapon. Most people literally cannot sit in silence with another human being around, especially in a café over drinks. We consider it odd.

Silence bothered Nic. 'So. If you might be

interested in bodyguard work, I might be able to get you a job.'

'I don't have a Dutch work permit,' I said. 'I lost the paperwork.'

'You wouldn't need permit. My clients are, um, very discreet.'

'Um, like pimps? I don't beat up on hookers.'

'Oh, no. Much more high class.' He lowered his voice. 'But one of the perks is, you know, girls.'

I kept my face still. 'I think I ought to get a beer for each guy I downed.' I hoisted the glass. 'You owe me two more.'

A smile inched across his face, slowed, faded back to the solemn frown. 'All right.' He was a busy man, he gave off an air of impatience, but he liked what he'd seen in the bar fight — he had to know I'd acquitted myself far better than he had — and he'd decided not to walk away from me. Not yet. He gestured at the waitress for another round, *sans* the jenever.

'Where in Canada are you from?' I knew all this would be checked tomorrow.

'Toronto.'

'I know it well.'

'Really?'

'Yes. Did you ever eat at the Rosedale Diner on Parker Street?'

'It's on Yonge Street. Best hamburger in town.' I could smell a test.

'Your parents?'

'Dead.' I shrugged. 'They left me a little money to see the world.'

'Which high school did you go to?'

184

'St Michael's College School. Then to McGill. Studied history, barely passed. But enough to get into Canadian Forces Officer Candidate School.' My legend as Peter Samson, Canadian scofflaw, had been built by the Company. Nic wasn't going to be able to dent it. I was Peter Samson, from birth until now, and there were school records and credit histories and a Canadian military record to support me.

Unless the Company had wiped out that identity. In which case, no records on Peter Samson would exist.

'You know Amsterdam?' Nic asked me.

I took another long drag of beer and stifled a belch. 'Pardon. Not well. I know Prague and Warsaw and Budapest better.'

'You've spent a lot of time in eastern Europe.'

'That's where the more interesting work opportunities are.'

'Such as?'

'Such as stuff I really shouldn't tell a stranger,' I said, with a kidder's laugh, and he laughed, too.

'No, really,' he said after an awkward silence. 'You put a man through a window for me, Sam. We're friends now.'

'Protecting stuff. I guess it's like protecting people. I just made sure the stuff got to where it was supposed to be.'

That was a kind and subtle description of smuggling, but if Piet was a smuggler like Gregor suggested, then I might be more interesting as a potential employee. Or at least I might get an interview. I just had to get close enough to scout them out, kill them all except the high-ranking one — which I assumed was Piet — and force him to lead me to the scarred man.

Simple.

Subtle worked on Nic. He lit a cigarette, sipped at his beer.

'Like to where?'

'Mostly to North America.' Getting a secret shipment to there was Piet's goal, I hoped. And I wondered, from the Turk's words, if maybe he'd arranged illicit passage to the States, and now the arrangement had gone sour.

'I might be able to offer you a job, but I need to speak with the client.'

'Your client's not this Piet guy who doesn't pay, is he?'

'Piet pays. Those dumbass Turks need to learn patience.'

I made a noise in my throat, shrugged. 'Look, I'm good at getting stuff to the States, protecting it, making sure nobody screws with it. If that sounds good to you, fine. If not, thanks for the floor show.' It was critical I not look too eager.

Nic waited a few seconds and then said: 'I think I can use you. The pay is excellent. Two thousand euros a week, in cash.'

'Well, I'm running low on beer money. So yeah, I guess, maybe.' I ran my finger in a circle along the beer smudge on the table. 'How do I get in touch with you?'

'You got a cell?'

'Yeah.'

He pushed a napkin toward me. 'Write it down.'

I did. I didn't put my name on it. 'Decide

186

quick,' I said with a shrug. 'I get bored, I might move on.'

He tucked the napkin into his pocket. 'All right.'

'Question,' I said.

'Yes.'

'You pulled a gun on me after I helped you. You're kind of an asshole.'

He cracked a smile. 'I have to be. I wanted to be sure you didn't really come after me next. You told the Turks Piet owed you money. You might have fought them just to get at me.'

'Yeah, I don't know your Piet. I said that just to get them to shut up,' I said. 'Didn't work.'

'The fists worked well enough. All right, Sam.' He tossed more euros on the table. 'Treat yourself to more blows on the head, or get yourself dinner. You did me a favor tonight and I think we can do business together.'

'Okay. You got my number.'

He got up and left. I had my back to the wall and I watched him go out of the door and across the long flat stretch of Dam Square, under the Nationaal Monument.

I stepped out into the night, and caught sight of Nic at a distant corner. He was heading south, in the direction of the Prinsengracht. It was full dark now, and I hung back in the shadows as he crossed a street and a bridge. I followed. If he turned he might see me, but no, he was back on his electronic nipple — the cell phone — talking.

I followed, but not too close. A car stopped, picked him up. He got in and the car roared off then turned toward Singel, a major street that made a large U-shape through Amsterdam.

I looked around for a cab. None.

I just started walking the direction he'd gone. You never know what you might see. And home — the Rode Prins — was the same direction.

Thirty seconds later a small blue sedan pulled up next to me. The passenger door opened. Mila. 'Get in, dummy.'

'You were watching me?'

She roared away from the curb before I even had the door shut. 'You could have screwed up, gotten captured. I would have had to kill you. Can't have you talking about us.'

It was hard to know with her if she was serious. 'If he'd grabbed me you would have killed me instead of rescuing me?'

'If you screw up the first job, no point in giving you harder work,' she said. 'Cut losses, move on.' She turned, revved fast, slowed as we caught sight of the car that had picked up Nic.

'I got into a bar fight.'

'Good way to stay in the shadows.' She sounded disgusted. 'You could have gotten arrested. Guess what happens when they run a check on your face, dumbass? You're on your way back to your boogey man Howell.'

'I didn't have a choice.'

'We're not like the Company, Sam. I don't do job reviews. I just cut you loose if you're a problem.'

'It's nice to know you have my back.'

She glared at me. 'Don't misunderstand me. I will have your back, always. As long as you prove it's worth having. Now all you prove is you like

188

to make stupid fight.'

'I made contact and he's trying to get me a job with the blond guy. Named Piet.'

We watched Nic's car turn onto Singel. 'Tell me all details.'

Mila drove with intensity while she listened, keeping just the right amount of distance behind. I wonder where she had worked, who had taught her skills. 'So he might be going to talk to Piet,' I finished.

'About you? A job applicant? You flatter yourself,' she said.

'I meant he made a call that said he had the goods. And he's having problems with a Turk who's making trouble for Piet, who was setting up a route. You understand smuggling? You don't just load your illegal goods up and hope for the best. You plan out the exact path your goods take, with all supporting documentation and people along the way to protect it and keep it out of the authorities' attention. Solid, unbreakable routes are a valuable resource. If their route has been messed up or compromised by this Turk, it might cause a meet to happen.'

She kept Nic in her sights as he turned onto another side street.

'These guys are weird,' I said. 'They're smugglers. So why do smugglers kidnap Yasmin and have her blow up a train station? Can you get me more details on the bombing, on the victims, the response, the investigation?'

Mila didn't look at me as she made the turn. A soft rain began to fall. 'All right. I'll get you what I can. But you don't have a lot of time, Sam, to be analysing these guys. You just need to find them and get Yasmin back. Don't lose sight of that.'

'Understanding them will help me find them.'

She snap-snap-snapped her fingers. 'Our time. It is going, Sam. You can't conduct psychoanalysis on a bunch of crooks before the Dutch police ID Yasmin on a security tape. Right now she's just some girl with a backpack. But if they can ID her . . . we're out of time, the damage to Zaid's company will be done.'

'If I was going to psychoanalyse anyone, it'd be you.'

She glanced at me. 'Analyse away. You will simply have to trust me that we are the good guys.'

'I've heard that before.'

'Yes,' she said. 'I know. Ah.'

Nic's car sped up, took a hard turn. She revved, followed close. In the street where he had taken the left, five streets led off, like the spokes of a wheel, each street short, intersected with another turn.

'You distracted me,' she said. 'Your fault.'

Nic was gone. The rain began to come down harder.

33

Ten days before, in an office in New York that hid behind a sign claiming to be a financial advisory firm, Howell raged. 'Find him. Find him, and bring me his head on a plate.'

'That's very Salome of you,' August said.

Howell touched his temple. The slow, arterial throb of a migraine began to pulse behind his eyes. 'He has to be heading to London. Has to be. That's ground zero for him. I want every office alerted to his profile. I want him found now, put under the control of our people, not under anyone else.'

'I want to know who the dead body was,' August said. 'Don't you think that matters?'

'Yes, of course,' Howell said. 'I want IDs on this guy, and I want to know how and when he died.'

'I think he died Friday night,' August said. 'Just from a visual check.'

'Christ,' Howell blanched. 'He must've killed the bastard right before I got there.' He got up and paced to the window. 'I should take you off this, Mr Holdwine. You're his friend.'

'My being his friend is the reason you should leave me on,' August said. 'I'm the only one he might surrender to.'

'Guys who leave bodies in tubs like party favors for us to find aren't interested in surrendering,' Howell said. 'I thought we broke him of escape when he couldn't get the passport.'

'You questioned him for how long? But you never got to know Sam,' August said. 'You don't know how he thinks. I do. Take me with you. Get me reassigned to your team.'

'All right,' Howell said. August Holdwine might just be a superior secret weapon against Sam Capra, he thought.

★ ★ ★

The past ten days had not been pleasant for Howell. First the discovery that Sam Capra wasn't whiling away an hour in the Brooklyn library; then the discovery that the Company had an agent who had left a dead body in a neighboring apartment; then tracking the stolen car to the truck stop, and then . . . nothing. For days.

Sam Capra could have hitched a truck ride to anywhere in the country. They had scant few customers to track from the truck stop in the window of time that Sam might have been there: most of them paid cash for their lunches and coffees. Three days later, one of the waitresses remembered that a man matching Sam's description had left at the same time as another trucker. No, she didn't know the trucker's name, but he'd paid for his lunch and fuel with a credit card.

Every credit card charge had been traced, until a trucker named Vince Trout was found who said, yes, he'd given a young man a ride to the Port of New York.

'The bastard is sneaking into Europe on a cargo ship,' Howell said. He was empowered to send teams to London, Rotterdam and Marseilles to scout crews, to see if anyone had seen a man matching Sam's photo. But hundreds of ships and the crews that might have seen Sam would be back at sea and not easily questioned.

'We could go public with his face,' August said now. 'Invent a story about him.'

'No,' Howell said. 'We don't want him front and center in the press. A possibly rogue CIA agent? We don't do that kind of self-destructive publicity. Horrible at funding time. We don't call them out until we've got them in handcuffs or a coffin.' He crossed his arms, stared at August. 'Or we catch him and we find out what the hell he's up to.'

'The guy he killed might have been sent to kill him. I think someone took the bait.'

'Then we want to find said someone. I have an ID on the dead guy. He's a low-level thug connected with smuggling operations in Paris. Simon Tauras, long criminal record. Nothing special.'

'Low-level thugs don't normally cross the ocean to try and kill a Company agent.'

'Yes, that's interesting to me,' Howell said. 'I'm going to follow that lead, see where it takes us. I want you to focus on seeing if there were any communications from ships out of New York that implied anything unusual. Like they found a stowaway. Or they had any odd radio transmissions.'

'It will take days to search that database. There are millions of conversations in it.'

'Then get started.'

The trail, gone cold, grew hot two days before Sam Capra arrived in Rotterdam. August discovered in the Echelon data-base — which monitored a vast number of the world's communications and could be searched for critical keywords — radio chatter from the captain of a Liberian-registered cargo vessel to the owning company about an approaching helicopter; the ship's captain was told the helicopter should be allowed to land. No further explanation.

Howell ran into a stone wall when he contacted the shipping company. The helicopter was explained as an at-sea inspection by the owners. The flight plan referred to didn't exist, though. So someone had maybe chased the ship out to sea for a reason; to find Sam, or to bring him back.

For three days the shipping company stymied him. Then they told him that the man he wanted to interview, the captain of the *Elisa Martin*, was already back out at sea and wouldn't be available for a face-to-face interrogation until he docked in New York's port in another week.

He decided to question the man by satellite phone, which he did, and ran into a wall of denial. Someone had paid well for silence, Howell thought.

'Let me at least send his face to the authorities. Say his passport may have been compromised, stolen by a known fugitive and whoever is using it needs to be contained immediately,' August said.

Howell agreed.

So. Rotterdam. Homeland Security had constant satellite surveillance going on all major ports in the world. Howell pulled strings to get the imagery analysed. It took a team of twenty and they found a dozen leads. They coordinated it with security camera footage from the port itself and caught a photo of a man who might have been Sam Capra, walking out of a secured crew area, next to a blonde pixie in leather jeans. The crew area was close to where the *Elisa Martin* had docked.

So Sam Capra was in Holland. Probably trying to figure out a quick way to London. He alerted the Dutch intelligence service, who promised to coordinate with the police in Rotterdam, Amsterdam, and The Hague, and the border police, all quietly. Eurostar and the ferry companies were alerted. The Dutch authorities had their hands full with a train station bombing and Howell could tell his request wasn't a priority. He contacted his counterpart in the British intel service, who, given that the Company bombing had taken place on their soil and they had lost several civilians, were most eager to find Sam Capra themselves.

He could not find any identification on the woman. Her eyes were masked by sunglasses, and the facial recognition software did not give any partial matches in the Company database. He asked the techs to expand the search; Sam had a friend, and he wanted to know who this most interesting woman was.

Howell badly wanted to go to the Netherlands. He wanted to find Sam himself because he suspected this would only end with a bullet now and he wanted to be the one to deliver it.

'If he's done this, it's for a good reason,' August said. 'Maybe he's doing the job we should have done months ago — finding the people who bombed our office.'

Howell said slowly, 'Yes, that has occurred to me. But that's my job, not his. And who's this woman?'

'He's gotten some help.'

'Yes,' Howell said. 'And who would bother to help Sam, and why?'

★   ★   ★

Howell and August took a flight to Amsterdam, hurried to a Company safe house that lay in a stately home along the Herengracht canal, and set up a communications point, waiting to hear. Waiting. Because someone was going to see or find Sam Capra in the next day. Sam was not going to be hiding; Sam was going to be looking for the people who had grabbed his wife. Howell felt certain.

August Holdwine stood at the window watching the rain hit the bridge and the canal and thought, *You dumbass, your only hope is if we find you and you are willing to talk to me. If you don't, you're going to jail for the rest of your life.*

And a jet-lagged Howell lay awake, listening to the rain patter against the canal and the roof's shingles and thought, *They won't risk another embarrassment back at the headquarters. They won't care what he's doing, even if it's right. Now I have to find out what he knows and then I will have to kill him.*

34

'There is a man trying to infiltrate our group,' Piet said. 'Nic told me about him. He is a former intelligence agent. He has been seeking a means to get close to me, and presumably to you. I'm pretty sure he's tied to your little bitch's daddy.'

Edward had just gotten off a plane, his flight delayed by bad weather, and he was tired and irritable. His stomach rumbled. The lunch he'd eaten in Budapest disagreed with him. The fish, he thought. That would teach him to eat seafood in a landlocked country. And he'd gotten word that Simon, his man dispatched on a critical errand in Brooklyn, had failed. Which meant Sam Capra was alive. This was a bad night. But he would not be afraid. Fear was for fools.

'Where is he now?' Edward asked. He put down his suitcase. He took a calming breath.

'Earlier he was at a bar. Nic can tell us.'

'And he wants to see me?' Edward said. 'Bring him to me. I will put him to good use.'

'And your little bitch?'

'If anyone is my little bitch, Piet,' Edward said, 'it's you. You will undo my work if you speak of her that way. She's one of us now. Be nice.'

Piet sucked in air and crossed his arms. Edward hated him. But Piet was necessary.

'You better be getting what you need to get out of her,' Piet said. His voice was a low growl.

198

'Otherwise, you've risked us all for nothing. And nothing doesn't pay my bills.'

'Life is getting what you want, and I'm better at life than you are, Piet.'

'Her father caved?'

'Caved, collapsed, avalanched.'

'You're overconfident,' Piet said. 'Bahjat Zaid is behind this infiltration, he is trying to outflank you.' He had his plaything, the *wakizashi* sword, pulled free from the custom holster on his pants. 'Let me go Van Gogh on her ear, send it to him. He'll behave.'

'You don't touch her. Ever.'

'I'm starting to think you have feelings for the little bitch . . .'

On the last word, ignoring the short sword in Piet's hand, Edward seized Piet by the throat and pushed him, almost gently, back into the wall. Piet brought the sword up quickly, the edge of it touching Edward's wrist.

'You know if you cut me, you're dead,' Edward said. 'The sword is a stupid prop, Piet. Carrying it, you look like a refugee from a bad samurai film. Now put your toy down or I'll yell out and my friends will come up here and kill you with their bare hands. That's their loyalty to me.'

After a long moment, Piet lowered the sword.

Edward released his grip. Piet was afraid of losing respect, of face. Easy to manipulate.

'The routes to get my goods — you did an excellent job. The pickup in Budapest went very smoothly.' It had been so hard to leave his treasures behind and get on the plane back to Amsterdam, but now the treasures were on their way, hidden in Piet's smuggling route. They would be in the Netherlands soon enough. 'Let's have a look at this spy and make him useful. Get the cameras set up. Please.'

The modicum of respect worked. Piet left with a curt nod and Edward went to Yasmin's room. He touched the place where the sword had lain against his wrist; he could still feel the edge of the blade. Piet was starting to be more of a problem than he was worth, but he needed him right now. Everything was lining up: the money; the goods; his future.

Yasmin lay on the bed — that was her privilege now.

Edward was proud of his fair lady, the woman he'd modeled from raw clay into a killer. He stood over her as she slept in an uneasy drowse.

After she'd dropped the backpack behind a book display inside the small magazine store in the train station they'd hurried her out to a van two blocks away and driven off. She had not panicked or freaked out or tried to flee; his invisible hold on her held. She had followed her orders without question. Without fear.

Edward could see the admiration for his work in the eyes of the others.

That night they moved her to the attic. Edward brought her favorite food, cinnamon pastries. He told her she had done a wonderful job, that she had done great good today.

'You eliminated a serious problem for us today.' He began to unbutton her blouse. 'You are a heroine to me, Yasmin.'

'Are they listening?' she whispered.

'No. You are one of us now. You proved that at the station. No one is listening to us. It is only you and me here, little bird.'

He slipped her blouse from her shoulders; she did not resist. He held up a small wooden dove. 'I saw this on a street vendor's table at the Albert Cuypmarket and thought of you. Beauty, strength. And wood can be shaped . . . into so many things, Yasmin.' He eased off the skirt they'd put her in; she lay nude and shivering on the narrow bed.

'There is no going back now, Yasmin. The bombing went well. You did your part exactly as we asked.'

Bombing. She didn't blink at the word.

'Your old dirty life is done.' He put the wooden carving — a dove — around her throat. It hung on a leather thong and he tightened the string, almost unconsciously, as he put it against her flesh. He felt the pulse of her throat through his fingertips.

Edward stood and undressed. His body was lean and muscular. He lay down on her and kissed her throat, her face, with gentleness. She did not kiss back. She lay still.

'You're troubled by what you did?' he asked. 'We went through this a thousand times.'

She didn't resist his kisses. He took her, with urgency. She closed her eyes. He finished, lay next to her, then took her again, this time with gentleness. She lay as though not feeling his touch. He didn't care.

The whole time, he whispered, 'This is how

you stay alive, Yasmin. Do what I say and you live.'

Now he sat and he watched her, thinking, until he heard a commotion, a struggle downstairs, and he knew Piet had readied the show for the cameras.

He woke her. 'Yasmin? Wake up.'

The first thing she saw was the gun he was holding.

'Is that one of the . . . ?' she began and then she blinked past the bleariness of sleep.

'No. No, it's not.'

She blinked and sat up from the pillow.

He sat next to her on the mattress. 'Listen. I have a duty for you, but one you will like. Would you like a shower? Some food?'

She nodded.

He led her to a bathroom, and fresh soap and shampoo and a toothbrush. When she started to take off the dove he stopped her. 'No. I want you to wear it always. A hope for peace.'

He gave her fresh pants, a shirt, underwear. Demi brought up bread and fruit for breakfast. He thanked Demi, and so did Yasmin. Demi gave her a surprised glance as she went back downstairs.

'It's nice to be one of us. To be free from the closet, isn't it?'

She nodded.

'Come with me.' He felt a thrum of excitement in his chest; it was just like going back on stage.

He brought her down into the main dining

room and there they were: Piet, Demi, six other men including the twins who often stared at her. Now they all stared at her. And in the middle, where the dining room table should have been, there was a man tied to a chair. Thick rope bound him; a gag protruded from his mouth.

He moaned as Edward and Yasmin entered, his face bruised and beaten.

'Do you see this man, Yasmin?' Edward said.

'Yes, I see him.' Her voice was flat.

'He's a terrible man, Yasmin. He has been working on a scheme to take you from us and to kill you if he cannot take you away.'

'To take me and to kill me?' Her tone was quiet, unruffled.

'Yes, to take you back to your father. He contacted one of our people with a mouthful of lies; we followed him. Do you know this man, Yasmin?' Edward grabbed the former spy's head, twisted it toward her. He'd been beaten badly, but she studied the face and finally she shook her head.

'Your father knows we are protecting you from him. Your father sends people to destroy us. In secret. Like this man.'

She said, 'Well, that's wrong. I don't want to go back to what I was.' And she spat in the man's face. The gob of saliva hung off a clotted eyebrow, dense with dried blood.

The group gave a soft murmur, watching her.

'Are you sure you don't know him? He has tried to infiltrate us, through Piet.'

'I don't know him.' She looked at Edward.

The man bound to the chair stared at her and Edward took the gag from his mouth. 'I just . . . I just want the money I'm owed. By Piet. That's all. I don't want to know about anything else.'

'You know about me. From who?' Edward said.

'I don't know . . . ' the man said in Turkish, and then Edward started to beat him. Yasmin tried to look away and Demi said, 'Don't you dare. Don't you dare look away or we'll tie you to the chair,' so she didn't.

Under his fists, Edward saw the blood leap in its little splatters and the teeth break. He stopped and picked up one of the man's hands. 'I have ten ways to make you talk, right here. Bahjat Zaid sent you, yes?' he said, and he began twisting the fingers hard.

Finally the man screamed, 'No, no. All right, Zaid sent me,' and then a torrent of words that Yasmin couldn't follow, and Edward, leaning close, his hand on the man's shoulder, gentle now, like they were friends.

'You were going to steal our shipment when it arrived in Rotterdam?'

'Yes . . . trade it for Yasmin. I would get it and then trade it for her. So I could take her back to her father. I will tell you all. Please just don't . . . '

'So your route to smuggle our goods from here to America, that was all a lie? I just want to be sure I understand. You have nothing to fear if you tell me the truth.'

'Yes. It was a lie. All a lie. There was no route.'

His breathing came in hard jolts.

Edward stepped away, wiped a speckle of blood from the toe of his shoe. He gestured at Demi, standing by a camera. He snapped fingers and said, 'Action!'

Demi started the video camera.

Edward pulled out a gun, its barrel capped with a silencer, from the back of his pants. He handed it to Yasmin. He could hear the sudden gasps of the others.

'Act one,' he said. 'Kill him.'

She took the gun in her hand. She looked at him in confusion.

'It's not a test, Yasmin. It's a duty.'

The man was broken, blood dripping from his mouth. His gaze met hers.

'Yasmin, do it. Now please, my to-do list is not getting shorter,' Edward said.

She didn't raise the gun; she stared at the beaten man.

'Yasmin . . . ' He hoped he wouldn't have to threaten to kill her again.

'I'm deciding where to shoot him,' she said. 'I don't want to hit the ropes instead.'

Edward smiled, a teacher's pride in his student. The man began to babble in his own tongue, begging her not to shoot, pleading for mercy.

She raised the gun, steadied its grip.

'Yasmin!' the Turk yelled in perfect English. 'Your father is trying to help you. Whatever they told you, it's a lie! Don't do this!'

'My father is the liar.' The gun wavered a moment. She blinked and fired.

The spit noise was soft; the bullet hit him in the chest. The chair fell over. He was still alive; he screamed in agony.

Yasmin fired again. The bullet struck the man's throat. He spasmed and then went still. One of the men laughed and then they all clapped for her. She just stared at the dead man, as though he might fade from her sight. She didn't lower the gun; she was a statue.

'That's a wrap. Demi, load the footage onto the computer. Blur our faces if they're visible. Then we'll get it ready to premiere it for her idiot father.' Edward took the gun from Yasmin and lowered her arm, like settling a marionette back onto its wooden stage. 'You are perfect now.'

She cupped her elbows as if she felt cold, and she seemed confused. He took her chin in his hand.

'Your father is now under our heel. He will not give us any more trouble, Yasmin.'

She glanced at the eyes of the others, all on her. 'May . . . may I go back to my room? Or do you need me to help you clean up?'

'Go upstairs.'

She obeyed. The group watched her in silence.

'I wonder,' Piet said, 'if that girl is playing you.'

'She is not.'

'I think she might do anything to survive,' Piet said. 'She knew it was her or that Turk. You said she was a scientist, right? I think she just might be stone-cold. Don't turn your back on her. She's shot a man now. It will be easier the second time. Always is.'

'Shut up and get rid of the body,' Edward said. Piet could do the dirtiest job, given his mouth. 'And Demi, I want that tape ready to send. I want her father to start his day with his lovely, perfect daughter.'

35

I opened my eyes.

I heard a baby crying and for one sweet moment I thought it was mine and Lucy's Bundle, and that all was right in the world. That London had never happened.

But the ceiling was weird, a blue peaked roof with white beams cutting across it at an angle. I was in Amsterdam. Morning light shone on my face. I could still hear the baby. I got up and went to the small window that overlooked the Prinsengracht canal and saw a harried mother walking by, pushing a stroller. The night's rain had gone and it looked like a pretty morning.

I had not thought much about being a father. When Lucy had told me we were going to have a baby there was at first the shock of surprise and joy. Then I thought of my dad, who'd taken me and my brother to six continents by the time we were ten, who was busy saving the world and often ignoring us. He had been a good father in some ways and an indifferent one in others. I would not repeat his mistakes, assuming I got that chance.

A knock at the door. I kept my gun close and opened it. Mila, dressed like a young account executive, a neat gray suit, muted scarf, stylish shoes. She carried an expensive briefcase and a bag of groceries. She was a little chameleon.

'Are you job-hunting today, Mila?'

'Yes. I hope to work with a better class of people very soon. Get showered, I'll make coffee. We have a busy day.'

I showered fast, dried, dressed in jeans and a black T-shirt and a jacket. When I came out to the small kitchen she had breakfast pastries on a plate, coffee steaming from the percolator. Her laptop was open and a video was playing on it.

Yasmin, shooting a man. The video reached its end, started again.

Mila munched on a roll, sipped coffee. 'The quality of the film is dodgy, but impact is there.'

'My God,' I said. I rewound and looked at the murdered man's face.

The man executed was the Turk I'd fought in the bar the night before.

I hit the space bar on the laptop and the video stopped — Yasmin frozen, raising the gun. Her face was clear in the video. Every other face, except the dead man's, had been digitally blurred.

'Let me guess,' I said. 'Blackmailing Bahjat Zaid, chapter two.'

'This arrived in his email at six o'clock this morning. He forwarded to me via a secure line.'

'So they've made her into a bomber and a murderer,' I said. 'They can't, or won't, take her to a bank for her Patty-Hearst-joins-her-captors moment, so they're manufacturing them.'

Mila made a noise as she sipped her coffee.

'Did Zaid send that man?' A slow anger started to smolder past the soreness I felt from last night's fight. 'He hires me, he hires this guy, we don't know about each other? I don't like it.'

'He could have named you before they killed him if he'd known.'

'Yes, but now they'll be on guard like never before. We both took the same tack, trying to connect to Piet, and now I'm screwed, Mila. My job just got a thousand times harder, just when I'd started to get close to Nic.' I stood and paced the floor. 'Get Zaid here. We have to talk. What the hell is this shipment that his other hired gun was supposed to steal?'

'He told me he was leaving Amsterdam.'

'Where is he?'

'I don't know.'

'Then let's find him.' I sat down, reopened the email he'd sent on the laptop. The original email source — from Yasmin's captors — had gone through an anonymizer service and was untraceable. But I looked at Zaid's email to Mila. Encoded in the source headers was information about the provider. I looked at it, plugged the information into a website that provided information on server locales. 'Zaid sent this from Hungary. Why the hell is he in Hungary? He's hiring me to save his daughter, and instead of being here, close to the action, he's in Hungary.' I heard my voice rise. 'That's where Yasmin worked. Why is he *there*?'

'I don't know, Sam, and yelling at me is not going to put a GPS on him. His company has a facility there. He might simply be tending to business.'

Right. The one Yasmin worked at. 'I do not like this. Zaid hiring another agent to attempt a rescue — we could have tripped each other up.

210

We could have killed each other, mistaking each other for members of the gang. I assume the Turk was given the same orders I was — rescue Yasmin and wipe out the kidnappers.'

She shrugged. 'Perhaps. We need a different approach.'

'No, we don't even have the full story. Zaid wanted the Turk to steal whatever's being shipped so it could be exchanged for his daughter. We need to know what that shipment is.'

'I will find out,' she said.

I considered. 'Okay, I was in the bar before Nic was. Maybe I can say I heard the Turk make a threat that will concern both Nic and Piet.'

She gave me a slight smile. 'Eat your breakfast. You must be prepared to frighten Nic very badly.'

I watched the tape again. 'What will they ask Zaid for now? They did this because they knew the Turk was chasing them, but they did it to ruin her again. Now there's footage of his daughter bombing a station and executing a man. What if she hasn't been brainwashed? What if she's a willing participant?'

'Nothing in her background suggests violence.'

I stared at the video. Watched Yasmin become a murderer again. 'It's like they want Zaid to suffer. This is personal.'

'That is your guess, you could be wrong,' Mila said.

'Here's the problem. I don't know how I can get leverage with Nic, and therefore Piet, and rise above suspicion.'

'We could grab Nic, force him to tell us.'

'No. You want this whole group eliminated, then I have to get inside. I have to get them all together. Nic is the key right now.'

'So how will you convince him that you are necessary?'

'Any operation like this faces a challenge,' I said. 'I need to know what their challenge is, and be the cure.'

'How will you find that out?'

I considered. 'Gregor told me that Nic lives above a coffee shop in the Jordaan. I know his last name is ten Boom. That's a start.'

36

It took me a while to find Nic. He was not listed in the phone book. I could have called Gregor, but I didn't want him any more scared. The Jordaan is an older neighborhood, not far from the Prinsengracht, that's gotten a bit trendy. It wasn't a canal district; the streets were narrow in some stretches and wide in others, even with parking for cars in the middle of the street. The buildings were the narrow, tall sort favored in Amsterdam: the roofline was a jumble of angles and heights. Many of the shops were appropriately hipster, or aimed at students: bookshops, clothing stores, and many places to get coffee or beer. The ninth coffee shop I tried, yes, there was a ten Boom listed on the door buzzer to the corresponding doorway. I was standing at the bottom of the stairs when I heard Nic's voice, raised, feet coming down the stairs.

Hell.

I bolted out the front door and hurried into line in the coffee shop. If he came in for his morning jolt I would have a bitch of a time explaining why I was here. I thought. Hmm. Maybe it would show initiative that I had found where he lived. More likely it would freak him out.

I heard the door jingle behind me. Best to face the music. I looked over my shoulder. It was a pretty young woman entering. And beyond her,

Nic, on a cell phone, talking with animated gestures. He unlocked a bicycle, pulled it free from its railing and got on it. He didn't bother with hands on the handlebars, like many of Amsterdam's daredevils, and he rode off, still jabbering on the cell phone.

I ducked out of the line, smiled at the pretty girl and hurried back to the building's lobby.

His apartment was on the top floor. I ran up the stairs, found the door, listened. Silence inside. I knelt before the door. Mila had pronounced my plan 'stupid' yet had geared me up.

The lock was a simple one: with two picks I had it open in forty seconds. I eased the door open and stepped inside, shutting the door without a sound.

The apartment was unkempt. Half-full beer glasses, left over from last night and smelling stale, sat on a coffee table. Yesterday's newspaper lay scattered across a couch. I moved soundlessly through the littered den, the small kitchen. Three doors beyond the kitchen. I opened the closest: it was a small bathroom. Then the next one. And froze.

An elderly lady lay asleep in a bed, snoring. An empty vodka bottle stood guard on a night table. Her hair was a mess and the slightest odor of dirtiness wafted above her. I eased the door shut.

Damn. This was too dangerous. But this might also be my only chance . . . I tried the other door. Nic's room. And it was as spotless as the other rooms were dingy. Most of it was taken up by a desk, with three computers sitting along it.

Above the monitors were rows of books on database design, programming languages, and many books on computer hacking and security. Perhaps he was more than a spammer. A scattering of photos sat on a side table. A younger Nic, without the ponytail and the beer weight, standing next to the woman who lay in the other room's bed. She looked younger and healthier and next to her was a man who looked like a much older version of Nic.

Nic, the wannabe badass, was a computer geek who lived with his mother.

I'd come equipped. I needed information and most information these days is parked on computers. I tapped the keyboard's space bar. There was a login prompt, asking for a password. I slipped a USB portable drive into one of the ports on the first computer. The software loaded on it started its work to crack the login password. Mila said it was NSA-based technology and didn't say how she'd gotten her dirty little hands on it.

While the cracker attempted to, well, crack, I searched the room. Nic had a gun, a Glock, under his bed. Nothing else.

The woman's snoring rose in volume, snuffled, went quiet.

The computer pinged. I was in. I removed the password cracker and slipped in a different USB drive, one designed to copy his entire hard disk. Mila had promised me that it would work much faster than a conventional drive. It started its work and I went to the listing of his most recent applications and documents to see what he'd

215

been working on. He'd been looking at PDFs. I opened them all up.

He'd been reading and capturing news website accounts of the Centraal Station bombing. I scanned them. Nothing I didn't already know. Five killed. Four Dutch, one Russian. The Russian's name had not yet been released, the police said, because of difficulty locating his family. The bomb had gone off in a small book store; it had been left behind a cardboard display of books that were on sale. Police speculated it was not left in the open area of the station because there was no place to easily dump a backpack without it being spotted.

Next up were pictures of the devastation and I'd looked at them for five seconds before realizing: no way these came from a news website. These were crime-scene photos, the kind simply not made available for public viewing, taken by the police.

They were gruesome. People buying their papers, their magazines, chocolate candy for a snack or a bad-for-you breakfast. One cashier, just doing a simple, honorable job. All dead. Their shredded bodies lay among the torn and burned remains of the shop. Blood splattered the walls. Limbs torn from the corpses.

It brought back the most horrible memories of the Holborn bombing.

How did Nic have these photos?

There was a police analysis of the bomb, stamped as classified.

What had he said last night at the urinal? *I got the goods, the cops don't know.* I thought he'd meant smuggling goods, but I was wrong. The smug bastard had hacked into the police database. He was following the investigation.

A chill touched my skin. Nic was far, far more than he seemed. I had badly underestimated him.

I examined the details of the bomb. A small amount of Semtex explosive, believed to have come from an inventory stolen in the Czech Republic six months earlier. Simple.

But. But.

There was nothing in the report about *how* the bomb was detonated. I paged through the rest of it. There should be a timer, or a cell phone to trigger the blast with a call. None was present. Even a devastating blast should have left forensic evidence of how the bomb was activated and blown.

The next page was labeled *unidentified electronics*. I glanced through it; there was gear in the knapsack that had been annihilated in the blast but left enough fragments to indicate that it wasn't from a cell phone. The police were still piecing it together. Maybe that was the detonator. But if it wasn't obviously a cell phone or a timer, what was it? I could see a half-melted grid, no bigger than a hand — it looked like a honeycomb, forged from metal. I had never seen its like before. Apparently it had blown through the paperback display and into the intestines of one of the victims, preserving it from the worst of the blast.

The police did not yet know what this gear was and that troubled me.

Next door the snoring rose again, and then stopped. I could hear movement in the bed. I stopped typing. The rustling stopped, but the snoring didn't resume. I glanced out the window. It was a straight drop four stories down to the café's awning.

I waited. No movement. Maybe she was awake and staring at the ceiling. I checked the portable drive; halfway done. Maybe Mom was used to the soft insistent click of the keys; she might just assume that Nic was home.

I looked at the files on the people who had died in the blast. The four Dutch citizens were the cashier and three customers, including a nineteen-year-old girl, a forty-five-year old man, a fifty-year-old woman, and a twenty-seven-year old man. They were wives and husbands, fathers and daughters, friends. Each had in their electronic dossier a photo from either a driver's license or a passport.

The file on the Russian was blank except for an autopsy report. No name. No age listed, no passport number listed. No photo.

Weird. The Amsterdam police, among the best in the world, didn't have a read on who the fifth victim was. That astonished me.

I looked through the rest of the files that Nic had stolen from the police databases. Found a video labeled *toezicht* and dated the day of the blast. *Toezicht* meant surveillance. I activated it.

The security camera feed had gone into a central security station; if the tape had only been at the store it likely would not have survived the blast. I had five minutes of the feed that Nic had managed to filch off the police servers.

I watched the last moments of the lives of innocent people.

The young cashier at her station, giving change with a slightly bored frown. She kept scratching her ear. Customers coming and going, most not lingering long. I did not see Yasmin, which meant she must have dropped off the bomb before this section of the feed started. Dozens of people, leaving and arriving and leaving again. The store was busy — it was amazing that more people hadn't been killed. I saw a man stop before the book display; next to it was a newspaper display. He reached for the paper and then the screen went white-hot blank.

I backed up the film and froze it. Five people in the store, caught in the camera's unblinking eye. The four Dutch I could see and guess at from their photos in life. The Russian was the man reaching for the newspaper display when the bomb detonated. I backed up, a frame at a time. He stepped back from the newspaper display. He was in profile, his face turned slightly away. He backed toward the magazine display. And then I saw his face.

I know him. It can't be.

37

Behind me, in the hallway, a door opened. Feet shuffled on hardwood.

'Nic? *Bent wakker u?*' Are you awake?

'*Ja*,' I called in my best impersonation of Nic. I couldn't stay. I pulled the drive from the port. I could hear the bathroom door shut and then water running in a sink, the flush of a toilet. A shower started. And beyond that, I heard the front door open.

Nic was home.

No way out the front. I tapped carefully on the computer, making sure I was not leaving traces of my time there. I logged out and the screen returned to its prompt page. I put it to sleep.

I put my leg out over the window. I could still hear the crash of the water in the shower and I hoped Nic wasn't heading straight back to his room. I pulled myself out, standing on the sill.

I couldn't go down: I looked up. There was a beam extending from the brickwork, several feet above my head. Most of the buildings in Amsterdam had them; I presumed they were used to haul large pieces of furniture up to the homes, given the narrowness of most Dutch stairwells.

It was quite a jump. I waited for someone on the street to notice me but no one was looking up. I gathered my thoughts; let the muscle memory of hours of parkour training settle in. I could do this. I raised my eyes to the beam. I jumped. I extended my hands to catch the beam.

I missed.

I fell. I reached and barely seized, with my palms, the brick ledge below the windowsill I'd been standing on. My body hit against the brick and pain lanced up my arms. My fingertips burned like fire but I didn't dare cry out. I used my feet to muffle the impact and that gave me leverage to strengthen my hold on the brick. Parkour hardens the hands and the arms and the abdominals but I was too out of serious practice. I glanced down. The street was mostly empty. A woman walked out of the café, past the bright yellow awning, didn't look up.

I heard the door open. Nic, inside his room. Whistling. I was screwed. I heard a clatter on his desk; he was probably only a foot away from me. He might even see my hands if he looked out the window. I heard him speaking rapid Dutch to his mom, annoyed, telling her he didn't have time to chat.

Thank God. I risked a pull up and saw through the window that he was walking away from me, down the hall. But he'd left the bedroom door open.

Parkour is about effective movement from place to place. Efficiency. I made my mind a knife. I cut the problem into small steps that could be done in one fluid movement. I had been hanging onto the window for less than ten seconds. I had no time to spare.

I pulled myself up cleanly. I managed to get a foot on the sill and I stood the rest of the way. Nic's mom called to him from her room, complaining about him not bringing her breakfast. Nic told her to piss off and go back to bed until she was sober. His voice got louder, walking back in the direction of the bedrooms.

I had to make the jump again. I jumped and this time I closed hands around the beam. I swung my legs up quickly, hearing Nic's voice berate his mother and her answering bray. I heard a shout from the street — I'd been seen. All I could do was to vanish quickly, before the police were summoned. I moved to the top of the beam and eased myself out of view onto the roof. On the roof no one could see me. I lay and I stared at the sky and I caught my breath. Slowly, I slithered off Nic's roof onto the neighboring one. I made my way, carefully, silently, staying out of the street's sight. It seemed to take forever.

A little girl in one of the attic apartments watched me, goggle-eyed, as I reached the end of the block, a dozen buildings away from Nic's house. She was maybe four, bright-eyed, apple-cheeked. I waved and she waved back. Then I put a finger to my lips and so did she, laughing. I pantomimed cranking open the window; she did.

I slipped through the window into her room. She stared at me. I patted her head and pantomimed silence again. She laughed again. I slipped out of her room, heard bedroom noises that sounded like a mom getting dressed, bathroom noises of a shower. I was out of the apartment in moments, and heading down the stairway.

38

'You know the dead Russian? How?' Mila said. She'd plugged the portable drive into her own computer and was looking at what I'd stolen from the thief Nic.

My voice felt thick. 'The day of the bombing in London . . . I gave a presentation on a guy who we believed was tied to financing for international crime rings, ones that even reach into governments. We called him the Money Czar, a guy no one could put a finger on. Nothing on him, he was a blank slate; we only had the one picture and mentions of him by a couple of informants who ended up dead. This is the guy. This is the guy I was hunting, that I wanted to catch. I thought the scarred man might have been working to protect the Money Czar. Instead, the scarred man kills him.' I could hardly breathe, my chest felt cut from stone. 'They killed my *target*. Who the hell are these people? What are they after? Why did they take my wife?'

Mila stared at me.

'This was no ordinary bombing,' I said. 'This was a hell of a lot more. This was a murder. I need to go through everything we lifted off Nic's laptop. I have to find a reason for him to bring me into the operation.'

'Then let's find you one,' Mila said, leaning over the computer.

39

'I don't think I can bring in new people right now,' Nic said on the phone. I suspected he'd gotten a lockdown order from Piet. They were in panic mode over the attempt of the Turk to infiltrate them. Or, a scarier possibility, he figured out someone had been in his computer or his room. No one new was going to be trusted; the Turk had soured my chances.

But I had no options. I had to sell him on me.

'Listen, Nic. That's cool. But you got to get me some money, man, because I have some information that's worth real money to you and your boss.'

'I doubt that, Sam, but . . . '

'Before you got to the Grijs Gander, the Turk was talking about moving a valuable shipment for you. To the United States. I don't think you should trust him, mouthing off in a bar. You need delicate goods moved, I can do it. Fast and safe and cheap.'

'He talked about a smuggling route. In the bar.' Nic's voice rose slightly.

'He said it all in Turkish to his friends and I picked up enough,' I said. I glanced at Mila, who was listening in. 'He said he'd make Piet pay if he didn't get his money. He said he'd phone in an anonymous tip to the cops if Piet didn't give him what he wanted.'

'I . . . I can't have this talk on the phone.' The

225

nervousness in his voice increased.

'But it didn't mean anything to me until they started going off about your friend.' Of course, if they'd tortured the Turk and he'd told them a different story from mine . . . I could be in very great danger. But such were the risks. 'Well, I will give you a better and more secure route than that Turk and I know to keep my mouth shut. I need steady work, Nic.'

'I will have to call you back. But no promises.'

'Look, fine, you and your friend get fried. I don't care. Good luck to you.' I hung up.

Mila raised an eyebrow. 'You hooked him hard.'

I didn't answer her.

'Sam.'

'What?'

'Don't let emotion trip you up.'

'I'm not emotional. Do you see emotion? I am the embodiment of a poker face right now.'

'This Money Czar. If he was working with the scarred man, if he was the money man, why would the scarred man kill him? And why would they kill him this way? Two bullets in the head and dumped into a canal is far easier.'

I didn't have an answer, and that was part of the problem. Two birds: the scarred man made Yasmin Zaid look like a murderer and he'd eliminated the Money Czar — but why? I had assumed the scarred man bombed our office to *protect* the Money Czar. Clearly not.

The phone rang in my hand. I let it ring five times.

'He's pissing himself,' Mila said.

I let it ring twice more before I answered: 'Yes?'

'I might be able to get you some work. Just understand that my boss is extremely cautious right now.'

I'll bet he is, I thought. 'I like a cautious boss.'

'I will meet you at the bar we were at last night and take you to Piet.'

'No. In the open, the sunlight. Where I can see you and your friends coming. I know a bar . . . ' But then Mila was shaking her head. 'No, I tell you what, Nic, as a show of good faith, you pick.'

'Do you know the Pelikaan Café on the Singel?'

Mila nodded. I said: 'Yes.'

'Meet me there. Noon.'

'All right. I'll see you at noon.' Nic hung up.

'Well.' Mila unclipped her earpiece. 'They bit. But they might well grab you, force you to talk someplace of their choosing. There will be no immediate trust. We'll have to prepare for that eventuality.'

'Why not have them meet here on our turf?'

'Because I wish to protect our turf,' she said. 'You must treat the Rode Prins as your safe house. I know the Pelikaan. I know what we will do. Hurry, we don't have much time.' She rose and I touched her arm.

'Did you get a hold of Bahjat Zaid?'

'No,' she said. 'No one seems to know where he is.'

227

'Look, I think he gave them something from his office in Hungary, the one that Yasmin works at. *That's* what they're smuggling across Europe.'

She bit her lip.

'He's an arms manufacturer, Mila. What the hell is he giving these people? He's paying ransoms and they're never going to give her back to him.'

'You and I have our orders, Sam. We rescue Yasmin, eliminate her kidnappers as witnesses and as a threat. Do that, and you don't need to worry about whatever he gave him.'

'Do you know? Be totally honest with me.'

'No, I don't,' she said, and I believed her.

'I still have to know what they want to get to America.'

'First things first. Yasmin. This gang. That's the way to find out the truth about your wife, Sam. Stay focused.' Her voice got a new steel to it. 'I have some leverage for you with Nic. Most unpleasant.'

'What?'

'On his computer.' She opened a file. Photos. Photos of youngsters, in awful, provocative poses. Boys, girls, a range of ages, a range of poses, from coy to hardcore. I saw a list of names, of emails. I looked away.

'He's a child molester?'

'Perhaps. At the least he is a broker of smut. It seems that if you want a photo to your specifications — Nic can provide it.' The steel in her voice faded and she cursed under her breath.

I thought of the odd glance he'd given the little girl in the café by Dam Square last night, and felt ill. 'Okay. That's leverage. I can force his hand.'

'And then,' Mila said, 'you can cut it off.'

40

Howell studied the video feed in the security center at the Rotterdam train station. There. The cameras caught the man he'd seen on the port coverage that looked like Sam Capra. The blonde-haired pixie in the huge sunglasses walking a few steps in front of him.

'The train they're boarding?' he said.

'That was the 10:15 service to Amsterdam,' August said, checking a train itinerary.

'I want every record of a pair of tickets bought together on a credit card.'

'They could have paid cash, or used a prepaid ticket,' August said.

'Or they could have made a mistake,' Howell said.

Ten minutes later Howell had a name, en route to Amsterdam. Most people traveling on the 10:15 service already had their tickets; but one pair, in car five, were charged to a credit card belonging to a woman named Fernanda Gatil.

He called the CIA office in Amsterdam and gave them the name, requested a full work-up on Fernanda Gatil, told them to put her name out on the wire to the Dutch border stations. He wanted to know where she worked, where she lived, every detail of her life. He wanted photo enhancement on the images pulled from the train station security cameras; he wanted to know who this woman was and why she was traveling with a man he felt reasonably sure was Sam Capra.

41

Ten after noon.

Nic the scumbag was late. I sat outside the Pelikaan, on the south side of the canal, sipping a half-pint of Heineken. The sunlight shimmered on the water.

I wondered, for the first time, who the Turk was that Zaid had hired. A soldier of fortune? An actual smuggler? Someone, like me, with his own personal vendetta against the scarred man? Bahjat Zaid was a panicked father who hadn't put his entire trust into Mila or her secret employers. After I calmed down a bit on the way to this meeting, I could not blame him. I didn't know if *my* child was dead or alive, either.

I was getting closer to the truth and to Lucy. I knew it. This was the most important meeting of my life. I tried not to sweat. I tried not to think too much. Just play the right note and I'd be in.

Nic worked his way through the strolling Saturday crowds. He gave everything and everyone a disdainful look. He did not look happy.

He sat across from me. In the daylight he looked pasty, robbed of sleep. I wondered if he'd figured out he'd had an intruder in his room, parsing his hideous secrets. But probably none of them had slept well last night after learning of the Turk's attempt to infiltrate them.

'Hello,' I said. I absolutely had to keep the

contempt from my voice. *I know what you are.*

'I'm having a very bad day,' he said. The waiter stopped by the table; Nic ordered a Coke. The waiter brought it and vanished. No one sat near us.

'So. This Turk compromised your route?'

'It was all bluff,' Nic said. 'The Turk was a liar.'

'Was?'

'I mean is. Forgive my English.'

I had to sound like a guy desperate for a job; which I was. 'Nic. Listen. I've moved plenty of stuff from eastern Europe to Holland, to England and America. I know how to get contraband of any sort through. If you want to risk that the Turk has screwed up your planned route, let me design an entirely new route for you, with new transport. Be safe.'

Nic sipped his soda. I waited. If they'd depended on the Turk to set up transit for their goods to the US, they couldn't use whatever he'd arranged so they had to be desperate. Unless they'd already found a solution. But the Turk had died a few hours ago, and maybe I was their best chance of keeping their operation moving forward. Nic would have been sent to take my measure.

'Why are you so desperate for work?' he asked.

'I like eating and sleeping under a roof. And I need a foothold in the Netherlands.'

'Why here?'

'A few minor difficulties for me in eastern Europe. I need to focus on smuggling goods to the West.' I took a long sip of beer. 'I wouldn't mind a slice of the action of whatever you've got going. What is it? Counterfeit cigs or luxury goods? Designer drugs?' All of those were trades worth billions — nearly twenty per cent of the world economy these days is in illicit goods.

'You must be in dire straits to be hanging out in seedy bars looking for work to appear.'

'Actually I'm just a big karaoke fan. And if you'd said dire straits there last night, I would have sung one of their hits.'

A smile flickered and vanished. 'What's your full name, Sam?'

'Peter Michael Samson.'

Nic's phone rang. He opened it, listened carefully. He kept a poker face, mostly — I saw the slightest tug of a smile at the corner of his mouth. He got up from the table, walked to another empty one, made a second call. He listened, watching me. I raised my glass to my lips, whispered behind the camouflage of the half-pint.

'Did you get that?' I said.

Mila answered. 'Yes.' The transmitter was hidden beneath my collar, thin as a toothpick. Hard to detect under my starched shirt. Hence dressing for the meeting like it was a job interview. Mila had slipped the transmitter into my clothes. State of the art; I wasn't sure the Company had field gear this good. It made me wonder again exactly who I'd decided to work for.

'If they have passport records access . . . they could be digging my name up right now.'

The Company could have killed the Peter

Samson legend, eliminated the IDs, the passport records. And surely there would be a trace put on any queries made against my old, discarded names, as well as watching for any use of them.

Which might bring the Company right down on Nic and his friends. But that couldn't happen before I got what I needed from them. Not before I had the scarred man in my grip. Not before I had got Yasmin to safety and knew the truth about Lucy and my son.

I watched Nic. Nic watched me. Minutes passed. Long enough for whoever he had working for him to access a Canadian passport database? They had hacked into the Amsterdam police servers; why not the Canadians' as well? I had underestimated Nic before.

I said nothing more to Mila; she was close, watching us from an empty office space across the Singel canal.

* * *

On the Herengracht, in the grand Company safe house, August pushed open the door of Howell's office. Howell glanced up from looking at photos that had come through passport control in Rotterdam. Thousands of faces, none of them Sam Capra. He felt dizzy.

'Sir, we just got a query hit on one of Sam Capra's old legends. The Peter Samson identity. It just came, moments ago, from an IP address from an internet café in Amsterdam. Looking for passport information, military records, criminal history.'

'Where?'

'Over on Singel. A few minutes away.'

'Let's find out who's so interested in Sam.' God, he thought, maybe it was Sam himself, checking to see if the old identity was still active. That little bastard finally made a mistake. 'Any record of the passport being used to enter Holland?'

'No, sir,' August said. 'Do you want me to kill all the documentation tied to the identity?'

'No. No. Leave it active. Let's see where it leads us.'

He and August and an ex-Marine, Van Vleck, permanently assigned to the Company office in Amsterdam, hurried down the steps into the bright spring day. 'We can call the Dutch police . . . ' Van Vleck said.

Howell raised a hand. 'Absolutely not. We handle this ourselves.' He glanced at August. 'This may get ugly. If he's there, we take him down, and you can talk to him later. Don't hesitate.'

'I won't, sir,' August said. 'We'll catch him.'

42

Nic closed the phone and I lowered the beer glass from my mouth. He approached the table. He might have been told that Peter Samson no longer existed. He could have taken a picture of me with his phone, sent it to Piet or even the scarred man — in which case I was dead. I looked at what was on the table: cloth, lovely flowers in a small glass vase, half-pint glass. If he came back to the table knowing I was a fraud, I could kill him with the vase. Shatter the end, put it against his throat. The glass in the vase was heavier than the beer glass.

Nic slid into the seat across from me. He straightened the ponytail and smiled at me.

'You were wanted in Croatia last year for smuggling.'

That was sadly true of Peter Samson; he was such a loser. 'That's so last year.'

'I guess so. The charges were dismissed.'

'Bribes work.' I shrugged. 'And a witness decided not to talk.'

'What were you moving?'

'Whatever needed moving. Illicit explosives from the Czech Republic. Old weapons from Ukraine. Opium moving through Turkey.' I shrugged again. 'I'm not a product specialist. I move whatever needs moving to Canada and New York.'

'And being a mover made you a good fighter.'

'The Canadian Army made me a good fighter.'

'I have a friend from Prague. I asked him about you last night.'

Gregor. 'Yes.'

'He said you could do a good job, but he also said that he thought you might have sold out some people who tried to screw you over, a pair of brothers.'

'The Vrana brothers were screwing over the people who brought me into the deal. Internal politics in a group aren't my concern. I'm only about the money. Sorry if that makes me sound bad; it is what it is.'

'So your loyalty would be to . . . me.'

'Are you the one getting me my money? Then, yeah, my loyalty is to you.'

He watched me for a minute, deciding. 'I might have a job for you, then. But I need you to do me a favor if you want to land work.'

'I'm not really in the favor business.'

'Then think of it as an investment. My boss, Piet, has become a liability. I think he needs to be cut out.' There it was, bluntly. Nic wanted Piet gone. Probably to take his place, to take his cut. Or to take his power. 'If you can get us a route to America, then you and I — we don't really need Piet in the picture. Or in the profit.'

'And if I don't want to get into your messy office politics?'

'Then we're done.'

He was using me. This was survival of the meanest. Nic was using Piet's mistake in trusting the Turk to bolt up the food chain.

But then, so could I.

'What's your beef with your boss?'

'Brains make more money than brute force.' The hacker didn't like the muscle.

'No doubt you're smarter than your boss.'

'There is no doubt. Piet is a moronic whoreson. He waves a sword around, if you can believe it. A *sword*. Do you know how unprofessional that appears?' The superior tone I'd heard in his voice last night returned.

'What is it you're shipping?'

'They're not large packages, but they must be well hidden. Extremely valuable and not easily replaced.'

'Not an answer. What *is* it?'

'That you need not know. It is not toxic or poisonous or dangerous.'

I didn't believe him. But I didn't press it. Not now. I had a new card to play. Basically, Nic wanted me to tattle on Piet, make him look bad, hope that the scarred man would cut Piet down. Even loose networks are brimming with egos and ambitions. This might be the fastest road to the scarred man.

'You want this job, you'll help me,' Nic pressed.

'And I design you a perfect route to smuggle your goodies, with documentation and containers and a well-greased captain and the right bribes, and you take my route, and you shut me out? No.'

'We must trust each other a little, Sam. I'm proposing you and I work together; this job, all the other jobs that come. I'm in demand right now and I need a partner who's not an idiot and is reliable. I don't want to have a boss who thinks he's a ninja.'

I put an edge of nervousness into my voice. 'Look, I'm going to put my ass on the line here. I don't know you people. I've got resources to smuggle whatever you need smuggled, but I need appropriate guarantees.' I sounded like a man who was talking too much, and that's what I wanted Nic to think. I wanted a scent of desperation, to close the deal. But to close it with someone with power. 'If you can't give them to me, I need to talk to someone who can.'

'I can't take you to Piet's boss. Doesn't work that way.'

Compartmentalize. Keep each node of the network safe. That was clearly their operating standard here. It was smart. 'Then we're done.' Bluff time. I stood.

He needed me. I knew that. I was his chance for a power grab.

'There is a great deal at stake.'

'The only great deal I care about is a great deal of money.'

'You will get a cut and a bonus for helping me oust Piet.'

'Can't I get a job without bloodshed?'

'Not these days.' He lowered his voice. 'Look, we need our goods moved from Rotterdam to New York. I don't know where the goods are right now except they're on their way to Holland from Hungary. Piet knows, all right? You can talk with him and see if you're willing to take this on. Both the smuggling job and helping me get him out of the game.'

That was as much as I could hope for now. I stood. 'All right. Let's go.' And as I stood, I saw Howell. Hurrying down the north side of the Singel canal. Heading in our direction. Behind him walked August. I kept my smile in place.

It meant we'd made a mistake. But Mila had left a trail for us to follow if that happened.

Then I saw Howell and August and another man, clearly a Company agent, turn hard into the doorway of an internet café. A neon coffee cup steamed in the window. Same building where Mila was watching from the top floor.

Choice. Help Mila or go with Nic. I wanted to help her. But I couldn't walk away from Nic. That way led to Lucy and my son.

I followed him, wondering how Howell had found us. From the ID check Nic had done? Maybe, if his associate who searched for the Peter Samson name had hit an electronic tripwire.

Nic walked directly beside me, hand across my shoulders. I couldn't look behind me. Couldn't see Mila. I had to think of a way to warn her.

'Trouble is coming,' I said.

'What do you mean?' Nic jerked a glance behind us.

'You. Playing your boss.'

'He won't be my boss for long.'

'I had a boss once, a guy named Howell,' I said in a conversational way, 'a total ass, and I feel he's always behind me.'

'Then you should have dealt with him the way I'm going to deal with Piet.'

I couldn't say more. I had to trust that Mila had deciphered my warning. The moment Nic pulled up ahead of me I tore the tiny earpiece from my ear and dropped it on the street.

43

Mila hurried from the empty office space, running down the narrow staircase. Howell was close; if he interfered in the sting, all was lost. The top three floors were offices; the ground floor housed a small internet café, popular with students and college-age tourists. She reached the bottom foyer; to her right was Café Sprong. Right now the internet café held a half-dozen surprised kids, hands lifted off their keyboards. Three men in suits stood inside, two holding guns. An older man — she recognized him from the Company files as Howell — was saying, 'Just everyone stay calm, we're working with the Dutch police.' He was hurrying from laptop to laptop, clicking on the keyboards. Searching.

They'd found her and Sam.

The one closest to the door grabbed at her arm. He was a big man, blond, Scandinavian-looking, with apple-florid cheeks.

Mila fought down the overwhelming urge to throw him through the neon-coffee-cup window. 'Excuse me,' she said in a low, hard growl.

He didn't raise the gun but he pulled her inside. 'This is police business. Do not be alarmed, we are seeking a criminal. Were you accessing the café's internet connection?' he said to her in slightly mangled Dutch. She shrugged like she didn't understand.

'Is this a joke?' she said in English, braving a smile. 'Or a movie?'

'Do you have a laptop? Or a smartphone?' he asked in English. 'Were you on the web?'

'No.' She only had a small purse. The wireless kit she'd used to talk with Sam was taped to the small of her back, under her suit jacket. Her gun lay strapped to her ankle. He looked inside her purse, found her smartphone. He tapped her browser. She waited.

The big man put the phone back in her purse. 'Thank you. Police business. Please don't try to leave.' So she didn't.

But if they were looking for her — shouldn't they have just rushed to the roof? Perhaps not. Maybe they knew she was here but not who she was. She stayed put, but every muscle was singing. Howell didn't have a weapon out. She decided how she would fight; the order in which she would kill them. The big blond, and then the dark-haired man, then Howell. The decision put her mind at rest and she watched Howell like everyone else.

The barista argued in Polish-accented Dutch with the armed men that they couldn't just come in here and do this, and the men ignored him. Howell stepped away from a frightened girl to a back table where a young Chinese student sat. The boy's hands quivered above the keys and Mila thought: he looks quite guilty.

She watched Howell turn the laptop away from the Chinese boy, study it, tap on the keys. Mila could see a terminal window appear on the

244

screen. A spill of data, white letters on a black screen.

Howell closed the laptop, gestured with one hand toward the gunmen. The big blond hurried forward, frisked the boy roughly, nodded an all-clear.

'Outside,' said Howell in English.

'You're not cops!' the barista shouted. Too much caffeinated courage, Mila thought.

Howell glanced at Mila as he walked past; she knew she should drop her stare. Everyone else, cowed by the guns, had. She couldn't. She just couldn't. She didn't glare. She just looked at him.

He met her stare for a moment; if she had known they'd seen her on a security tape feed from the port, dressed in leather and wearing giant sunglasses, she would have killed them all where they stood. But Howell, intent on his prize, didn't linger on her face. He followed the man and the Chinese boy outside without a backward glance.

The other man — thick-necked, with dark hair — lowered his gun and said in perfect Dutch, 'Our apologies. You may return to your work. That man has been conducting serious cyber-crime attacks using the café's server. We apologize for frightening you all but we didn't want him erasing his data before we could stop him.'

The barista started to argue again, saying 'We didn't know, you can't just come in here like that waving guns, you could have *shot* us.'

The thick-necked man kept a broad smile in

place. 'Our apologies again.' He turned and hurried out as the café broke into rapid-fire talk, the barista yelling at the man's back, reaching for the phone, vowing to call the police.

Mila stepped out after the muscle. He broke into a full run, hurrying after Howell and the blond. He caught up. Howell carried the boy's laptop.

Mila looked across the canal toward the café where Sam sat with Nic.

Gone. Both men gone. Choice: follow the Company thugs or try to find Sam. The Chinese boy might be a link back to the scarred man's group, and she wanted to see what the Company people did. She followed Howell and the others, keeping back a discreet distance.

She dug her earpiece from her purse, slipped it back into place and hurried toward her car.

44

Nic put me in the back of a van. He held up a blindfold.

'You asked me to trust you,' I said. 'That works both ways.'

'It does. But I'm not going to let you see where we're going. You don't need to know. Everything within our group is need-to-know. You get to that point, you'll be told.'

It wasn't a bad thing for him to believe he had full control of the situation, so I allowed him to put the blindfold on me.

He said, 'I'm going to search you', and he did, thoroughly. From hairline to throat to belly and below, down to my heels. He was thorough, but he missed the transmitter under my collar. I'd made the choice to keep it alive and broadcasting despite knowing that if he found it he would kill me immediately.

I didn't fight the search; I told him once it tickled and he ignored me. I heard him go back up to the front of the van, crank the engine, and, with a sway, we pulled back out into traffic.

'Where're we going? Am I going to see Piet?'
'Yes.'

I wanted to ask: *and his bosses?* The scarred man and Yasmin might be there. The scarred man would recognize me; I had to assume if he'd taken Lucy he knew my face. I didn't want to end up tied to a chair like the Turk. But I had to take the risk.

The van drove for a long while; I figured given the number of short, sharp turns that we weren't heading out of Amsterdam, but rather that Nic was trying to shake off any possible tail. Or confuse me. I wondered if Mila was sticking close to me. I could only hope she had dodged Howell and August. Otherwise I was alone. How on earth had he found us? It had to be the hit on my Peter Samson ID from Nic's computer guy. He must have been working in the internet café, perhaps masking his work behind its server. But Howell and August were in Amsterdam, hunting me no doubt, and they'd cornered Nic's hacker. Which meant Howell might be hot on the trail of Nic's people, and, in that case, he'd ruin my chance to find my family.

There is a time on every job where you say, screw caution. I'm not foolhardy. I'm not stupid. But sometimes you have to be the battering ram. Howell was getting way too close. So my time to find the scarred man was running short.

'I want to tell you how to handle this,' Nic said. 'Piet will be there, and so will another man. You don't need to know his name.'

I realized I was holding my breath. 'Okay.' Let the other man please be the scarred man. Please.

'You will tell them exactly how to set up an alternate route.'

'And in return, I get money and work?'

'Yes. But I want you to make Piet look bad.

You tell Piet's boss that you know of Piet through smuggling in Moldova — that you've worked the same routes. That Piet sold girls that he moved, along the way, and pocketed the money before delivery. He cheated his clients.'

My guts twisted. 'Piet is a human trafficker.'

'Piet is mostly a mover of commodities.' I could practically hear the shrug in Nic's voice. 'Women from Moldova, shipped to Britain and Germany and Israel for the whorehouses. Babies sold to adoptive parents in Italy, brought in from Macedonia and Albania. Mass-produced counterfeit goods, brought in from China to western Europe. It doesn't much matter. He moves what needs moving.'

A sick tickle feathered the back of my throat as the van stopped. I could smell a tang of fuel, of exhaust, and in the distance I could hear the purr of freeway traffic.

'We're here, Sam. Showtime,' Nic said. 'Do good and I'll do good by you.'

45

The fourth blow to the face produced their desired results. It was Howell's experience that hired computer hackers were easily broken. Their loyalty was earned only with money and to access to technology. The Chinese boy — who, according to his ID, was a graduate student in computer science at the University of Delft — made it through two black eyes, a torn lip and a badly cuffed ear before he screamed out an address. It was a warehouse off the A10 highway, which ringed Amsterdam. Van Vleck stepped back from beating the hacker and August checked the address with his smartphone.

'And who will we find there?' Howell asked.

'Nic. Nic.'

'Who's Nic?'

'Guy who hired me.' The boy broke into a babble of Mandarin, calling Howell a worthless stump of a penis, and Howell slapped him and told him in Mandarin that his mother was a disgusting whore and to not talk to him that way. The student's mouth twisted in shock and pain.

'And Nic hired you why?'

'We have a back door into a passport monitoring exchange . . . used by North American and European governments.'

'And you were checking Peter Samson's

passport and records.'

'Yes. To see if he was for real.'

'Who does Nic work for?'

'He does work for hire.'

'For Samson?'

'No, Nic wanted to be sure Samson was who he said he was. He was hiring Samson.'

'For what kind of job?' Howell's voice sharpened. He leaned close to the battered face and he could smell the milk and stale coffee on the student's breath, under the coppery blood from the ear and the nose.

The Chinese student started to cry. 'I don't know any more. I swear. I was just supposed to verify his story as he told it to Nic. That he was a Canadian named Samson.'

August gestured at Howell and they stepped out of the van, where the hacker couldn't hear them.

'If Sam's risking using a legend he's trying to get close to this guy Nic,' August said, 'so maybe he has a lead on whoever took Lucy.'

'We'll know soon enough. Let's go see who's at this address.'

'Shouldn't we wait for recon?'

'Sam Capra is close, August,' Howell said. 'No way in hell we're waiting.'

'That's not standard protocol.'

'Neither is letting his friend be part of the search team,' Howell said. 'You coming or staying, Holdwine?'

August got back into the van. He did not notice the small blue car, keeping its distance behind them.

46

Nic kept me blindfolded until I was inside. When he shut the door it made a steely echo. He pulled off the blindfold and I could see that it was an old machinists' shop. The equipment to reshape and refine steel into tools remained in place.

Near the entrance, the shop was crammed with boxes and pallets along two walls. I could smell the tang of curry and the yeasty aroma of spilled beer. A metal table, scattered with papers, stood in the center of the room. Windows, smeared with dust, let in a slant of brownish light.

Two men — twins — stood on either side of me. One was armed with a Glock, the other with an assault rifle. Both had dead eyes. One was shaved bald, the other had scant reddish hair. Smiles with cruel mouths.

'These are the twins,' Nic said as if I hadn't noticed they shared the same scowling face.

The twins searched me for weapons and wire. They found nothing; they too missed the little transmitter in my shirt collar.

I looked to see if any of these guys sported the same Novem Soles tattoo as the killer in my apartment. No, no sign of it. So maybe Nic and the twins were just hirelings.

Sitting at the table was the dyed-blond man I'd seen on the videos. Piet. The trafficker.

He was taller than me, six-six, wide shoulders,

narrow hips, the curve of powerful arms under the sleeves. He looked like a guy who'd fight with gusto. His nose had been broken in the past and he had eyes like two dots of oil. Cold and unyielding. Under the iced eyes and the twisted hook of nose he wore a smile like a scar left by a jagged knife. I had a sense that smile had been the last thing seen by many people. He was the kind of guy, I guessed, who thought cruelty was funny.

And yes, he had a little sword. A *wakizashi*. It sat on the desk and gleamed in the faint light.

There was no sign of the scarred man.

I smiled back at Piet.

'I understand you can help us, Mr Samson,' he said in English.

'I'm sure I can.'

He got up and walked around me. I doubt I looked forbidding. Old jeans, worn shoes, an old gray jacket. Mila had bought my clothes second-hand, clipped out all the labels. I looked like I was neatly dressed but desperate. I met his gaze but then I let my eyes drop. Let him think he was the alpha.

'So. I have fifty parcels I need to get inside the United States. They cannot be discovered; they cannot be seized. I need them there in ten days. They must arrive together; they must not be separated during shipping. At the same time, I want the most secure 'cover' for them imaginable. How would you do this?'

'How big are the parcels?'

'Less than a meter across, a meter long.'

There were fifty of them? Okay. 'And heavy?'

'No. Five kilos.'

'Then I'd probably disguise them as leaded crystal glassware from Poland. Mark it as fragile, but it explains the weight. You could also do frozen fish.' I shrugged. 'If the goods can be packed in ice without harm, then it's a good call.' This was standard smuggling tradecraft. 'Or electronics from Finland. They ship tons of cell phones and related equipment. If it's electronic goods, then that would simplify the camouflage in case it's X-rayed. Or an easy route is counterfeit cigarettes. Fake British or French or Turkish brands.' One out of three cigarettes smoked in Canada today is counterfeit. It's big business.

'I want you to make sure it's not X-rayed.'

'I have a contact in Rotterdam who could make sure the container's not singled out.' I was lying, but it didn't matter.

'And what about dealing with American customs?'

'I have a friend on the customs staff in New York. He has three children currently in college and grad school, and so has large bills. He's rather open to not inspecting whatever I say.'

'And where would you get the appropriate export documentation, and the packaging, and the manifests from a legitimate manufacturer?' Piet asked.

'Well, before I give away all my trade secrets, I'd like my money first,' I said.

Piet stared at me.

'Why did you come to Amsterdam?'

'I came for the waters,' I said.

'Ha!' Piet said. 'One of my favorite movies. *Casablanca*.'

I used a line from Bogart's character, the barman Rick Blaine, when he is asked to explain his presence in the intrigue-filled city. I smiled. 'I needed a change.'

'You were based where?'

'Prague and Croatia. I stayed there after I got out of the army. I liked the country.' I looked at Nic, then back at the smile. 'What's in the fifty packages?'

'You don't need to know.'

'Where's Edward?' Nic asked suddenly. After all, my performance was supposed to convince Piet's boss that Piet was untrustworthy, more trouble than asset, and Piet appeared to be alone. There was no one to convince. Edward. Edward was the scarred man. Edward. I let the name roll around in my brain. Edward. The man with the question mark close to his eye who'd taken my wife.

'Edward isn't here,' Piet said. 'Left it up to me to take the measure of this man.'

'This man ended up in a bar fight last night defending your good name,' I said, 'and I don't even know you.'

'Yeah, interesting, that. Thanks for the good turn. Not really used to altruism.'

'I was looking for you,' I said.

'You and the Turk both,' he said.

'Popularity is a curse,' I said. 'But I wasn't really looking for you until the Turk started threatening you. That was an opportunity for me and I took it. But I hope you don't have more loudmouths around here.'

Piet glanced at Nic. Then back at me. 'I'd like to hear what you heard the Turkish gentleman say last night.'

'The Turk was talking to one of his friends at the bar before Nic here showed up.'

'You speak Turkish?'

'Enough. I used to run goods down to Istanbul. Excess Russian ordnance bound for Africa, mostly. The Turk said he had arranged to smuggle something to America for you. And that he was going to get you to give up some woman you have, in exchange for the smuggling going smoothly.' I watched his face as I laid down the trump. Nic wasn't so good an actor; he jerked his head toward me at this unexpected twist.

'Some woman,' Piet repeated.

'Yes. He was going to guarantee that whatever you were smuggling wasn't harmed, wasn't captured by the cops, if he got some woman who's with you. Yasmin?' I shrugged. 'I may not have the name right.'

He didn't blink. But his hand, curled into a fist, unfolded, fingers close to the *wakizashi* sword. Like its weight called to him. Then he made his hand a fist again. 'And that was all?'

'Yes.'

'And on that basis, you fight for the honor of my name?' He laughed.

'No. I thought you might not want him screwing up your deal. I need a job. I didn't realize until later that what I heard might be valuable to me.' I shrugged. 'You can't use his route to America now. But you could use mine.

256

I'm guessing, if you're using the Turk, it's because you don't have a regular route into America.'

'But we don't know you.'

'You want my creds? Ask Petrova in Kiev about me. Ask Djuki in Athens about me.' I threw out the name of two traffickers.

'Petrova is dead,' Piet said.

'I hadn't heard.'

'Last month. She was shot by a rival.'

'Oh. Too late to send flowers, I guess.'

Now Piet flicked a smile, like he was tossing a card to me, sure my hand would crash. 'Djuki went missing a few months ago.'

'He's probably hiding.' The fact I knew their names was not cred enough. I didn't expect it to be. 'Or he's in China, running Gucci and Ralph Lauren counterfeiting action.'

'And if I could reach him, I'd hire him over you. Him at least I know. You could just be cleaning up the mess left behind,' Piet said. 'You could work for Yasmin's father, too. Same as the Turk, just coming at me from a different angle.'

'That's a theory.'

'What did you work on with Djuki?'

'Girls from Moldova and Ukraine, shipped to Israel and to Edinburgh and Toronto. I moved guns from Albania and Uzbekistan to Mexico. I shipped in fake cigs and fake Windows software from China to Canada and the US, mostly Houston and New York.'

'You moved girls with Djuki?' He raised an eyebrow.

'Yeah. Twice. You find him in China, you can

257

ask him about me.' I shrugged. Djuki wasn't hiding; he was dead. He was a Greek trafficker who'd been turned by the Company, spilled information on his routes and methodologies for a hefty sum and immunity, and then been killed when he tried to vanish when the Company put him back out in the field to serve as an informant. Djuki was scum. I'd met him once or twice and the Company had entrusted me to put out the word he'd gone to China to work deals on that side.

'Where's his scar?' Piet asked.

And my mind went blank.

47

I didn't blink. 'There are so many to choose from.'

'The most embarrassing one.'

I swallowed, trying to picture the photos in the smuggler's thick file. Not on the face. Not on his chest. Then I smiled as I remembered Brandon, my boss back in London, cracking a joke.

'Across his ass,' I said. 'His girlfriend gave it to him with a kitchen knife. She should have had your *wakizashi*.'

He smiled at me using the Japanese term. 'And why did he get it?'

'He was screwing around with girls he was shipping to Israel and Dubai,' I said. 'Breaking them in for the customers.' I couldn't let the disgust show on my face. Most of the girls trafficked were from the former Soviet republics, desperate for work; they'd been promised waitressing or secretarial jobs; they were going to be broken with rape and heroin before they met their new pimps. 'Girlfriend didn't approve. He was lucky she cut his backside and not his front.'

'And how did you see the scar?'

I'd seen it in his file, of course. I hoped Djuki's explanation as to the scar's origin was accurate. If it wasn't I was dead; Piet would kill me on the spot if I couldn't kill him first. 'He kept up his practice of breaking in the girls when needed. I saw it then.'

Piet gave me the slightest of nods. I was inside the circle, at least for now. My creds proven by knowledge of a rapist's ass scar.

'Make your calls,' he said to me. 'The goods will be here in two days. You will arrange a pickup of them when they arrive, repackage them for shipment to America, and then get them past customs and onto the ship in Rotterdam. You'll be paid fifty thousand in euros. If you need help forging documents, my boss Edward is an expert forger.'

Repackaging the shipment. Oh, yes. That would be it, the key. I would need help. I would need the whole gang together to help me.

And that's when I could take them down, rescue Yasmin, and find out the truth from the scarred man. The opportunity dangled before me, bright as a diamond.

I hid my sudden relief by holding up hands. 'Wait a minute. You've cut the Turk loose, right? I'm not coming aboard if he's about to bring the law down on you.'

'He's not a worry for anyone any more.' This was one of the twins speaking, the bald one.

'Oh,' I said.

Piet said: 'The Turk is a former MIT agent.' MIT was Milli Istihbarat Teşkilu — Turkey's CIA. 'He got run out of the agency for malfeasance. He bribed a group of Turks here to let him work with them to get close to me; I won't ever work with those guys again. He tried to screw me over, he failed.' He leveled a stare. 'The twins are very good about finding out what we need to know about people.'

The Turk was like me, then; Bahjat Zaid had found a fellow reject to try and save his daughter. 'Well, I don't fail when I take on a job.'

Piet glanced at the twins and then at me and said: 'You want to break in a girl, Samson?'

'What?'

He jerked his head toward a door. 'I got eight girls heading to Nigeria and Israel. Two still giving me a bit of lip, even with the horse in their veins to settle them down. But nothing settles them like getting broke in.' A second test; if I was experienced as a human trafficker, I shouldn't blink much at raping the merchandise.

'Go choose one you like, give her a ride,' Piet said.

'You said we could have a turn,' the bald twin protested. 'Why does *he* get first pick?'

I thought how pleasant it would be to kill Piet. I had not killed but once before and it was not an experience that I had liked. No human being would. But with Piet, I wouldn't blink at it at all. It would be a service to humanity. Part of my heart, the part that thought I might be a husband and father again as soon as I found Lucy and the baby, said don't be so ready to kill. But this guy . . . if Edward had taken Lucy, had this monster been near her?

Had Piet touched my wife?

It took a total gripping down inside my heart to say, 'Do you move a lot of women?'

'My best revenue stream. From Moldova, mostly. Doing more from Russia and the Baltics as the economy worsens. About thirty a month. Usually special requests. Can't keep up the

261

demand for the young ones. Come see.'

I glanced at Nic, who trafficked in pictures of kids. Filling specific demands. Welcome to the personalized world of human suffering.

I followed Piet down a short hallway to a side office. The twins and Nic followed me. I smelled rotten fruit, burned steak, and a chemical stench, with sweat an uneasy undercurrent.

He opened the door into a dimly lit room, a side parlor to hell. In the flickering gloom I could see eight women along the wall. Manacles cupped their ankles and their wrists. The chains threaded back to the concrete on the floor. The women sat huddled. They wore their tops still — stained, torn. But their skirts and jeans and underwear were gone, robbing them of dignity. I saw bruises and tears and emptiness in faces that had endured too much horror. I felt a hot red rage glow in my brain.

But if I killed Piet and Nic now to free these women, I ruined any chance of getting close to Edward, to finding Lucy and the baby.

But I could not permit this. Rewrite the scenario, I told myself. I had to contact Mila, let her know that these women were here. But being the new guy, if this operation got compromised, I would be compromised. They would kill me on the spot.

Impossible choice. I needed an option, fast.

'Which one you want? The redhead?'

Six awful little words. The redhead looked to be seventeen and I could see her lip quivering in horror, in fear.

'Just don't hit the faces or the tits. You got to

whip one, do it on the back of her legs. No one ever looks at the back of their legs,' one of the twins said.

'No,' I said. 'No thank you.'

'What's wrong with you? They're like ripe fruit. Pluck one.' Piet laughed. 'We'll both take one. Seal our friendship. And we won't get cut on our asses like stupid Djuki, will we?' He laughed, and I saw the women shudder. I tried not to think about what he'd already done to them, what he'd do to them if I left them in his grip. He prodded the closest one with the tip of the *wakizashi* and she burst into shuddering tears.

I looked at Piet's neck and thought about how I would break it.

Nic had followed us, watching me, seeing me dipped in this inhuman litmus test.

'I'm a businessman,' I said. 'I don't stoop to sampling the goods. That's for the muscle.'

'Eh?' Piet didn't like that. I'd implied he was not a boss, that he was muscle. I could see rage rising in his stare. He stepped back from the terrified woman and the edge of the sword glittered in the faint light from the hallway.

'Are you serious?' I said. 'Is this going to be how you test me? Whether I'm willing to break a girl?'

Piet's mouth worked.

One of the young women — the redhead — looked up at me. I'd spoken English and who knew if she understood.

'Don't talk to him this way,' Nic said. 'What the hell is wrong with you?' Tension, tight as wire, strained his voice. I stared at him.

At this point I was only just inside the circle. But only just in wasn't good enough. I needed to be all the way in. I glanced at Nic. Rock, meet hard place. If I played Nic's game of betrayal, Piet might never let me near Edward. If I didn't — Nic was unpredictable. I didn't need Nic. I needed Piet.

I gave Nic a last smile. He was a traitor to his friends and he was a scumbag who used children. I didn't mind paving my road with his bones.

48

'I want in,' I said to Piet. 'But on my terms.' Then I turned and launched a hammering kick into Nic's face. He crumpled. I didn't want him talking so I slammed a second kick, precise, into his throat. Not hard enough to kill but enough to keep him nice and quiet.

Piet had a gun out, leveled at me, before my foot was down. It was good to know he had more than that stupid for-show sword. The women screamed and retreated against the wall; I raised my hands.

'He's your problem. Not me.' I pointed at the sprawled Nic with a tip of my toe. Nic made gaspy, breathy noises, eyes blinking in shock. 'He's setting you up. He wants to take over your operation.'

'Outside.' Piet gestured with the gun, screamed at the women to be quiet. They fell into a snuffle of tears and whispers. He gestured toward Nic. I pulled Nic to his feet, shoved him staggering out into the hallway and back to the main room. I pushed him as the twins hurried out and Piet shut and locked the door. Five seconds I was alone with Nic, but that was all I needed as the twins and Piet rushed up behind us.

'What the hell is your problem?' Piet said.

'He's busting on you,' I said. 'Selling you out. Check him.'

Nic moaned through his ruined lip and broken teeth. He started to sit up, consciousness rousing, and Piet pushed him back down to the floor with the barrel of the gun.

'He wanted me to lie about you to Edward. Say that you had been stealing girls from shipments for another client, reselling them.' I kept my voice steady, looking at Nic as his eyes widened in horror. Because, you know, I was telling the truth. It's always easier to tell the truth than to lie. 'He wanted you out, and himself in as lead trafficker. He figured there's more in live women than in photos of little kids. He's working for someone else who wants your business and betraying you is the cut.'

Piet kept the gun glued on Nic, who stayed still and bubbled blood from his mouth where my heel had smashed lip and teeth. He ran a hand along Nic's pockets, under the jacket.

At first I thought Piet had missed it. He stood, not even aiming his gun at Nic any more. Then I saw the thin little tube in Piet's hand, pinched between thumb and forefinger. He held it up to Nic's face. Nic blinked.

'What is this?' Piet asked, in a whisper that sounded like dirt sliding off a coffin's top.

'I don't know, it's not mine,' Nic mumbled. 'He's a goddamned liar, Piet. Who are you going to believe, him or me? You know me.'

'Yes. Yes, I do know you Nic.' Piet inspected Mila's little transmitter. He tried to cut it apart with his thumb, failed. He opened a knife from his pocket and sliced into the microphone and unpeeled it apart carefully. I'd had seconds to

266

slip it into Nic's pocket. It would be cutting my only link with Mila, assuming she hadn't been grabbed by Howell and his men, but I had to do it. It was my way to save Piet's victims. My heart beat out a hard, skittering rhythm in my chest.

I watched Piet's face as he inspected the state-of-the-art device. 'Goddamn it.' he said. 'This is like freaking spy gear. Who are you working for, Nic?'

'No one . . . I work for you. He's lying. You don't know him, you know me.'

'Yeah, and you've had the hate for me for weeks,' Piet said. 'You think I'm blind? You always had your goddamn precious nose up in the air around me. Who do you work for? Stand up.'

Nic stood. The light in his eyes shifted. Darkened in rage, the anger of the trapped animal. 'I don't work for anyone but you and Edward. He's tricked me. He's tricked you. He planted that on me.'

I shook my head. But Piet raised the gun from Nic to me.

'I guess I have a choice to make,' Piet said.

49

'Call in reinforcements?' August asked Howell. They sat in the van, half a block from the address provided by the Chinese student. It was a gray block of industrial space. Multiple buildings, but the complex looked mostly deserted. Two vehicles parked in front of one door at the end. The rest of the parking lot space was empty.

'You're rather timid,' Howell said. 'Surprises me.'

'One man's caution,' August said. 'I don't want my friend dead when he's more valuable to us alive.'

'I like the idea of moving now. No witnesses around,' Van Vleck said.

'I want this kept quiet. I don't want to attract the attention of the Dutch authorities. What do we have in the van?' Howell asked.

'Four assault rifles, bulletproof vests, infrared goggles.' August looked at him with a scowl. 'There's only the three of us.'

'I can count, Agent Holdwine.'

'I think, respectfully, we should call in backup.' August glanced at Van Vleck. 'Capra is trained. We don't know about the other guy. We should go in with overwhelming force.'

'Two vehicles here. One van, that brought Capra and his contact. The other car's small. There's not an army inside.' Howell smiled.

'Let's go, gentleman. I am tired of Sam Capra being a problem for us.'

Van Vleck and August started putting on the bulletproof gear.

'Get that young man to his feet,' Howell said, gesturing at the Chinese hacker. 'We'll use him.'

50

Mila parked her car a block away from the warehouse, at a small café. She pressed her earpiece and closed her eyes for a moment. She heard most of the conversation between Piet and Sam, the offer to Sam of one of the captives to rape. Her breathing grew very calm; a hot hollow rage expanded in her chest.

She wore a black trenchcoat over her suit — she had a gun for each pocket and now she also carried a retractable baton. It was her favorite weapon and she imagined beating Piet and Nic senseless with it.

She heard Sam's advice to search Nic and the discovery of the microphone and knew what Sam had done. She applauded him. But he was cutting her loose, severing the one tie between them so as to delve closer to these monsters.

But if Howell blundered in now he would ruin their chance to break inside the ring.

Mila watched the van, crouching from behind a corner a block away. She saw the back of the van open; the Chinese student they'd grabbed lurched out, hands bound. She could see the kid's face was battered and bruised, a wet smear of blood below his nostrils. Then the two thick-necked men. Then Howell. All armed.

The three men stopped at the door. She could see the Chinese boy shake his head. They'd stopped at an access keypad by the door. The

Chinese boy, hands shaking, entered a code.

The four men entered. Mila hurried toward the van. They were going in full throttle, so more worried about their front than their back.

She slid under the van and she began to count, watching the door. Her timing would have to be impeccable if Sam was to survive.

51

'Him or me?' I asked. Nic looked too shocked to speak.

'Or both?' Piet said. 'I don't need trouble.'

'But you still need help,' I said. 'Or you wouldn't even have bothered to talk to me. Nic thinks you're a joke. He ever make fun of your sword?'

The corner of Piet's mouth jerked. Sometime in those months, Nic's disdain had been noted and filed. 'Everything you said is correct,' Piet said. 'Here. Fine.'

And he handed me the gun. 'Kill him.'

Final test. If I was a cop or a plant, I wasn't going to gun down an unarmed man. This was the line that no one with a shred of decency left would cross.

What decency did I have left? I raised the gun; my head crowded with Lucy and the baby. This man had helped kidnap and assault women, shipping them into slavery. He was smuggling weapons. He was hacking into government databases and stealing information. He was trading in photos of assaulted and abused children.

And I was what — a courtroom on two legs?

I guess I was.

Him or me. And with me, my family.

I fired.

The bullet caught Nic in the chest and he fell

back. Bad shot. It didn't kill him outright. Sorry, Nic. He looked at me with a wrenching stare of agony and hate and I fired again and his face didn't matter any more.

I wouldn't see it again, except maybe in my dreams.

I pulled my shirt loose, wiped my prints off the Glock, and handed the gun back to Piet. My hand didn't shake. And for one moment the past five seconds seemed like a life that happened to another man.

'Well,' Piet said into the silence. He stared down at Nic's body.

'Well,' I said. Well, well, well. Who was I now?

'Let's get to work.' He gestured at the goods. 'I like your ideas, but I've already got a load of goods to use as camouflage. You reinforced my opinion as to what would work best.'

Nothing like brownie points from the trafficker. I inspected the boxes. Counterfeit cigarettes.

'You're going to ship your super-duper top-secret stuff inside illicit cigarettes that you then sell in the United States and double your profit. Two birds, one stone.'

'I maximize my efforts.'

Piet was much smarter than he looked. He gestured at the boxes. 'About a million euros' worth.'

I pointed at the shredded, destroyed microphone. 'You better hope there wasn't a tracker in there. Whoever he worked for will be coming when contact gets cut.'

'Which is why we're going to move everything

right now. The women, the cigs.' He turned to the twins and started issuing hard orders in rapid-fire Dutch.

How could I get the women to safety without blowing my cover? Right now, I couldn't. The thought hurt.

I heard a soft ping. A door opening. I couldn't see the front door from here: the boxes and boxes of illicit cigarettes made a labyrinth between here and the front door.

I was counting on the arrival being Mila. Which meant I wanted Piet heading out the back with me, abandoning the captives and his goods. 'Are you expecting anyone?'

'No,' he whispered. We leaned against the wall. Stacks of boxes barred part of our view. He gestured at the twins, who took up positions ahead of us, closer to the door.

I saw a figure step into view. Not Mila. A thin young Asian man, walking in, wearing an ill-fitting jacket and loose jeans. He had thick black hair cut in a bad slash; tufts stuck up like little exclamation points.

'He works for Nic,' Piet said. 'Hacker.' For some reason he retreated back toward the table.

The Asian kid stumbled forward into the dim light and I saw he'd been beaten. Really worked over. One of the twins — the bald one — said, 'Hey, what are you doing here?'

The answer was a bullet that sang out and caught the bald twin in the throat. He sagged to the floor. His brother bellowed a shocked scream and started blasting the boxes with his assault rifle. Puffs of brown powder danced in the air:

the fragments of cigarettes, tobacco exploding into miniature clouds by the impact of the bullets ripping through the boxes.

And someone, from cover near the front, shot out some of the lights. I saw the Asian kid scream and run and then he caught a bullet and sprawled to the floor.

Chaos. Near darkness. I couldn't let them shoot back — this could be Mila. Piet ran around one corner of the stacked boxes and I followed him.

Ping. Another light shattered. One light left, directly over the metal table.

I saw a figure standing near us, laying a round down toward the remaining twin. A dark-haired man. Piet fired before I could react and the man toppled, screaming in English. Both he and Piet raised to fire and I yanked Piet back, out of the line of fire. I needed him alive for now.

'Goddamn it, what the hell . . . ' Piet coughed.

'These have to be cops,' I said. 'Who else would give Nic a wire like that? We need to get the hell out.'

We ran and an explosion of bullets tore through the cardboard maze.

52

I heard a clang, metal landing on concrete, and then a blast tore open the biggest stack of the cigarette boxes. Flame erupted from the flying debris; the hot, sweet scent of tobacco crowded the air. The thrum of the blast nearly deafened me. I turned as Piet fired back and I saw him drawing aim on a man through the tendrils of smoke.

August. The Company was here.

I grabbed Piet's arm, spoiling his shot. The bullet pinged to August's left and he ducked behind an unused machinist's lathe. He hadn't seen me.

'What the . . . '

'Just run, come on!' I shoved Piet toward the exit. I ran back toward the attackers, vaulted over the lathe and hammered both feet into the side of August's head as he risked standing up. He sprawled. I didn't think he had seen me yet. I had to keep it that way without killing him. I grabbed his gun.

The remaining twin ran toward me, expecting me to put a bullet in August's head. Instead I raised the gun I'd just taken off August and fired right between the twin's eyes. He had about a second to look surprised before he collapsed.

I ran like hell.

If Howell took me back into custody, now, I was done. I would spend the rest of my life in a prison. I couldn't prove that I worked for Mila's secret do-gooders, that I was trying to infiltrate a criminal's inner circle. I would just be a bitter ex-employee keeping company with a slaver. I would vanish back into Howell's prison, sealed in stone. Or be dead and buried, unmarked, unmourned. Everyone who thought I was a traitor was going to think they were right.

I heard a roar from the lathe. Howell's voice. Yelling.

I ran past Nic's body. Piet reappeared, gun in hand, and laid down fire behind me, driving Howell back into cover. I could see Howell returning fire, and then — in a moment when Piet paused to reload — fire coming from the front door.

Someone was shooting at Howell from the other side.

He turned, returning fire. On the other side of the steel door I heard the captive women screaming and sobbing.

'Come on,' I grabbed at Piet.

'No. I'm not leaving these bitches here.'

'They're not worth your freedom. They're not worth losing the big job.'

I could see on his face he hated to give up — but he listened.

We ran down a hallway and hurtled out into the clouded light of the gray day. A Volvo van was parked in the rear.

Piet held out an electronic key. The van's lights blinked; it made the oh-so-welcome click of locks opening. We jumped inside; Piet jabbed the keys in the ignition and slammed into reverse. We roared backwards, straight, Piet not taking the time to spin out and turn yet.

Howell came through the back door when we were about thirty feet away.

He saw me, and a scowl swept across his face. He had been wrong to give me a moment's trust. I *was* a traitor. A criminal.

The evidence was running away before his eyes.

Piet jerked the wheel and we hurled around the edge of a building, gunning out of their sight.

'They'll throw up roadblocks,' I yelled.

He just spun the wheel around and floored the van. We exploded out of the industrial park, revving onto the service road, dodging around several slower moving cars.

'Got to get enough distance then find new wheels,' he said. 'We can carjack someone. There's a school nearby, a mother won't fight us.'

'But she'll see our faces.'

'You still have a bullet?'

'Let's do this the easy way. I can hotwire anything.'

'Takes too long.' He slammed a frustrated hand against the wheel. 'I hate losing those whores.'

I was free from agonizing about the captive women; Howell would make sure they were safe. Now I just had to keep Piet from killing someone else so we could catch a ride.

'Those weren't cops,' I said. 'They'd already have blocked out the industrial park. They didn't. So who the hell was Nic working for?'

Piet didn't answer for a minute so I did. 'Rivals.'

'Rivals?' Piet said. 'You mean other traffickers.'

'Or maybe whoever the Turk was working for,' I said. I wondered if Piet would now mention Bahjat Zaid's name.

'Well, we are going to take care of *that* problem.'

I loved that *we*, although he was horrifying company. Fine for him to think we were a team; easier for me to slide the knife past the ribs when the most happy time came. I fought down the thought. Enjoying killing people? That was a downward slide in which I had no interest.

He pulled into another sprawling industrial park that wore a concrete gray anonymity. He wore a mulish frown on his face; he seemed almost eager to find a victim, to vent his rage.

He spotted a young man carrying a box, walking toward a Mercedes parked at a remove from the others. 'Him. We'll take his.'

'I don't want you to kill someone over a car, Piet. Every small crime we have to do is a crack in the chances of pulling off the bigger job.'

'Don't talk to me like I haven't worked before,' he said, annoyance in his tone.

'I'm not. But you kill only when absolutely necessary.' That was true. 'This isn't necessary yet.'

His face reddened. He did not like being lectured.

'I'll take care of the car. Without killing the guy. You stay here. Keep your face out of sight. I don't want him to see you.'

'He'll see you. If he does, you kill him.'

'He won't see me.' I slipped out of the van as Piet kept driving, slamming the door, running. The guy, bespectacled, thin, started to turn toward me and I hit him, a single precise blow at the base of the neck. He crumpled and I caught him. I pulled him out of sight, gently set him down in front of a cluster of other parked cars, where a narrow strip of anemic grass lay and the concrete wall of the office park. His breathing was regular.

He had Mercedes keys in his pocket and I fished them free. Piet was already out of the van and running toward me. I ran to the Mercedes, unlocked it and slid behind the wheel.

'That was extremely smooth,' he said. But his tone of voice wasn't admiring. 'Where did you learn to do that?'

'Canadian Special Forces.'

He said nothing more. I peeled out of the industrial park. 'Where to?' I asked.

'I'm not sure I trust you, Sam,' he said. And he tightened the grip on the assault rifle he held.

53

Mila ran. She'd fired four rounds into the machinists' shop, with calculation. She wanted to confuse, to unsettle. She'd winged the blond in the arm and had forced Howell and his men to concentrate on her for a full minute, which hopefully had given Sam time to flee.

Then she'd retreated, running across the parking lane and around a corner. A Closed sign — *Gesloten* — hung in an office and she'd worked the lock with a kit in her pocket, ducking inside before she could be spotted. She slammed the door closed and hurried to the curtained office window to watch.

Five minutes later Howell and his two men emerged. No sign of the Chinese hacker. The big blond clutched his arm, his jacket sodden with blood. The other man stumbled, hit in the leg. Both men looked more pissed than hurt. Howell's face wore blind rage.

The van pulled away. So. Howell was not treating a crime scene like a crime scene. Maybe he would call the Dutch police; but then there would have to be explanations as to how Company personnel had arrived at the warehouse and engaged in a gun battle. And although the industrial park looked neglected and empty, someone nearby might have heard the shots and summoned the police.

Ten seconds after the van roared off, she made

her decision. Howell wasn't waiting for the police, but that didn't mean he wasn't calling them and they might arrive within minutes. She had very little time to scope out the building.

Mila slipped back inside the old machinists' shop. The smell was of close-in gunfire, acrid; the sweet smell of tobacco.

She saw a spill of blood drops, heavy, near one of the lathes. The Chinese student had taken a bullet in the head. She glanced down at him, didn't see breathing. The ID on him was still in place and she took that; anything that could delay the police investigation was to her advantage. She checked an abandoned office. Empty. She hurried through the entire office space, tense, her breath tight, expecting to see Sam's dead body. But there was no sign of him.

Then she headed down a short hallway and found a shuttered steel door. Here. They had to be here.

Mila picked the lock with care, as quietly as she could. The mechanism eased and her hand went back to her gun. She took a deep, calming breath, leveled the weapon and kicked in the door. Screams greeted her. Eight women, half-naked, bruised, chained to the wall.

For a moment she faltered. A pain as sharp as a steel blade went through her chest, made her spine ache. She stared at the women and they stared back at her. Then a surge of indignant strength rose in her bones. Revenge was its marrow. Had Howell not realized these women were here? Or did he not care? Or was he calling the police anonymously to report their presence?

It didn't matter. She could not, *would* not, leave them.

Most of them kept their gaze low to the ground, but one, a redheaded teenager, glanced up at her.

Mila tried English. 'It's okay. It's all right. You're safe now.'

The red-haired girl spoke to her in Moldovan. 'Who are you?'

Mila switched to Moldovan. The words tasted like a sweet she'd loved as a child. 'You'll be safe. I'm getting you out of here. The bad men have gone.'

'Who are you?' the redhead asked again.

'A friend. I want you to do exactly what I say, because we may not have much time. I'm going to get you to safety. And then home.'

'We have no money to get home,' one of the other women said. Her lips were purple with bruising.

'I know,' Mila said. 'I will take care of you all.' She stepped back out in the hallway, knelt by Nic's body. In his pocket she found a set of manacle keys. In his palm she saw Sam's transmitter, stripped apart. She scooped it up from the dead man and tucked it in her pocket.

Her hands shook as she unlocked the women from their restraints. Her head flooded with forgotten sensations: the low rumble of the traffic on the boulevard, the odor of cheap pizza, the warmth of a gun in each of her hands, the breeze through the open windows of the warm Israeli night as she walked through the rooms of the damned, the one man that she'd left alive roaring that he'd hunt her down and kill her one day for what she'd done. She shoved the memories down.

A couple of the women started to moan and cry, in Moldovan, hardly believing that their horrific ordeal might be over.

She was thinking: they need shelter, doctors, documents. She was not thinking about Sam Capra. For the moment, he was on his own.

54

'You're an asshole,' I said, watching the gun pointed in my direction. 'I just saved your life. If I wanted you dead, I could have shot you in the back when we were running to the van.'

'But I don't *know* you. And you walk in and everything goes to hell.'

'Everything went to hell because of Nic turning against you. I gave him to you and everything that happened since then confirms he was trying to screw you over.'

'But I don't know you.' Logic wasn't his strong point. 'I've lost everybody. Everybody.'

He was scared.

'Listen, Piet. I have a few friends in Amsterdam. Maybe you know them. Gregor, he used to run a watch shop in Prague, he's living here now. He was a friend of Nic's. We did a bit of business last year. Ask him about me.' I was gambling huge here, that Gregor would play along. Welcome to the tightrope.

'I know Gregor. The watch geek. Who else? Give me another name. One is not enough.'

The only other person I knew was Henrik, the soft-spoken bartender at the Rode Prins, and I'd only talked with him once or twice. But — if he was smart, he could cover me. I had no idea if he knew what kind of work Mila and I did. And by giving Piet the Rode Prins, I was giving him my hiding place in

Amsterdam. Mila would kick my ass.

But it didn't matter if Piet tied me to the Rode Prins; he was going to die soon. 'I drink at a place called the Rode Prins, on the Prinsengracht. You know it?'

'I had a drink there, once.'

'A bartender there, Henrik, he knows me.'

'And what's your drink?'

'Usually beer.' Henrik had served me only once, but I'd drunk the beer on his recommendation. I held my breath. 'I'm not real original.'

He worked his phone, presumably summoning up the Rode Prins number from an internet search. He pressed the button so I could hear him make the call.

But to Piet, I was Peter Samson. I was just Sam to Henrik. Oh, Jesus.

Henrik's voice came on. 'Rode Prins.'

'Henrik, please.'

'This is he.'

'Henrik, this will sound very strange, but do you know a gentleman who goes by the name Samson who drinks there now and then? Not Dutch.'

A pause. A painfully long pause. The barrel of Piet's gun felt screwed into my temple.

Henrik said, 'Samson? You mean Sam?'

'Yes, is that what you call him?'

Thank God, thank God.

'Yes, everyone calls him Sam. Dark hair, tall, mid-twenties.'

'Yes. What is he?'

'You mean what nationality is Sam? I don't know. Wait. I saw him once take stuff out of his pocket to get his money, set it on the bar. His passport was Canadian. I remarked on it then.'

'Do you know what kind of work he does?'

'No idea. He is one of those who doesn't talk much about himself. Is he in some kind of trouble?'

'No, he's not. What does he like to drink there?'

'Heineken. And, you know, I have a business to run, and you sound like a goddamn stalker. You like Sam's green eyes, maybe?' Henrik got a little contempt going in his voice. 'You want a date with him? He doesn't swing that way as far as I can tell but you could leave your number.'

Piet hung up. Silence stretched for five long seconds. 'I like you don't talk about what you do. I don't like people who talk too much.'

He dialed another number. 'Speak and you're dead,' Piet said.

'Hello?' a voice said.

Gregor. I could be dead in the next ten seconds.

55

'Gregor. This is Piet. Do you know a man named Samson?'

A pause that ripped my heart from my chest. 'Yes. But not well.' Establishing that all-important distance. 'He's in town,' Gregor said.

'What does he do?'

'Um. I would describe it nicely as transport work.'

'And?'

'I don't know what else. Muscle when needed: Sam's dangerous in a fight.'

'Who did he work for when you knew him?'

'Big Vlad, but he's dead now. Pissed off some Nigerian and got himself macheted in the bathroom. He worked with Djuki, too.'

'Is Sam reliable or not?'

'Reliable. Kind of a know-it-all. But he can move all sorts of goods. He had inside contacts at legit shippers. Made things easier.'

I could feel the air give in my chest, a hollow breath. Gregor was repeating words he believed to be true.

'Thank you, Gregor. How are things?'

'Fine but slow. Do you think people don't wear watches so much with their phones telling them the time now?'

Piet didn't answer his question. 'I can throw some major business your way. Very soon.'

'Good. Okay.' Now I could hear the tension in

Gregor's voice; the eagerness to be done with the conversation.

'Thank you, Gregor. We'll speak soon.' Piet clicked off the phone. The barrel stayed in place.

'What the hell more do you want? A résumé?'

Now I pulled the car over to the side of the road, earning a honk from a truck behind me. I turned to look at him.

Piet was scared to death.

This stone-cold mother was in deep trouble. He'd lost his ally, who had betrayed him to an unseen enemy. He'd lost his distribution point for a lot of counterfeit goods and his slave trade. He'd lost two men that he'd counted on. He'd lost a warehouse full of goods and slaves that his clients would be expecting him to move. He had just lost a great deal of money. He'd been made by Nic, and he was being chased. This, on top of the Turk blaring his name around town. Piet was rapidly becoming a liability, and he knew it.

'It's gonna be okay, Piet. Chill.' And I carefully pushed the gun so that it was aimed at the van's floorboards and not my body.

He let me.

'You don't want to tell your boss about the day going bad,' I said.

'Shut the hell up and let's go have a beer. At that Rode Prins.'

289

56

We stepped into De Rode Prins. It wasn't too busy; a group of young men sat at the biggest table, laughing, drinking beer, talking sports. A woman sat by herself, sipping lager, studying a guidebook to the city. In the back, a group of Scottish tourists downed beers in the corner and munched on plates of cheese, sausage and fried lumps of something mysterious; an older man in a nice suit sat at the far end of the bar with a small glass of jenever, reading a newspaper. I could love the Rode Prins because it truly was a quiet neighborhood bar. From the wall, the red-splattered prince looked down on us all.

No sign of Mila. Henrik stood behind the bar and I gave him the slightest of nods.

'Some guy's looking for you,' Henrik said.

I raised a thumb toward Piet. 'My friend. He found me.'

Henrik nodded. Piet ordered two Heinekens for us; we sat at the opposite end of the bar from the man in the suit.

Dilemma, I thought, as Henrik brought us our beers. Piet seemed calmer. He needed me, badly. He was on my turf now, and I could beat him senseless, haul his sorry ass upstairs and question him hard for the location of the gang. And then I would probably kill him, since I could hardly hand him to the police while I still had work to do. But right now, with an infiltration and an attack on his resources, Edward might scramble, run to distant corners, and take Yasmin Zaid with him. I needed Piet alive, and I needed him as camouflage.

'Not a good day for you,' I said in a low whisper.

Piet sipped at his beer. He should have been running straight back to his boss Edward. But no one likes to be the bearer of bad news.

I began my slow squeeze. 'I can see the mess you've landed in. You've got your regular business here. Maybe Nic helps you forge documents on his computer. You make most of your money from the women, moving them from eastern Europe to here. And you got hired for a truly big job, with this Edward dude. You broke out of your comfort zone, having to get goods to America.'

He glanced at me.

'Why do you think I left Prague all of a sudden? Man, I've been there.' I shook my head, sipped at the beer. I had killed two men less than an hour ago and now I sat in a bar, drinking. They'd never feel the cool comfort of beer in their mouths again. Fine. They'd made their choices. If I hadn't killed them, innocents would have died. I wasn't going to dwell on what I'd done. I wasn't proud of it, either; it was what it was. But it was important that Piet think I was as awful as he was. My hand didn't shake as I picked up the beer glass. It stayed steady.

'Edward isn't going to take this news well, is he?'

'No.'

'And he doesn't fire people.'

'No.'

'What is he like?'

Piet considered. 'Very smart but he's a dick. He's English. He mentioned once he used to act, on the stage, I don't know where, maybe in some backwater. Expert forger — I think he might have worked in intelligence once. He's good at getting people to follow him. Talks like he was raised around money. He throws money around, too.'

'How do you know so much? He should keep his mouth shut.'

'Edward likes to be the most important man in the room. That often involves bragging.'

Time to play. 'You might have to fire him.'

'Fire him?'

'You know, some clients interfere with profitability. That's what happened in Prague. I fired clients who tried to screw me over.'

He laughed. 'And now you're running.'

'No, I'm laying low. It was best that if I didn't want to be fired from this good sweet world that I relocate for a bit.'

'Why are you telling me this?'

'Because I know how a guy like Edward works. He's got critical goods he needs moved. They want to use our networks, our connections, because they need us. But if the job goes wrong, they don't hesitate to kill us.' I felt like I was slipping entirely into a new skin; I finished my beer, gestured at Henrik for another round. 'The point is, we're businessmen, and guys like Edward are bigger trouble than they're worth.'

'I can't fire this guy. It would bring so much heat on me.'

'I wasn't suggesting you should,' I lied. 'You just have to be prepared for every eventuality.'

'When I tell him what happened . . . '

'The fact you've waited is going to piss him off,' I said. Right now I needed to be the voice of reason, someone Piet could trust. 'He might run.'

'No. The job is too important to him.'

'And the job is what?'

His gaze slid back to me.

'How many friends do you have left, Piet?'

'Lots.'

'And I'm sure, now that this Edward might be gunning for you, they'll be lining up to help.'

He let the sarcasm hang in the air for a long moment. 'Why would you help me?'

'Money. I'm very predictable. And hell, man, I'm sort of deep in this now.'

'If I don't do this job, I have not so much money. I need it. Badly.'

I wasn't particularly interested in his financial woes. These guys were all the same: big risks, big payoffs, and they blew it on bling and expensive girlfriends. 'Here's the deal. You're crippled right now. I still have my resources, to help you move what the mystery meat is that you're shuttling for this Edward guy. You've lost your team, you've lost some of your capital. You take me on as a partner, just for this job. I get half.'

'Half!' Red crawled into his cheeks and he didn't bother to keep his voice down. The Scots and the old man glanced at us.

'Half,' I whispered. 'I'm pulling your fat from the fire.'

'You underestimate me, Sam, very badly.' The words were stone cold.

'I think I'm estimating your sorry-ass position just fine. Good luck with Edward. And good luck with the police, or Dutch intel, or whoever's gunning for you. Between those two, I predict a week full of puppies and rainbows for you, asshole.' I tossed euros on the counter, got up to leave. If he stayed, I would grab him when he walked out and haul his ass upstairs and let him see what a grieving husband and father could do to mortal flesh.

He let me take five steps before he spoke. 'I'll give you thirty per cent.'

'Forty-five.'

'Forty,' he hissed. 'I set up the job, I've done most of the work. You're just helping me reach completion. Forty.'

I needed to let him win the battle. 'All right, forty per cent.'

He risked a smile at me; it was the same smile he'd given the captive women and it took a certain amount of self-control not to slam my beer glass into the shine of his crooked teeth.

'Then you deserve to know who we're fighting.' He made his voice low.

'Yes.'

'It's not the police. It's a man. Bahjat Zaid.'

'I know that name.'

He raised an eyebrow.

'Military equipment manufacturer; I read *The Economist*, you know.' I risked a frown. 'Did you counterfeit his goods? Rip him off?'

'Not me. He has a grudge against Edward.'

'Legit business types don't hire gunmen.'

'Zaid does.'

So true. 'And this respectable businessman's trying to derail your big job?' I wanted to know if he would confide in me about Yasmin. 'Why doesn't he just call the cops?'

'He has his reasons.'

I took a sip of my beer. 'What are you smuggling to the United States?'

'Can't tell you.'

'Piet, I have to know. I can't get it packaged and shipped without knowing. Be reasonable.

His need to trust me won out.

'Military equipment.'

'What kind?'

'Electronics.'

I didn't like this vagueness but I wasn't sure he'd tell me more, not in a public place. 'What kind?'

'Experimental. Zaid has his reasons for keeping the police out.'

What reasons?

Piet finished his beer, watched the remaining suds inch down the empty glass.

What mattered was getting Piet and Edward and their group all together. I had to work that angle relentlessly.

So. Put the edge of the knife against Piet's fears. 'So you're in a mess. You're moving counterfeit cigs to the US, and you're hiding

Edward's secret military experimental equipment inside the shipments. Now you've lost your cigarettes *and* your means of smuggling Edward's gear.'

Piet clenched his eyes. 'I'm screwed, and I don't like being screwed.'

'So. We need goods to ship, to serve as camouflage for whatever Edward wants to get into America.'

'Yes.' For a moment he looked like a stressed owner of a small business, worrying over his accounts payable and an anemic cash flow.

'I have a solution.' One, I thought, that would get me close to Edward and Yasmin and the rest of the group.

'What?'

'We steal replacements.'

'Replacements?'

'Yes. Hijack a load of goods. Preferably counterfeit; that way, whoever you rob won't go to the police and we ship whatever secret stuff Edward wants in the US in the stolen goods containers.'

'It is a bold thing to steal a freight shipment.'

'Easiest thing in the world, if you know how to do it. But you and I can't do it alone. This Edward guy, he must have people, yes?'

'Yes.'

'Then we need them.'

'They are not robbers.'

'Neither am I, but circumstance dictates. Do they want to get this electronic gear, whatever it is, to the US?'

'Yes.'

'What is the gear?'

He leaned close to me. I could smell his deodorant, the soft stench of his scent, the beer on his breath. 'Weapons.'

'Weapons. For who?'

'Not your concern.'

'What kind?'

'Terrible ones,' Piet said.

I said nothing for a long, long minute, let the conversation in the other parts of the Rode Prins rise and fall. Then:

'Define terrible,' I said. 'Unlike you, I don't bite off more than I can chew.' I had to play my part right, and it was okay to be scared of the enormity of a job.

'You can't back out now.'

'Are you going to tell me the N word?'

'N word?'

'Nuclear.'

'Oh, my God,' Piet laughed. 'Oh, no. No.' He laughed again. 'No.'

'I need details.'

'Before I give you details, I need to talk with Edward.'

'Fine. I need to talk with Edward, too.'

'Why?'

'Because I blew Nic's cover and I saved all your asses. I want payment. I want my slice of this, Piet. I'm getting shot at and I deserve a stake in this deal.' I made my words a hiss. Apply the pressure, I thought, crack him. Crack him now. Make the world an anvil falling from the sky in a twisted cartoon to obliterate his head. 'I don't share a bit of information on the shipments until I talk to this Edward and his people. Not a bit.'

I could sense the desperation coming off him. A dozen telling signs: in the flick of the tongue on his lips, in the way he held the heavy glass. This was a man not easily rattled and he *was* rattled, badly, by the thought of failing Edward.

He didn't speak so I asked: 'When was your shipment supposed to arrive in Rotterdam?'

'Morning after tomorrow.'

'Then we don't have much time, do we?' Tomorrow wasn't enough time to plan a robbery but I hoped that their desperation would be as great as mine.

'Edward does not rush. Ever. He will not be rushed by my deadline.'

In the mirrored wall of the bar, I saw Mila walk past us. She did not look at us; but she caught Piet's eye.

He watched her pass with an appreciation that made my bones go cold. 'That's a prime little number.'

'Three or five?'

'Huh?'

'Little prime number. What, you don't like math jokes?'

'Math only exists for money.'

Mila vanished through a door into the back of the Rode Prins. I wanted to talk to her, now, find out what had happened.

He finished his beer. 'Come with me, Sam.'

I didn't want to leave but I set my beer down. 'Where are we going?'

'You want to meet Edward, you shall meet Edward. Let's go.'

Finally. It would happen. I was going in unarmed but I'd face the scarred man. Find my wife and my child.

Henrik watched us leave. I wondered if Mila was going to tail me again. But I never looked behind me to see. I couldn't have Piet becoming suspicious.

57

'I saw him.' Howell stood in the quiet of the safe house in Amsterdam. Outside the spring light danced on the shallow waters of the Herengracht; bicyclists pedaled by slowly, savoring the lovely day. He could smell gunfire and blood as if it were burned into his clothes. 'I saw Sam Capra. He fired on us. He left behind a warehouse full of goods that I suspect are stolen or counterfeit, and a room full of women I suspect are bound for sex slavery.'

'There has to be a reasonable explanation,' August said. A Company doctor was tending to his arm. He winced as the doctor closed a stitch.

'I think he went rogue long before his wife died. Has it occurred to *anyone* that he was the bad guy, not her? That Lucy wasn't the driving force behind him turning traitor?' Howell said. 'I appreciate your loyalty to him. But I am telling you, August, that it is misplaced and misspent on Sam Capra.'

'Or he thinks these people know where his wife is.'

'He shot at my men.'

'Did you see that?'

Howell hesitated. 'No.'

August thanked the doctor, who left without a word. Then he turned to Howell. 'Novem Soles.'

'What?'

'You asked him about the words Novem Soles.

Is it a group? Could these people be it?'

'These people are apparently cheap traffickers. I doubt they've endowed themselves with some grand Latin name.'

'What's Novem Soles, Howell?'

Howell crossed his arms. 'A term heard mentioned on some monitored lines tied to criminal rings, or to government officials who were on the take. I don't know if it's a group, or a code name for a person, or what it is.'

'That dead man in Brooklyn had a tattoo of a stylized nine and a sun. Novem soles, nine suns. I didn't sleep through Latin.'

'Maybe Sam Capra was working with these people on the bombing, and now they wanted him dead. Or maybe he's turned against us since we let him walk.'

'We've thrown him away; are you surprised he's landed with trash?' August said.

'The hard, awful truth is that the only survivors of the London office are the Capras. Someone recruited either Lucy or Sam, or both of them. They killed our people. They attacked us with impunity. That's what's unacceptable. He's acting like a criminal. Pretty it up how you want it, August, but he's a criminal, too.'

'You told him that you had proof he was innocent.'

'I lied,' Howell said. 'It was a considered decision to let him go, to see what he did.'

'Then let's use our contacts in the underworld here. Ferret him out. I'll talk to him.'

'You,' Howell said, 'are going home, soon as we can get you a plane.'

'Sir, don't. Let me stay.'

'You've been shot, Agent Holdwine. Go home.'

'You're going to kill Sam,' August said.

'Only if he tries to kill me,' Howell said.

'Sir, I request permission to stay. My injury is not that serious, and . . .'

'Permission denied. Get some rest, August. Read a good book, watch TV. You've earned some quiet.'

Howell walked out, shutting the door behind him. On the other side of the door, August considered. He still had the spare phone in his pocket, the number that he'd given to Sam in case someone came after him back in Brooklyn. It had never been used. He felt bad that Sam hadn't called him after the attack in his apartment. Either Sam didn't trust him, August thought, or he liked him too much to get him involved. But he still had a few hours in Amsterdam, to hope for the phone to ring.

58

'Do you know where De Pijp is?'

'Yes.' It was the same district as the Albert Cuypmarket, where Gregor's shop was.

'Drive there.' Piet gave me directions and an address and dialed his phone. 'Yes. Hello. Listen, I have bad news. The machinists' shop was compromised. Nic turned on us, he was spying. I have an associate who exposed him.' Great, he was claiming ownership of me. 'Nic might have been working for the same employer as the Turk. We were attacked, not by police, possibly by rivals. The twins are dead, our cover shipment lost. What do you want to do?'

This had to be Edward. And Edward would have to summon Piet for a meeting. Then I was set. I'd already killed two of them. I figured, from the video I'd seen, that there were about nine more who could damn Yasmin Zaid as a killer.

Nine targets and Edward. I had no weapons on me and couldn't have counted on taking any because I would be searched before I was brought anywhere close to Edward's inner circle. Fine. I would have to start killing them before he saw me, before he recognized me as Lucy Capra's husband. With what? My bare hands?

Bahjat Zaid wanted them all dead. But Zaid had lied to me, and avoided me, and given this group weapons, if Piet was to be believed, all without telling me. I didn't like being a pawn. So I didn't feel that I had to follow his orders to the letter. Grab his daughter and get out was good enough for me. And that alone was going to be a nearly insurmountable challenge.

'We lost the shipments, but my partner says he knows how to get replacements.' He listened. Then said yes three times. He clicked off the phone.

'Where are these shipments we can take over?' he asked.

'You can't steal a legit shipment,' I said. 'You can't redirect it, not if you want to be sure of total control of it. They could have GPID chips inside for the police to track it. You need to steal from counterfeiters. They can't run to the police and if they want to try and take you on you might be able to outgun them.'

'I don't want to steal in Rotterdam,' he said. 'These people could be my customers later.'

I hate people who think long-term. I needed him panicked, not logical. I tented my tongue with my cheek. 'We don't have time . . . '

'We will have to figure it out. Now. We're on a deadline. I miss it, Edward will kill us both.'

Well, I was about to ruin his plans. But what if Edward and Yasmin weren't where we were headed right now? I'd have to continue the charade to get close to them. Where the hell would I find illegal shipments to hijack?

I considered. 'The Chinese usually move their billions in counterfeit cigs in stages, shedding shipments in major cities as they move west across Europe.' I drummed a finger against my lip. 'So. I think Chinese counterfeits, being shipped into Western Europe, are our best hope. We can grab a shipment, relabel it, hide the goods and get it on its way to America.'

He was calmer. 'What do you need?'

'A team of at least seven, and guns. Silencers. We will need forged papers to replace their shipping manifests with our names in case we are stopped.'

'And how will we find the Chinese shipments?'

'I know a man,' I said. But I hoped I'd have Edward in my grip before I had to make that call.

★ ★ ★

The house was in a section of De Pijp that was a bit worn and tired.

If I could get the gun from Piet before we were in I could work through the house, eliminating them. I would be going in blind, though. But better to get the layout, see the faces, then strike. Assuming I got my hands on a gun.

God, I was assuming a lot.

I glanced at the rear mirror. It would have been nice to see Mila pulling up behind us, arms laden with, well, arms. But the street was empty except for two women walking along the sidewalk, carrying their shopping bags.

A man opened the door as we approached, his eyes hidden behind retro-style sunglasses. His mouth was a lush cruel curl. I tensed. I felt like I was walking into a gas chamber. This was what my life had come to: killing. I wondered what my baby looked like; I wondered what his skin felt like, what it would be like to know the curl of a hand around a father's finger.

You think the damndest things when you believe you're really about to die. Like you know you only have so many thoughts left.

The man who had taken my wife and child from me was inside. Waiting.

Piet said, 'He's clean,' but the sunglassed man guided me into the house with a fist in the small of my back and searched me thoroughly, his hand running along my back, my legs, my groin.

Beyond the entryway I could detect a scent of spicy food, of laundry detergent, of sweat. Another man, a blond, stood at the end of the hall. Three to kill. But I would kill them, somehow.

A young woman stepped out next to him. She wore jeans and a faded T-shirt and held a gun. She had brown hair, pulled back. Not Yasmin Zaid. She stared at me with flat eyes. Four to kill.

And on her arm, a nine paired with a sun, stylized. Just like the man in Brooklyn who I'd killed with my bartender's guide.

I wondered if the guy in shades could smell my fear, my tension. I didn't want to die. The realization was on me like a weight slamming between my shoulders.

'You're enjoying this,' I said as he ran probing fingers up my leg, toward my crotch. 'Those are some gifted hands.'

'Shut up. You talk when I say so,' he said in perfect English. Since his fist was close to my groin, I decided silence was the best option. I could see the gun in the back of his pants. Good to know. I'd already decided I'd take the woman's gun; she was holding it a bit loosely, as though it were more prop than weapon ready to use.

'This is Samson,' Piet said. 'He's all right. He — '

And he didn't get a chance to finish. The sunglassed man jabbed a hand hard into Piet's throat. Piet slammed against the wall, choking, and the sunglassed man — probably about six-four, two hundred very solid pounds — said, 'I'm not happy with you, Piet.'

Piet — big, tough sword ninja Piet — started to beg. 'Ah, Freddy, please. Please.'

'We all want to know how today went so bad. How Marc and Dirk died.' I guessed those were the twins.

'He can't answer you if he's choking to death,' I said. Piet gurgled and brought a bit of color to the dour room, turning a nice shade of robin's egg-blue.

Freddy shot me a look. 'I don't know you.'

'Marc and Dirk got killed because Nic sold us out,' I said. 'Nic's dead. The revenge is done, if that's what you're after. I killed Nic and I'm going to get us some goodies to hide your junk in.'

'They were our friends.'

'I'm very sorry. They died standing up.' He had the same tattoo as the woman, the nine that was partly a sun. It looked very fresh on his forearm.

These guys were Novem Soles? These guys

were . . . nothing. What had they done that ranked a Company file before the London bombing?

Freddy gave me a long, funny look. Piet started to kick the wall. Freddy's bicep looked like it was hewn from marble. He probably didn't keep a gun at hand because he could kill you with one blow.

The woman said, 'Freddy. Let's hear what Piet's come to say.'

Freddy dropped Piet, who coughed and rolled on the dirty floor. I helped him to his feet. I couldn't get my hands close to his gun, though. And Freddy had a gun out now and had it very close to my temple.

He steered us into a den at the end of the hallway and I thought: here we go, moment of truth.

But it was empty. No Edward. No scarred man. He wasn't here.

'Edward wanted to talk to us,' Piet said.

'Edward doesn't talk to people he doesn't know,' the woman said. She had an odd accent, as though British and Dutch had been pureed in a linguistic blender. She was pretty, in a technical sense that proportion and balance were in her features, but she was ugly at the same time. Like the rot in her soul had inched its way to the surface. I disliked her immediately, and intensely.

'That must make his social circle very tiny,' I said.

'Yes.' The woman seemed to be in charge. Freddy wasn't contributing to class discussion.

'My name is Samson,' I said. 'And you are?'

'Demi.' She gestured at chairs. I sat.

'Like the actress?'

'Like the actress. Did you know her name is very popular with Dutch parents?'

'I did not,' I said.

This wasn't right. They looked like low-level crooks, nothing that could pull off multiple bombings to rid themselves of enemies, or blackmail a corporate titan like Bahjat Zaid. But as my mind flashed across the video images from the Turk's execution, I felt sure that Freddy and Demi and Piet and the other guy had been among the masked crowd on the tape. I could recognize Freddy's bulk, the Dutch kid's slouch, Demi's crossed-arm stance.

The house was old, and it smelled, and they looked like youngsters playing at gangsters rather than being real criminals. On the TV a SpongeBob cartoon played, muted. I could smell burned popcorn wafting from the kitchen. A disassembled gun lay on the table. Sloppy.

'When's Edward going to be here?' I said.

'He's not,' Demi answered. She watched Piet slide into the chair next to me. The blue tint in his face had been replaced by a flushed red. He was pissed.

'What the hell is this?' he yelled.

'Edward said he's making sure the shipment reaches us okay. He'll see you when you've got the American side of the trip ready. Not before.'

I could hardly ask if Yasmin Zaid was here. 'Is this all I have to work with?'

'What do you mean?'

'There are four of you, including Piet. I need

more people to grab a shipment.'

'Piet was hired to arrange the shipment. We're not helping you at all.'

'But we need more people.' I gained nothing by taking down this group; it wasn't all of them and Yasmin and Edward weren't here.

'You don't get to talk to Edward, or anyone else, until you've fixed the cargo problem.'

I glanced around the den; it wasn't the room where they'd shown Yasmin shooting the Turk. This wasn't their base of operations. This dump was a backup safe house for them.

I was going to have get Edward's operation back on track. That was the only way to get him and the whole gang within reach, close enough to kill, close enough to get answers.

No choice. Starting tomorrow, I was going to have to steal a shipment of cigarettes from gun-toting Chinese smugglers to give me the man I was hunting.

Lucky me.

59

Gregor said, 'I don't do a lot of business with the Chinese.' He looked at me and then at Piet. He swallowed. 'Seriously, guys, I don't think I can help you.'

'I just need someone in the counterfeiting chain,' I said. 'You must know someone. No way are all these Rolexes entirely real.'

'I beg your pardon, Sam, but they are.' Gregor managed a moment's outrage. He turned to Piet. 'I honestly can't think of anyone to aim you at.'

I was going to owe Gregor big time. But killing Piet and removing all danger to him would probably be a good settling of the accounts. 'I need to know, Gregor. You must have a contact among the Chinese.'

Gregor looked gaunt and frightened and once again like he was fending off a cold. He shook out a garlic lozenge from a package and slipped it between his lips, sniffling.

'I have one or two. But I'm not sure they'd appreciate me giving you a name. The Chinese counterfeiters are very, very careful about their associates.'

'They are also very, very entrepreneurial,' I said, 'and I'm sure that we can make them an appealing offer.'

'What do you want them for?'

'We want to hire them to smuggle goods for us,' Piet lied.

Gregor clicked the garlic capsule against his teeth. 'Ask your friend Nic. Wouldn't he know?'

'Nic is dead,' I said.

Gregor dragged a tissue across his nostrils with a wide swipe. 'Really?' He looked at me as if to say: well done.

'Yes. So. We need a name with the Chinese. We'll pay, Gregor.'

He pulled a piece of paper close to him, wrote down a name and a phone number. 'You want Mrs Ling. She handles a lot of trade coming into Holland. I've gotten watches from her before. She has a legit export company, but she uses it as a front. I take fake Swatch watches from her, sell them online.' He finished his cigarette. 'I would not cross Mrs Ling.'

'I'm supposed to be afraid of a woman?' Piet snorted.

I had no intention of playing the fool. 'Tell me about her.'

'She goes nowhere without her three sons. I suspect their father is the devil and Mrs Ling won custody. These are vicious people. I do not deal with them unless I have to.'

'Where are the Lings?' My impatience showed. Fine. I'd face the badass Lings. I just wanted to get close to Edward. I'd thought of my child in that moment when I thought I might die and now I couldn't shake the thought of my baby.

'You can call them,' Gregor said. 'Don't involve me. Tell her you would like to propose a business deal to your mutual advantage.'

'He sounds like a Dickens novel,' Piet muttered. I hadn't expected literary knowledge from Piet. I reminded myself not to underestimate him.

'Thank you, Gregor,' I said. It occurred to me that Gregor could solve a couple of problems for himself as soon as we left by calling the Lings and telling them we intended trouble. Or that we were trouble. 'C'mon, Piet.' The plan on how to use the Lings to get rid of a chunk of the gang was already forming in my head but Piet said, 'Wait.'

I turned back. Piet stared at Gregor, who stared back.

'What?' Gregor said. 'What's the matter?'

'He's real nervous today. He's afraid you'll warn the Lings about us and so he's thinking about killing you,' I said. I believe in honesty in all dealings with people like Gregor. He was a crook, but he was not a vicious killer and rapist like Piet. Garbage has different levels.

Piet shot a look at me.

'But if he kills you, I'll kill him,' I said.

Piet shot out his arm and grabbed Gregor by the throat. Gregor tried to wrench away, his thin, delicate fingers plucking at the sausages that made up Piet's hand. 'Listen. You keep your goddamned mouth shut and you'll get a cut.'

'All right, all right,' Gregor choked. Piet pulled out the short sword and ran it along Gregor's jaw with a frightening tenderness.

'Let him go,' I said. 'Now.'

Piet pushed Gregor away. Gregor gagged and fell to the floor. He spat out the garlic capsule, huffing for breath.

'We're all cool. All cool.'

313

Piet stormed out of the watch shop.

'It will be okay, Gregor. He won't bother you again. I promise.'

Gregor didn't look at me. 'Please don't come see me again. Please. I don't want to stay in the business. I don't want to be tied to whatever you're doing. I have a wife. A child. *Please*.'

I'd pushed him too far and he wanted out; I couldn't blame him. He'd given me a lot.

'Okay, Gregor. Thank you for helping me.'

Piet had repaired to a café across the street.

I sat down across from him and he said, 'You do not issue the orders. The next time you do that in front of someone, I will take the *wakizashi* and I'll lop off a finger. Do you understand me? You're nobody here. *Nobody*.'

'I'm a nobody who's saving your ass and don't you forget it. The next time you decide to strangle someone who's helping us, I will take your *wakizashi* and drive it into your back. You understand me?'

He glared at me. 'Fuck you.'

'Listen to me. Edward and his people are just about done with you. That's clear to me if not to you. They've had their fill of your screw-ups. So either we get the shipment or they're going to kill us both.'

Piet said nothing as his beer was put on the table. I shook my head at the waiter. 'I will find out where the Lings have a shipment heading for Amsterdam, one we can intercept.'

'How will you . . . ?'

'I will. Trust me. But give me tonight to do it.' I stood. Piet stared down at his beer. 'Give me a

314

number where you can be reached.' He spouted one off and I memorized it. I didn't want to leave him but I had to. He could duck and run now. But I couldn't show him how I intended to find the Lings without tipping my hand on my past.

Because I'd heard of the Lings. One of the suits, the young one, had mentioned the name in the briefing, a minute before Lucy called me and the bomb went off. The Company was watching the Lings.

60

The Rode Prins was empty inside; its few customers were all outside basking in the sun. Henrik wiped down the bar and nodded politely as I approached.

'You saved me,' I said. 'Thank you.'

'You're welcome, Sam. I don't like that man. Not a bit.'

'I don't like him either. Where is Mila?'

'She is upstairs.'

I caught her coming down. 'We need to talk,' I said.

She turned around without a word and we went into the apartment. I started to speak and she delivered a slap right across my face. It stung.

'What the hell . . . '

'We did not bring you inside,' she hissed, 'just so you can find your wife, who is probably a traitor. We brought you in so you could do good. Actual, real good.'

'Didn't I?'

'You left those women there.' Agony layered her voice. 'It is beyond indecent, Sam.'

'The Company was there. My friend August was there . . . '

'And they abandoned the women. They left them behind.'

That couldn't be. I tried to think of a reason why Howell would have done such a thing. 'Mila

316

. . . they had wounded and they were operating on Dutch soil without clearance. They had their covers to protect . . . they would have called the police I'm sure.'

'You are sure. So they, and you, leave women chained like dogs in darkness?' Her voice broke.

'Mila, where are the women now?'

'They are with friends of mine. I will make sure they are returned home.'

'Mila, I did my best to protect them.' I took a step closer to her, her slap still stinging my cheek. 'I kept Piet from hurting them again or taking them with us. I'm sorry if I let you down.'

She bit her lip, clutching her elbows. 'You will have to fend on your own. I need to help the women.'

'You're abandoning me?'

'*You* abandoned *them*.'

'You know that's not true. I set it up so they could be freed. Mila, why are you being this way?'

She looked at the ground. 'Because I have to be this way, Sam. Listen carefully. If you have to leave Amsterdam, my employers own a bar in just about every major city in the world. Do a search for 'Roger Cadet' on your phone and you'll find the address for the closest one. Go there and tell the manager that Roger Cadet asked you to stop by and you will be helped, whatever you need.'

'Who's Roger Cadet?'

'The supposed owner. But he doesn't exist. It's just a password. But every bar's location is encoded with it so it'll show up on a GPS map.'

'These bars are a chain?'

'No. Each bar is unique. But each can serve as a safe house for you.'

I took a step toward her. 'I am so close, Mila. So close to finding this Edward jerk, and to finding my wife and child. To saving Yasmin Zaid. Please don't walk away. Help me.'

'You don't need me, Sam. You need only yourself, and your unbroken focus. Everything else is a distraction. And I have to help these women. I have to.'

She spoke from a place of pain and I couldn't argue with her. 'All right.'

'I can always be reached at this number.' She gave me a cell phone number; I repeated it and she nodded.

'Good luck, Sam.' She left. I didn't want her to go; but in one way it was easier. Because there was no way in hell she would agree to what I was going to do next. I went to my duffel bag, where I'd stashed it under the bed, and I pulled out the cell phone August had given me a lifetime ago in Brooklyn.

I went downstairs and I walked a half-mile away and stood on a bridge that spanned the Prinsengracht. A sightseeing boat cruised below me; a group of students, laughing, walked past me. I dialed.

It rang seven times before it was answered. 'Yes?'

'Hi, August.'

A pause. 'Where are you?'

'I need to talk to you.'

'You better be turning yourself in.'

318

'No. I need to see you. Face to face.'

'Um, I was shot today, you know.'

'Are you in the hospital?'

'No. Flesh wound in the arm and I took a blow to the head. The bullet is out and my head's hard as steel. But I get sent home tomorrow. They didn't have a plane available tonight.'

'I need your help.'

'You need help, all right, Sam. You know there was a dead body in the apartment next to you, don't you?'

'I knew that.'

'Did you kill him?'

'Yes.'

'Oh, Jesus, Sam.'

'Well, he started it,' I said. 'Can you come see me? Without Howell or anyone else?'

'You have to be kidding!'

'The guys I was with are tied to the man who set off the London bomb and kidnapped my wife,' I said. 'Now, if you want to grab me, you will ruin any chance of getting this guy. He's behind the bombing in Amsterdam and he's working on getting experimental weapons of some sort to the States. He sent the dead guy who tried to kill me. He's tied to the Money Czar we were investigating in London, Jesus, August, it's all knitted together and I'm this close to pulling it apart. I need your help.'

'You are so major-league screwed up, Sam. Look, come in; tell us all about it and let us help you.'

'I can't, August. They'll just put me back in

319

jail. Howell thinks I'm in with these people. I don't have time to explain to him that I'm not.'

'I'll lose my job if I don't report this conversation, and you know it.'

'Yes, you will.' I waited.

'Where are you?'

61

August arrived an hour later. Alone. I was at a back table in the Rode Prins, near the curtain screening the corridor that led to the kitchen. He sat heavily across from me. I'd kicked him in the side of the head and a purplish bruise stretched from temple to jaw. I could see the heft of a bandage underneath his jacket.

'How are you feeling?'

'Like hell. Howell's gone to a meeting and I told them I needed fresh air.' He stared at me. 'Sam. What in God's name are you doing?'

'One of the crime families the Company had an interest in are the Lings. They're based here. One of the Langley guys mentioned them in London.'

'Okay. They behind the grab on Lucy?'

'No. But I need to know if they are still being tracked by the Company.'

'What for?'

'I need to know where their shipments are. I need to steal one.'

His mouth opened, closed, opened again. 'Insanity doesn't agree with you, Sam.'

'It's the only way for me to get close to the guy who took Lucy. He . . . he has a hostage, August, so I can't force my way in. I have to draw him to me. But I need to know what we know about the Lings' routes.'

'You're crazy, Sam. I can't imagine what

you've lost. I can't. But I think your grief has damaged you. Badly. And you have to accept — you're not getting Lucy and the baby back. They're *gone*. You know they wouldn't have kept her alive for months. They wouldn't have been saddled with a baby.' He stopped, as if horrified by his words.

I stared at him.

'This is all . . . for nothing,' August said. 'You're not getting them back. I'm sorry, man, sorrier than you will ever know. But I . . . '

'Please just do as I ask. If we were ever friends.'

'Friends don't put friends in positions like this, man. I could lose it all.'

'You could. I already have. August, I know that you, as a decent man, are going to help me. You can't *not* help me.' I wanted to say *I saved your life today* but I couldn't play that card; he hadn't seen me and it wasn't fair.

'Howell will have my head.'

'Howell left a group of women behind in that machinists' shop.'

'What do you mean?'

'After you and the other agent were hit, and he chased me out, did he secure the building?'

'He did.'

'Did he tell you there were a group of sex slaves being held captive in the back?'

August paled, dragged a finger along his unshaven jaw. 'No. I didn't know. I swear.'

'I believe you. Because Howell is Ahab, and I'm the white whale,' I said. 'He's losing perspective, August.'

'I . . . I don't know.'

I took a deep breath. 'I knew about you and Lucy seeing each other before Lucy and I dated. She never mentioned it. You both kept it secret and I don't blame you; the Company doesn't need to be in your business. But I knew. And you didn't dump me as a friend for going out with your ex,' I said.

'Lucy and I weren't a good match,' he said. 'It only lasted a month.'

'Why?'

'I never trusted her.' He put his hands into his coat pockets and I wondered what I would do if he pulled a gun on me. I honestly didn't know. August felt like the last strand of my normal life and now I was asking him to do a job that was incredibly dangerous. I didn't know what he was suggesting to me about my wife. I just couldn't go there.

A long silence, and then he said: 'Can I call you on this number if I find out about the Lings?'

'Yes.' I tried to keep the relief from my voice. 'Thank you.'

'Don't thank me yet. No promises.' He turned and walked out of the Rode Prins without another word.

I sat and drank Henrik's good coffee and closed my eyes and thought it through how I would steal the shipment, given what I could guess about the limitations I would face.

Five hours later August called. 'We have an informant inside the Lings' operation. The Lings' trucks stop at a sweatshop in France. You do not hit them at the sweatshop, you hear me? You do not. You'll dirty up a current investigation into them.' He gave me the address. 'Their trucks are marked as being part of a company called Leeuw en Draak. Lion and Dragon.'

'Thank you,' I said. And meant it.

'Don't call me again, Sam. Good luck.' And he hung up. Now I'd lost my best friend as well. I mourned for all of ten seconds.

Then I called Piet. 'I have what we need.'

62

We waited in the rain, just north of Paris. It had taken us nearly five hours to drive south from Amsterdam, to the locale August had given me. It was early afternoon and the day was gray and sodden. Piet sat next to me, sharpening his *wakizashi* sword on a whetstone. Stroke. Stroke. Stroke. It made the flesh on my neck jerk. How sharp could you make a sword?

The sweatshop was off the E19/E15 express-way, hidden in a gray huddle of buildings. Early afternoon now and I thought how pleasant it would be to be rid of Piet. Very soon, I thought. Very soon. We sat and watched absolutely nothing happen at the sweatshop. Hours passed; twilight began to approach.

'How does a Canadian soldier get into this business?' Piet asked, breaking the silence.

I glanced at him. 'I was bored. How did you get into trafficking women?'

He smiled. 'I needed money for art school.'

'I didn't expect *that* answer.'

'An annoying percentage of young people in Amsterdam harbor a secret desire to be Van Gogh or Rembrandt. Anyway, I knew a guy. A friend of my mom's. He needed help getting girls to Holland. I helped him buy a van so we could move them, and eventually I took over the route.'

'Took over?'

'He got married and thought he shouldn't

traffic girls no more. What, you thought I'd killed him?'

'Yes.'

'No. Known him since I was twelve.' He rubbed at his bottom lip. 'He owns a coffee shop now.'

I really didn't want to know Piet as a person but some instinctive need to understand took control. So I asked: 'Why the sword?'

'The sword is who I am.'

'But it makes you memorable. I thought the idea was to stay under the radar.'

'It honors my mother.'

'She was Japanese?'

'Yeah. She came here in the early 1980s. Boyfriend brought her, dumped her, she stayed.'

I remembered Gregor called Piet a whoreson. Perhaps he meant it as more than an insult, as a description. His mom might have been a worker in the Rosse Buurt; many of the women there were not Dutch.

'I thought I wanted to study art, do Japanese-style stuff, like netsuke or watercolor painting. My mother did that in her spare time.' He shrugged. 'But art school didn't work out. They hated me there and a girl made trouble for me. Assholes. So I left.'

I had not thought of Piet as someone with smothered dreams. He read my expression. 'Eh, you thought I was just a snake.' He laughed.

'Well, I . . .'

'Man, we're all snakes. Gregor likes to pretend he's shed his skin, been reborn as an honest soul, but his scales are still there. And I suspect you're a very crafty snake, Sam.'

I shrugged. 'Sure. I got run out of the army. I spoke some Czech from my grandmother's side of the family. I couldn't find a real job in Prague so I made my own there. So you went straight from art school into trafficking?'

'Not right away. I used to do contract work for the police department in Amsterdam, designing their websites and brochures,' he said. He gave a long, low laugh. 'Then I saw how much the opposition paid.'

I glanced at him. 'That's a switch.'

'You make serious money by being a player. If I'd stayed with the police then I would have been a cog in their operation. I paid attention. I wanted to own cogs — not be one.'

'So you picked girls for your commodity.' My mind kept saying shut up, but it was a strange thought to sit here, making conversation with a monster in the shape of a man.

He shrugged. 'Good profit margin. Growing demand. Not likely to run out of raw materials.'

It was brutally cold accountancy. I wondered if it was a sort of twisted revenge on his mother. 'You sell people, Piet.'

'You sound like a schoolmaster.' He shrugged. 'I think of it as selling comfort and convenience.'

'Not to the people you sell.'

He flicked a smile. 'They don't have money. They don't count.' The smile turned greasy. 'You know, they live better here, even as whores, than they do back home. I've done them a favor, I have.'

'It would be one thing if they chose it. But most don't.'

He gave me a look of disapproval. 'I didn't know I'd offended your sacred morals.'

I had overstepped. I could show my loathing for him when I killed him, not before. 'I just think counterfeit merchandise is a lot easier to control than people.'

'I like the control.' His voice became a low slur of gravel. 'You should try it. I'll treat you to the choicest morsels from my next batch from Moldova. Got some girls coming in four days, an order from a house in London. You and me, we can break one of the girls in. You get a taste for this business, then fake goods will pale.'

If I looked at him I would kill him on the spot. And I needed him. So I watched the sweatshop parking lot.

He misinterpreted my silence. 'Ah. Maybe you don't like the girls. We get boys, too, not so many, but I know a couple of boys back in Amsterdam you might like . . . '

'No, thank you,' I said. 'Not interested.'

'You're weird,' he said, 'worrying so much about people. Other people don't matter; all that matters is you. You judge me. But you are no different than me, Sam. You lie, you kill when you have to, you live under a false name. I never shot anyone down the way you did Nic.'

'I did you a favor with Nic.'

'True.' He rubbed his lip. 'I keep thinking that I will be arrested any moment, because I don't know what he was transmitting, or who he was talking to. I need a big payday, Sam. I need to be

328

able to run and hide. That's a great luxury, to hide well. That's the mark when you're not a pawn no more, when you're a player.'

'Tell me about Edward,' I said. 'Is he a player or is he more?'

'What do you mean, more?'

'You said he's moving experimental weapons.'

'I think he's pulling corporate espionage — stealing from one company to sell to another.'

'What's he want to put into this shipment, Piet?'

'Not for you to worry about.'

'If we get caught I'd like to know what I'm serving time for.'

'You'll never see the light of day if we get caught on this job.' Piet's gaze went back to the warehouse. 'Ach, hello.'

A truck, marked with a stylized lion and dragon, pulled into the back of the warehouse where the sweatshop sat. Three Chinese men spilled out. Two wore black trench coats. Another, more portly, wore a regular tan jacket and blue jeans. He walked to the bay of the warehouse.

The two in trench coats stayed close to the truck.

'Let's go,' Piet said.

'No,' I said. 'They've got shotguns under the coats.'

'How can you tell?'

'See the way the fabric bulges, right below the arm? One guy was riding in the cab, but the second came out of the truck itself. They won't go into the building. They're guards.'

'Well, what are we supposed to do?'

'We can't grab the truck here. They're picking up extra goods — they've already dropped off fake cigs along the route. We go in now, while they're parked at a friendly spot, the Lings get a phone call.'

'Not if we kill them all.'

'I didn't sign on for a massacre,' I said. 'And it's bad business practice.' Interference with profit was the only argument that might sway Piet. 'The Lings would start hunting for us fast. We need to tackle the truck crew alone.'

'So how do we steal the shipment?'

'We don't,' I said. 'We hijack it.'

63

August was sitting in the hallway of the safe house, waiting for the pilot flying him to New York, when he heard the exchange between Howell and one of the operations techs:

'Mr Howell, we have a match on the description of the man at the warehouse based on the description you and August gave. Is this him?'

'Yes. Who is he?'

'Piet Tanaka. Dutch national, formerly a contract employee for the Amsterdam police.'

'What's he doing now?'

'He's dropped out of sight, sir. No listed address, no listed occupation.'

'August!' Howell called.

August got up and walked to the computer screen.

'This the guy you saw in the warehouse?'

August nodded. 'Yeah, distinctive face. That's him.'

Howell turned back to the tech. 'Find this guy. He's got Sam Capra working for him.'

'I don't think that's accurate,' August said.

'Don't you have a plane to catch, Agent Holdwine?' Howell said.

August left and found the pilot downstairs, ready to take him to the airport; Howell didn't wish him well or thank him for taking a bullet. Treason poisoned the air; they all felt it since Howell had seen Sam Capra leaving the scene of murder and trafficking. Treason put people in a sour mood.

64

After loading several boxes, the Chinese truck pulled back out onto the highway and we followed at a distance, three cars back. Piet was good; he knew how to tail.

'How are we going to get this truck grabbed before they stop again?'

'We force them off the highway.'

'What, in broad daylight?'

'Yes. In broad daylight. Right now, they're split up — two in the cab, one back with the goods and they are more on guard when they're stopped. They won't expect an attack now.'

'That's because attacking them on the highway is stupidity,' Piet said. 'What do you suggest we do?'

'Get behind them, then go past them,' I said. 'I want a better look at the cargo door.'

He inched up past the two sedans between us and the Ling truck and swerved back over. I studied the back of the truck. A sliding door, secured at the bottom by two separate padlocks. Hard to pick, roaring along at seventy miles an hour.

'Now go past them.'

He floored the van and hurtled past the truck. The cab door appeared to be normal, no modifications. I didn't give it more than a glance; I didn't want to attract the driver's attention. But I saw him, and he was laughing.

'Stay ahead of them.'

I studied the map, unfolded on my lap. There was another highway intersection, cutting across northern France, perhaps fifteen kilometers distant.

'Floor it. Get us there now. I have an idea.'

★ ★ ★

'This is insane,' Piet said but he smiled. The Ling truck would be here within minutes, and the van was parked on a bridge over the expressway.

'You understand what to do?'

He nodded. 'If this fails, you'll have wrecked everything.'

'If this fails, I'll be dead. So don't bitch. Just do what you're supposed to do.'

'Good luck.' He offered me his hand. I dared not show my revulsion for him. So I shook hands.

'They're coming,' he said, looking south. I could see the truck approaching in the heavy gray mist.

I put my legs over the side of the overspan and I heard Piet's van roar off, but my mind was on counting.

The truck should pass under me at fifteen.

Twelve, thirteen, fourteen . . .

I was wrong. The Ling truck hurtled beneath me at fourteen and if I hesitated I would miss it, landing onto unforgiving asphalt, tumbling into fast-moving traffic. I threw myself off and caught the last third of the truck, trying to land on all fours and roll with controlled parkour grace. A roll would be far quieter than hammering feet against the roof.

But my legs slipped and the truck veered slightly. I started to go off the roof's edge, on the passenger side. My legs danced in the air.

I swung myself hard, every muscle in my arms screaming, thinking if they see me in the wing mirror I'm dead. I yanked myself up with a jerk that felt like I'd torn flesh from my arms and settled into the slight depression in the truck's roof.

Then I lay very, very still.

Had they seen me? I had to assume radio communication between the cab and the guy in the hold of the truck. Either could have reported an unexpected sound or the passenger in the cab could have seen my blue-jeaned legs swinging out into the empty air when I struggled for a grip. Maybe they'd take the next exit, search for a place of privacy, then dispatch me.

No. I saw the next exit sign pass. A light rain began to fall from the granite-gray sky. The truck pressed onward.

I started to crawl along the length of the truck. Slowly, steadily, keeping my head down. I didn't want a motorist to see me. I risked a glance behind me. Piet had rejoined the highway and his van was there, staying close but not too close.

The rain increased, slickening the metal. I needed a firm grip for the next step and nature had just made my job harder.

I reached the forward edge of the truck. The cab's roof was about two feet below my hands. I could ease onto the roof, but I'd be more visible to anyone in approaching traffic. Cell phones were everywhere; I didn't want the French police getting phone reports of a crazy man truck-surfing the expressway.

The other choice was to ease down between the cab and the truck, into the narrow space, so that's where I went, feet first, my back to the cab. The truck jolted over a rough patch of road and my right foot slipped. Gravity seized me and I caught my hand in the jumble of cables at the cab's rear. My foot landed on the metal strut connecting the cab. Below me I could see the road passing between the crushing wheels.

I steadied myself. Now or never.

I inched my arm, holding Piet's gun, around the cab's corner. I planned to grab the passenger door, wrench it open and yank myself inside. All without the cab's guard shoving me back out into empty air at seventy miles an hour. The wind whipped hard around me, the rain seeping into my eyes.

I put my head around the corner and stared into a man's face, leaning out of the window.

65

The passenger's eyes were bright with shock that someone stood behind the cab; he looked to be about forty, heavy-set.

Time froze for three seconds. Then his shoulder made a sudden hard shrug, bringing up his arm.

I jerked my head back around the cab's edge as he fired. The bullet made a bright spark against metal, ricocheted out into the rain.

The truck veered hard, shuddering into the other lane, then whipped back.

They were trying to throw me off. I gripped the rain-slick metal and saw Piet's van race up to the driver's side, a spray of water fountaining from the tires. A muffled shot, from the truck, aimed at Piet.

I took a risk that the driver wasn't driving and firing at the same time — that it was the passenger shooting at Piet. All I had now was force, calculated and vicious. I went back around the corner and heard another crack of shot. I yanked on the door just as a hand from inside tried to pull it back.

I threw myself forward, the door's handle in a death grip. Then my feet gave way on the wet metal of the doorstep, my legs shot out and my shoes dangled inches above the tarmac.

I dropped my gun. It clattered onto the metal,

onto the road, and was crushed under the wheels.

The window, inches above my head, exploded. Shards blew out, stinging my scalp. The passenger, firing in panic. I wrenched my hand, shifted my weight, pulled my legs against the door for leverage, covered my head with my arm, all in one fluid move, like I was jumping onto a public housing railing in London.

I threw myself through the window, head first, my back slamming against the edge of it. I wriggled, trying to get leverage, elbowing the passenger hard in the throat, knocking him into the driver.

I had five seconds to win this fight. The driver whipped a gun from his left hand to his right, toward me. He fired, and the bullet skittered a path along the very top of my scalp, hot and vicious. I seized the gun's barrel and pushed down; he had to keep one hand on the wheel and he pulled the trigger in reaction. The next bullet hammered into the seat by the passenger's leg. He screamed and, in panic, wriggled past me. I threw a kick at him and he slammed into the door and crumpled.

Now I barreled hard into the driver, shoving him into his door. Where the bullet had grazed me, the pain was like a burning match dragged along my skin.

He knocked me back but my heels hit the windshield and I powered back into him. I threw hard, fast punches into his throat, eyes.

The truck veered wildly and he dropped the gun, but I felt the tires leave the asphalt and brush along an unpaved surface, grass, a skid beginning.

I levered my foot up, snaked an arm around his neck. 'I'll break it,' I said in Mandarin. 'You listen to me. The man with me, he will kill you. I will not. All we want is the cargo. He will kill you if you do not cooperate. I will let you live. Do you understand me?' And I gave his neck the slightest wrench. He nodded.

I grabbed the gun and pressed its heat to the driver's ribs. 'Drive. Normally.'

The driver settled the truck, guided it back onto the highway. We earned a roaring honk from a Mercedes that powered past us, the driver shaking a fist, blind to the struggle inside the cab.

The van pulled alongside us, like a teenager sidling up to the dream girl at a dance. A bullet hole marred its roof. Piet leaned forward — with extreme caution. I waved.

'The man in the van will kill you,' I said again. 'Do you speak English?'

'A little,' the driver said.

'Don't let him know you understand. He's crazy. I'm your only hope right now, you got me?'

The driver nodded. The passenger, unconscious, did not contribute to the discussion.

'Tell the guard in the trailer that we're pulling over, and he's to lay down his weapons, come out with hands up. You tell him any different, I shoot you in the knee.'

The driver obeyed, speaking into a walkie-talkie.

I gestured for Piet to drive behind us and, at my order, the driver took the next exit. I blinked away wetness on my face. We pulled four kilometers or so down the road. Now I saw empty stretches of land with a shawl of gray mist hovering above the ground. Cows grazed. Maybe a dairy close by. No sign of people, and the road was an old, narrow affair, rough around the edges. In the distance I saw a rough stone building; it looked like a storage facility.

I said in Chinese, 'Remember, do what I say, no matter what I say to the man in the van. We will walk to the storage shed and then we'll take the truck. You understand me?'

The driver nodded.

Piet crept up from where he'd parked the van, a gun at the ready. I pulled the driver out, keeping the gun on him.

I turned and heard a creak of metal. The back of the trailer opening, Piet jumping back. The driver called in Mandarin: *Do what I told you.*

'Don't shoot!' the guard yelled. He came out, hands raised.

Crime is a kind of war. But while soldiers will die for their country, few people will die for lords like the Lings. Loyalty is a smoke that inches up from the ashes of greed in this world. A change in wind scatters it.

'How do I know you won't kill me?' the driver said in Chinese.

'Because you'd already be dead if we wanted you dead,' I said.

Silence while he decided. He opted to trust

the calm in my voice. The guard was maybe forty, tired-looking, a little heavy. His mouth trembled as he blinked at the cows on the soft turf.

'Here,' Piet said, handing me his gun. 'Kill them.'

'Not out here,' I said. 'Shots will echo across an empty field and I'm not dragging dead weight into the woods. I'll take them to that shed. You check the cargo. If there are any RFID chips on there to trace the goods, tear them out. The Lings could be monitoring the shipment. I'll take care of these guys.'

Piet looked at the Chinese and smiled. 'God they're dumb. Standing here while we talk about killing 'em and they don't have a clue.' But maybe the guard did. He looked like he was about to break into a panicked run.

'Calm down,' I said in Mandarin. 'It's okay. Come with me.' Then I told the driver to haul down his unconscious friend and carry him. He obeyed, putting the knocked-out passenger over his shoulder.

The guard said, in stuttering Mandarin, 'This is my first run. I used to be a schoolteacher, my brother-in-law, he got me involved, I don't know much about doing the runs . . . ' He wore a Yankees baseball cap.

They walked ahead of me, and we went over the fence and toward the shed. I glanced back. Piet had vanished into the truck.

The shed was old and when I kicked the door the weathered lock shattered. I gestured them inside.

341

'Please,' the guard said. 'Please don't.' Terror ragged his voice.

'Sit down,' I said. They sat, the driver laying the unconscious cab guard down first.

'He has to think you three are dead. You understand? But I am not going to hurt you.'

They nodded. Their eyes stayed on the gun.

I took a step back. 'You,' I said to the guard. 'Toss me your hat.'

He pulled off the Yankees cap and threw it at me. I caught it and covered up my bloody hair with it. 'Your wallets, your papers.'

They tossed them over to me, trembling, and I studied them. 'Stand up now. Turn around.' Slowly they did, shivering, and I quickly hit each one of them, hard with the butt of the gun, and they collapsed. I punched each until they were out cold. Then I fired three shots into the rotting wall. Motes of wood and dust danced in the air before my face. I wiped the blood off my knuckles, in the dirt.

I walked back to the truck. Piet studied papers. The manifest on the truck indicated these were Turkish cigarettes, bound for London. Of course they weren't. They'd been made in China, mostly likely in a factory half-hidden in the ground.

'Any tracking chips?' I asked.

'No,' Piet said. 'Nice cap.'

'Then let's go.'

'I want to see the Chinese,' he said.

'Well, then, go look,' I said. I would have to shoot him. He studied me.

A small blue farm truck suddenly appeared on

342

the road, inched past us, the driver — an old woman — giving us a long, curious stare as she went by.

It rattled him. 'Let's just get going. Get you bandaged up, clean off the blood in the cabin. I'm driving the truck. You're driving the van.'

And we drove away. I kept my eyes locked on the little shed in the rearview mirror. No one came out of it.

★ ★ ★

We arrowed into Belgium, past the empty buildings of the old border station, and the lights along the expressway, activated by the cloudy day, glowed white in France, yellow in Belgium.

I had no cell phone — Piet had insisted, still nervous that he might be betrayed again. No way to contact Mila. There was no built-in phone in the van but there was a GPS. I wouldn't have the weapons; I wouldn't be able to set a trap. I felt dizzy from the loss of blood from my scalp wound.

And I decided I wasn't going in blind.

It was time to see if Mila had been telling me the truth.

66

I did a search on the van's GPS monitor, entering in the name Roger Cadet. Mila had said that would show me her employers' bars that I could use as a safe house.

One result: Taverne Chevalier, off Avenue Lloyd George, in the diplomatic district. As we edged into Brussels I flashed lights. Piet pulled over and I walked up to the cab.

'I need a drink and a meal, and I need to make some phone calls.'

'What phone calls?' Piet said. 'We keep going.'

'This isn't the only deal I've got. Either we stop or you decide to trust me with a cell phone.'

'No calls.'

'I have to work the next deal after this one. And I have to work it now.'

Greed lit Piet's eyes. 'What is this deal?'

'Military goods. High profit margins.' I was already thinking of the call I needed to make.

'Where do you want to stop?'

'I know a place.'

* * *

Taverne Chevalier was one of those places that looked rather humble but was zealously guarded by posh types as their private, unpretentious discovery. The bar itself was a finger of dark mahogany. Taps for a large assortment of Belgian and Dutch brews lined the bar, and it looked like some ales were being served in old-fashioned ceramic pitchers. I heard a variety of languages bubbling from the crowd. Hipsters in their requisite black-framed eyeglasses, men and women who wore the carefully neutral smiles of bureaucrats. Brussels was a city of diplomats and dealers, and I thought that if Mila and her mysterious bosses had half a brain between them they would have planted bugs on all the tables, recorded every conversation.

'Not the time for a drink, and if we need to eat, we could get fast-food.' Piet did not sound happy. We had parked the truck in a lot a few blocks away and he was very nervous about leaving the shipment.

'I know the owner here,' I lied.

'You can't do business here. Too many people.'

'Trust me,' I said.

Piet laughed. 'I like it when you make a joke.'

I leveled him with a stare. 'What are you drinking?'

'I think I should go back to the truck. We can be in Amsterdam in a couple more hours.'

'And we will be. Follow me.' We went to the bar, waited for a pretty girl to take our order. I ordered two Jupiler lagers and when she brought them I slid money to her and said, 'I'd like to see the manager, please.'

'She's busy, sir.'

'She'll make time for me, I think. Mila sent me.'

The girl vanished into the back of the bar, and a few moments later a stout, fiftyish woman appeared, a frown on her face. 'Yes, sir?'

'I'm a friend of Roger Cadet's,' I said, using the pass name Mila had given me back in Amsterdam.

She nodded. 'Any friend of Roger's is welcome here.'

'Is Roger here? I'd like to speak to him alone.'

Her glance slid to Piet. 'I can find out if he'll see you.'

I turned to Piet. 'Stay here, drink your beer. I'll just be a minute.'

'No. You could be calling someone, telling them where the shipment is. We stick together.'

I put my mouth close to Piet's ear. 'This is a byway, a stop. I have private business with him on this weapons deal, but I can use your help and you'll earn a cut. We're partners, yes?'

He was torn; he wanted the money but he didn't want me apart from him. 'I don't like this, Sam.'

'Listen to me. I took the risk back on the truck. I'm not messing you over. We're solid, Piet, all right? I must pay respects. Do you understand? You could bolt out the door and steal the shipment while I'm in there, and I'm trusting you that you won't.' Lose Piet and I might well lose Edward for good. But I had to take the calculated risk. 'I won't be but a minute or two.'

The manager cut through the crowd of diplomats and skinny beautiful people and we went upstairs. She glanced back at me. 'You're new.'

'Yes. And in trouble. I need weapons, a cell phone.'

She unlocked a door to the left of the landing. I glanced back down the stairway. No sign of Piet.

I stepped inside the door.

'I'm Eliane,' the manager said after she shut the door. 'You're supposed to call first.'

'I couldn't. No phone.' The small room was lined with shelves, some of which contained weapons. A cot, neatly made up, stood in the corner. I wanted to fall on it and collapse. Instead I searched the shelves. Found two Glock 9mms, spare clips, silencers.

'What else do you need?'

'I have to fight a large number of people,' I said. 'They will be heavily armed and I'll be alone. So I guess I have to kill them.'

Eliane blinked. 'You're going to kill them all?'

I swallowed. 'I don't know.' Hell. Was I? If I left some of the group alive, couldn't I leave them for the Dutch to interrogate, possibly to glean useful information? Zaid's insistence that everyone be killed to protect Yasmin's good name nagged at me. The girl had been brainwashed. That wasn't a crime. His reputation might survive.

Eliane moved to a box, opened it. The box was marked with a logo I recognized. Militronics, Zaid's company. Gear from his own company would help free his daughter.

'Do you have restraints?' I asked.

'Yes, but I thought you were going to kill them, not take them hostage.'

'Let's keep our options open. Let me have several sets.'

She showed me a thick banding of plastic wrist cuffs. 'And this. A flash grenade,' she said. 'Modified police issue. Do you know how to use it? Here is the activation button, here the timer.'

'Thanks. Where am I going to hide these?' I could hardly go downstairs loaded with gear in front of Piet. 'My van is parked about a kilometer away. Can you get this stuff there?'

'Yes,' she said. 'This man with you — he is not good.'

'He's a cold-blooded murderer and a slaver. I have to ambush him and several others at a meeting.'

'Then we mustn't make a mistake,' Eliane said. I liked her. I'd been judged by so many people lately, from Howell to August to Mila and Eliane just seemed to want to help me. I could have kissed her.

I gave her the keys and the description of the van. 'And I need a cell phone. Programmed with a number where I can reach Mila.' I took off my baseball cap and she gasped at the encrusted blood. She insisted on examining the wound.

'It's superficial, but it needs tending,' Eliane said.

'No time, and it would make him suspicious. How much time do you need to get to the van, load it, and get back?'

'Ten minutes.'

'Give me cash. A thousand euros, if you have it. I need to impress him that I cut a deal with Mr Cadet.'

She went to a safe in the wall, keyed in a combination then fingered her way through a pile of bills and handed them to me.

It felt human again, to not be pretending to be someone I wasn't, to not be with scum like Piet. I wanted to savor the moment. Eliane was like a cool mom for people on the run.

And just like a mom, Eliane looked at me as though my thoughts were written on my forehead. 'We have jobs to do. Go.'

She was right. I hurried back down the stairs. Piet had found a corner table and was sitting in a sullen funk, wolfing his beer.

I sat down and slid him a hundred euros. He blinked at me.

'Cadet owed me some money,' I said. 'And gave me an advance on the next job.'

'This wasn't worth the stop.'

'It was to me, Piet.'

I gestured at the waitress. I had to give Eliane time to find the van, plant the goods where he wouldn't see them.

Jimi Hendrix's 'Purple Haze' began to play on the speakers. Not louder than the talkers, but enough to impart the necessary funky vibe to the suit-infested pub. I saw Piet lean back slightly and let the feel, the groove of Taverne Chevalier ease into him. It had been a long, hard day. The mind, the body, wanted to relax, let the adrenaline burn itself out.

We ordered the specialty, thick Ardennes ham sandwiches, but Piet downed his beer in four long gulps and said 'No, coffee, please,' when the waitress asked if we wanted another

349

round. I agreed: coffee.

'Get the sandwiches and coffee for take away, please,' Piet said.

'No,' I said. 'I am sitting here, like a human being, and having my dinner.' I leaned forward and made my voice a hiss. 'I got grazed by a bullet and lost blood today, Piet. I jumped onto a truck. If I want to eat here, we're eating here. We're taking a short break.'

How much did he still need me? I could see him weighing the balance by the way he glared at me. He could get up, walk out, force this to a fight. Shoot me in the darkness of the parking lot where we'd left the truck and the van, leave the van behind. The stop had raised his suspicions.

Hurry, Eliane, I thought. I couldn't risk a glance at my watch or the clock. He watched me, a hard awful light in his eyes, so I took refuge in my beer.

Some of the suits — men speaking in hushed German — pushed past our table, making their way to their own. Piet scowled. 'I hate these suits. Rule-makers. They think they run the world. All they do is set up walls and rules and then argue amongst themselves about what those walls will be.'

'Men like you and me, we tear down the walls,' I said. I couldn't help thinking of my first few months in London, Lucy and me sitting in a wine bar on the side of Paternoster Square in the soft light of the old city, happy to be together, and excited to be doing good work.

Good work had been my family's specialty and my family's tragedy. I had killed now to stay alive, and I wasn't worrying about it, but I wouldn't have wanted to describe those moments to my father or mother. My own life had marked me with my own permanent stains, the damned blood that didn't wash off the guilty hand.

'Eh, tear them down, they build them back up.' He fell silent as the waitress set coffee down in front of us. 'We'll take our food to go, miss,' he told her.

'But . . .'

'No, Sam.' His voice was like a knife. 'I don't like this bar. I don't want to be here a moment longer after I'm done with coffee.'

This wasn't a fight I could win, and I knew now that the closer we were to delivering the shipment to Edward, the more Piet would seize command. This was his deal; I was a replacement player. Fine. Let him think I was cowed. 'All right, Piet.' But I didn't really hurry.

'You've got time to finish your coffee,' he said. 'I need to make a call. Stay here.' And he stood up and left the table, stepped outside the Taverne Chevalier. Panic inched up my bones. If he was running I would lose the only thread I had to Edward, and to Yasmin, and to whatever happened to Lucy. I couldn't see him on the front window of the bar.

My gut said, he's dumping you, follow him.

The waitress placed the bag with our order on the table. I slid her money and got up from the table.

I stepped out from Taverne Chevalier's front door. Piet stood twenty feet away, closing the cell phone. Staring at me.

351

67

I raised the bag of sandwiches. 'Are you ready to go?'

'Yes,' he said. 'Come here, Sam.'

I did and he pushed me along the street. Then into the barely-lit doorway of an art supply shop. 'What, you're going back to art school and need supplies?'

'Hands on the door.'

'Why? What's wrong?'

He ran probing hands along my legs, my arms. Searching to see if I had anything I shouldn't have had. He pulled the wad of euros from my pocket.

'That's enough. I don't have a phone, I don't have a weapon. You're really getting our partnership off to a great start after I saved your ass. Give me my money.'

He pushed the wad back into my hand. 'There. Sorry,' he added, almost as an afterthought.

I pretended to be angry. 'Christ. I pulled your ass out of the fire, I found you the Lings' shipment, I took the bigger risk today. If someone's not going to trust someone, maybe it should be me not trusting you.'

'Perhaps,' he said. 'I think you think I'm not as smart as you, as tough as you.' He was threatened by me; I'd jumped onto a moving truck and hijacked it. *Stupid.* This was about

352

machismo. 'Come on.'

'Let's sit here and eat, if the bar's making you nervous. I don't like cold food.' I had to give Eliane time to return. Otherwise I'd have to pretend I'd lost the van key in the tavern and we'd have to come back and his suspicions would skyrocket.

He seemed to feel a bit guilty about his rant so we sat on a bench on the road and ate our sandwiches. I saw a vaguely female form race around the corner on a scooter. I could tell it was Eliane and hoped that Piet couldn't. He seemed engrossed in his food, though, hunger winning out over the desire to make time.

'I need to go to the bathroom,' I said when the sandwich was done.

'Me, too,' he said.

I wanted to go back in alone; I needed that van key. Eliane was behind the bar, drawing a beer. She glanced up, caught sight of me, but gave no sign of recognition. Piet was close behind me.

We both went into the bathroom; I finished first and stepped back into the hallway. Eliane was three feet away, and she brushed by me, calling out orders to the barkeep. She pressed the key into my hand and it was in my pocket a moment later.

Piet's hand clapped me on the shoulder. 'You're right, a break helped. I got new life. Let's get going.'

We walked out into the darkness, the laughter and music of Taverne Chevalier fading as we headed down the avenue.

He kept his hand on my shoulder. In my pocket, I worked the key back onto the ring.

'So. Back to Amsterdam?' His phone call had to have been to Edward, now that we had the cigarette shipment to camouflage his military gear.

'Yes. We're meeting Edward and his people. We'll get the shipment ready with their goods and on its way to Rotterdam and then we'll get paid and you and I will go celebrate.'

'How long do we have until the meet?'

'Three hours.'

'All right,' I said.

The parking lot was in sight; I could see the truck, the van parked next to it. Nearly there. Within three hours I would either be dead or I'd have killed Piet and the kidnappers and found Yasmin. And have Edward talking to me about where my wife and child were.

'You know, Sam,' he said, 'you're right. You have proved yourself, more than once. Here. You drive the truck.'

I stopped. No. Not what I wanted.

'No, that's fine. You drive it,' I said.

'No. You drive the shipment. As a sign of trust in our partnership.'

I felt a chill settle into my bones. Either he was being sincere or he'd seen the key passed from Eliane to me.

Trust or suspicion. I still needed him; I didn't know where the rendezvous was, and if I showed up without him I'd never get inside. 'Fine, whatever, let me have the truck keys.'

He dug them out of his pocket, and traded

them for the van keys.

'Just follow me,' he said.

'What if we get separated in traffic?'

'We won't,' he said.

I got into the truck. Maybe that's all this was: he was tired of driving the truck. Maybe that's all it was. But the phone, and the weapons, were now out of my reach. And once we got to the rendezvous point, there was no need for me to go near the van.

I was still heading, defenseless and alone, into the snake pit.

68

Amsterdam, well past midnight. The night was a mirror of the city, the lights of Amsterdam reflected in the sky by a sprinkling of stars peering through the tracery of clouds. It was not a city that ever slept deeply or soundly. Too much business in Amsterdam needed the night.

I followed Piet. There would be ten of them, including Edward, if the count in the group in the video held true. We'd have to meet at a place with privacy, for the weapons to be repackaged with the cigarettes. Some of the gang would be dispatched to unload the cigs. Another group would probably be inside the facility, guarding whatever Edward's prize was. That division of targets might make it easier for me, but not for long.

Yasmin would be held separately, I guessed. I should be able to make a sweep and not worry about her in the crossfire.

Don't you need a gun, a little voice chimed in? That was, I told myself, only a temporary problem.

Piet drove to the southern edge of Amsterdam and stopped at what appeared to be an old brewery. An unweathered sign announced in Dutch that the brewery was closed for renovations. Another truck was there, unmarked. Next to it was an Audi sedan and I felt my heart jump.

The silver Audi I'd chased through the streets of London, with Edward and Lucy inside. Different license plate, but I recognized the scuff on the back bumper where he'd scraped through the jammed street to get away.

He had taken my wife. And I was close to him now. I felt a primal rage rise in me, the raw anger we like to think was banished with cave fires and wall paintings. But I couldn't be angry. I had to be cold.

Thin lights flickered in the windows. They were here. This was it.

Time to live or die.

Piet had already walked back to the truck as I got out. 'Van keys, please,' I said.

'Why?'

'I left my smokes in there.'

'I didn't know you smoked.'

'Well, I do,' I said.

'Well, hell, you got a whole truck of cigs right there.'

'I don't feel like opening crates.'

'Fine. Go get them.' And he pressed the van keys into my hand.

I turned and went back to the van. He went around the back of the truck, presumably to open up so the unloading could start.

Go.

I could only guess where Eliane had hidden the gear. Under the driver's seat.

They took your wife and your child. Be cold.

I made a show of searching the seat for the cigarettes in case Piet was watching.

Then I put my hand under the van's seat.

Nothing. I leaned over, groped under the passenger seat. Nothing. No way Eliane would have hidden it under the back seats. I glanced into the emptiness of the van.

And felt the barrel of the gun press against the back of my head.

'You tried to fool the wrong guy,' Piet hissed. 'Stupid move.'

'What the hell are you doing?' I asked.

'Your guns, your phone, your little devices. The phone went off, someone in Amsterdam trying to call you. Why do you have this stuff?'

I didn't answer him and he pushed the barrel of the gun harder against my head. 'To protect myself.'

'From me?'

'No. From *them*.'

'Them?'

I turned to look at him; he kept the barrel on my face, so that the gun slid along my cheek, settled below my eye. 'Edward and his people. What do you think they'll do to us the moment we've delivered the goods? They'll kill us, man. They don't need us anymore. We're two and they're, what, a dozen?'

'They won't hurt us.'

'Edward's not just a smuggler, Piet. I know who they are. The people who blew up the train station.'

His face went pale. 'How the hell do you know? Who are you?'

'Peter Samson, just like I said. My friend at the bar got me the gear,' I said. I didn't blink. I didn't look concerned. Because old Piet had tipped too much of his hand, confronting me outside.

If you are heading toward a rendezvous with very bad criminals, and you think you have a spy on the inside, coming with you, and you have brought said spy close to said very bad criminals, it might be a very bad idea to let the very bad criminals know that you have put them in grave danger of exposure. So I figured he hadn't said a word in warning to Edward.

All this cut through my mind in seconds. Along with the realization that Edward's team, having heard the low rumble of the truck's arrival, should be stepping out of the old brewery within seconds.

I didn't have time for Piet any more.

'Aren't you going to shoot me?' I said.

'I want to know who you work for,' he said. His life depended on information now. He'd brought the spy close, now he needed to know who I was. It was the only way to redeem himself with Edward and his people. 'Tell me, goddamn it, or I'll kill you.'

I said nothing.

'Who are you?' he raged. And then he took the gun off me because he remembered he had a better way to hurt me.

He pulled out the *wakizashi* from under his jacket, lifted the blade.

He stepped back to launch his swing; he wanted to scare me, to have me know I couldn't stop the sword from opening me up. So he stepped back too far, and he gave me room. He slashed the *wakizashi* toward me with a singing hiss. I pivoted and blocked it with a kick. The blade went halfway into the thick sole of my work boot. His melodramatic toy of a weapon stuck. For one sweet second he was so surprised he didn't know what to do.

So I grabbed the handle of the van for leverage, and kicked him with the other foot. My work boot caught him hard on the chin and he flew back, teeth flying, lip splitting.

I landed on the asphalt, awkwardly, one leg. I yanked the *wakizashi* loose from the thick, rugged sole and advanced on him. I pointed the tip at his groin.

His front teeth were gone. He tried to skitter backwards on the pavement. 'No, please.'

I yanked him to his feet, put the blade at his gut. He let out a broken-toothed mew of surprise; he thought I was going to eviscerate him.

Then I heard the brewery door open. The van was between us and the doors. I slammed a fist hard into his bloodied mouth and he crumpled.

69

I hurried into the van, crawled to the back. The gear was there, where he'd tossed it. I pulled out the two Glocks, one mounted with a silencer, the explosive charge, the cell phone.

I heard footsteps skittering on the pavement. At least two people. I wished it were more.

'Piet?' a man's voice called. Then in Dutch: 'Hurry up, Edward's pissed, we're going to be behind schedule.'

They stepped into my range, in the intermittent light of the moon. One of them saw Piet lying on the black of the pavement. He rushed forward; the second man was smarter, stopping, then falling into a protective crouch, gun at the ready.

Through the barely open back door of the van, I shot the first one in the knee. I have always heard that the pain is excruciating. The silencer made a quiet hiss. He fell with a raging howl, clutching at his leg. I shot the other one, standing over Piet, in both knees. He dropped, his knees hit the pavement. I slammed a fist into his throat and he went silent. I kicked the first guy hard and he went quiet, too.

Two down.

I ducked out of the van and ran for the door. It had been propped open. Oddly — and I didn't like anything that suggested oddity right now — the large bay doors to the brewery remained closed. With the truck here, I expected them to be opening in greeting. I didn't want to be caught in the open.

I hung at the lip of the parking lot door. No sound, no voices — only a distant murmur.

I risked a glance. The old brewery's entryway was empty, dimly lit by fluorescent lighting. Concrete floor, brick walls, high, grimy windows. I smelled the soft waft of sausage and pizza. I rushed the door. Beyond that was a brick hallway of old offices, most of the doors shut, one door open, faint light gleaming from inside.

I could hear voices, speaking in Dutch: 'You're cheating.' A man's voice, young, rough.

'You cannot cheat on a computer game.' A woman's voice.

'You know a trick.'

'Knowing a trick isn't cheating, whiner,' the woman said. Laughter from more people.

I stepped into the doorway. Five of them, four men and a woman, sat with their backs to me, hands holding video game controllers, a fictional bloodbath erupting on the screen. They were killing Nazis in the computer-generated rubble of Berlin. The room wasn't so much an office as a big storage room, and I saw a large heavy metal door.

'Hey, assholes,' I said. 'Game over.' Not a brilliant line but I wasn't thinking witty.

They all did this little jerky dance of surprise: jerk, freeze, stay frozen. The woman, Demi — I recognized her from the house Piet had taken me to — was closest to me and I pulled her close. She stiffened with terror. They dropped the

362

game controls and behind them on the screen I could see their players immediately fragged by an SS squadron.

I put the gun against Demi's head. 'Drop the weapons . . . slowly.' Three of the guys had guns in the back of their pants; I'd seen them when they stood up. Two of them obeyed. The third, a muscular youth with a hateful glint in his eye, took his out and hesitated.

'You won't get away with this,' he said. I remembered his name. Freddy.

'Do you want to die? Seriously? Drop the gun.'

He didn't, and I needed an example, so I shot him in the knee, too. All his bravado evaporated as he screamed and fell. He also dropped his gun.

'Okay, then,' I said. I kept my voice steady. 'I want Yasmin Zaid and Edward. Where are they?'

None of them answered.

'If you don't know you're useless to me.' I let the gun's aim go to the next guy.

'Past the vat room,' Demi said in a hoarse whisper. 'Down to your left. There's an old wing of offices. She's guarded.'

'How many others here?'

Her lips tightened.

'Do you think I won't shoot you because you're a woman? Get over yourself,' I said. 'How many others here?'

I knew they weren't pros when Demi said, 'Five' and Freddy gasped, 'Twelve, and more coming,' at the same time. I believed Demi. God, I hoped she was right.

'That metal door,' I said. 'Open it.'

One of the men obeyed. Freddy yelled, 'Don't help him, don't.'

'Do you want to dance again?' I said. 'Shut up.' He went quiet.

I could see inside — it was a cold room, like a giant refrigerator.

'Cell phones on the floor. Empty out your pockets.' They obeyed: five cell phones hit the floor.

I gestured them inside with the gun then slammed the door and locked it. Five more, and I didn't know if that included Edward.

I continued down the hall. The main brewery floor was dark. Thin light gleamed from up high. I could see the squat bulks of six old copper vats, concrete flooring separated them. A catwalk encircled the square of the floor up high, a few rooms and offices above the catwalk. The walls were white tile.

I heard footsteps approaching, above me on the catwalk. A man, with an assault rifle buckled across his chest. You walk on a catwalk, you tend to look down through the metal mesh. He saw me.

He opened fire. I ducked low behind a rounded vat and the shots drumming the copper sounded like a jangling of cymbals.

I could see in the distance, on a half-lower level, a long wall with a metal rectangle. The bay doors. That's where most of them would have been, I thought, when the fight began, waiting to do the work of the loading. If I stayed pinned down here they'd rush me.

I climbed inside the vat. It was low and dark and the singing of the bullets made it sound like crawling into a gong. The catwalk formed an L-shape over the opening. I waited.

The rifleman stopped shooting. He was looking for me, not wanting to waste bullets, and he'd thought I'd just hide behind the vat. I listened for the soft scrape of his feet above me and threw myself into the opening, firing into the space between the flooring and the railing. He jerked and then he fell to the cat-walk. I didn't know if he was alive or dead but he was down and not shooting at me.

But all surprise was gone now.

I ran into the loading bay area, jumping over a railing, dropping to the concrete floor. I saw a man running toward me, raising a pistol. Two more men following him. Old pallets of bottles sat to my right and I dodged behind them. Gunfire exploded the tops and shattered sprays of glass, splinters, and stale beer fountained above my head.

Three to fight. I went still. I had a Glock in each hand, Piet's *wakizashi* tucked in my back belt and an explosive charge in my jacket pocket.

The gunfire stopped.

An awful echoing silence filled the room, the smell of cordite, of old beer.

I could hear a hissed argument in Dutch. 'You go', 'No, you go', cowards daring each other to find some courage. I thought of the people they'd helped kill at the train station. I tried to calm my mind, think of efficiency, like running along the edge of the building in parkour, find the line.

One called out in Dutch, 'Throw down your guns, you can't get out.'

I moved as quietly as I could to the corner of the large pallet I'd hidden behind. I raised the Glocks, aiming down each corner from the beer pallet.

No sign that anyone was coming.

Behind me, on the far side of the huge room, I heard a muffled scream from a woman.

70

Yasmin.

I didn't have time to wait the three stooges out. The old pallets of beer were stacked in five long rectangles at one end of the dock space. Maybe forty feet between me and the external doors. I could hear at least two voices two pallets away. Like a run to make. Break it down into steps then commit each action as part of a more fluid movement.

My mind shifted to a gear it hadn't been in since I tried to save Lucy in London. Overhead a bay of fluorescents loomed. I gunned the lights. The room plunged into semi-darkness; the only light now came from the glow of the vat room.

Yasmin screamed again.

I studied the room with a *traceur*'s eye. Pallets to leap on, railing to jump, walls to bounce off. I could try to use parkour to outflank them. I wasn't sure how steady the pallets were and usually I ran with hands free, not holding guns.

I saw movement to my left and I risked standing and firing a shot, then fell back to the floor. A babbling scream rose from the other side of the pallet.

I hurried down the passageway formed by the pallets. Suddenly glass crunched under my heels.

Gunfire exploded around me, from three sides. In front, behind me, to my right.

Surrounded.

I retreated left, in the direction of the man I'd shot. I could hear feet scrabbling around, two closing behind me to cut off my retreat back to the vat room.

But I wasn't retreating. They were only looking for me between the pallets. If I wasn't where they expected I could gain a momentary advantage.

I did a standing jump and yank onto the fifteen-foot-high pallets and ran along the edge. I saw movement to my right, another guy rounding a corner where I'd been crouching twenty seconds before, and I fired. Missed him. He fired at the same time I did and I felt the bullet tear up through the jacket and score along the flesh of my back. Then heat hit my shoulder, a sting that rose into agony.

Below my feet, bottles broke, the pallet coming apart at the top. The stack gave way. Beer flooded my shoes. I knew if I tumbled into the mess I'd be cut by the jagged glass and an easy mark.

I jumped to the roof of a forklift, looking down to see a surprised face hiding behind its bulk. I fired wildly and the surprised guy went down, bullets punching into his shoulders. I jumped to the next pallet, hit the wood and didn't look back. The pain in my shoulder seared. A warm throb of blood coursed down my back. I was hurt.

I couldn't be hurt. I couldn't. I jumped off the stack and landed on concrete.

And one of the two had doubled-back on his run. I landed three feet in front of him.

He raised an assault rifle but he didn't fire. 'Drop your weapons!' he screamed.

I dropped both the Glocks.

'On the floor!'

I went to my knees. My hand twisted behind me for the *wakizashi*.

'Hands where I can see them!'

My hand closed on the *wakizashi*'s handle. I turned the sword and it sliced through the thin leather belt I wore. Thank you, Piet, for being bored, for sharpening the sword while we waited in the rain outside the sweatshop for the Lings' truck. If I'd pulled it free he would have seen it, but I made my right hand dangle. 'I'm shot in the arm,' I said. 'I can't lift it.'

He took a single step toward me. 'Who are you? Police?'

'Yeah, because the police come in one guy at a time,' I said. 'Don't be an idiot. I'm not police.'

I heard the crunch of glass behind me. My feet were in shadow; the only light coming from the vat room. Whoever was behind me would see the *wakizashi* any second.

'Who are you?' the first man yelled again.

Two more steps from behind me. The guy coming up behind me would see the blade. In three. Two. One . . .

I fell backward into the scattering of glass and rolled, my jacket protecting me from the floor full of sharp edges. The *wakizashi* swung through flesh down to bone on the leg of the guy behind me. He screamed, and the guy with the rifle froze in surprise. I yanked the sword free from its mooring of flesh and swung the *wakizashi* back, twisting to put the edge forward, and slashed through the thigh of the man before me. He bellowed and staggered back, bullets spraying into the floor as he fell. Seriously, are any of us prepared to be slashed with a sword? No. For an instant, the pain must have been so hot and fresh in the man's mind that he forgot to shoot me.

That's the key. You must ignore the pain.

I could hear someone else approaching. God, how many were there? I kicked both the men unconscious. I yanked the flash charge from my jacket, activated it and tucked it under one man's arm.

I hurried on the other side of the pallet, moving as quietly as I could, ignoring the pain.

C'mon, I thought. I heard footsteps. One set, closing fast, spraying a panicky round of fire down the passageway formed by the pallets. Bottles shattered and beer gushed.

I heard someone kneel on the glass-covered floor, murmur a name, and then the light and sound burst like a little bright warhead. A howl. I hurried around the corner, saw a man — but only one — writhing in the glass, blinded and deafened by the flash bomb. I picked up a beer bottle and smashed it on the back of his head and he went groggy. A second kick to the face left him cold; my shoulders hurt too much to try and punch.

A dozen. I'd taken out a dozen. I was barely on my feet. Still one. Still one more. Edward. I checked my Glocks. Empty. One of the men had a gun with a full clip and I took it.

I crept out of the space between the pallets.

The glass from the beer bottles was like a signal; every movement producing an audible crunch under my feet, a terrible telegraphing of my position. I moved as carefully as I could. My ears rang from the concussive blast and I was bleeding freely. Everything hurt.

Lucy. The Bundle. Yasmin, the girl I'd been sent to save, the key to the man who had stolen my family and my life. Focus. Don't give up now.

I heard nothing except the distant sobbing of the young woman.

She was valuable to Edward. Maybe the orders were to guard her at all costs.

Then I heard her voice rise into a scream. I could hear the echo coming from a hallway to the right.

Maybe Edward had gone after her, decided to make his stand close to his prize.

71

I tore down a small hallway, gun extended, ready to shoot any shadow.

Yasmin's screaming stopped. I skidded into an old circular chamber, lined with stone. It smelled of wood and spilled beer and a more recent tang of gunfire. The darkness was gray and blue and a sputtering light flickered at one side of the chamber. Three side doors, the farthest one half-open. I heard a hushed voice inside, murmuring. I strained to hear the words.

Don't be afraid. Just do as I say and all will be well. A man's voice, a low growl, full of impatience and hate.

My father has sent someone else . . . Yasmin's voice, wavering. *Please.*

I inched closer to the door.

Be quiet. And it was Edward's voice, the voice on the tape, the voice of the man who had stolen my wife. *He'll come here soon enough.*

Damn straight. Anger and hate roared up into my head and I kicked in the door. In the guttering light behind me I saw them, him crouching over Yasmin, her mouth twisted in fear. She sat on a bed and Edward had positioned himself between me and her. The scar — like a little question mark — gleamed by his eye. He held a gun in his hands.

He started to raise it.

I needed him alive. 'Drop the weapon!' I fired

and the bullet went just wide of his head. He dropped the gun. I didn't see fear in his eyes. I saw a raw calculation.

'Kick it over here!'

He obeyed. He was a big guy, broad-shouldered, muscled, bigger looking than in the videos.

I stepped on his gun. 'On the floor, now. Hands on your head.'

Yasmin was crying. Edward obeyed, scowling.

'Yasmin, it's okay. Your father sent me. I'm getting you out of here. Come here.'

She slowly inched away from Edward. He seemed to shackle her with his stare, directed fully at her, not at me.

'I know you,' Edward said as she slowly made her way toward me.

'I know you, too.'

'London.' His voice was a snake moving across stone. He had a soft British accent. The bastard smiled. 'You ran very fast. It was almost funny to watch. You made me think of a spider with its web burning. No place to go.'

'My wife. Where is she?' Yasmin was halfway between us, wiping tears from her eyes.

'That's my sole value to you, yes? Information?'

'Where is my wife?'

He laughed. 'Worth something to you, I see, knowing her final resting place. Are you afraid of knowing how she suffered?'

My skin prickled cold. No. 'You tell me and you get to live.'

'Even if I've killed Lucy? I still get to live?'

Edward laughed again. I didn't like the laughter. A man only laughs when he holds the upper hand.

'Do you mean the American woman?' Yasmin stopped two feet short of me, her hands clutching her elbows, shivering. In real life her voice was a bit higher than on the tape. 'The American woman with the baby? Lucy, yes?'

My gaze jerked to her. 'Where is she?' I hollered.

'I don't know where she is now . . . ' She seemed to fight for control of her voice. 'I don't know . . . '

Edward said, 'You want to know where your wife is? You let me and Yasmin leave. It's the best deal you're going to get today, Sam.'

I heard a footstep behind me, in the doorway. I'd missed one.

I turned and fired.

And the voltage hit me like a steam train slamming into my bones. I fought to keep the grip on my gun but the shocks, coursing along bones and tendons and spine like lightning, made it drop from my grasp. I fell to my knees. I stared at the black leather boots in front of me.

I looked up.

Lucy. Holding a Taser. Every sound was a blasting roar in my brain. Every sight a nightmare. I tried to slap the Taser needles from my body but then I saw, as if in slow motion, her thumb worked and the shattering surge hit me again.

Her boot came back, rocketed toward my head.

Darkness.

PART THREE

14–21 APRIL

'Systems do collapse, and are replaced by others. The state is only here because people choose to believe in it — because they trust its systems . . . This, then, is the threat of crime to modern society: not that it will overcome civilization with violence, but that it will undermine trust in, and thus the viability of, the system.'

— Carolyn Nordstrom, *Global Outlaws*

72

Piet Tanaka opened his eyes and blinked away blood. He took a hard, shuddering breath. The hiss of air over ruined teeth hurt so sharply he jerked up. A weight lay atop him. He shoved the form away. A man. One of Edward's thugs, shot, unconscious.

Piet pulled himself up from the concrete. He could hear the shattering sounds of gunshots inside the brewery.

It was time to leave. The job had gone very wrong. He didn't care who was winning on the inside: that fool who'd tricked him so badly or Edward's people.

He saw the van's keys, stuck in the driver's side door. He lurched into the van, started the engine, and accelerated into the night. When he realized his sword was gone he felt a feverish rage take hold of his heart. Sam, you rotten bastard.

Two kilometers down the road he had an idea. He needed a safety net. Sam worked for someone. Fine. Sam's bosses would want information. They could hide him. It was time to defect.

It had been a bar in Brussels where the manager got Sam his gear; well, Sam had used another bar in Amsterdam to establish his bonafides, and said he knew the owner. De Rode Prins. The bars must be connected, and there he could look for Sam's bosses to make a deal. He blinked through the pain — his tongue kept probing where his front teeth once were and his gums gave off a hard throb — and he headed for the Prinsengracht. The bar would be closed. But he could break in, find out who Peter Samson worked for.

73

Pain — from my head to my shoulder to my back — forced open my eyes. I slowly sat up. Everything hurt. Dried blood on my head, my cheek, drool stuck to my lips. I was in a small stone room. No bed; file cabinets. My shirt and my jacket were hiked up.

Then I saw Lucy, sitting across the room from me.

I blinked at her.

'Hello, Sam.'

'You cut your hair,' I said. My voice sounded thick, heavy, broken.

'I'm supposed to kill you,' she said. Five words to end a conversation before it started. I could hear a truck's engine rumbling in the distance. The plonking sounds of crates being moved. I heard those sounds and I couldn't wrap my head around the words she had just spoken to me.

'Lucy . . .'

'I told Edward I would take care of you, but *take care* has a whole range of meanings.'

'Lucy. Where is the baby?' My mind swirled with a thousand questions but that was the one that knifed through the shock.

'Sam. You'll die if you don't listen to me.'

I looked at the flat of her stomach. Her dark blouse was neatly tucked into blue jeans. 'Where is our son?'

'He's not your concern, Sam.'

'He's my only concern. Now that I know what you are.' Hello, anger, boiling up in my chest.

'Will you please listen, monkey? I am trying to save you.'

'You. I don't even have the words for what *you* are.'

'You'd rather argue with me than live?'

'What you are. I know what you are now,' I said.

'Smarter. Quicker. Stronger. Richer. You could try those on for size.'

The woman I loved. I *thought* I loved. She sat there, wearing the face and the body that I knew so well, that I'd treasured; she spoke with the voice that had murmured love into my ear, she regarded me with the intelligence that sealed the deal to spend my life with her. But she was a stranger. I hadn't known her.

Let me say that again: *I hadn't known her.*

She had been a complete and utter lie and she had stolen far more than three years of my life. The scale of the lie staggered me. She had stolen my sense of who I was, and what I knew in the world. The marriage was done and I didn't even have time to grieve for it. All this flashed through my head in a second, not even in words, just a coldness that covered me.

'All right, smart and rich,' I said. 'Where is our child?'

'Don't you want to know why?'

'No. I'll ask and you'll lie, or you'll not tell me. You've done what you've done and that's it,' I said. 'I don't understand it but I don't *need* to understand it. I only need to stop you.'

'Well, that's not going to happen.' Now she showed me a half-smile, the one when I used to tease her and she'd tease back.

'Fine. We'll play it your way. Tell me why. You're clearly dying to,' I said. 'You seem to have a reason for keeping me alive. Just to taunt me?'

'I'm not heartless, Sam. I do have regard for you. You were a good cook. Good in bed. Thoughtful company. You were a good husband.'

'I was good camouflage,' I said. 'I was a good pawn.'

'I'll bet you insisted to the Company that I was innocent. Very chivalrous.'

'Very naïve.'

'No. I'm just very good at fooling people,' she said. An emptiness seemed to hollow out her words.

I got to unsteady feet, my head rocking. 'What is going on here, Lucy? Who are these people, what are you doing?'

'Sweet mystery,' she said. 'I'm supposed to find out what you know and shoot you. But I can't. I can't just shoot you in cold blood, Sam. I think . . . '

I took a shambling step toward her and she raised the gun. 'It's not cold blood if you attack me. Then I do what I have to, Sam. And I assume you don't want to die.'

I stopped. 'Yes.'

'I'm glad I didn't wreck your will to live, then.' I couldn't read the emotion in her face. She wasn't smug, despite her earlier words about being smarter and richer. She looked unsure.

Like she wasn't used to seeing consequences staring back at her.

'I want to know where our son is.'

'You say nothing to the police, to the Company, that I'm alive. You don't mention me and, in a week or so, I'll be in touch with you. I'll tell you what you need to know to find the baby. You can have him. Just say you never saw me, okay?'

'Is the baby all right?'

'He's safe, Sam.' She glanced up at me. 'A healthy, beautiful boy. We made us a good one.' She stood and I saw a swallow work her throat. A silencer capped her gun. 'I really need to go. Now. So here's what we're going to do. I am going to leave. You are going to be quiet and not make a sound. Edward and I will be on our way. Eventually the police will come and you will have to answer questions. You keep my name out of it — and I'll know if you do or not — and then I'll let you know where the baby is. Mention me and you'll never, ever see him.'

'Why would you let me live?'

'I stole three years of your life. This is restitution.' Her voice was unsteady. The spouse always knows. August had said that, so had Howell. The spouse always knows when treason is in the house. I hadn't.

'That's not reason enough. Why?' She had to have another reason. One based on her own advantage.

'Don't be an ingrate,' Lucy said.

I thought of our three years together, how

every word, every action, had been choreographed to protect her.

'Did you ever love me?' I asked. I hated asking; it didn't matter. She didn't love me now. Any question was sentiment. I'd lost years of my life as surely as if stranded on an island or walled in a prison. The only thing that could matter was my child, not my ego.

'I must have. You're still breathing.'

She looked past my shoulder. Out the window. And I heard the blast of gunfire. She slammed the door, locked it. I staggered to the door. I started kicking the lock, trying to break it.

The gunfire stopped. I looked out the window. A van roared into sight, spilling three men out onto the pavement.

One of them was Howell.

74

Piet had parked his van on a side street and stumbled along the Prinsengracht. He remembered walking along the grand canals with his mother, hand in hand, before Mama would go to her job, kneeling before the disgusting strangers. He'd dreamed of living in one of these nice homes, with the canal glistening in the morning light. He'd become a great artist and have a studio along the Prinsengracht or the Herengracht. It had never happened, and now it never would.

Most of the windows were dark but the apartment immediately above the Rode Prins had every light blazing.

He staggered to the Rode Prins's front door. What was the barman's name? Henrik. He could ask for Henrik. Maybe Henrik was the manager; maybe he lived above the bar.

The job had gotten too messy. Information on Edward could buy him passage. He'd go someplace quiet like Panama or Honduras. Warm, under bright skies and slack laws. Lots of girls there that could be shipped up to brothels in the States and Canada. He'd start over. You could always start over when you had good people skills.

Heavy velvet curtains covered both the front windows and the door. He knocked on the door. Once, almost timidly. He didn't want to attract police attention. He didn't see that a small camera, hidden in the doorway, watched his moves. He knocked again, slightly louder, and was very surprised when the curtain on the front door slid slowly open. A woman stared at him through the glass and to his surprise he felt a shiver. Odd, the night wasn't cold. Maybe he was losing blood.

'Samson sent me. He needs help. Please.'

The woman seemed to study him. She was a nice little number, maybe thirty, but a bit older wasn't always a drawback. Blonde hair, petite. Through the pain he assessed her, out of habit, as though she might bring him value. He remembered her now; he'd seen her in the bar before, when he drank beer with Sam. A prime little number, he'd joked.

'I don't know who Samson is and the bar is closed.' She spoke with the very slightest muddle of some eastern European and British accent. Her words were hard and precise. He liked the accent. He'd developed a taste for hearing broken English with Slavic pronunciations, usually in a begging scream. He knew how to deal with Slavic girls.

'I don't care if it's closed. I want to see Henrik or whoever runs the place. I got information to sell.' He remembered the name Samson had used at Taverne Chevalier in Brussels. 'Roger Cadet. That's who I want to see, whoever works with Roger Cadet.'

'What sort of information?'

'On who Peter Samson is chasing.'

'His name's not Peter Samson,' the woman

385

said. Now he really didn't like her tone, a bit clipped and impatient. Bitch needed a lesson in respect, he thought. 'It's just Sam,' she said.

'Well, Sam what-the-hell-ever. He works with you, right? You and the people in Brussels with the same bar? Can you make me a deal or not, bitch?'

She smiled at him. 'Yes, I think I have a deal for you.'

He lowered his voice to a hiss. 'Your boy is fighting some badasses right now. He needs help.'

'And you want protection from those same people. Your type, it is very predictable to me.'

He didn't know what she meant. He didn't care. 'I got stuff of value.'

She looked hard at him. 'I am Sam's . . . superior. Come inside.'

She opened the door and he stumbled in. She closed the door behind him and shut the curtains. 'Christ. Thank you. Can I get a drink?'

She went to the bar, poured a stiff shot of jenever. He eased onto a stool and drank it down. The alcohol seared his lacerated gums. 'Sam kicked my teeth out.' He sounded like a whiny child.

She stayed on the other side of the bar and poured him another. 'Yet you are here.'

'Sam had backing. You don't just show up at a bar and leave armed to the teeth.' He slammed the second one down. Warmth seeped through him.

'My name is Mila,' she said. 'And I'm not

offering anything in trade. You will simply tell me where Sam is.'

Piet spat blood onto the bar, feeling nauseous. 'Nothing's free in this world.' He poured himself a refill and gulped the jenever again.

'Pain is.' She raised a small black stick. A baton. It telescoped out to an arm's length. And she lashed it hard across his nose and mouth. He screeched in agony as the jenever glass shattered in his face. He swung blindly toward her and missed. She vaulted over the bar and began to hit him with a precision that rivaled a surgeon's, delving past nerve and blood vessel to diseased tissue. He felt his nose break on her second blow. He lunged, trying to close his massive arms around her pixie's frame, and she shattered his knee with a blow. Air vacated his lungs.

Her fist closed around his testicles and agony replaced breathing. Then she hammered her forehead against the broken nose and he lay flat on the floor.

He opened his eyes. A lock of her blonde hair, daubed with his blood, lay between her eyes. She was breathing hard.

'Do not move,' Mila said. 'Do not raise your hands. Do not do anything except breathe and listen.'

He gasped and he listened.

'I know what you did to the women in the machinists' shop,' she whispered. 'I know. I know what you are. In the old days, Piet, you would have been the captain of a slave ship. Or a Nazi commandant, whipping laborers to death. You are cut from the same foul fabric. I know what you are. I know every inch of what you are.'

He moaned and writhed. His knee. The thought that he might never ever walk right again scratched past the pain in his brain.

'The bar has a concrete floor. The walls are soundproofed. None of that is an accident,' she said. She ran the edge of the telescoping baton along his shattered knee. 'You will tell me what I want to know or I will rape you with this baton.'

A cold terror enclosed his heart. He looked up at her and saw, in a flash across her face, all the women he had sold. Past her shoulder he saw the red prince, in his portrait, the splatters of paint marring his face. He could see his own blood splatters, low on the bar's front.

'Do you understand me?' Mila said.

'Y-yes.'

'Where is Sam?'

He babbled out the address of the brewery and directions. She moved the baton toward his groin. 'Please . . . please . . . '

'Shut up. You don't get to ask for please. You don't get to ask for mercy. Those are human concerns, and you are a human being in species only.' She stood. He sobbed, clutching his knee, moaning in pain.

'Stand up,' she said.

'I can't, I can't, you bitch.'

'It would take ten of you to make a real person. You shot one of the Moldovan girls in the calf when she fought you,' Mila said. 'I know. She told me. *She* managed to stand. I'm just seeing if you're made as tough as those women were. Stand — or the baton goes up your sorry

388

ass. Ten. Nine. Eight . . . '

On two, he was on unsteady feet, shuddering in pain and rage.

'Listen,' he said. 'It's not my fault, it's just a business . . . I had to make money. My parents are ill . . . '

'Shut up,' she said. 'You are Piet Tanaka. You never knew your father and your mother is a dead whore. I don't care that you hurt right now. No one cares. You made your choice about life. Your whining bores me.'

Tears leaked from his eyes. 'I told you, I can provide information . . . '

'Those girls you send. To Israel, to Britain, to Spain, to Africa. They don't get mercy. They don't get to cut a deal. They don't get traded to the police. They get used up and then they get killed. They get raped two dozen times a day.'

'Please . . . ' Piet tried again.

'I think you need to know what it's like. To be taken into a dark room and know that you are only there to be used. To be hurt. To be treated as less than human.'

Piet grabbed the brass railing along the floor, in front of the bar, squeezing it in agony. He sobbed.

She pulled a phone from her pocket and dialed a number. 'Hello? Nadia?'

Nadia was the name of one of the girls. He remembered: the redhead.

'I have him. He has a broken leg, a broken nose, and he's beat up good. He can't get away from you. He can't hurt you. Do you want me to bring him? You all could do with him what you like.' A pause that lengthened. 'Are you sure? It might make you feel better. No. All right, then.'

She rang off. 'The women don't want to ever see you again. I guess they're better than you.' Mila shrugged. She closed the baton.

'Please . . . please.'

'The girls are also better than me.' She pulled a gun from the small of her back and she shot him in the crotch. Pain beyond imagination. He screamed and writhed and howled and clawed at the concrete.

Mila began to count. Leisurely. 'One-Amsterdam. Two-Amsterdam. Three-Amsterdam,' while Piet sobbed and shuddered on the concrete. When she reached eight — one count for each young woman she'd saved from him — she put a mercy bullet between his eyes. He jerked, his corpse hissed out a purring breath, and lay still.

She didn't look at him again. She picked up the phone and called Henrik. He answered on the third ring.

'I need you to clean up a very serious mess. Use the dump site out past the airport — and keep the bar closed today until you hear from me.'

'I understand,' Henrik said.

She unlocked the door, relocked it, and hurried to her car, arrowing onto the still streets. She started to shake about five minutes out of town, thinking of the dying man's terrified eyes. A gaze that pled for a mercy she could not give.

Do you think he ever thought of the women's

390

eyes? Mila asked herself. He never did. Ever. Let it go.

She did and she drove. She wondered if Sam Capra was still alive, if she would ever tell him what she'd done. She thought not.

75

I felt the lock give. I pushed open the door. My back was soaked with sweat.

I ran upstairs, slowly. I could hear distant shots. The men lay where I'd left them, except for one. He was by the wall.

All of them had bullet holes in their foreheads.

I ran up to the vat room. The guard I'd shot on the catwalk was down by the stairs now. Bullet hole in forehead.

I stumbled up the hallway to the storage room. The spill of cell phones still lay on the floor; the video game had run its course, showing an empty battlefield. The steel door was partly open; I pried it back. The five I'd corralled into the freezer room sat slumped. All of them shot dead at point-blank range.

I felt stunned. Edward had killed his entire team.

Why?

I hurried back up to the loading dock area. It smelled of blood and beer.

I could surrender to Howell, tell him about Lucy.

And hope that he believed me? If Lucy was already gone, I had no proof. And Howell would not let me escape again.

So.

No surrender.

I had to get out without being seen.

I heard the back door crashing open. I ran. Or rather, I half-stumbled, half-ran. I darted through the wide open rooms, ran past the dead men. A window in the brickwork faced an empty field and a slightly decrepit windmill. First one I'd seen since getting to Holland.

I pulled myself up to the window, worked the lock, shoved it open.

'Stop! Sam Capra!' Howell's voice rang out like a bolt from the blue. I stopped. I shouldn't have. But I did. I looked behind me and he had a gun leveled at me, two men behind him, Glocks aimed at me.

'Step away from the window, Sam.'

'She was just here,' I said. 'Lucy. She was just here.'

'Step away from the window and we'll talk about it,' he said. He wanted me alive.

'You don't believe me,' I said. 'I know. She was just here. I came here to rescue a hostage they have and Lucy is with them. You were right. I was wrong.'

Howell's voice was stone. 'Let's talk about it, Sam. Come tell me what you know and we'll find her.'

I looked at him, in his pressed, perfect suit and his steel-rimmed glasses and his stage actor's voice. I hated him. 'I'm going to find her myself. She's alive. She lost the baby.' I didn't want him asking about my child.

'Just come down, Sam.'

They were going to shoot me; that was my last invitation. 'How did you know where I was?'

He nearly laughed. 'Our informant in the Ling

393

organization wasn't happy you robbed their shipment. She called us. We tracked the truck with a GPS device the Lings keep hidden inside the cab. I can guess how you found out about the Lings. August went for a long walk the other night, didn't he?' He shook his head. 'You should be ashamed, ruining your friend's career. Get down from the window, Sam, or I shoot you in the back.'

I considered my options. Get shot or throw myself through the window or surrender. None were good. He would not let me escape from him again. I'd be bound and tied and kept with a pistol to my temple and not given a mockery of a life in Brooklyn. I'd be back in that prison that wasn't supposed to exist, the plaything of Howell's internal affairs group inside the Company.

I got down from the window. I staggered and I put my hands in the air. And the three of them closed in on me, with fists and guns.

76

They cuffed my wrists, they shackled my ankles, and they dragged me to their van. They shoved me inside; Howell sat across from me. He briefly examined my injuries; his fingers probed my head, my back, my shoulder.

'Jesus, Sam, you're a mess.' Then he told his two puppies to start processing the scene. The van door slammed closed. We were alone.

'I need a doctor,' I said. I enjoy stating the obvious.

'You'll get one if you cooperate. How did you know August was in Holland?'

'I saw him, when I stopped a guy from shooting him at that machinists' shop,' I said. 'I stopped those psycho twins from shooting you, too. And you're welcome.' I could smell my own blood sticking to the clothes on my back, my arm. My injuries were untreated; I'd been Tasered and then tranquilized. My limbs felt heavy and awful and disconnected from bone and tissue.

'August got sent home because he was hurt. I'm glad. I think he would have affected my judgment regarding you. He is actually your friend, useless as that position is to him.'

'I can explain all this. Sort of.'

'Listening.'

I took a painful breath. 'I've been undercover. Kind of.'

'Governments and police agencies give cover. You pretending you're someone else is just breaking the law, Sam. Sort of, kind of.'

'Please, I want to talk to Langley. This guy, Edward, that took Lucy — he's moving illicit weapons of some sort.'

'Is that who shot at us as we arrived?'

'Yes. I don't know. Was it a truck?'

'We didn't see a truck leave. A man in an Audi shot at us as we arrived.'

'Audi. That's him. Please, take me seriously. Call the ports.' But Edward wouldn't use Rotterdam. Not with this heat. He'd move the weapons out of France, or Belgium, or Spain. 'Here, I can tell you what was in the Ling shipment. You can stop it. Call Langley, get authorization. I'll talk to them . . . '

'Maybe Langley doesn't want to talk to you, Sam. Maybe Langley just wants you to go away and stop being a giant pain in the ass.'

I swallowed. 'What I said about Lucy is true. Please. She was here . . . '

He raised a hand. 'I'm going to offer you a deal, Sam. I want you to consider it carefully, because right now your life is in my hands in a way it never was before. I don't like your answers, I put a bullet in your brain and we're done. I have permission to do whatever I need to do to you.'

'The Company won't let you execute me. They want to know what I know. They want the connections I've made here. They want information and I have it.'

'The Company doesn't know that I have you

396

yet, Sam. Right now, you and I get to write our own history. You were found in a building full of dead bodies.'

'The woman, and one of the men — they have tattoos like the guy in Brooklyn who tried to kill me. Novem Soles. You asked me about it, well, here they are.'

He stared at me, ran a finger along his chin. 'And you killed them all?'

'No! Edward killed them because he didn't need them any more.'

Howell folded his arms and he looked at me with a glare I had not seen on his face since I had been his prisoner in Poland. 'I think you're the sole survivor, Sam, but I think these people were your colleagues. I think they helped you blow up the London office and I think they helped you escape me in New York. The guy in Brooklyn could have brought you your money and papers to escape, and you killed him to keep him quiet.'

'He tried to kill me. These people sent him to kill me.' And then I wondered: Edward or Lucy? It had to be Edward who'd dispatched the assassin. Lucy had let me live twice.

'And where's the lovely Mrs Capra?'

'She Tasered me and she left. Look at my chest. I've got the Taser rash.'

He opened my shirt and inspected the needle marks.

'So she works with these people. Goodness, after all those months you kept insisting on her innocence.' His tone was mocking.

'I'm a good husband,' I said. 'You don't

397

assume your wife is a traitor or a criminal. I saw her taken by Edward. She saved my life. Twice.'

'I think you were both working with this group, gang, whatever. I think she turned, and then she turned you. I tend to go for the simplest explanation.'

'That's because you're simple,' I said. 'Life isn't. *This* isn't. I don't understand why Lucy's done what she's done.'

'Where's your baby?'

I looked at my knees. I didn't know what to say. I didn't want him to know she'd offered me my child for silence. A silence I'd already broken. So I looked up and said: 'Lucy lost the baby.'

He studied my face for a long time. 'Where is Lucy? Where will she go?'

'I don't know. But I'm going to find her and I'm going to find out the truth,' I said.

'Uh, no, you're not,' Howell said. I swear bureaucrats have a smug voice they save for moments like this, ones they can savor.

'Yes, I am. Look, Howell, if I was guilty and I was caught, I'd be cutting a deal. I don't want your deal. I'm not going to confess to anything I haven't done. Put away your knives and your water-boards because I will never confess to what I haven't done. Ever. All I care about is finding Lucy.'

'Convince me, Sam. Tell me the whole story of what's happened since New York and maybe I can help you find her. Who got you off the boat? Who's been funding you and supplying you?'

'I can't.'

'You helped a man escape who fired on me and my men.'

'*I* didn't shoot at you. I killed men firing on your agents. They used to give medals for that.'

He grabbed my shirt and slammed my head against the van's wall. It hurt. My body felt wracked with pain. 'I want the whole truth, Sam. Everything.'

'Why don't you believe me? Why? Why?' I screamed into his face. 'Why don't you even *try* to believe me?' Spittle from my mouth sprayed his face. He leaned back.

I fought for calm. Pain wracked my body. I'd been beaten, shot, and the implacable doubt on Howell's face made me blind with rage. He just stared at me.

'Why aren't we at a Company safe house?' I asked. 'Why aren't you recording what I'm saying, in front of witnesses? Where are the Dutch intelligence service? None of this is protocol.'

'Pot, meet kettle,' he said. 'Sam, you have no place to lecture me on right and wrong. The whole Company is going to know soon enough that you are a traitor.'

The word was like a lash against my skin. 'I'm not a traitor.'

'You want me to believe you? Then tell me everything.'

I blew out a long hiss of air. I had to give him more to get to a position of strength. 'This Edward used the Centraal Station bombing to kill the Money Czar we were investigating in

London. A supposed financier for criminal networks, the biggest ones that connect back into government. I don't understand why Edward killed this man, but he did,' I said. 'He's smuggling contraband, bad stuff, into the States and he needed that shipment I stole as camouflage for whatever he's shipping. It could be a bomb, it could be plague, it could be people. I don't *know*. I could have found out if you hadn't interfered.'

'Let's say you're telling me the truth and that you *are* innocent. How did you find these people, Sam? How did you learn about them? How do you know any of these details? Who helped you find this Edward, who got you into Holland?'

It was the wrong question. Realization bolted into my bones. 'Don't you care about what his operation is?'

'I don't believe a word you say until you tell me who has been helping you.'

'Where is your curiosity about Edward's shipment?'

'First things first.' He pushed a photo at me. Me and Mila, at the train station in Rotterdam. Then another one, at the train station in Amsterdam. 'Who is this woman?'

I pretended to frown at the photo. 'Someone who rode on the train with me. I don't know her.'

'You do. We questioned a conductor on the train. You traveled together. You sat together and talked.'

'Oh, her. Yes. Lovely face but horrible breath. I

offered her an Altoid. That was the extent of our interaction.'

'Bull. Where have you been staying in Amsterdam?'

'In hostels. Cheap, pay cash. I'm young enough to look like a wandering grad student.'

'Which hostels?'

'Let me get this straight,' I said. 'I have just told you that the guy who bombed the London office is smuggling seriously dangerous goods into America, and you want to know what hostel I stayed at?'

'If he can smuggle this stuff in, it's because you provided him with the camouflage,' Howell said. 'What I've caught you doing is helping this guy.'

I heard a noise outside, like a man falling against the side of the van and sliding to the pavement. A yell.

Howell whipped out a pistol, aimed it at my head.

'I'm tied up,' I said. 'I'm not the threat.'

He moved the gun away from me and I hammered my foot hard into his jaw. I hope I broke it because I was really tired of hearing him talk. Shutting up for a long while would do Howell a world of good. He slammed against the side of the van and I launched myself toward him, my hands useless and bound behind me but I didn't care. I wasn't rational. I just wanted him to shut up and listen to me. I wanted his silent belief.

I hit him hard with my head, slammed my skull upwards to catch him under the jaw. He gurgled and a freshet of blood oozed from his mouth. I slammed my head into his and he went down. I lost my balance and collapsed on top of him.

The van door opened and I expected to see one of his puppies there.

Mila.

'Finally,' I said.

She sliced my plastic restraints off and I helped her put the two Company guys into the van; both were unconscious but not seriously injured. She slammed the van doors shut, locked them, tossed the keys into the field behind the brewery. We got into her car and she gunned it toward Amsterdam. The day was going to be a cloudy, gray one; it matched my mood.

'Thank you,' I said.

'You are welcome.' She sounded weary.

'How did you find me?'

'Your friend Piet.'

'Piet is not my friend.'

'Piet came to the Rode Prins. He was panicked. He thought he could trade information for sanctuary, for whoever you worked for.'

'And Piet talked.'

'Piet talked.' Now her voice was cool iron.

'Is Piet still talking?'

'Piet is done talking.'

'What did you do to him?'

'Such concern for the rapist and the slaver.'

'My concern is not for him. My concern is for you.'

I put my hand on hers. She shrugged it off.

'Don't worry your bloodied and beaten head about me, Sam. I'm fine. Never felt better.'

'You killed him.'

'He needed killing.' She raised an eyebrow. 'Did you find this Edward? Did you find Yasmin?'

'I found my wife.'

77

Mila's resources included a doctor; I woke up in the bed in the apartment above the Rode Prins with an old man poking at me. He was bald and frowning and his breath smelled like hard-boiled eggs.

'You're a wreck, young man,' he said to me.

'Yes.' In more ways than one, I thought, but I'd sooner die than admit that.

'I stitched and bandaged your head. And cleaned out your shoulder. The muscle will be sore, you should rest it. The back injury required several stitches, like a furrow it was. So drink fluids. Rest. I leave you some pain pills. Do not abuse them.' He turned to Mila and said, 'I know you are no Nightingale, woman. Make sure he rests.' He extended a finger but did not wag it.

Mila nodded. The doctor packed a bag and scooted an array of medical equipment back into the storage room. I watched him. Rather I stared off into space and thought about what I was going to do now.

'Are you hungry?' Mila asked. 'Henrik made potato soup, it's very good.'

'I'm mostly thirsty.'

She brought me cold water, and I drank it greedily. I felt like a bus had hit me then backed over my body several times just to ensure a high level of misery. I drank more water and then yes,

404

I was hungry, and I ate a huge bowl of the potato soup, dotted with Gruyère cheese and with bits of ham.

Mila watched me eat and said nothing. But she was Mila, and she waited until my spoon scraped the bottom of the bowl. 'I am sorry, Sam.' She said it like the words tasted funny in her mouth.

'I know you are.'

'Can you tell me all that happened?'

I explained. Mila listened in silence. When I was done she said, 'So your Lucy is a traitor.'

'She is,' I said. The canal outside was very quiet. I listened to my own stupid heart still beating. Okay. She was a traitor. To me, to her country. Okay. I had to deal. I'd heard the words for months, from Howell and even from August, and I hadn't believed them. I hadn't *wanted* to believe them. No fool like a fool in love.

I don't mind calling myself a fool. We've all been fools at some curve in our lives. But I had been so sure that I knew her.

Why didn't she kill you?

I thought, even weak in bed, that I could go downstairs and rip the beer taps from the bar, smash every window, knock down the brown walls. My rage felt like strength enough. Even with the pain in my body and my head.

Why didn't she kill you?

That was the question that defied both brain and heart. She could have put a bullet in my head. And why hadn't she let me die in the bombing in London? No way that she loved me. That entire life had been a cheap fiction, sold

405

with great competence and warm smiles and teasing kisses and long, shuddering nights, joined at hip and heart.

'Why did she leave you alive?' Mila said, as though she could see my thoughts hovering about my head.

'There has to be a reason,' I said.

'Your child?'

'She has hidden him somewhere. If I keep quiet that she's alive she'll call me and tell me where he is.' I kept my voice steady.

'Sam. My employers and I, we can help you . . . perhaps, to find your child.'

'She'll never call. My son is her shield. We're not done. She and Edward took Yasmin. I am going to find her.'

'Where?'

'I am going to call the Company and alert them, and alert Customs. Maybe they'll find Edward's shipment; they have the resources. Howell didn't believe me. Someone will. Maybe August Holdwine.'

'Try, if you like, but this Edward is no fool. He'll disable the GPS trackers. There will be entirely new manifests for those cigarettes, there will be no way to trace them. Their crates will be labeled as an entirely different product now. Customs won't shut down Rotterdam on what they'll consider a prank call. And if the Company believes you to be a traitor, they'll think your warning is simply a lie or a diversion. Your friend will be trumped.'

She was right. 'Howell was a lot more interested in who'd helped me than my phantom

406

shipment. He's after a group called Novem Soles. I think he thinks you're it.'

'Did you speak of me?'

'No. Never.'

She stood. 'I didn't think you would. I am glad I don't have to kill you.'

'Well, I'm glad too, Mila.'

'Rest now like the doctor said.'

I closed my eyes. I kept thinking, in all the spin of information that I now had, that I was missing some vital element — a fact or an insight worming its way through my brain that could provide an answer. It all went back to London. The bombing to protect the man that Edward himself later murdered. Somehow, that was key. Work I'd done in London was worth all this grief to Edward and his people.

'I will. For a bit. But we're going to London.'

'Why London?'

'I want to see Zaid. He put us on this job and ever since he's been avoiding us and he knows more than he's ever been willing to share. He gave Edward weapons to smuggle. Now that the shipment has reached Edward, maybe Zaid is supposed to get Yasmin back. So we go to Zaid's unannounced. Surprise him.'

'I will have to see.'

'Your bosses won't approve? Is Zaid one of your bosses?'

She walked over to the table, set the glass on it. 'No. But he is connected to them.'

'Who am I working for, Mila?'

'Me.'

'I think I've fought hard enough for you to

deserve an answer. I could have given you to the Company. I didn't. I wouldn't.'

'You might do anything to get your child back.' She raised a hand before I could interrupt her. 'Sam. You work for me. Let's leave it at that. If you wish to stop working for me, you may rest here, for however long you need, until you feel ready to leave. And we will not bother you if you do not bother us.'

'You have resources I need to find my child,' I said.

'That is an uncomfortable truth. For you.'

I looked out the window. 'You dropped out of sight for a while, Mila.'

'I was busy.'

'How are the women?'

'They're safe. We'll get them back to their families, or find a place that's safe for them.'

'I'm glad you helped them but you could have let the police handle them. I needed your help.'

'I could *not* let the police handle it,' she said. 'I needed to. The police deport them, they just go back to Moldova where they could be targeted by the recruiters and the traffickers for revenge. Such has happened before. They need protection, them and their families. I had to arrange that.'

'I understand.' I closed my eyes. 'I am going to find Bahjat Zaid. I am going to go to London in the morning. Either you can arrange the travel or I'll risk using one of my forged passports and getting picked up at the airport or the ferry. Howell will be looking for me. Get me into England, if you're so clever.'

'You won't give up, will you.'

'I have a child to find. I cannot give up, Mila. My kid is to me what those women were to you. Innocents who cannot be abandoned. I can't stop.'

She got up and closed the door. I sat in bed and I swallowed one of the pills the doctor had left and then I fell into dreamless sleep.

78

Monday in London. Gray, bleak, the sky smeared with rain. My body hurt but not as bad as yesterday. I'd slept the rest of the day until early the next morning, gotten dressed in new clothes Mila brought me, and we'd taken a private jet to London. Very posh. Mila's deep-pocketed employers must have given us the okay to chase down Bahjat Zaid. She used one of the new passports for me and there were no problems with immigration. Mila had a Jaguar waiting for us.

It was strange to be on British soil; where I'd been happiest, where I'd faced the worst day of my life.

Zaid's office was near the Bank of England Museum, in a modern tower. Mila and I were dressed casually: slacks, shirts, jackets. I wore a dark cap to mask the bandage on my head. Zaid's secretary at Militronics gave us a chilly smile.

'Mr Zaid is not available,' the secretary said. 'He was called away on a matter of urgent import.'

I glanced at Mila.

'Urgent import?' she said. 'Do you really talk like that?'

The secretary frowned. 'Perhaps if you'd care to leave a message?'

'You tell him that Sam and Mila came by to

talk to him about his daughter. We know where she's been.'

The secretary's frown deepened. 'He left to go see his daughter, sir,' she said. 'But I will relay the message.'

'When did he leave?'

'About ten minutes ago.'

We left. We stood on the busy street corner. 'Yasmin's contacted him,' I said.

'Or they've finally worked out an exchange,' Mila said.

'We need to find where he's at. Because if they're delivering Yasmin to him, then Lucy and Edward are there.'

We walked back to the Jaguar. 'You drive,' she said. I got behind the wheel and she opened the glove compartment. A modified netbook, wired into the car's satellite system, lay inside. She slid it out, opened it, and began to type furiously on the small keyboard.

'There are cameras all over London,' she said. 'For traffic and security. We have limited access to the grid. Let's find out if we can see when Bahjat left.'

She found a video feed that displayed the front of Zaid's building, rolled it back to the time Zaid stepped out of the building. A Mercedes was brought to the curb, the driver got out, Zaid got inside. He headed up Princes Street.

Mila opened another window on the netbook. Found him turning onto Gresham Street. Followed him making a turn onto St Martin's Le Grand, past the Museum of London. Then it looked like she lost him. She rechecked the video. He was heading north on Aldersgate Street. She tapped keys and a map of London appeared in the corner, turning the camera stations she'd tapped red so we could see his route through the city.

It was time-consuming, trying to spot his car in the press of autos, backtracking when she missed it, hoping he hadn't made a turn when the video feed wasn't snapping images.

A few more dots and she said. 'He's gone to St Pancras. I'm a fool. Driving fast, now, come on!'

'What's at St Pancras?'

'The Eurostar arrives there. The train. From Holland and Belgium. Edward may have decided now to give Yasmin back.'

Driving in London is often an exercise in madness and patience. I drove like a man possessed.

'This doesn't make sense. Say Edward has decided to give Yasmin back,' I said. 'They could easily have asked for Zaid to come to Holland. But they take the risk of moving her, a kidnapping victim? So they want something from Zaid, goods he couldn't bring to them.'

'Sam,' she said. 'If Lucy is here with them, and we catch them, would you like me to kill her for you? I know it may be hard for you to do so.'

It was the single strangest offer I had received in a life full of bizarre opportunities. 'Thank you, no. I don't want you to harm her. I will deal with Lucy.'

'Unwise. I have no baggage with her to slow me. I am worried enough if you are emotionally stable for this, knowing she is a crazy loser bitch.'

'I won't hesitate if need be.'

'The words 'if need be' are hesitation,' she said, and she was right.

'I want to talk to her.'

'The child. Forgive me. I mean no cruelty. But you don't even know if she had the baby, Sam. You have no proof the child is alive.'

'I don't think she's lying about this.'

'She's lied to you every second of the day for the past three years. Now she tells the truth?' Mila made a disgusted snort. The tires lost their hold on the road, hissed wetly as they grappled for the grip. I eased up and the car regained its footing as we sliced through an intersection.

'She could have killed me. Why would she spare me and lie to me?'

'A thousand reasons. She wanted you found, alive, with all those dead people. Again, you alive is a distraction for the Company. You attract blame and investigation. She wanted to feed you false information. She is cruel and she toys with you. Leave her to me.'

'You don't touch her, Mila,' I said. 'You do not touch her. I want to know where my kid is. She knows.'

Then Mila said the truest thing I'd heard in months: 'Your wife has made herself bulletproof to you with that lie, Sam. You do not know that there is a baby any more. Or that it is even yours.'

'It's mine,' I said.

'She lied about everything else. Perhaps she and this Edward were lovers here in London.'

'Thank you for the head screw.' Then I made

my words bricks: slow and steadily added, building a wall. 'I have considered all these options, long before you did,' I said. 'I knew maybe she'd fooled me, maybe she was a traitor when I saw the evidence. But it was all circumstantial. She saved me then, she saved me now. She knows where my child is. It's the ultimate insurance policy and she wouldn't give that advantage away.'

'It's only insurance if you believe her. You cannot properly interrogate her. I will. I will get to the truth.' Mila set her mouth in a firm line. 'You are not much use to me if you are distracted by this loose end of your kid.'

Loose end. I wondered what forge had formed Mila, that she could think such a way. I was afraid to know. I thought of her solicitude for the captured Moldovan women back in Amsterdam. She could be kind. She could be cruel. I thought Piet might have suffered mightily at her hands. She might also be right. Lucy would dance a dance with me; she would play on our past, on the embers of my feelings for her, on the obvious wish that I had that she had loved me. Mila would not dance. I almost felt a tremble of fear for Lucy — misplaced and ill-advised — thinking of her at Mila's mercy.

Unleashing Mila might be the quickest path to my child.

My child. I didn't want to think about what Mila was saying. I had to know. I couldn't walk away from the possibility of my child, lost in the world, or worse, being raised by a woman like Lucy Capra. Lucy and Mila were both willing to use my child to reach their goals; I was willing to let them think they could use me, but I would use them. It's an ugly world when we fight over children.

I veered the Jaguar into a parking garage. We were here.

79

St Pancras is a huge rail and underground station. It has undergone a serious, high-cost beautification process in recent years: massive, pale blue steel arches sweep against original brickwork. Glass ceilings lend an air of openness in the concourse. High-end shops and restaurants fill the walkways. A sign advertises the world's longest champagne bar. Thousands of commuters and travelers moved through the station but I walked through St Pancras alone.

Mila stayed with the netbook in the car; I had a microphone nestled in my ear. She was watching Bahjat Zaid on the video feed, having hacked into St Pancras's security system. We were running a big risk; the security system might notice it was being invaded and a security team might decide to investigate if they discovered the hack was occurring so close to the station. Security was naturally heavy — if not obvious — at such a critical travel hub.

'Found him. He's waiting near the champagne bar on the upper level,' Mila said.

'Is he alone?'

'Yes.'

'Are you reading anyone watching him?'

'No.'

I headed upstairs toward the impressive stretch of the champagne bar; it was packed with beautiful people and a few tired looking travelers. The bar ran for hundreds of feet, only broken by waiter stations. Stretches of wood were designed for solo travelers to sit with their laptops; other lengths were actually booths for four. Its far and only wall was glass and steel, and it faced the Eurostar station where trains from the Continent arrived and departed.

Zaid sat in a booth, alone, in his Armani suit, his polished gleaming shoes, and he looked as bent and as ill as though he'd been consumed by a cancer. The confidence I'd seen in him was gone. He wiped a trace of sweat from his forehead and he kept a briefcase close to his legs. Very close. I sat to his left, where he couldn't see me so easily, where a square bar formed the entrance and where the waiters, nattily attired, gathered their poured flutes and moved with grace back to the tables. I stayed on the other side of the bar and hoped my sunglasses and the dark cap would keep him from recognizing me. I ordered the cheapest glass of champagne on the menu but didn't touch it.

Zaid kept scanning the crowd. Eagerly, nervously. He craned his neck around when groups walked alongside the Eurostar. Waves of people came and went. A crowd to my left was getting a bit loud, fueled by a magnum of champagne. Zaid kept glancing toward them. I turned away. I couldn't risk him seeing my face.

'Do you still have him?' I said into the mic.

'Yes,' Mila said into my ear.

'He's nervous, constantly scanning the crowd. I can't risk him seeing me.'

417

'You don't think you should just go up and speak to him?'

'Not if he's getting Yasmin back. Edward could see me . . .'

'You are afraid of Edward?'

'I am afraid he'll kill Yasmin if he spots me,' I said.

Mila said nothing, but I could almost hear her sneer.

I felt a tap on my shoulder. I turned. Bahjat Zaid looked as though he meant to stagger toward his death bed: sweating, pale, mouth twisted into an angry tremble.

'Get the hell out of here,' he said. 'You must leave. Now.'

'Is Edward bringing Yasmin here?'

'I am ordering you to leave,' he hissed.

'I know you've given Edward weapons for keeping his videos of Yasmin's crime spree to himself. Are you swapping your snazzy briefcase for your daughter?'

He looked as though he might vomit on my shoes. 'Leave. Now.'

'Answer me and maybe I will.'

'I give them the bag, they give me Yasmin, and this nightmare is done.'

'What's in the briefcase?'

'Cash. Nothing more.'

'After all this, they just want some cash? What did you give them in Budapest, Mr Zaid? What experimental weapons?'

Pure hatred came into his eyes. 'Your services are no longer required. I will have my daughter back and she is safe. No one can talk about her now. They will be here at any moment. They could be watching us now. You being here may cost me my daughter's life.' He so badly wanted to scream at me. To punch me. But he couldn't. He couldn't draw attention to us.

'You yell and bring the cops down on us, and I'll tell them everything your daughter has done since they grabbed her.' He stared; I think he was too stunned that I was here, or unsure of his next step. 'You lied to me, you lied to Mila. And when we needed you, to help your own daughter, you hid from us.'

'I did what was necessary. If you ever wanted to help Yasmin, you will go. Now.'

I took a tiny sip from the flute, to show I had no intention of vacating my seat. 'I might get up and leave, or I might not. Cooperate and I'll play along with you. Who's coming? Edward?'

He nodded as though it cost him physical pain. 'Yes. I was told you were dead.'

'Then he won't be expecting me, will he? Go back to your seat at the bar, Zaid. You've got champagne to toast getting your daughter back. Shouldn't you be rushing her home?'

'I am taking Yasmin to a psychiatric center where she can be cared for, where she can forget all she was forced to do.'

'I wish you luck.'

'Leave. This is suicide for us both. This Edward — he is both insane and calculating. You can't beat him. I beg you.'

'Go sit yourself down. Right now.' My voice was cold and measured.

He retreated, slowly, unused to the idea that here was someone he could not get rid of. He returned to his spot at the bar and sat down. He made a production of not looking at me. I moved to another part of the bar, further from the entrance and from Zaid, so I couldn't be easily noticed.

How much backup could Edward and Lucy have here? I had to assume they had contacts to help them in London. But if they were arriving on the Eurostar . . . what, with Yasmin in tow? No. Yasmin would be squirreled away somewhere, and Zaid was trading the briefcase for that location.

'Did Zaid signal to anyone else in here?' I asked into the microphone. He could have his own security backup, after all.

'Not that I saw,' Mila said.

He wasn't taking any chances with his daughter's life. Except that I'd changed the math.

Twenty minutes passed. Champagne drinkers came and went. Friends met, lovers toasted, business types dealt. A low, constant murmur of talk, broken by the happy pop of corks leaving bottles at velocity. In my ear, Mila sang Coldplay songs, bored, until I asked her to stop. Zaid kept eyeing his watch, as if willing Yasmin to appear. He kept a glass of champagne in front of him, and another glass across the table. Waiting.

And then she did. I saw her before Zaid did. She was walking unsteadily, as though she'd been doped. Edward held her arm; he was almost holding her up. Half of Yasmin's face was hidden by a scarf.

I glanced around the bar. There might be backup here, but it wasn't Zaid's.

Behind me, Lucy.

80

She sat at my booth. And for one second I thought she would kill me where I sat.

'You are a bad father,' Lucy said. 'I told you if you want the baby, back off.'

'Irony is wasted on you,' I said.

'You're going to make things difficult for me, aren't you, Sam?'

'You don't know difficult.'

'Don't open fire here, Sam. So many innocent people. Not to mention expensive, easily broken champagne bottles.'

'Edward thinks I'm dead.'

'Not any more, monkey. He's seen you. You will let this exchange happen, or I will never tell you where Daniel is.'

'Daniel.' The name cut like a knife.

'Our son. I named him for your brother, like I said we should.'

I felt my heart shift in my chest.

'Don't interfere,' she said.

'What is Zaid giving you for his daughter?' Now, thirty feet away, Edward and Yasmin approached Zaid. They stood by the booth, facing him.

'He's giving us,' Lucy said, 'everything he's worked for in his life. You could learn a lesson here, Sam. He's doing whatever it takes to protect his child. Back off and Daniel will be yours.'

Yasmin blinked, heavily. The scarf hid the rest of her face.

Zaid handed Edward the case. Edward spoke softly and Yasmin sat beside her father, sagging into the booth. Edward remained standing.

'Stay in your seat, Sam, and I'll tell you where Daniel is. Don't interfere,' Lucy said.

Edward turned and hurried away, carrying the case. Zaid embraced his daughter. She seemed very small in his arms. She did not hug him back.

'Reunions are lovely,' Lucy said and I wanted to tell her to shut the hell up. 'You and your son can have a reunion, too. Just stay seated.' She leaned forward, plucked the tiny earpiece from my ear, and crushed it under her boot. 'Who are you working with?'

'A crazy woman. I only say that because now she can't hear us.'

'Sam, come with me. Daniel is very close. I can give him to you now. And then we're done.'

She'd protected me twice before. I so wanted to believe she'd just give me my son. That, I know, is both the definition of optimism and insanity.

I glanced back. Zaid still held Yasmin, heaving in the massive relief that his child was safe.

Yasmin kept her scarf over the bottom of her face. They sat, perhaps waiting for Edward to clear the area. I remembered that no one knew Yasmin was missing. She nodded once in answer to words her father spoke. Tears ran down Zaid's face.

'I can get you immunity,' I said. 'You could

negotiate a deal. You don't have to keep running. Is that going to be your life now? Dodging and hiding?'

'Immunity? That's a laugh. I made my choices, Sam. I know that.' I heard a catch in her voice, for the first time, a prick of regret.

Zaid held his daughter's hand. He picked up the champagne glass and drank it dry, a nervous gesture. Yasmin stayed still as stone. I couldn't imagine the levels of therapy she'd need to get her life back.

'Lucy. Why would you turn your back on your whole world?'

Then, on her wrist, I saw the little sunburst inside the nine. Same as the thugs in Holland, same as my would-be murderer in Brooklyn. 'Lucy, my God.' I jabbed at her tattoo.

'Get up,' she said. 'We're walking out now.'

I saw Edward hurrying past a statue of a man in a windblown coat, looking up at the glass ceiling as though expecting a storm. Then he had vanished in the mass of people heading downstairs. I hoped Mila was tracking him; I wanted her to forget about me. Yasmin was safe.

We were up and walking. I risked a glance back at Zaid just after we passed and saw him jerk slightly as he set down his champagne glass. Cough. He coughed again. Then Yasmin eased out from the booth and hurried toward the entrance.

I stopped. Yasmin Zaid didn't. In her eyes was cool resolution. She was hurrying past us, not giving me or Lucy a glance. Or glancing back at her father. She went down the stairs, the same way Edward had gone.

I took a step forward and felt the gun rub up against my spine. 'This way, Sam. You want to see your son? This way.'

Zaid still sat but his head had sagged forward. No one around him, intent on their bubbly, on their laughter, on checking their phones, noticed. I couldn't see if he was breathing or not. Poison, I thought.

'He's dead,' I said. 'She killed him.'

'Yes,' she said.

His own daughter.

'What the hell has Edward done to her?' This world, where wives betrayed husbands, where children poisoned parents, I felt my chest go hollow.

'Edward's made her into his own. You honestly don't want to know. We're walking, Sam.'

A server stopped by Zaid, noticing his state, knelt close to him and screamed.

'Your son,' Lucy said. 'Your son.' Like it was a prod to keep me going. I walked.

Further down the concourse, Edward waited for Yasmin. She closed the distance between, and his right hand closed around her wrist. His other hand held the briefcase.

'Just stick to me,' Lucy said as we went down the stairs, 'and you'll get your kid back.'

'No, I won't,' I said and I turned and grabbed the gun she had set in my side, under my jacket. Transport police swarmed past us, hurrying to the champagne bar. 'You shoot me now, you won't have time to get away.' Our lips were an inch apart, like lovers saying goodbye at the train station in an old black and white movie.

'Sam, don't. Why can't you just walk away from them? For your son's sake?' Her voice begged.

I glanced down the stairs. I could see Edward and Yasmin looking back at us, at Lucy and me locked together. I took the risk. I pivoted and grabbed Lucy's gun, twisting fingers around the barrel, forcing its aim toward the floor.

81

Over Lucy's shoulder I saw Edward drop Zaid's briefcase and raise a heavy, odd looking gun out from under his trench coat. Larger than a revolver, it had a strange black section connected to it, with a metallic grid pattern on it that looked familiar, that gleamed for a moment in the bright light of the concourse.

The firing boomed loud and the heat of the bullet passed between Lucy and me. We both fell, part way down the stairs, but neither of us relinquished our grip on her gun. In the stunned silence after the gunfire, screams erupted all around us, a choir of chaos.

Edward fired again. The bullet kicked the green stairs, very close to Lucy's head, and, still fighting, we tumbled down the rest.

Lucy powered a fist into my face as we got up. Hard, right below the eye. I wouldn't let go of the gun.

'Let go or Daniel is gone!' she screamed.

I didn't let go. 'Maybe they'll trade me you for him,' I said.

She hit me again, as the crowd scattered, no one looking at us, so I tripped her, yanking her backwards over my leg. She landed hard on the floor and kicked me in the thigh and I landed on top of her. The panic in St Pancras was now a fully-fledged stampede, hundreds of people running, seeking cover; if we lay here on the floor we would be trampled.

I yanked her to her feet. The pistol was gone, lost in the shuffle. I didn't assume she was still unarmed.

'You listen to me,' I hissed in her ear. 'You're nothing to me now. *Nothing*. And you're nothing to your friend, because he just took off with his girlfriend and tried to kill you. So. I'm your only hope.'

'Screw you!' Anger and fear shredded her voice. She tried to pull away from me, but I was stronger and I was madder. Her face was white with shock that Edward had risked killing her.

I yanked her to her feet, wrenched her arm up between her shoulder blades. In the stampeding panic no one accused me of being ungentle-manly. We were swept out into the street by the crowd.

I pulled her close to me, our faces as close as our wedding kiss. 'If you try to run from me, I will catch you and break your neck.'

She shook her head. 'Then you won't get your kid back.'

'No, you'll be dead. And I'll still find my kid. There is no place on earth you can hide him from me, Lucy. Do you understand? I will never give up. Ever. I will find him. And you will be in a coffin.'

Her hand went behind her back. I hadn't frisked her yet, swept along by the sea of panicking commuters. I saw the flash of steel in her hand; knife, short, curved. I dodged her swipe, felt the blade nick my ear.

'Sam, stop, please! Just let me go!'

So you can kill me? I thought. I powered a fist into her stomach — the same stomach that the last time we'd been husband and wife I'd kissed, feeling the tremble of our child inside — and she folded, dropping the knife. I grabbed it.

'Why'd he try to kill you?' I said. She was groggy and she stopped to dry-heave along the sidewalk. Confusion and emotion felt like a storm blossoming in my chest. I'd loved her. Crazy, opera-singing love, beyond-death love. But to love her was to die at her hands now. I forced down the swell of emotion I felt.

'I don't know. He's turned traitor on me,' she managed to gasp.

'He doesn't need you,' I said. 'This is almost funny. You betray everything for this guy and he betrays you. It's rich.'

'I don't work for *him*.'

'Who do you work for.'

'Not Edward. We have the same boss.' She gave me a sideways glance.

I sensed the beginnings of a deal. 'Who? The guy who made you get the tattoo?' I could see that the fight wasn't out of her yet. You couldn't beat the fight out of Lucy. It had been one of the traits I loved about her. I put the knife in her back, under her jacket. We walked.

I looked at her and saw tears on her face.

'Don't cry,' I said. Almost automatically. I used to say it as a husband; Lucy's tears, a rare occurrence, were always like nails in my flesh. 'It won't work on me.'

We were close to the parking garage. I pushed her along; she went. 'Why is he turning on you?'

429

'I didn't know Yasmin would kill her dad,' she said. 'She was just supposed to be returned in exchange.'

'For what?'

'The other part of the weapons. The chips.'

'What weapons? What chips?'

She went silent. Making the point that she had critical information I needed.

I pressed on. 'Well, Yasmin just murdered her dad. So I think this ransom, this kidnapping, was all a big fake she and Edward engineered. Why?'

'I can't explain myself,' she said. 'You think I can explain other people?'

'Did she go Patty Hearst? Brainwashed into joining her captors?'

'It's one survival mechanism to play along. Trust me, I know,' Lucy said.

She'd just compared our marriage to a kidnapping. I shook my head. 'Your charade is over,' I said.

'Yes. But it's another thing to kill your father. Or your husband. I made them save your life here in London. That was the deal.'

'You'll regret it,' I said. We hurried up the incline of the parking garage.

'No,' she said. 'I don't think I will.'

Her words made me feel cold; because if she had Daniel she had the trump card. She had it all.

Mila stood near her car, watching us approach. Her expression was blank.

'You caught her,' Mila said. 'Congratulations. Hello, Lucy. I've heard so much about you.'

Lucy studied Mila. 'I don't know you.'

430

'You will.' Mila stepped forward and put plastic cuffs on Lucy's hands. I pushed Lucy into the back seat and sat next to her to keep her under control. Mila stormed the Jaguar out of the garage and I explained to her the chaos that had carried us out of St Pancras.

'I have no idea where they would go,' Mila said. 'I lost them on the feed.'

'I know where they're going,' Lucy said quietly.

'With you captured, I'm assuming that their plans will change,' I said.

'Sam's not dealing with you,' Mila said. 'You're dealing with *me*.'

'I told you, Sam. Daniel is close. Let me go and you can have him within a few hours.'

'I don't believe you. You didn't know I was going to be at the station. You thought I was in Holland, probably in a hospital bed. You wouldn't have brought Daniel with you. No way you're carting a kid around while playing hired gun. You've hidden him somewhere, Lucy, and the deal is you're going to tell me or I will hand you over to Howell and the Company as a murderer and a bomber. Howell was entirely right about you.'

'Kill me now, then, because I won't just tell you. You have to let me go.'

Mila said, 'You won't tell him but you will tell me.'

'She's charming,' Lucy said. 'But he won't shoot me, little Miss Russia. Do you have a name, by the way?'

'You can call me Mila,' Mila said. 'I plan on

beating you senseless, by the way. Just so you know, I will enjoy it.'

'She'll talk without violence,' I said to Mila.

'Is this where you thought you would end up?' Lucy said. 'I mean, you joined the Company because you wanted to avenge your brother. Now you're a hunted dog, and you don't have your kid. You've lost everything.'

'No. I still have you.' I stared ahead into the traffic.

Lucy said, 'What will you do with me?'

'First, you will tell us where Edward and Yasmin will go,' Mila said. 'Sam, shut up. That's an order.'

'Yes, Sam, that's an order,' Lucy said.

Mila pulled the Jag over in a screech of tires. She launched herself toward the back seat and she hit Lucy, hard, two snapping blows to nose and mouth. Blood gummed under her nostrils, in the corner of her lips.

'Listen, Mrs Capra,' Mila said. 'Let us be clear as the crystal. You're nothing to me. You don't speak to Sam unless I give you permission. You are going to talk to us, or I am going to kill you.'

'I doubt your superiors want me dead,' Lucy said, her voice a half-scream. Blood dotted her spittle. 'I have information to barter.'

'You do not understand who Sam and I work for now. I do not work for a government accountable to voters who do not bother to inform themselves on basic issues. I do not work for an agency worried about budgets controlled by petty politicians. My only rule is that I have to return the car clean.' She flicked a little smile. 'I don't have to be a good example to anyone. I don't like you. I don't like what you did to my friend Sam. I don't like a woman who uses her child as a pawn. You are an infinitely bad mother and an even worse person.'

'I know what I am,' Lucy said through the blood on her lips. 'And I'll make a deal with you. I will take you to where I think Edward and Yasmin will go. I'll answer your questions. I'll tell you where Daniel is.'

'And your price for this jackpot?' Mila asked.

'You let me go. When you've recovered Edward and his goods, which I promise you will be of great interest. Guarantee me that. If Sam says you'll do it, I'll trust him.'

Cars honked madly, Mila veered back into the flow of traffic.

'You have no reason to trust me,' I said.

'Yes, I do. I know you. I know your word is good.' Lucy looked at me and for a moment I could think we were back in our Bloomsbury flat, a young couple, happy, a baby coming, in love.

'You let her go and she cannot testify to the Company that you are innocent,' Mila said. 'They will never take you back. They will never stop looking for you. A life on the run, Sam, think long and hard about it. Are you going to drag your child along for the ride?'

A trade-off. My child for my freedom. At least this way I could find my kid, see him, hold him, be a father. Lucy had to deal with me, fairly, or she was dead. She knew it. Her game was over. She wasn't going anywhere until I had my kid safe in my arms.

I glanced at Mila. She gave the barest of nods. I leaned back. 'Fine, cooperate and we'll let you go.'

'If you survive,' she said.

Mila said, 'Where will they go?'

'New York,' she said. 'We were to meet with my boss.'

'For what reason?'

'You get Edward, and you'll know.'

'This boss. Your tattoo. This is Novem Soles — the Nine Suns?'

Lucy nodded.

'What is it?'

'A group that wants power and doesn't care how they get it. I can't give you a single name, though. I don't know them.'

'But you got the tattoo.'

'They make you do that.' She shrugged. 'It's part of owning you. They made me, like they made me do everything else.'

'Made you? Like you had no free will? What's Edward smuggling?'

'Only he and Zaid, and maybe Yasmin know. I don't.'

'You're lying.'

'I have no reason to lie,' she said. 'I don't know what it is.'

'Where will they go right now? To New York on the next flight?'

'I think Yasmin will go home,' she said. 'She and Edward have unfinished business.'

82

London's Adrenaline Bar occupied an old power station on the border between Hoxton and Shoreditch; it was all open space and brick walls and a gorgeous long steel bar, much bigger than its brothers, the Rode Prins and Taverne Chevalier, and the bartenders were serving actual cocktails, precise with the measurements, using fresh ingredients. I saw a proper martini being mixed (shaken is still the fastest way to chill, and bruising the liquor is a myth), a bull and bear made with genuine Kentucky bourbon, an excellent bottle of French Bordeaux being opened. The barkeeps had been well trained. My kind of bar. The tables were low and long and rustic, more French farmhouse than elegant, but cool looking. I had thought given its name that it would be a frenetic dance club; rather Adrenaline seemed an ironic name, a place where cool control would win the day more than frantic action.

We walked through it, keeping hold of Lucy by the arm. It was easy for a moment to think about the loveliness of a proper bar, rather than to think about my traitorous wife.

I liked the open space, which somehow seemed warm and inviting. Bright, forceful modern art and bold photographs hung on the walls, all done, Mila said, by local artists, many of whom patronized the bar.

'You'll see movie stars here as well,' she said. 'I have to do my damnedest to keep us out of the guidebooks so we don't go touristy.' I knew artists had reclaimed once-blighted Hoxton for their own, and the developers followed the artists, quickly pricing most of them out of the territory they'd staked. A large outdoor patio held sculptures and large blow-ups of photographs; it held a circular stage for live music, currently empty as it was mid-morning.

A thin, well-dressed man approached us. He was handsome, in his early thirties, wore a perfectly tailored suit and spoke with a West African accent. 'Mila, hello. How nice to see you.'

'This is Kenneth,' Mila said.

'Kenneth, help me,' Lucy said. 'They're holding me prisoner.'

He ignored her. Mila introduced me, just as Sam, and he shook my hand.

'Give Sam whatever he needs,' Mila said.

He nodded and regarded Lucy.

She said, 'I'll scream.'

Kenneth said, 'I believe you have no interest in speaking to the British police, do you?'

Lucy shut up.

Upstairs was a much bigger office than the bars in Amsterdam or Brussels; it housed an array of computer screens. Mila locked the door behind us and sat at a keyboard, began to type. The back of her computer monitor faced us. I pushed Lucy into an office chair, handcuffed her to it and sat across from her.

'You want us to take down Edward to help

keep you safe? Then you talk to me.'

'Go to their house. Zaid's house. That's where they'll go.' She turned to Mila. 'Since the bar's open, I'd like a Scotch.'

Mila ignored her. I went around and looked at what she was doing. She turned off the computer.

'Your wife is correct,' she said. 'We have to go to Zaid's house.'

'Why?'

She looked at Lucy. 'Come with me to get your wife's Scotch.' She leaned down close to Lucy and wheeled her chair into a small, empty, windowless room. She slammed the door and locked it.

'What's going on?'

'My employers insist I go to Zaid's country house and make sure there is no evidence of his connection to us.'

'What do you mean? Wipe out his computer?'

'Yes.'

'He was just murdered in full sight in a train station. The police will be swarming over his residences.'

'That is why we must hurry. Remember Zaid telling us that his estate was equipped with bunkers for the government in case Britain was invaded during the war? I think if he has kept secrets from us on what he has given Edward, those secrets will be there. It is his best hiding place.'

'But why would *they* go there?'

'It is hiding in plain sight. Zaid covered for her while she was so-called kidnapping victim. He told us, remember, that no one knew she was missing, not even her mother. So now she cannot be missing. Whatever they are up to, she must be in sight now or she would be suspected.'

I ran a hand through my hair.

'You're right. That underground complex would be the perfect hiding place. Do we know who's living there?'

'A small staff, I would suspect. He keeps a sizeable stable of horses.'

'I love horses,' I said.

83

Zaid's death and the gunfire at St Pancras dominated the news the rest of the day. No one else had been seriously injured and the shooters had escaped. The police were already at Zaid's London home, interviewing his family. I saw news footage of Zaid's blonde wife, walking into her London home in Belgravia, filmed at a distance. Yasmin, with no scarf on to mask her face, walked with her mother, a supportive arm around her shoulders. Mrs Zaid had said that her husband had gone to meet their daughter, who was returning from a trip, and that Yasmin had phoned her to say she'd been running late and, when she arrived, her father was dead from an apparent heart attack.

She'd killed him, vanished in the panic, and then boldly returned, her face uncovered, for her 'meeting'.

'She poisons her father and now pretends to be the doting daughter.' I felt sick. Yasmin would have to vanish before poison was identified in her father's body. We did not have much time.

On the television, I watched Yasmin Zaid and her mother step away from the press of the reporters and go back into their perfect house. *My daughter belongs to me*, Zaid had said a million years ago, back in Amsterdam. He had been so, so wrong.

Early the next morning I drove past the Zaid country estate in Kent, not far from Canterbury. High stone walls rose and fell with the gentle sway of the rolling landscape. I followed the road, looking for signs of cameras or monitors hidden in the trees or the fence itself. I drove a few miles past the property and then drove back again. I wanted to get a feel for the terrain, based on the satellite map Mila had shown me, together with the plans of the house she had somehow obtained the night before. The complex lay under the Georgian mansion, stretching toward the western edge of the estate. Near the end of what would be the far side of the complex were stables. A private airstrip lay on the far western side and stretching halfway across the ample property was a small river, which seemed to start in the grounds itself, and a number of small creeks. It looked like one tunnel ended close to the stables, which lay about two hundred yards from the wall. A private road fed from the wall past the stables. No guard, at least right now, but a heavy gate with a keycard reader.

I drove past again one more time, then wheeled back to the closest village.

* * *

I keyed in the phone number.

'Hello?' A woman's voice, crisp, undaunted, apparently, by the tragedy that had befallen her master.

440

'Stables, please.' I hoped this would work. Even with Zaid dead, his horses would have to be cared for. Someone should be on duty.

'One moment.' Then the phone rang again.

'Hello?' This time a crabby man's voice.

'Hi,' I said. 'I'd like to speak with whoever handles purchasing for Mr Zaid's stables, please.'

'This is a most inappropriate time, young man. We have had a death in the family,' the man scolded me.

'Oh, I'm so sorry, I didn't know. I am so sorry.' I could not have sounded sorrier.

'Goodbye then . . . '

'Sir? Could you please tell me who I should ask for when I call back?'

'That would be Gerry and he's not here today. Who's calling, please?'

'I'm Mike Smith, with Service-First Equestrian, we're a brand new firm and I think we could give Gerry great service at a very attractive price.'

The voice surprised him with a laugh. 'You better give Gerry service, or he'll yell your ears off. Just fair warning.'

I laughed a false salesman's laugh. 'Yes, sir, I appreciate the candor. Might I ask if you know who supplies Mr Zaid's horses now?'

'Um, yeah. Blue Lion Horse Supply. They're close by.'

'Very fine company. But we have better deals with our suppliers we can pass on to you.'

'Save your pitch for Gerry. D'you want to leave a number?'

'No, sir, I'll call back next week and make an

441

appointment with Gerry. Sorry to have bothered you.'

'All right then. Good luck. Bye.' The man hung up.

A search on my phone gave me a listing for Blue Lion Horse Supply and I drove the two miles to the business; it was in a standalone building of old stone and a paved parking lot.

I walked inside. Horse feed and equestrian equipment lined the walls and the shelves. A young man stood at the counter, tapping on a keyboard and frowning at a computer.

'Hi,' I said. 'I'm from the Zaid place. Gerry sent me.'

He gave me a nod.

'We were supposed to get a delivery of feed yesterday, and it didn't come. Gerry sent me to pick it up.'

The guy frowned and said, 'We delivered your supply two days ago.'

'Well, we don't have it and Gerry's out today and so I'm supposed to come get the stuff.'

'Hold on, my brother does the delivery to the Zaids. Alec?' he called and got a answering 'What?' from the back office. 'There's a guy from Zaid's out here and he . . . ' The clerk turned around and I had the gun square in his face, an apologetic smile behind the Glock.

★ ★ ★

I tied the brothers up in the back office, tight, gagged them, hung the closed sign in the window and found the delivery pickup. A

442

delivery for another client was already loaded; good, it would save me time. I pulled a knit cap marked with the words BLUE LION off Alec's balding head.

'Guys.' I knelt close to them. Now I had to scare them a bit. 'I went through your wallets. I know where you live. So you're going to stay nice and calm and if anyone finds you before I come back here, you're going to tell them someone who doesn't look like me took your truck. You aren't going to mention Bahjat Zaid. You aren't going to describe me. Because I'll vanish, and if it takes five days or five months or five years, if you piss me off, I'll be back and you won't see me coming. You boys understand me?'

The brothers nodded.

'Okay. I'll be back with your truck real soon. Be good.'

I called Mila from the parking lot. I said: 'I'm ready.'

She said, 'I'm going inside now.'

84

Mila had gained access to the mansion by flashing a false identification that stated she was with Scotland Yard. The news crews, which had been there the night before, were gone.

Mila stood in the foyer after she'd been admitted by the sallow-faced housekeeper, Mrs Crosby, who stood with a stricken look on her face, a handkerchief in one hand.

She said, 'Two police inspectors have just left . . .'

Mila gave a polite, slight bow. 'I apologize for intruding upon your grief but I work in computer forensics and I need to access Mr Zaid's computers. We need to see who he had been in contact with, if anyone might have threatened him.'

'Mr Zaid was a fine man,' Mrs Crosby said. 'He didn't deserve what happened to him.'

'You were with him a long time?'

'Yes, me and my husband both, we've been in his employ here for almost thirty years.'

'Excuse me,' a voice came from beyond the foyer. Mrs Crosby went instantly silent.

Mila turned to see Yasmin and Edward stepping out from the study. Mila gave no expression that she'd seen either of them before, but her stomach lurched.

'Hello,' Edward said. 'I'm Edward Maxwell, a security consultant for Mr Zaid. May I be of help?'

The housekeeper was strangling her silken

handkerchief, twisting it into a tight rope.

She's afraid, Mila thought. This woman is scared to death.

'Well, I hope so,' she said to Edward. 'I'm Inspector Mila Smith, from Scotland Yard.'

'Forgive me, but I've never heard of a Scotland Yard inspector with a Russian accent.'

'I am a naturalized citizen and married to the world's greatest Manchester United fan.' She offered a small, polite laugh as Edward shook her hand. He smiled.

'Mrs Crosby,' Edward said to the housekeeper, 'it's all right. I'll assist the inspector. I'm not sure why the police are taking such an interest in Mr Zaid's heart attack.'

'We're not convinced it was a heart attack, sir,' Mila said mildly.

Edward gave no reaction; Mrs Crosby let out a small gasp.

Edward said, 'I think it would be best if you went home, Mrs Crosby. Unless the inspector needs to speak to you.'

'No,' Mila said softly. 'That won't be necessary.' It was as if they were in agreement; no non-combatants on the field.

Edward took a step closer to Mila. She made herself not look at the question-mark scar.

Mrs Crosby nodded and left.

Yasmin didn't smile. She didn't speak. She didn't watch the woman leave.

Mila waited until she heard the soft jingling of the housekeeper getting her keys and a back door shutting. 'So. Mr Zaid's computer.'

Edward's tone chilled. 'I'm afraid that I can't

let you have access to Mr Zaid's systems. There is confidential information on them regarding Militronics business.'

'I understand, sir, but I do have a warrant.' Mila reached inside her purse.

★ ★ ★

I pulled the cap over my head and turned into the gate. I waved the key card over the pass.

The gate didn't open. Maybe because people up at the house were busy dealing with Mila, confirming her story. Or fighting with her.

A voice squawked from the speaker by the card reader. 'Yeah, who are you?'

I put on my best English accent. 'Alec at Blue Lion Horse sent me. He didn't have some of the horse feed in yesterday's delivery for Mr Zaid and I'm bringing it now.' I didn't look directly at the camera; I looked at a notepad, checking the details of the delivery. What I was delivering wasn't horse feed but a story to a guard who was probably already nervous, given that his boss had just been murdered. But it is the nature of underlings to trust their eyes and I wore the cap, I drove the truck bearing the Blue Lion logo and name on the door, I lobbed the right name.

Silence for ten seconds. 'Someone will meet you at the stable. Wait there.'

'It won't take long, will it? Because I've got other deliveries, mate.'

'I'll see you there.'

'Thanks.' I rolled up the window.

The gates opened and I drove through.

85

Mila's hand closed over her pistol. But she sensed Edward take a step forward. She looked up and Edward held a gun on her.

'You,' he ordered Mila. 'Drop the purse. You're not Scotland Yard. Honestly, couldn't they find a British bird to play a British bird?'

'No.'

'Edward . . . ' Yasmin started.

'Just a moment, love,' he said to her. His gaze bore into Mila. 'Who are you with? Sam Capra's bunch?'

'Yes.' Very carefully, her fingers pressed a button on a small device next to the gun in her purse. In her head she started a slow, measured countdown.

'And who exactly are they?'

'We work for Mr Zaid.'

'Ah. Clear your hands from the purse. Then drop it on the floor.'

Slowly, Mila made a show of sliding the purse off her shoulder. Her gaze locked on Edward's and the only time her glance wandered was to evaluate where she would strike him: the throat, the eyes, the base of his nose where the bone would spear into the brain if you hit it just right.

'Yasmin, get the guards on the radio.'

Yasmin stumbled toward the hallway.

'I told you to drop the purse, bitch,' he said to Mila.

Her purse hit the floor. Edward leaned down, keeping the gun fixed on Mila, dragging the purse toward him and five seconds later its zippered opening exploded in a blast of dazzling light.

★ ★ ★

No welcoming committee was waiting at the stable when I parked the truck. I didn't see a soul.

I grabbed my bag and got out then dropped the gate of the pickup, took a bag of feed and half-dragged another bag off the edge of the pickup's rear gate; I needed to look like either an eager-to-please delivery man or a delivery man hurrying to finish one job and get to the next. I stepped inside the stable, slung the bag over my shoulder and waited. Zaid's beautiful horses nickered, perhaps anticipating a run or exercise. I was sorry to disappoint them.

Three minutes later, a truck topped the rise of the hill. Three men inside. An awful lot to receive a delivery. Either Mila had already failed, or they were cautious.

Three against one, and me already coping with injuries. I hurried to each of the stalls and opened the doors, led the Arab horses out via the back gate. I swatted them gently on the sides to urge them to run. Two broke and bolted past the corral, the others cantered. They were such beauties. I remembered my dad teaching me and my brother to ride, one humid summer when we were in Virginia, not melting in a Third World housing project, and the joy you could feel from the wind in your face, from the bridled power of the horse.

I went back into the stable and waited. The truck stopped before reaching the building as the guards caught sight of the horses rounding the stables. One man, a redhead, jumped out to try and catch the horses. The other two, wearing holsters, kept the truck headed for the stables. They pulled up next to the Blue Lion pickup. Got out, but left their guns in their holsters. They moved like professionals and I wondered if they were just hired security or if they were part of Edward's organization. I didn't really want to kill rent-a-cops who'd just taken the wrong job patrolling a quiet English estate.

The way they fought would show me who they were.

As they stepped inside, I swung a heavy bag of feed into the first one's face. The man toppled and as the weight of the bag spun I nailed the second guard with a kick below the throat that sent him sprawling out onto the porch. My shoulder ached from the weight of it and I staggered after the kick.

The first man — thick-necked, with a blond burr of hair — rolled into a martial artist's stance and yanked a small knife from a sheath on his belt. Not a cop-for-hire then. That simplified things. He swiped at me with the knife and I hammered my palm into his face, then grabbed both his wrists and slammed them against the top of a stable door. They broke. He screeched and staggered backwards, staring at his bent wrists.

The second man, a wiry African, coughing blood, lunged at me, drawing his gun, yelling an order to surrender. I ignored it and rammed a fist into the man's hand, knocking the gun to the floor. The bolt of pain shot up my arm to my wounded shoulder, and I was too slow pulling back. The African slammed three hard, brutal blows into my ribs. Bruises still fresh from Holland thundered into agony. I couldn't fight for long.

I stepped inside the African's swing and head-slammed him and the man went to his knees; I gave him a kick, square in the groin, and I meant it. The African collapsed in huffing agony. He looked up at me as a man expecting to die, fear shining bright in his eyes.

I relieved him of his gun and yanked an earpiece from his ear. They were wired to check-in, and so reinforcements might be here soon. The man with two broken wrists looked at me in shock. I leveled a kick into him that drove his head back against a stall gate and he crumpled.

I pulled out my gun.

'Where's the entrance?' I said. 'To the underground rooms?'

The African shot me the finger. Honestly, I thought. I knelt down and twisted the finger back to within a millimeter of breaking it. The African howled.

'Are they paying you enough? Really?' I asked.

'The back . . . the kitchen.'

I yanked him to his feet, hustled him into the kitchen.

'Pantry,' he said. A bit more steel in his voice now. He was going to get cute. But I still needed him.

The small kitchen held a pantry at its back and I opened the door, keeping the gun aimed at the African. Another door stood behind the narrow shelving; made of new, reinforced steel. I tried pushing it. Locked.

'Open it,' I said.

'Door only opens from the inside.' He was right. There was no knob or bar.

'Okay.' I slammed the African into the pantry shelving once, twice, and the guy cracked his head and dropped, unconscious. I checked the window; no sign of the redhead. He'd be back in minutes, or radioing his friends who'd gone into the stable and wonder why they weren't responding.

I opened my bag, found the strips of plastic explosive and the wires, and began to shape the charge around the door.

86

The blast was more light and dazzle than heat and, as Edward screamed and staggered back, Mila drew her baton from the small of her back. The first blow grazed Edward's jaw, the edge of the baton bloodying the skin. Mila slashed again, aiming for Edward's chest, but he caught her arm and twisted her forearm savagely. She slammed the heel of her other hand into his face. A fist hammered into the soft of Mila's throat and she went to her knees, Yasmin attacking with blows and kicks. Edward grabbed Mila's hair, spat in her face, pounded her head against the table twice, then a hand wrenched the baton from her grip.

Yasmin, panting and mewling, smashed the baton across Mila's head and Mila fell onto the fine Persian rug.

'She *hurt* me,' Edward said. Blood welled along his skin, dotted his shirt. Mila looked up and Yasmin Zaid leveled a gun at her. Her thin mouth — with a stitched lip — jerked, wavered, slid back to a mostly straight line. The hand shook slightly. The eyes were blank of feeling. Whatever personality that once ruled this woman was gone, hollowed out and replaced with an emptiness that twisted Mila's stomach.

'Stand up,' Yasmin ordered.

Slowly Mila stood.

'Where's Sam Capra?' Edward said.

'Gone. Hunting that wife of his.'

'She got away from him? I'm supposed to believe that? And you just came here to confront us? Please. Do I look moronic?'

'You don't look smart,' Mila said.

'Is Sam Capra *here*?' Edward asked.

'No. I came alone.'

'These people you work for, who are they? Are you CIA? Or are you MI-5? What?'

'You should be so lucky,' Mila said. 'We're worse. We're focused. You won't know how to fight us.'

Edward backhanded her. She held her ground and her strength seemed to enrage him.

'I am not breakable, you pathetic small freak,' Mila said in a hoarse whisper.

'We'll see. Yasmin, bring her with us. Where are the guards?'

'They went to see about a delivery at the stables.'

Edward froze. 'Have they come back?'

'No.'

'Radio them. You, come with me.' He grabbed Mila, put the gun close against the cool of her throat. He hurried her down a hallway.

'Your friend, Piet. When I killed him,' Mila said, 'it was like beating a crying sack of flour.'

Edward didn't slow. 'You did me a favor.'

'Ah. Yes. You slaughtered your own people back in the brewery.' Mila turned her head and spat in Edward's face. Edward slammed her into the wall, drove a brutal fist into her stomach.

'You're trying to delay me. It won't work.'

'I know what you are,' she said to Edward. 'You worked with a slaver. You're no better than he is.'

453

'You don't like that Piet was a slaver?' Edward laughed. 'When I'm done with you, when you've spilled every secret about who you work for, I'm going to sell your ass to a man I know. You're not too old to be broken into the trade.'

'We don't need her,' Yasmin said, coming up behind them. She centered her gun on Mila's forehead.

'I feel sorry for you,' Mila said and Yasmin's aim wavered. 'Whatever he did to you, time can undo. I know people who have been through worse than you and they can recover.'

'What he did was set me free.'

'If there's a shred of Yasmin Zaid left under the brainwashing, you know that's not true.'

'I am what I wanted to be, always — free of my father,' Yasmin said. But her mouth wavered, her hand shook.

'You traded one bully for another,' Mila said.

'Don't shoot her,' Edward ordered. 'I want to talk to her. Did the guards report any problems?'

'Some horses got loose,' she said. 'They're chasing them down.'

He frowned. 'I don't like it.'

Yasmin, gun now to Mila's neck, hurried her to a wall hanging. Edward pushed it aside, pressed a release, and a door opened. Dim light showed stairs going downward.

'Churchill planned to use the estate as a base for a resistance, if needed,' Edward said. 'The resistance is here all right. It's just not the one he envisioned.'

He shoved Mila through the door.

★ ★ ★

The explosive felt soft and claylike under my fingertips, and for an odd moment I thought of playing in the mud along a river in Thailand with my brother Danny when we were young.

I heard the sound of a footfall behind me.

'I'm holding high explosives,' I said. 'So you probably don't want to shoot.'

No bullet came. I'd given him room for doubt. I risked a glance over my shoulder and saw the redhead aiming a gun at my back.

'Put the explosives down.' He spoke with a Serbian accent.

I answered him in Serbian: 'You're the smartest guy I've met here.'

'What?'

'Put the gun down. You're making me nervous. You don't want me nervous. *You* can only kill *me*. I can kill us both.'

An edge cut his voice. 'Put the gear down, stand up, hands on your head.'

The gear was in place and I slid the triggering device into my sleeve.

'Now!' the redhead yelled. He looked at me like I was the prize, a promotion, or bonus. Normally I applauded ambition. Not now.

Slowly I stood, turned, locked my fingers on the top of my head.

'Move back from the door.'

I obeyed, taking five steps.

'Where's the trigger?' the redhead asked. He was the smartest, after all.

'In the gear bag.' The edge of the triggering

455

device lay cool against my wrist. I took another step backward, getting the redhead between me and the door. The guy was doing it all wrong but I wasn't going to correct him. Not my place.

He knelt by the gear bag. Explosives apparently made him nervous, as they would any sane person.

'It looks like a silver cylinder,' I said, and it was true. But the guy didn't do what I hoped; he picked up the bag instead of searching its jumble and gestured at me with the gun. 'Let's go outside.'

'Don't jostle the bag.' I made my eyes frantic-wide. 'Not at all. Because it's a sensitive button, it gets pushed, then it's boom, boom.'

The redhead stopped so I turned and I pretended to stumble over the outstretched arm of the unconscious African, dropped one hand and the detonator device slid into my palm.

'Then you come find it. Not me. I'm not touching this again.'

'All right,' I said and I covered my ears and head as I dropped to the floor and pressed the detonator.

The blast juddered the heavy door and blew it off its hinges. The noise thrummed my bones as I leaped up and slammed a fist into the redhead's face. Already concussed and dizzy the man collapsed.

I bolted through the mist of grit and down a set of stone stairs into the darkened tunnel.

87

I put the map Mila had shown me into my head. Mila had told me there was a sharp bend after you entered the tunnel from the house and that was where the old complex lay, where Zaid would have done his secret work, and where the truth about this weapon would be.

I ran. Low dim lights illuminated the tunnel and the air smelled damp. I could hear in the distance a rushing of water. As I went down the tunnel, the sound increased in volume and then faded as I ran deeper into the ground. The passageway opened into a large open space, hewn from rock. Concrete blocks, gray with age, constituted the floor. The air was cool. Low-hanging lights. A metal table filled with an array of computers. Personal photos dotted it: Bahjat Zaid and his family; a picture of Yasmin as a girl, standing with her father, the sun slanting across her face.

I shut the door behind me and flipped the lock, then I sat at the computer at the center of the table. Gear that looked like external hard drives attached to the machines. Each held a small slot, too small for a CD, more like a flash drive connector but narrower. Each bore a Militronics stamp.

I moved the mouse. The computer's monitor awoke. Someone had been here, and recently. The screen showed what looked like a oversized barcode image, full of encoded data that meant nothing to me.

I looked at the file's name: DNA 017. This was someone's DNA analysis? The software had an Open Recent Files option.

There was a list of files under the arrow: DNA 001 to DNA 015. I hit the More option under the last listing. It showed a numerically ordered list of files, the last being DNA 050. Fifty files, fifty DNAs.

In each corner was a picture: DNA 050 was a girl who looked to be about twelve.

They were analysing the genetic profiles of children? Why?

I started scanning the files. Most were children; a few were men; the rest were women, most appearing to be in their forties and fifties. They looked like normal, everyday people. Some of the photos looked like passport images; but some did not; the people, all well dressed, walking, several of them waving at the camera. I recognized none of them and no names were attached to the files.

Who were these people?

I looked at the drives. There was one mounted on the computer's screen. Maybe all the answers were on the external drive — a backup I could take with me. I selected Eject on the icon.

But the drive didn't eject. Instead, a small chip did, from the drive. I held it up. It had a flat shiny surface, a grid on it echoing the one I'd seen on the weird gun and on remnants of the bomb. On the table lay a plastic case sized for the chip and I slid it into the protective case, then put the case into my shoe.

Then the door unlocked and opened as I began to sit down at the computer again.

Edward and Yasmin stood there, with a gun locked on Mila's head. The same unusual gun I'd seen him fire inside St Pancras.

'Hands up, Sam,' Edward said.

I obeyed.

'Finally. Face to face.' He smiled. 'Wow. You're a piece of work, man.'

I didn't speak. I thought of him slapping Lucy in the car. I thought of him driving away while my friends burned and died.

'I don't blame you for trying,' he said. 'You are much tougher than I ever thought you would be. We figured you for, you know, a PowerPoint jockey mostly. But no. I really have to say, you surprised me.'

My gun was on the table, less than a foot away from me. Even if they killed me and Mila, I could not let them walk. Whatever they were planning, my God, against innocent people, against *kids* . . .

'If you move or resist us,' Edward said, 'your baby dies. It just takes one call.'

He knew where my child was.

'Stay still,' Edward said. 'Yasmin, take his weapons.'

She obeyed. She brought the gun and the knife to Edward.

'Why?' I said. 'Why my wife? Why kill all your friends in Holland?'

'Why should I explain a thing to you? I don't care if you die confused. Yasmin, search him.'

She came back to me and her hands, shaking, roamed my body. She didn't think to check my shoes . . .

'Who do you work for, Sam?'

I nodded at Mila. Mila said nothing.

'And who does she work for?'

'She won't tell me.'

'Where is our troublesome Lucy?'

'Gone.'

'Dead,' Mila lied. 'She wouldn't tell Sam where his son is.'

'I will put your mind at ease about one point, Sam.' Edward smiled. 'I sold your son.'

They were the four worst words I'd ever heard. Worse than 'Watch what happens to men like him,' when my brother was killed. Worse than 'I'm supposed to kill you', said by my wife. For a moment I thought my knees would buckle.

'I sold him to a trafficker. He's keeping him close at hand for me. He'll kill him if you or Lucy make trouble.'

I have no words for the horror, the rage. White hot, like I'd been crafted from lightning.

I spoke the only words that occurred to me: 'I'm going to kill you.' I should have bargained. Said I'd do whatever. Just don't . . . just don't hurt my kid. Sell him? Vomit rose in my throat. I swallowed the sourness down.

Edward laughed. 'No, you're not.' He gestured me away from the computer. I stepped away. Then he did something odd. He ejected a computer chip from the side of the gun where the unusual grid lay and inserted a new one from his shirt pocket. The chip was just like the one in

460

my shoe. The gun was a bit bigger than the standard Glock, heavy and glossy and very dangerous.

'Are you giving a demo? Did you get his . . . ' Yasmin started.

'Never mind,' Edward said. 'I want to take them to the shaft.'

I didn't like the sound of that. Mila was in handcuffs. Yasmin took me by the arm, pressed a gun against my neck, and guided me out of the lab. We walked — me and Yasmin first, then Edward and Mila. The corridor was narrow, not enough room to fight. And if I fought, he had my son killed.

'Your father just wanted to save you,' I said to Yasmin. 'He gave up everything to save you.'

'My father wanted to control me.' She virtually spat out the words.

'Someone's controlling you far worse than your father ever did,' I said.

'Shut up,' Edward said.

I wanted to keep him rattled. He'd make a mistake, maybe. 'The DNA analysis for the kids and the other people? What's that about?'

'You'll be free of all worries by then,' Edward said. 'Don't burden your mind with it.'

This was the end of my life. No way out, no exit. We walked down to a dark room that was a widening in the corridor. I could smell the earthy tang of artesian water.

'Just kill them,' Yasmin said. Her voice shook. We knew what had been done to her and she didn't like us being around. We were from her

461

old life, outside the cocoon where Edward had trapped her.

The hallway's splinter opened up into a narrow room and the concrete ended at a heavy steel door. We went through the door into a round stone room. At the end of the room was a large hole, nearly seven feet across. In its depths I could hear a rush of water. I remembered seeing the start of a river on the property map. This must be the underground route of that river.

'Take him to the edge, Yasmin,' Edward said. She eased me along. Edward kept one gun trained on Mila's throat, the other on me.

'You behaved so your son lives,' Edward said. 'You are a good father.'

'You don't need to hurt my kid. Ever.' I was going to die for a son I'd never see. Okay. It was what it was. But I wished I'd gotten to hold him, to see his face, look for the clear bits of me and Lucy — yes, even Lucy, the Lucy of my dreams, the honest one — in his face.

Edward's mouth twitched. 'I'm sure he'll have a good life.'

I had nowhere to run, nowhere to fight and in my last moment I decided dignity was the only exit.

Let me go, Lucy had said, and I hadn't. I couldn't. It had got me here. 'I'm sorry, Mila,' I said. She nodded.

Edward raised the odd, heavy gun that he'd slipped the computer chip into and aimed it at my chest. He was seven feet away. I wondered if I'd die before I hit the water, if I'd drown. I didn't want to drown. I thought of my father, my mother, the weird life they'd made for me, my brother. I thought of Daniel. I held onto him.

The barrel of his gun centered on my chest.

He fired.

I kept standing and like an idiot I looked down at my chest, where a gaping hole should have been. My T-shirt was unmarred.

Four feet away from me, Yasmin staggered, stunned. Blood welled from her chest.

Couldn't be. The gun was aimed directly at me. Impossible. She was four feet to my left, and Edward's aim hadn't veered.

Edward laughed. Mila's mouth dropped open. I caught Yasmin at the edge of the shaft, felt the life pulse out of her as I held her in my arms.

'One man's science,' he said, 'is another man's magic.'

'What . . . what?' I managed. She couldn't be dead. The gun was aimed at *me*.

'I don't need her any more.' He raised the gun again.

'While you die in the dark, I am going to kill your baby,' he hissed. 'Just because I can.'

He fired two more shots. I held Yasmin, tried to turn us both away but there was nowhere to go. The bullets hammered into her and I fell into blackness. I fell into dark water, Yasmin still in my arms.

88

I stayed under the water. If I surfaced he would just shoot me. The cold was a shock. Illuminated by the crooked lights above the stone shaft, the water was gray.

I kicked down, steadying myself against the stone wall, trying not to rise again. If I broke the water's surface he would kill me. He had to believe me dead.

My lungs felt like they would explode. I heard a distant scream, perhaps Mila. Or, I wished, Edward. Mila was not the screaming type and I was sure Edward was. A crazy, disjointed thought to keep my lungs from shredding. But no Mila crashed down to join us. Yasmin's face turned to mine, an inch away, eyes half open in the water. I touched her throat. No pulse. A little wooden dove on her necklace floated between our faces.

The lights went out. In the distance I heard a heavy grinding — the stone door shutting. Total darkness. My lungs seared with the burn of spent oxygen. I eased to the surface, tried to breathe as quietly as I could. I failed. My gasps echoed against the stone.

No shot came. Edward was gone, and I was buried in a horrible, suffocating darkness.

★ ★ ★

I groped for the side of the stone shaft and explored it with my fingers. But it wasn't smooth concrete; it had to be a more ancient well with hewn stone that might give me a chance to climb it.

I didn't think I was badly hurt. I could feel furrows along my wrists where the skin had parted as the bullets had hit Yasmin as I held her and my already-wounded shoulder hurt very badly.

First try I made it up about five feet before I fell and slid back into the water's embrace. I didn't bother to rest. I clambered back up.

I am going to kill your baby. Just because I can.

I made it ten feet. At least I thought I had. The pitch dark could be playing a cruel trick on me. Then I ran out of handhold and flailed, found another grip, lost it. Stone hit my chin and opened the flesh. Blood was a seeping warmth down my front.

The cold water revived me. I started to climb again. Fell again. Climbed again, but now I started to recognize the stones by feel. I used the same path and, after a half-hour of agony, I felt the smooth lip of the top of the shaft.

I pulled myself up and lay, spent, my ribs afire with pain, the rest of me shivering and cold. I groped for the wall. I found it and searched, found the stone door.

It was bolted, locked into place, and over the lock was a smooth metal plate. It was engaged on the other side. I had no way to pick it, and no light to see by. Yasmin had taken my flashlight when she searched me.

I am in my grave.

The thought nearly paralysed me. Someone would come. But how long? How many days? Maybe never? Did anyone else know this complex even existed?

I am going to kill your baby. Just because I can. And the kids on the computer. They were part of Edward's sick plot.

I slid to the edge of the shaft. I could hear running water. The river would have to surface at some point. But I couldn't know what turns or twists the stream might take.

How many minutes can you hold your breath? How long?

'Long enough,' I said to the empty blackness. 'Long enough.'

I put my legs back over the shaft. It was one of the hardest things I'd ever done. I didn't want to drop back down into the awful inky darkness. It had taken so long to climb up. I could just wait. Sit and wait and hope that someone found me.

I thought of Daniel.

He needs me.

It was a strange thing to be needed. I hadn't known it in a long while. The need that Lucy had for me was false, a need curled in the grass like a coiled snake. My parents didn't need me after Danny died. They hated me for living. Daniel, though, he needed me, and he didn't even know it.

With that, I dropped into the black.

89

I dove down. Yasmin's body was gone. I could feel the tug of the moving current beneath the relative quiet of the shaft.

She'd sunk and she'd been swept away.

I filled my body with oxygen, heaving in slowly, deep, saturating breaths. I pushed my fear of the water deep back into my brain.

Then I went down. The dark water was cold and clutching. It felt like death grasping at me. I stayed close to the roof of the cave that met the end of the shaft; it was smooth stone, worn by the ceaseless knife of the water. The current shoved me forward. I brushed hard against the rocks that scraped my back and my head. Agony lanced my ribs.

Ten seconds in the deep.

No pain. No fear. I pressed on. Trying not to panic, trying to stay streamlined like a torpedo to move me along faster. The blackness was complete, like nothing I had ever experienced. I kicked, kept my hands out in front of me to try to protect myself from any hidden obstruction in the pitch black, told myself I had all the time in the world.

Fifty seconds. So I guessed. My lungs began to burn. Panic tugged at the edges of my mind. A little tug and then tearing.

I saw a blossom of dim light to my left and hurled myself toward it. The light grew brighter.

I kicked, I swam, trying to cut through the current to the unexpected glow. I saw a stone circle, dimly outlined from the light above, just like the shaft I'd fled. I kicked upward, fighting the urge to let the stale air — precious gold — out of my lungs. The shaft here was narrower. I went up.

And exploded into air.

I took long, huffing breaths. A grate lay two feet above my head, brown with rust. I breathed like I'd never breathed before. I tried to push open the grate. It was locked into place, with heavy iron bolts. I couldn't get up the shaft to the rest of the complex.

But the sound of the water was loud, and this must have been the rush of current I'd heard heading from the stables into the complex. I tried to pull the grate from the stone and I realized I was getting nowhere and losing precious strength.

I wanted to remain in this pocket of light and air, but I couldn't. My kid needed me. Mila needed me. Had Edward killed her? I thought not; he wanted to know who she worked for.

I had to go back into the darkness.

I took the long, low, heavy breaths, looking up through the stone shaft like a baby glimpsing a distant world at the end of the birth canal. I filled my body with air and kicked back into the blackness.

The cold river swept me away. I could feel a sudden shift downward in the angle of the ceiling. Going down, further from the ground, from the surface and the sacred air. Don't panic.

Whatever you do, do not panic.

I fought the urge to turn back to the last shaft. Then I felt the stone not only above me but below me. The tunnel had narrowed into a grave. I tried to turn back, panicking now, the bubbles exploding from me in a rush, and the water swept me forward between the stone jaws.

Narrow, black stone scraping both sides of me. My mother, my father. My brother, staring into a camera, silently pleading for his life. I would be with Danny again. My child. Lucy. I didn't want my last thought to be of Lucy. I thought of my brother, imagined I felt his strong hand taking mine.

Then no stone pressed against me. Above me, no rock. Light, a thousand miles above me. I kicked. Weakly. My muscles trying their last. Then my head burst above the water into the sweetness. I gasped, wheezed, turned into the water and vomited. I was in the river, bright with sunlight, alive.

I heard a buzz. A plane. I remembered the private runway on the map. And lying in the cold, gray wash of the river I looked up and saw Zaid's LearJet.

Edward was gone.

90

I lay on the bank until I found strength enough to get to my feet. I walked to the stables. The guards were gone, either to the hospital or to the main house, I guessed. I headed back into the complex.

I checked all the computers; all the hard drives were gone, all the backup drives, the strange drives for the chips. The chips were gone as well.

I checked my shoe. The chip I'd taken was still there.

Edward had put a chip in the gun before he'd shot Yasmin. So the chips somehow worked with the guns. The bizarre gun that shot Yasmin when it was directly aimed at me. That gun that shared a strange metal grid with the bomb that had killed the Money Czar back in Amsterdam.

I got into the delivery truck and drove to the empty plane hangar. No sign of Mila.

He'd taken Mila, because he wanted to know who was after him.

I drove down to the canal. I drove past where I'd climbed out from it and about another half-mile I found Yasmin's body. I waded into the water and I pulled her free from a thickness of rushes. I picked up Yasmin's body and carried her to the truck. I wasn't exactly crazy about the idea of driving back to London, with no license in my name, in a stolen delivery truck, with a corpse in the back. But I couldn't leave her body.

The gun that had killed Yasmin had not been like anything I'd ever seen before. I wanted to see the bullets.

91

Adrenaline thrummed with music, guitars battling under androgynous singing. Most of the crowd was in the building's courtyard listening to an impossibly trendy band play. I parked the pickup behind the bar in the reserved owner's space and used the private back entrance, carrying Yasmin's body on my shoulder, keying in the code Mila had given me to open the door. No one saw me. Lucy was still locked inside her windowless room. I left her there; right now if I looked at her I might kill her. I had to stay focused. I locked the doors behind me. The room had been soundproofed but I could still feel the distant beat of the music.

There was medical equipment in a closet, just as in Amsterdam. I found a scalpel. I spread plastic sheeting on the floor and carefully cut into Yasmin's bullet wounds. I couldn't shake either the image of the treasured daughter she had been, in her father's eyes, or that of the empty shell she'd become.

I found one of the bullets and carefully pulled it out. I wiped it clean and took it to the table.

The bullet was longer and slimmer than usual. Malformed slightly from the impact on entering Yasmin's body, it carried a grid on its nose that matched the grid I'd seen on the bomb shrapnel and the gun. I pulled apart the bullet. Inside lay a complex web of miniaturized technology.

I took photos of the dismantled bullet and loaded them onto the computer on the desk.

Then I took one of the phones from the shelf, checked it, and called a number in New York City.

It rang three times. 'Howell.'

'It's Sam Capra.'

'Sam.'

'I have my wife.'

'You *what?*'

'I have captured my wife.'

A long shocked silence.

'You were right, Howell. She betrayed me, the Company. I have proof.'

'Slow down.'

'Have you intercepted that cigarette shipment?'

'No. The customs people in Rotterdam haven't tracked it.'

'Listen. Lucy's connected to a group — your Novem Soles — that has stolen a prototype for some kind of high-tech gun. I want to send you photos of a bullet. I need it analysed.'

'No, you need to come in, Sam. Do this right.'

'No. I will send you the photos. I think that maybe they're targeting kids with these guns.'

'Kids?'

'I saw a list of fifty people that I think may be targeted. Mostly kids, a few men and women. Give me an email to send this information to you.'

'Bring in the evidence. Now, Sam.' Howell lowered his voice. 'All could be forgiven if you really have Lucy.'

But if I told him everything, I'd have to give him Mila as well. I wasn't prepared to do that.

'Give me an email, that's the only way we're doing this.'

Reluctantly he did. I hung up. I went to the computer and used an anonymizer program to access a series of servers, finally ending up on one in South Africa hosting a popular celebrity gossip site. It was a Company front. I used an inactive account there I'd once had as Peter Samson to send the photos I'd taken. I'd give Howell a couple of hours before I called back.

I changed into dry clothes I found in a closet then unlocked the soundproofed room. Lucy sat on the floor, chained to the wall.

I looked at her as though she were a complete stranger.

92

Lucy drew back against the wall. 'You look like crap.'

'Edward has this weird gun. You aim at one person and it kills another. Tell me about it.'

She shook her head. 'I don't know what you're talking about.'

'It uses a computer chip.'

'I don't know, Sam.'

'He has a list of children to target. Children, Lucy.'

'I honestly don't know.'

'He told me he was going to have our son killed. Just because he can.'

I could almost see the next *I don't know* forming on her lips. Then her mouth went slack. I waited to see what she would say.

'He said that he sold our son, Lucy. Is that true?'

She tried to stand. 'You have to listen to me, Sam, please . . . '

'Did you help him sell our child?' I screamed in her face.

She shook her head. Then she nodded. Then she shook her head again.

The number of people I have wanted to kill — not *needed* to kill, but *wanted* to kill — is very few. The men who killed my brother, who set me on my life's course. Piet, for raping and selling those women into slavery and smiling

475

about it. Edward. But now I wanted to kill Lucy. I felt my hands close around her throat and she didn't fight me, she just looked up into my eyes.

My fingers began to tighten against her flesh. Then I shoved her away from me.

She closed her eyes. 'Edward's keeping Daniel so I cooperate with him.'

'Where is he?'

'I don't know. After he was born, they took him from me . . . I had only held him once. Just the once, and I'd kissed him and given him his name . . . I couldn't stop them. The birth was hard, Sam. I wasn't strong enough then.'

I knelt by her. 'And?'

'And. He said he put Daniel with a trafficker. That he would sell Daniel to a couple back in the US and I'd never find him if I didn't obey him.'

She turned away from me. I turned her face back to me.

'I don't believe for a second that you're an innocent victim, Lucy. You might feel guilt for me, maybe even for our child. You let me live. But you have stayed with these people . . . '

'Because they had Daniel! Edward is very good at finding your one fear and capitalizing on it.'

'You put the bomb in the office,' I said. 'You had money going through accounts that the Company thought were closed. You are not the innocent victim of a kidnapping here. They had no leverage over you then.'

'I didn't know it was a bomb. I got in over my head. It was supposed to be a drive that just

476

copied the hard drives. Edward wanted the files from the office. All of them.'

'Like the files on my investigations.'

She nodded. 'I didn't know it was a bomb until Edward told me. I was in the car. I knew you were inside. He got out of the car because the remote for the detonator wasn't working and he had to get closer to the building. It had a twenty-second delay. He got it working and then he got back into the car and he realized I'd called you. Then everything exploded. I saved you, Sam.'

'And let everyone else die.'

'I had to make a hard choice, just like you do,' she said.

I took a steadying breath. 'If you want to help me, you'll tell me what I need to know. This weapon. It uses a chip. The chip I got was connected to a computer that had a DNA profile on it. You put the chip into the gun. It uses nanotechnology to somehow key a person's DNA to the bullet.'

Slowly she nodded.

I sat across from her. 'This is how I think it happened.'

She pulled her knees up to her chin.

'Edward is British but he's working in Eastern Europe. He works for one of these transnational crime rings our office was targeting. He finds out about these DNA-guided guns being developed in Hungary, maybe from the scientist informant that could have handed me the Money Czar. He kidnaps Yasmin to get leverage over her father. The ransom was these guns. But Zaid only delivers the guns, not the chips that make them work.'

Lucy looked up at me. 'Yeah, he screwed over Edward.'

'And Edward realized he had items of huge value in these guns. So he wanted them for himself. I'm thinking this whole operation was funded by the Money Czar. Edward wanted him out of the picture, so he had Yasmin kill the guy to make her look like she'd willingly joined her captors and to assure silence from her dad.

'But no one in the Amsterdam gang knew the Money Czar. Only Edward did. Edward's gang helped kill him and none of them knew that wasn't a bombing to show possible buyers that the technology they were smuggling worked, that it was simply a murder. And when they were done being useful to him as a cover, he killed all of them.'

I raised Lucy's jaw with my fingertip. 'Novem Soles. Nine Suns. Who are they? Is it Edward alone?'

'They're the ones who said I had to come work for them.'

'You didn't have a baby to be used against you.'

'No. I had you.'

I shook my head. 'Wrong. You didn't do this to protect me.'

'Yet there's that troublesome fact that I got you out of the building. No matter what I've done, Sam, I did that. You're welcome.'

I turned my hand into a fist and put it back in my lap.

'The bomb in Amsterdam. The police couldn't figure out how it was triggered. But it had some sort of scanning grid on it, the same as that gun, the same as the bullet. The bomb goes off if the person with the right DNA gets close enough.'

She nodded.

'Our office wasn't bombed because of the Money Czar. The bigger threat was one of the guys who'd pointed us toward the Money Czar — the scientist who was working on nanotech research. We were targeted because we were investigating that connection to a researcher in DNA technology, in nanotechnology. When he had to silence the scientist in Budapest, the next target who could help him use the technology was Yasmin. Did that scientist used to work with Yasmin?'

She nodded.

'These guns, these bullets, that bomb, it's all using nano-technology to tie the weapon to a person's DNA, isn't it?'

'Yes.'

'The Money Czar gives him money to bomb London, to wipe out my investigation. Then he uses the money to set up the group in Amsterdam. They thought they were going to be smuggling badasses. He pays off Piet and Nic to run a criminal smuggling operation for him so they could get the guns away from Zaid and to the United States.'

Lucy wiped at her face. 'Yes. A bullet encoded with DNA won't miss. Snipers can fire into crowds and know they will hit whoever they want to hit, unerringly.'

479

'So. Who are these fifty people they're targeting? Who are these kids?'

'I honestly do not know. I don't know what he's doing. Edward tried to kill me. Did you forget that? I can help you, Sam — I can help you.'

Deal with the devil, I thought, part two.

93

Moonlight broke through the clouds above Brooklyn, like a smile in the night.

Time was scarce. The burglar had to assume that there were hidden camera feeds in the empty apartment, scrolling data onto a hard drive. There might only be minutes for the burglar to find what was needed.

The burglar headed straight for the bathroom. A comb, a brush and a toothbrush lay on the shelf under the mirror. The burglar held up the hairbrush and examined it. Sam Capra had a full head of brownish-blond hair. Several strands lay entwined in the stiff bristles of the brush.

The burglar hoped some held surviving follicles. The brush went into a plastic bag, to be joined by the comb and the tooth-brush. A slide of the gloved fingers along the bag and the job was done.

Then out the door, down the stairs, back into the moonlight-dappled night. The burglar slid up the dark heavy balaclava that hid his face and walked off into the black. The key to dealing properly with Sam Capra lay rustling like a whisper in the plastic bag.

94

I called Howell back three hours later.

'What did you find?'

His voice sounded grim. 'The photos match a set of prototypical weapons being developed by the Company.'

By the Company? Oh, my God. 'Being developed for you by Bahjat Zaid.'

God or nature or biological accident gives us these awesome brains and this is what we do with them. We think of better ways to kill. Ways that make murder as easy as taking a breath.

These guns could change history. Kill a CEO, kill a president, kill a pope, kill a good guy, kill a bad guy, with total confidence that the bullet will find its mark.

Howell said, 'Sam, do you know what the goal is? Of this man having these guns? Why's he doing this?'

'Profit, I'm sure — he must be selling the guns to someone who has an agenda. He has the DNA of fifty people. One of my contacts, Piet, said there were fifty packages Edward was smuggling. Fifty. Fifty means something, but the fifty people aren't famous.'

'Would you recognize them if you saw them again?'

'Maybe. I don't know.' My head pounded.

The guns were a ticket back to having my life back. If the Company forgave me my sins, then I had a chance of getting back and keeping my son without looking over my shoulder for the rest of my life.

'New York,' I said. 'He's shipping the guns to New York.' Piet had told me that.

'Why? To who?'

'I don't know.'

Silence. Then: 'You listen to me. If you're setting me up for another fall, then you will seriously regret it.'

'I have bigger problems than you, Howell. I know you're just doing a thankless job. I'm sorry I'm your headache. I really am.'

'Sam . . .'

'When I find out more I'll call you.'

'You are still a Company officer.'

'I am not.'

'You are — and I am ordering you to come in.'

I hung up. I went downstairs and found Kenneth, the manager of Adrenaline. He came back up to the office with me. He sucked in his breath when he saw Yasmin's body.

'I didn't kill her,' I said.

'All right,' Kenneth said.

I explained what had happened, without telling him about the specific nature of the weapons. Best to keep that to myself. When I told him Mila had been captured, he said, 'How can I help?'

'Kenneth, who runs this? Who do you work for?'

'I work for Mila.'

'Who does Mila work for? This technology,

483

this level of resources — you folks have serious clout.'

Kenneth said, 'Mila should have told you.'

'Mila may be dead.'

He sat. 'She works for the Round Table.'

'Round Table? Like King Arthur's Round Table?'

'Mila likes to pretend they date back to a distant time, but it's simply a name. They're a group of powerful and wealthy people who have joined forces over many years and I don't know more than that. I do know I can make phone calls and certain resources are arranged for Mila, or for whoever, working for her.'

'Okay, I am working for King Arthur.' I nearly laughed. With all the insanity of the day, I felt on edge.

'No, sir.' Kenneth seemed alarmed that I believed this.

'And the Round Table owns the bars? Adrenaline, De Rode Prins in Amsterdam?'

He nodded. 'Under a front company.'

'Why do you work for them? What's your background?'

He studied me for a moment. Then he said, very formally, 'Ten years ago I was accused of murdering a former girlfriend. I was innocent, but I was convicted and I went to prison. Mila's employers helped me prove my innocence and they found the real killer. I owe them. And I have an interest in justice now I did not have before.'

'Is that Mila's background, too? Falsely

484

accused and saved by the Round Table?' Just like me.

'I cannot say because I do not know. Does it matter, right now? We must help Mila.'

'All right. I need transport to the United States. For me and for a prisoner inside that room. I can't cart her through first class in chains. Can you arrange that?'

'Yes. I can put you on a cargo plane.' Kenneth went to a phone and picked it up to make a call. He hesitated. 'Do you think Mila's dead?'

'I hope not. I hope I'm going to get her. Because I think whoever has her wants to know about the bars, and this Round Table.'

'They won't break her.' He said this with certainty.

I went back to the closet where Lucy was locked. I considered what would I do if I were Edward. The chips he'd keep with him, but the guns required end-user certificates, the documentation necessary to ship military-grade weaponry. He wouldn't risk forged documents on a shipment to America; too easy for authorities to seize the guns. Hiding the DNA guns among the thousands of containers coming into America, nestled inside a set of counterfeit cigarettes, meant far less risk.

Mila was Edward's bonus. He knew that he and his employers were facing a formidable enemy in whoever Mila and I worked for. It was the only reason she'd been kept alive. Edward was, if anything, a constant opportunist.

I stared down at Lucy. 'We're going to go get on a plane shortly. If you try and break away from me, or create a scene, I'll shoot you. Do you understand me, sweetheart?'

'Yes, monkey.' Lucy held up her wrists. 'I understand you.'

95

The cabin was bare but functional. Me, Lucy and the pilot and co-pilot. They did not ask questions about our guest in chains.

'They've been told that she's a prisoner of the CIA,' Kenneth said. 'I thought you would appreciate the irony.'

'Thank you.'

Lucy ate the sandwich that I gave her and drank from a bottle of water.

The plane left England behind, soaring out over the dark heavy steel of the Atlantic.

'I have a question for you. How exactly does the chip get the DNA?'

'I could bore you with the detailed science, but you put a hair or a blood sample on the chip and it encodes the bullets with the target's DNA. Then the bullet's like a guided missile.'

'But he shot at you and missed.'

'He didn't have my DNA on the chip. It acts as a normal gun without the DNA enhancement.'

'Does he have a chip with your DNA?'

She started to answer and then fell silent.

'He could and you don't know.'

'If he's smart he does. Edward won't let anyone betray him.'

'I've been thinking hard about why you turned traitor, trying to see how someone like Edward, a psychopath, could lure you away from your life with me.'

'Well, when you were investigating these criminal networks, I used to see the numbers you crunched. You look at these crime rings, you see how much money they make. Billions and billions. Twenty per cent of the world's economy comes from illicit goods now. It's easy money. You just need the right mix of skills. Smugglers, hit men, hackers. The right network. And then . . . ' She looked at me coolly. 'I'm a business person. They offered me some money. I knew I could clean it through Company accounts and make it vanish. At least, I thought I could. It wasn't going to hurt anyone, giving them the files.'

'Tell me about Novem Soles.'

'I have a contact. He got me my money, but I've never met him.' She finished her sandwich. 'I don't even know how they got their name. But I found an old legend about nine suns on the internet. Chinese. It says that there were once ten suns, but they wouldn't come out just one at a time during the day. All ten would come and their heat and power would incinerate the world.' Her voice had grown very soft. 'The emperor asked the father of the ten suns, Di Jun, to ask the suns to appear just one at a time, so the earth would not be remade in heat and flame. But the suns refused. So Di Jun sent an archer named Yi, with a magical bow and arrow, to frighten the suns, to make them obey. Instead Yi shot nine of them, so only one sun would remain.' She risked a smile. 'Because the nine suns, returning, would destroy the world, annihilate whoever tried to tame them. I don't even know if that story has anything to do with the Nine Suns, or why they use a Latin name if it's based on a Chinese legend.' She smiled but there was no joy in it. 'Nine people who could remake the world, that's how they think of themselves.'

'Is Edward one of the nine? Or is he a flunky?'

'I don't know.'

'These fifty people. What's special about them?'

'I said I don't know.'

'That's a lie.'

'No, it's not.' Lucy drew her knees up to her chin. She peered at me above them. 'When you asked me to marry you, I almost said no. Not because I didn't want to marry you. I did. But I felt like you wouldn't be enough. I wanted a lot from life. I wanted money. I wanted respect. I wanted to work hard for ten years and then have enough to live on. Not work my fingers to the bone clawing up some male-run bureaucracy, not putting my life in danger for a bunch of ideals.' She slid her legs out in front of her and for a moment we were back in London, drinking lager in our apartment, talking about our future. 'I knew you didn't care about that. And for a time I thought I could live without the money. I couldn't.'

I didn't say anything. She was quiet for nearly forty minutes and I thought she'd fallen asleep. Then she said: 'I think I will tell you a little bit about who I work for,' she said.

'Why the change of heart?'

'Because do you think the Company's really going to welcome you back? Even if you help them? Maybe they'll give you a pardon. Maybe. But they'll never, ever let you work for them again. They won't trust you. They won't think you can follow orders. Orders trump all.'

'Are you telling me this to offer me a job?'

She stretched out a leg. 'Consider it a lifeline. I think the Company will simply kill both of us when they're done.'

'No.'

'Oh, not them officially. But there are rogue groups running inside.'

I looked hard at her. Could I have been so wrong for so long? The thought was a fist in my chest, in my brain. 'I wasn't enough for you. Marrying me wasn't enough,' I said.

'Marrying you was . . . Marrying you was the right thing to do. I loved you. It was an act of optimism.'

'I don't believe you loved me.'

She raised an arm, slid up the sleeve, and I saw a trio of round, brutal burns on her upper arm. 'That was the price of making that phone call that got you out of the office. Edward thought I'd betrayed them, leaving you alive. A dead patsy is more valuable than a live one who can deny and possibly disprove the frame.'

'But you did frame me.'

'You were alive. I knew they might let you go, that there was a chance. Better prison than a grave.'

'Why wasn't I enough? Wasn't I a good husband?'

490

'You cannot possibly care about my opinion.'

I started to answer and she raised a hand. 'No, you don't care about me. I see through all this talk. This is about the baby.' She smiled and then the smile went away. 'My trump card.'

'Don't talk about Daniel that way.'

'I know. He's a person. Who grew inside me for nine months.' She wiped a hand against her lip. 'When we found out I was pregnant, do you remember . . . ' It was a sign of her psychosis, I thought, that she even had to ask.

'I remember.' It had been right after dinner; she'd taken the test without telling me of her suspicions. And brought me the test, with its little affirmative plus, and I'd whooped and hollered and she'd worn a stunned smile on her face.

'Well, I thought, that's that. I won't work for Novem Soles any more. I will walk away. I will cover my tracks and I will stop and no one will ever know that I ever sold bits and pieces of information. I will have this baby and I will love Sam and that will be my real life.' She rubbed at her lip and she dropped her gaze from mine. 'But they don't let you walk away. You don't submit a letter of resignation. They told me they would kill you.'

I said nothing.

'So. My choices were let you die and then be faced with a life I didn't want, with a child, or to keep working for them and figure out a way to cut loose and to set you free.'

'You could have come and told us that you were in trouble. Cooperated with us. You've used

491

me, you've used our kid.'

'I couldn't come back after the bomb. I couldn't do prison.'

'There are worse things than prison.'

'Is that a threat? *You* won't hurt me.' A half-smile played on her face. 'You won't. You're the good guy. I'm the mother of your child.'

'Where did you have the baby?' I said. 'You owe me this, Lucy. Tell me.'

'I owe you nothing. I saved your life. We're square.'

'There is a Company airfield in Maine, near Damariscotta. If I tell the pilots to land there, they will.'

'I thought we were going to New York.'

'No. I think I should give you back to the Company.'

'Sam, we had a deal. You stop Edward, I walk.'

'But you don't know where he is, you say. I'll bet you'll tell the Company. I bet they'll make you talk.'

'But the guns . . . '

'My son takes precedence. Maybe these people haven't even fixed their targets yet. Maybe the fifty people are just to see if they can encode a chip; they may not be targets at all, just DNA samples that they stole somehow.' I crossed my arms. 'I can't wait to see what Howell does when he gets his hands on you. Oh, I was just the warm-up, sweetheart. You're the main course. You made him look very bad. Hell hath no fury like a bureaucrat screwed.'

'He'll kill you, too.'

'No, I'll get forgiven. He'll say he authorized

me in secret or some bull. He'll be clean. He'll have his traitor in his pocket.'

'The Company won't let you land at their airfield,' she said.

I stood up. 'I can be talking in five minutes with Howell. I'll have clearance.'

'You weren't always so stubborn.'

'Where did you have the baby? Tell me and we'll keep going on to New York.'

She decided to believe me. 'Strasbourg. A private clinic called Les Saintes. On the tenth of January. He was given the name of Julien Daniel Besson.'

'Who took him?'

'A woman.'

'Who does Daniel look like?'

'Babies all look like Winston Churchill at first. But he has your eyes, Sam.'

'What is this broker's name?'

'Edward didn't tell me. I don't know. That's how they kept me in their pocket. It was insurance.'

'And they gave you money for my son?'

'Our —'

'You just lost the right to call him yours, Lucy. Don't you *ever* call him yours again.'

'No.'

'Only because they haven't sold him yet. Jesus.'

She stared at me and she knew the deal between us was dead, that I was never going to let her go without having my child.

'What's going to happen to me?' she said.

'You tell me everything and then you tell the Company everything. I want my name cleared.'

493

'Your name is never, ever, going to be cleared. Sam, there will always be someone in power who believes you knew. That maybe you didn't do anything wrong, but you knew what I was doing and you kept your mouth shut. Either hoping that I would stop, or I would never be caught. You're a good husband. That made you a bad agent.'

'Then I'll focus on being good at my job. Where is Edward delivering the gun chips? Where in New York? You cooperate with me and I'll be your advocate with the Company.'

She considered this and for several long seconds there was only the whine of the engines. 'At the new Yankee Stadium. Since Edward tried to kill me I'm assuming he thought that you were going to capture me and he wanted the plan protected. He won't change it if he thinks I'm dead.'

'What time is this meeting?'

'At eight tonight. As the game starts. The season's just begun.'

I stared at her. I thought of our last morning together, our lives so normal, our lives such a lie that it clenched the air in my lungs.

She said, very softly: 'Do you remember once that I asked you, if we knew a day was our final day together, what you would say to me?'

I remembered. 'I'd say anything but goodbye. I never wanted to say goodbye to you.'

She looked at me and I couldn't tell if there were tears in her eyes or if it was the dim light of the cabin. 'I think I'll say my goodbyes now, Sam.'

494

96

Lucy and I walked free of the private plane. Our papers had been stamped and the customs official waved us through. Thank you, Kenneth and flight crew. Borders. Do they even matter any more?

We exited the airport and walked along the short service road. A car pulled up and I pushed her into the back seat and then followed. I'd phoned ahead.

'Hello,' August Holdwine said.

'Mr Nice Guy. You just committed professional suicide,' Lucy said as he pulled the car away from the curb.

'Career advice from you is rich,' he said. 'How are you, Lucy?'

'I should have married you. Not him,' Lucy said.

'Be nice. August is going to get the credit for your capture,' I said.

'You're not surrendering to the Company?' Lucy jerked her head to look at me.

'No. I'm going to go get our kid. Thanks again, August.'

August glanced at Lucy in the rearview. 'I always thought it was iffy to trust you. I hate being right so often.'

I could feel the defensiveness rising in her. 'You're betraying the Company yourself, going out of bounds to help Sam.'

August said, 'You got a limited imagination, Lucy. Certain people in the Company might entirely approve of what I'm doing. As long as it nabs you.'

Lucy opened and then shut her mouth.

'You mean we have help?' I asked.

'No. You have me,' August said. I wasn't sure how tough we could be. I was injured, and August had been shot in the arm. We weren't exactly a pair of badasses.

Lucy seemed to study these words, as if they hung in the air above August's head.

'Where's Howell?' I asked.

'Summoned to Langley. Whatever technology you found these guys have, it has set off a firestorm.'

'The rendezvous is in one hour,' Lucy said. 'I suggest you drive a little faster, since you're in such a hurry to be a hero.'

'There has to be a reason they're meeting at Yankee Stadium,' August said.

'A demonstration,' I said. 'You want to prove a bullet can truly, without fail, seek out a single target among thousands? A crowd is the best way to make your point, without a doubt. So who's the target?'

'Any of the star players,' August said. 'And the governor was scheduled to throw out the first pitch, I checked, but he had to cancel.'

I looked at her, thinking of the photos of the kids I'd seen on Zaid's computer. 'Kids. Are they going to kill a kid at this game?'

Lucy said, 'I told you, I don't know if there's even a demonstration. That's between Edward and the buyer. It seems awfully risky to me.'

I said to August, 'Do you have a liaison with the NYPD?'

'Yes, but I ask them anything, they'll want to know my source. And I'm supposed to be on leave.'

'Do they know that?'

'I imagine not.'

'Say the tip's anonymous. Call. Find out if there are any groups of kids being brought in.'

August phoned his contact. 'Hey, Lieutenant Garcia, this is August Holdwine at the Manhattan CIA office.' Pause. 'Yeah, I'm fine, thanks. I'm kind of dodging channels here but I thought I better talk direct to you. Do you have any groups of kids coming in for today's game? We picked up some chatter that talked about targeting a kid.' He listened. 'Okay, no, I don't have more than that.' He listened some more. 'Can you give me a rundown?'

'If Edward sees you coming, our son is dead,' Lucy said. 'Just so you know.'

'Not if he gets caught first.'

'I wouldn't be willing to risk it,' she said, as though I were the bad parent.

August got off the phone. 'Twenty-seven kids groups there today, everything from orphans being brought in from a Catholic orphanage in Queens to Boy Scouts and Girl Scouts and prep school groups. They're going to put extra security around them all but Garcia needs to know more.'

'We don't have more.'

'This is getting people's attention, Sam.'

497

August glanced at me in the car. 'I suspect the police are going to want to talk to me as soon as I get to the stadium. I can't back you up if I'm chatting up Garcia. They'll want threat assessments . . .'

'Good.' I raised my hand.

'Like a cop can stop that bullet once it's fired. Nothing can,' Lucy said.

'We find him before he ever fires,' I said.

'You risk our child to save a stranger's,' Lucy said. 'I should have killed you in Amsterdam, Sam. At least our son would be safe. If you're wrong . . .'

I had been so wrong about so much. I couldn't be wrong now.

97

'I expect he'll be alone,' Edward said into the phone. 'Do you have the sample for him? In case I need it?'

'Yes. I took the precaution. I'll see you shortly, Edward, and I look forward to the demonstration.'

'Yes, I think the whole world will be impressed,' Edward said. Bright sunshine kissed New York City; the sky gleamed a faultless blue. He felt happy. He was nearly done with his trudge along a very dark road. He missed Yasmin, to his surprise. He had made her, shaped her into the person most useful to him, and he wondered if he had given her up too easily. Ah. Soon he would have enough money where he could attract a woman who required much less effort to bend to his will.

A marvelous day, it was, to prove that fear works wonders.

98

It was a gorgeous afternoon in New York. The sun smiled down like a saint. August already had our tickets and we moved through the crowd.

August's phone rang. He answered and listened. 'Yeah, I don't have more information, Garcia. Kids. Credible, I don't know how much. You can't take the risk, though . . . yeah. What? What? Um, okay.'

He hung up the phone. 'Garcia had to go; he's dealing with the governor's security detail.'

'You said . . .'

'He un-cancelled. The governor is here to throw out the pitch,' August said. 'His son apparently begged him to do it.'

The governor of New York was in his late forties, a man named Hapscomb, popular, but with no plans for higher office. 'That's it,' I said. 'Surely if you want to demo a weapon, you kill a prominent person.'

But killing a governor — it lacked the impact of killing a president, or a religious leader. It seemed a smaller stage for Edward's ambitions, especially with such a powerful weapon. And none of the people in the photos were politicians, at least none that I recognized.

We watched thousands of people settling into their seats. The game would begin in minutes. I scanned the ring of the stadium, looking for a likely spot for a sniper to fire from. But the security details would already be watching those.

Lucy saw what I was doing and shook her head. 'As long as he's in range, Edward doesn't have to set up a careful position to shoot the governor,' she said. 'He can just fire. The bullet will do most of the work, if there's nothing in its way.'

'If he's delivering the guns here, too, he needs seclusion.' I held her between us, a firm grip on her arm, steering her through the crowd, August on the other side of her.

Fifty guns. Fifty bullets. Fifty states. Fifty governors? But none of the people in the files were governors. 'This is the product demo, isn't it? And then the buyer will move onto the next targets.'

'You've missed the other timing advantage of this gun,' she said. 'God, I thought you were smarter, Sam.'

Any fool could assassinate. Fools had been doing it for centuries. But now, with these guns. 'With fifty guns all at once, you can hit many targets,' I said. 'Mass assassination. You kill a governor, security goes up on all the others. You kill them all at the same time and . . . '

'What would it do to this country?' Lucy said. 'Oh, it would be a shockwave. How do you fight a weapon like this? And, psychologically, what does it do? Every governor, dead within minutes of each other. Their replacements, dead in another month. No one is really going to be rushing for those jobs then, are they? You have a profound shock to the political system if you cannot guarantee that leaders stay alive. What does it do to America if the leadership pool gets rapidly thinned, if no one will lead because they're going to be killed? It makes the world weaker. It makes it easier for the criminal networks to do their job, to commit more crimes. Maybe even to take over.' She smiled. 'You know, the crooks run parts of Colombia, of Moldova, of Pakistan. Why not here? Why not in the West?'

'Who's this buyer?'

I watched August hurrying down toward the field. He hadn't waited to hear more. He was heading straight for the field, and the security detail for Governor Hapscomb.

I scanned the stadium.

'Let me go and I'll tell you where he is,' Lucy said.

'The baby?'

'No, I mean Edward. You can't have it both ways, Sam. I'm keeping where the baby is a secret.'

She knew. She knew and she knew where the meeting site was. God*damn* it.

'Tell me!' I grabbed her shoulders. 'Lucy, for God's sakes, don't do this. Tell me!'

'Hey, buddy,' a deep voice rumbled behind me. I glanced over my shoulder. Three guys, thick-necked, short haircuts. Five hundred pounds of muscle, glaring at me.

'You don't need to talk to the lady that way. Let go of her arm,' the good citizen said.

'The lady is pure evil, like it's any of your business,' I said.

It did not occur to the good citizen that, in an equal-opportunity world, a woman could be pure evil. 'You let her go,' he said, not backing down.

Lucy began to moan as if in pain.

The slugger slugged me. Hard. I saw it coming and ducked back but he still connected with my face. Lucy launched a hard kick that caught me on the collarbone.

I let go. She ran. I saw her heading toward the large section of private suites.

It might be perfect. Elevated. Private. Lower a window, fire, leave in the resultant chaos.

The good citizen grabbed me. 'Asshole, you're done.'

I saw two police officers racing toward us. So I played the victim. I screamed, 'Please help me, help me, he's gone crazy!'

Every bit of subtlety helps. It shifted the cops' reaction ever so slightly, the guy tackling me looked the bigger threat. You never want to look the bigger threat. But of course the cops were going to take us both down. They couldn't risk doing otherwise.

The cops — one heavy, one skinny — took us down. I got the skinny one and a hard sharp blow and he was on his knees. I seized the gun from his holster, slamming my fist into the back of his throat and ran into the crowd, the gun high. The other cop couldn't risk the shot, not with the crowd between us.

I saw Lucy. Then I heard the roar rising from the crowd.

I risked a glance toward the field. And saw August, bolting out onto the field, as the governor stood on the mound with a teenage

503

boy, presumably his son, ready to throw out the first pitch.

And the realization hit me like a bolt.

His son. *His son.* It wasn't the governor at all. And it wouldn't be all the governors to come.

It would be their kids. Their husbands. Their wives.

99

Next to the stadium's main outdoor private suite area, an interior bar with a view of first base was closed for repairs. No place is more deserted in a stadium than a closed bar. Inside, the buyer looked down over the field and said, 'Let's get started.'

Time to begin an extraordinary audition. Edward thought, in a flash, of the first time under the lights, his brain burning with the right lines, eager to pretend to be a whole new person.

Edward lowered the window of the closed bar slightly and placed the rifle into the gap. There was no rifle sight; he didn't need one. But he didn't want to risk the demo going poorly, so he aimed toward the mound. And saw the big blond man barreling out onto the field, deftly stiff-arming a policeman who tried to stop him.

Interference. No. Edward pulled the trigger without hesitation.

100

Governor Hapscomb saw the runner — screaming that he was a CIA agent — plowing past an errant security line, heard the rising gasp of the crowd, and had he been alone he would have simply stared his attacker down. But he had his thirteen-year-old son Bryant with him, and he could not bear the thought of Bryant being harmed. So he threw himself on his surprised son, in case the crazy in the nice suit was armed, just as the bullet shot out over thousands of spectators, its nano-sensors seeking the one true match among thousands.

★ ★ ★

I saw the flash at the edge of the main-level outdoor private suites. Through a slightly opened window near the seating area. Right where Lucy was headed, a few rows above us.

I caught her and pressed the cop's gun against her ribs.

I wrenched her around so I could see the mound. Screams erupted from the massed crowd. The governor and his son were down on the mound, not moving, August buried under a pile of police.

'Let me go!' she screamed. 'Let me go and I'll tell you where the baby is!'

'Just tell me!' I hadn't stopped Edward's bullet.

I'd failed.

She threw a fist against my jaw, I wouldn't let her go, and we slammed into the railing.

* * *

'Sam Capra,' the buyer said. 'There.'

Edward tore his stare away from the mound. He couldn't tell if the Hapscomb boy was down or not. Sweat exploded down his ribs. He ejected the chip and slipped the new one in. The gun whirred, the match being made, the bullet given its own soul. The coding process would be done when the green light appeared.

He couldn't wait. Edward raised the rifle and fired.

* * *

'Tell me!' I said, clutching her close. We spun, her fighting me.

'Daniel's in . . . ' and then she stiffened. I heard the impact of metal hitting flesh and she fell in my arms.

'No!' I screamed. 'No!'

* * *

'This hasn't gone well.' Edward had to pick his words carefully or the deal would fold. 'I think the governor took the bullet meant for the child.

He covered him just as I fired. This isn't a normal situation, since we'd usually strike without warning . . . '

He turned to his buyer and the knife flashed across his neck. Edward staggered, tried to close up the wound with his hand as the blood gushed. Pointless. He fell against the wall and thought *no no it hurts and I'm afraid I'm afraid* —

The buyer stepped away from the spray of blood. He could see panic arising not only from those close to the field but in a nearby section, where Edward's second bullet had scored. No sign of Lucy. No sign of Sam Capra.

He collected the briefcase of DNA chips. Technology could always be refined. This demo might have been too extreme. Fine. Time was on his side. Resources were on his side. There were networks of rogue programmers, hackers, scientists, assassins, all eager to help him refine Bahjat Zaid's prototype.

He had the chips, and the rest of the guns would arrive in the next few days. He could collect the shipment, and even if those prototypes were lost, he could recreate as many guns as he needed based on the gun he had. And he hadn't transferred the funds. He folded the gun; it telescoped down into a wide metal tube which he put in his briefcase.

There were worse days.

He stepped out, the panicked crowd rushing pell-mell and no one noticed him hurrying toward an exit with brisk efficiency. Thousands began to pour out of the stands, the police trying to effect an orderly evacuation.

He was close to the gate when he heard a voice say, 'Hello, Howell.'

101

Howell kept his bags close to him. His pinched frown told me he could feel the gun in his ribs.

'Move and I'll kill you,' I said.

'So. Turning yourself in.'

'Don't bull me. You're the buyer.'

Howell took a deep breath. 'Kill me and Mila dies.'

'She'd call that a fair trade,' I said.

He kept walking. So did I. I was careful to keep the gun under a fold of my jacket.

'You left your wife to die?' Howell asked.

'She's not my wife any more.'

'Ah.'

'Who are you?'

'Howell.'

'Who are you really? Who do you work for?'

'The Company.'

'No, you don't. The Company hired Zaid to develop these guns. You would have gotten them without stealing them.' He'd used Edward to steal them. Of course. If the guns were stolen before they were ever delivered, then Howell would never be suspected. He'd chased me to keep me from tracking down the guns, or perhaps he'd hoped to double-cross Edward and steal them before he had to pay millions for them. Using me to see if I could locate the trail, do his dirty work.

'Part-time,' he amended. 'I have another job.

510

We can use a man like you.'

'Novem Soles. You asked me if I'd heard of it because you wanted to know if she'd talked. Not because you were on its trail. You were protecting Novem Soles.'

'Sam, that deal . . .'

God, everybody wanted to make a deal. I was sick of deals. 'No. Where is Mila?' Now we were out of the gates, streaming into the parking lot.

'She's being questioned. We want to know about you the same way you want to know about us.'

'You got Lucy to turn. She *worked* for you.' And that was worst. He'd used her. She'd gotten her orders from someone inside the Company. I believed her. She hadn't known it was a bomb she'd planted in the London office until that final minute, when Edward left to make sure the detonator worked and she called me . . .

Howell gave me the equivalent of a shrug.

'Where is my son?'

'I don't know.'

'Don't lie to me. You will simply tell me where my son is.'

'Actually, I don't know. Your wife handled all the arrangements for the baby broker.'

'That's not what she said.'

'And you believed her?' Howell cleared his throat. 'This is my car.'

We got inside it, him sliding over from the passenger side, me keeping the gun on him, sitting in the backseat.

'Yeah, now I do. You're the asshole, Howell. You're the king of the assholes.'

'I can make your troubles go away, Sam. I can clear your name. I can stop being your inquisitor and be your champion. We get rid of Mila. You forget about the guns. I can get the Company to see you infiltrated a dangerous group in Holland. We'll say you were on a secret job and we expose your wife as the, well, traitor she is. Was.' He turned his flat stare onto me. 'I can even help you find your child.'

'We'll pretend, in other words, that it never happened.' His pet phrase he'd used with me in that distant prison where I had been the only inmate.

'Yes,' he said.

'No,' I said, and I shot him. The bullet sprayed through his heart and he jerked. The sound of the shot was loud but no one was right by the car then. Immediately afterwards a group of Boy Scouts hurried by and they glanced at me and Howell sitting in the car. He stayed sitting up, his head down a bit like he'd decided to grab a nap, like the shooting, to use a phrase he favored, had never happened. I just got out and walked away from him, sifting into the crowd.

Let me go. Now I'd let it all go. Everything. All of it. Gone.

102

When a Company exec dies in a baseball stadium parking lot, right after an attempt is made on a governmental official, the case gets taken from the NYPD and the Company takes over the investigation. The Company was most interested in the nano bullets and the gun, and the shipment manifest tied to a container of cigarettes.

The fifty people I'd seen on Zaid's computer were indeed the kids and spouses of America's governors. No one is targeting them now, and they sleep safe in their college dorms, their beds at home, their cradles. Including Bryant Hapscomb, shielded by his father's body; the bullet couldn't change course fast enough. Thousands attended the governor's funeral. He died for his child, although the world believed him to have been the target. It did not occur to anyone that a thirteen-year-old boy was the target and that the governor simply threw himself on his child, covering him in the same millisecond that Edward pulled the trigger.

A few days after the shootings at the stadium, I sat in the Round Table's New York bar, an elegant space called Bluecut, drinking a Boylan Bottleworks Ginger Ale, my favorite soda, waiting for Mila to show up. The bar sat on the edge of Bryant Park, not far from the hubbub of Times Square, and it was a beauty. Perfect mahogany curve, fine chairs, the right tools with which to lift cocktail creation to an art. A glance, even in the early afternoon, told me that it was a Destination. Every person at the bar, every person at a table had their own story. Soft jazz — but not light jazz — filled the air, played on a grand piano by an African-American woman with a shock of blonde hair and fingers delicate enough to impress Monk or Mozart. I liked this Bluecut bar a lot, but I felt itchy waiting here. I had things to do.

I ordered a Glenfiddich for Mila and had it waiting for her. She had been kept in a rental office near a port; she'd been found by a member of a Salvadoran cleaning crew. Howell had been questioning her. Her broken arm was the worst of it, but the burn marks on the soles of her feet were taking a long while to heal.

August slid onto the stool. He pointed at Mila's drink. 'Can I just down that?'

'It's for my friend Mila, but go ahead.'

'If she drinks that, she's my friend too.'

I thought it best not to mention that Mila was the one who'd grazed him with a bullet in Amsterdam. 'Go ahead, but it's eleven in the morning,' I said. 'Try the ginger ale, it's perfectly cold and good.'

'But whisky means good tidings,' he said.

'I thought whisky was for wakes.'

'One man's wake is another man's good tidings,' August said. He cupped his hands around the glass. 'The police identified you, you know. Lucy getting shot got captured on a security camera. They know you didn't do it.'

'I know. They haven't bothered me.'

'The Company sat on it. It took a lot of grease and muscle and loss of face. NYPD is quite particular about its officers being bested in terms of control of their firearms.'

I sipped my ginger ale. 'So now the Company is shielding me?'

'They — we — oh hell,' August said. 'None of us are fools. While I was being suffocated under the weight of New York's finest, you were killing Howell.'

'If I did, they're ignoring it. He's the biggest embarrassment to the Company since . . . '

'Since Lucy. You can say it.'

'Officially, there are no prints.'

'Then it didn't happen. Like Howell always said.'

August cleared his throat, studied his drink, took a nice healthy sip. 'The Company has deputized me to offer you your job back.'

'Why you?'

'They think you'll only listen to a drinking buddy.'

'I *would* only listen to you, August. You were a real friend to me.' I clinked my green bottle against his whisky. 'But I have to find my kid. And the Company, except for you, was quick to think me a traitor. Not a nice vote of confidence.'

'Sam, you must understand . . . '

'I do. I don't want them. They had no faith in me.'

August savored his drink over several small sips. 'This is why I needed the drink. You're a bad influence. I can only hope you are going to

515

find gainful employment.'

'I don't care about a job. I have to find my kid.'

'How? Edward is dead, Howell is dead, Lucy may never wake up.'

'I lean on the right people back in Europe, I'll find him.'

'The Company isn't going to let you go quietly into that good night.' August lowered his voice. 'They're going to keep a watch on your passport. They're going to be shadowing you when you might not expect it. This whole Howell working for a secret group has them shaken. They'd like to pretend it isn't as frightening as it actually is. They want to know what you're doing. Who you're going after.'

'They can try and find out, as long as they don't get in my way. Are you sticking with them?'

'Yes, I must get my semi-suspect hands on my retirement benefits.' August shot me a sidelong look. 'I'm sure, though, we'll see each other again.'

'I'm sure, too.'

He got up and fished in his wallet.

'I got it,' I said. 'Least I could do.'

'Yes, but I have a job,' he said.

'No, really, I got it. Thank you, August.'

'You will find your son, Sam. I know you will.'

'I know I will.' I watched August leave and wondered if anyone was shadowing him. I could smell the whisky left in August's glass and I ordered one for myself.

I was just starting on its replacement when Mila slid onto the stool.

516

103

'Hello, Sam.'

'Mila.'

'I promised we would have a drink together when all was done.' Her bruises were healing but there was a sadness in her eyes instead of the steel I was used to in her gaze. I gestured at the bartender. He brought her a Glenfiddich without being told.

I said, 'That doesn't go with painkillers.'

'Americans have obsessive worry about drug interactions. So risk-averse.'

'With such a nice place, why did you go drink at Ollie's?'

'I would like to buy Ollie's bar, as he said. He won't sell.'

'Two bars in one city?'

'Brooklyn and Manhattan are two different concepts.' She glanced around. 'My, I like bars. Bluecut is really marvelous.'

'I like bars, too.'

'Good,' she said. 'Would you like this one?'

I glanced at her. 'I like this one just fine.'

'You misunderstand. Would you like to own it? Bluecut, and all the bars we have? The Adrenaline in London, the Rode Prins in Amsterdam, Taverne Chevalier in Brussels? We have many more: in Las Vegas, Sydney, Miami, Paris, Moscow, all around the world. I think we're up to thirty.'

She had to be kidding so I laughed. 'Sure. You and I can go have a drink in each one. After I have my son back.'

'Sam. My employers are interested in retaining your services. You did extraordinary work for us.'

'Was Bahjat Zaid part of your Round Table? One of the rich and powerful members?'

She didn't show surprise that I knew the Round Table name. She said, 'Yes, he was. He supplied us in the past.'

'He wasn't such a nice guy.'

'He was a desperate man, trying to save a daughter. He made poor choices.'

I started to shake my head, but Mila deserved better than scorn. 'I don't even know who you people are.' And I remembered what I'd said in London to the suits, about networks that came together only to do work, snapped apart and reformed in new shapes, some so powerful and with such reach that they had infiltrated government. I'd talked about criminal networks that way; perhaps the Round Table was such an informal network, but a force for good. Novem Soles could be its opposite, the dark to its light.

'Together, we stopped Edward. We stopped Howell. You know we're on the side of the angels.'

'I've had enough mystery. I *have* enough mystery. I have to find my son.'

'Sam. Do you trust me?'

'Yes.' That wasn't a hard decision. I did trust Mila. She was halfway to crazy, and she was unpredictable, but I could see a core of decency that ran through her clear as iron in stone.

'There's a reason certain people inside the Company don't want you to find your child,' she said quietly.

'What?'

She slid a piece of paper over to me. It read: AGENT CAPRA CAN ONLY BE CON-TROLLED BY HIS DESIRE TO FIND HIS CHILD. ALL FILES ON CAPRA ARE CLASSIFIED DUE TO and then long black lines of redaction. 'That is from a highest classification file. Whoever has taken your child, the powers that be wish to keep that person's identity a secret. Out of a desire to control you.'

I stared at her. 'I don't believe this.'

'I think the Company would like to help you. I am not at all indicting the CIA. But there is a secret cabal inside it, I believe, connected to Howell; perhaps he only was their tool. These people will block you at every turn. If you try and work inside with them, your quest for Daniel will be futile.' She took a long, savoring sip of her whisky. 'I do not like being the bearer of bad news.'

'Why would this be so?' But then I thought of my work in London. Criminal networks, tied into governments. It had happened across Europe, now it was happening here.

'Because we don't yet know all her secrets, Sam. Lucy's and Howell's. Maybe even yours.'

'I don't have secrets.'

'Sometimes you don't know . . . what you don't know,' she said.

'What does that mean?'

519

'You need to find your son. We need your talents, from time to time. You need a cover. So, I propose this: to the public, you will be given the ownership of the bars. All of them. Run them, keep them profitable.' She smiled. 'The bars give you a reason to go wherever your search for your son, or wherever our assignments take you. A cover that the Company cannot question. You do, after all, have a background in working in bars, and you need gainful employment. You will do jobs for us when needed. Jobs that require your skill set, your vision, your sense of action.'

It was a profound compliment. 'They'll still suspect. And now you're saying I'm working against the CIA.'

'No. Against someone — probably several — inside it, who have no loyalty to the CIA, or to your government, or to humanity, for that matter. Have you not wondered if Howell had a master?' Only Mila could say the word *master* and have it sound cruel rather than funny. 'This Novem Soles, Howell was their boy. Even with his high rank, he must have been nothing to them, just a flunky being paid. Worse will come, I think.'

I studied the bottom of my whisky glass.

'We will help you. I swear to you, Sam. Please say yes. Here.' She slipped me a DVD. 'Security tape from the clinic Lucy said she had the baby at. You will see a tall dark woman leaving Lucy's room, carrying a baby, the day after your child was born.'

I didn't dare to breathe.

520

'We can help you ID this woman. Pick up the thread.'

Find the line, I thought, just as I had raced to find it in the parkour run on that long ago morning in London, the last normal morning of my life. Find the line.

To have a life again, I could take this secret life, for a while, to find my son. I felt the old tickle of adrenaline begin again, along my spine, curling into my brain.

I stood, turned to face the small scattering of customers in the Bluecut. I jumped, without a wobble, onto the fine leather barstool and cleared my throat. The elegant piano player stopped. The sparse but cool midday crowd looked up at me, startled.

I put on my host's smile and held my whisky glass up in a toast. 'Ladies and gentlemen, I just acquired this bar. The drinks are on the house.'

Acknowledgments

Many thanks to the amazing people who helped me, in different ways, with this book:

David Shelley, Ursula Mackenzie, Thalia Proctor, Daniel Mallory, Nathalie Morse, Kati Nicholl, Richard Collins, Sean Garrehy, Sarah Jones, Shirley Stewart, Peter Ginsberg, Nathan Bransford, Dave Barbor, Holly Frederick, Sarah LaPolla, Carolyn Nordstrom, Steve Basile, Kevin Casey, Dan Edwardes, James Whitaker, Georgina Tripp, Tracy Edmonson, Wesley Skow, Jurgen Snoeren, Marc van Biezen, Judith van Doorn, Johnny Zhao, Janice Gable Bashman, Sam Bashman, JT Ellison, and as always William, Charles, and Leslie.

TRUST ME

Jeff Abbott

Luke Dantry tragically lost his parents when he was a teenager — his father was murdered by a crazed operative, his mother died in a terrible accident. Brought up by his stepfather, Luke now works with him on his research, monitoring extremist groups on the internet. Yet within the seemingly harmless world of the internet lie untold dangers. And Luke suddenly feels the full force of them when he is kidnapped at gunpoint in an airport car park. He's an ordinary guy who's led a blameless life, so why has he been targeted. He just knows that he must escape — somehow.

RUN

Jeff Abbott

Everything changes the day two government agents appear unexpectedly at his door. Ben's business card was found in the pocket of one of America's most dangerous assassins, who has just been shot dead. Whoever killed him now has their sights set on Ben. With no idea why he has been targeted, Ben has to act quickly. And in a world where suddenly nothing is as it seems, and no one can be trusted, Ben's only option is to run for his life . . .

FEAR

Jeff Abbott

Miles Kendrick is in a witness protection program, hiding from the mob and haunted by his best friend's death. With the aid of psychiatrist Allison Vance, Miles is trying to hold onto his sanity and to recall the events of that tragic night. But when Allison is blown to pieces by a bomb planted in her office, Miles becomes caught up in a deadly conspiracy. Targeted by a deranged FBI agent, Miles must run for his life — and force himself to remember the terrible truth about the death of his best friend . . .

PANIC

Jeff Abbott

Things are going well for young filmmaker Evan Casher — until he receives an urgent phone call from his mother, summoning him home. He arrives to find her brutally murdered body on the kitchen floor and a hitman lying in wait for him. It is then he realises his whole life has been a lie. His parents are not who he thought they were, his girlfriend is not who he thought she was, his entire existence has been an ingeniously constructed sham. And now that he knows it, he is in terrible danger. Evan's only hope for survival is to discover the truth behind his past.

ABANDONED

Cody Mcfadyen

The woman had been missing for almost eight years. Someone watched her, stalked her, and held her captive in the dark all that time. No ransom demand, and no suspects. No answers, even now that the woman has been found — thrown from an unmarked car in front of a beachside wedding — alive, but unbearably traumatised. All she can do is scream. Tracking a kidnapper who appears to have no motive, FBI Special Agent Smoky Barrett and her team are plunged into the most sinister and disturbing case of their careers. Then they start to find the others . . .